Legend
of the
Tumbleweed

Kirby Jonas
6/7/03

Books by Kirby Jonas

Season of the Vigilante
The Dansing Star
Death of an Eagle
Legend of the Tumbleweed
Lady Winchester*
Disciples of the Wind (co-authored by Jamie Jonas)*
The Secret of Two Hawks*

*Forthcoming

Legend of the Tumbleweed

Kirby Jonas
Cover art by author

HOWLING WOLF PUBLISHING
POCATELLO, IDAHO

Howling Wolf Publishing
P.O. Box 1045
Pocatello, Idaho 83204

For more information about this and Kirby Jonas' previous books, or if you would like to be included on the author's mailing list, point your browser to *www.kirbyjonas.com* or send a request via postal mail to Howling Wolf Publishing at the address above.

Book design by Serephin Multimedia (*www.serephin.com*)

First Edition
Library of Congress Cataloging-in-Publication Data

Jonas, Kirby, 1965–
        Legend of the tumbleweed / Kirby Jonas. -- 1st ed.
                p.   cm
        ISBN 1-891423-02-9
        1. Title.
                Library of Congress Catalog Card Number 99-62565
                                                                CIP

First edition: November 1999
Printed in the United States of America

On the number one best selling novel, Death of an Eagle

"Kirby Jonas is one of the best of the young writers who breathe a new freshness into the traditional Western."
Don Coldsmith, author of the Spanish Bit Saga

"Finally, a voice as real and honest as thunder rumbles from the canyons and tinderbox towns of the wild Old West. The voice belongs to Kirby Jonas. Every shining detail carries the stamp of authenticity and drums like the hoofbeat of a sure-footed horse at full gallop."
Mike Blakely, author of Shortgrass Song

"Death of an Eagle establishes Kirby Jonas as one of America's most promising Western writers. He writes with the passion of a young Jack London. For anyone who likes Westerns, Jonas is must reading."
Lee Nelson, author of The Storm Testament series

"Death of an Eagle is a tour-de-force of poetic description, sharp period dialogue, and the kind of action that whitens one's knuckles. Kirby Jonas is one of the best new finds in an American genre that continues to grow and deepen."
Loren D. Estleman, author of Jitterbug

Acknowledgments

I can't imagine any book of mine involving a tribe of the northwestern United States not having my friend, the Honorable Clyde Hall, somewhere in the acknowledgments. Clyde is a métis, half French and half Shoshone, and his dear friendship and vast knowledge of the plains tribes is indispensable to the authenticity of my work.

Likewise, I owe a debt to Dr. Karl Holte, who is always ready to give counsel and detail on plants of the West. Karl, I seem to be forever learning from you.

Thanks to brother Jamie, who is always ready to drop what he is doing to read my imperfect drafts-and help them to become less imperfect. Without your help, brother, these books could never be what they are. And to Mom and my wife, Debbie, whose common sense and gut-level emotion blend together to fill in some raggedly awkward gaps.

Thanks to the Darryl Darger clan, to the Keith Perkins family, Pat Davis, Janet Tolman, Donald and Allen Wadsworth and Scott Summers, who are not only helping hands but great inspiration. And Natalie, thank you for your smile! Of course my undying appreciation goes out to my new friend, Dr. Loui Novak, who has gone all-out to make my writing career as pain-free as it can be. Loui, without you the world would be a darker place.

Thank you to my new friends, Quinn and Amy Moyes, both of whom I barely know yet who happily agreed to appear on my book cover as the models for the characters of JoAnna Walker and Slug Holch.

And, in Legend of the Tumbleweed, perhaps more than any previous book, I would be remiss in not including mention of my good friend, Chris Taft. An author himself, and a student of life with an ingrained understanding of the idiosyncrasies of the human mind, Chris has helped me through more tough spots in building characters than any one other person. Chris, my undying thanks.

As for Steven Medellin, the king of the computer. Most of you know I do the artwork for the covers, but it has always been Steve's magic that makes the final product come to life. Steve, you are an inspiration I couldn't work without.

Here I have to add, with deep humility and respect, my deep thanks to James Drury, "The Virginian". Jim read Legend of the Tumbleweed for me and added his much-needed opinions. He also gracefully let me use his face to portray the character of Flint Drury on my back cover. Jim met me only recently, but to me he has been a friend since I was three years old. As a child in Bear Canyon, Montana, Jim was the first "cowboy" face I ever remember seeing, and as such he is the man who, besides my father, I owe the most for instilling in me the love of the West. Jim, we may be new friends, but you gave a young boy reason to dream, and no matter where our paths should lead, I could never forget you. Thank you for making the portrayal of western characters your career, and thank you for countless hours of entertainment. The screen would have been a duller place without you.

Thanks, last of all, to those Wyomingites, at the Buffalo library and elsewhere, who were willing and ready to help an annoying snip of an author along in his search for truths and legends about Wyoming's people and its natural history, past and present. Long live Wyoming, the Cowboy State!

Kirby Jonas

Author's Note

For years, I've been telling my readers about this mysterious book which started a budding author on his way. Here it is at last, in all its glory.

Legend of the Tumbleweed began life in 1976, when I was a student in Mr. Jarvis Anderson's sixth grade class. It is the book I credit with instilling in me the desire to hold tight to the Western novelist's pen.

At the time, I was an avid reader of Louis L'Amour novels, an avid fan of John Wayne movies and, on television, Gunsmoke, The Virginian, Cheyenne, The Big Valley and The High Chaparral. Consequently, those elements played a major role in my first draft, a whopping forty-nine pages long! The inclusion of a number of classmates was another interesting twist and as it turned out one of the main reasons I decided to continue writing.

As a grammar student and all the way through high school, I was beyond painfully shy. In answer to any query, a teacher could expect a quiet and simple answer-generally a yes or no. They seldom got much more unless they managed to get me alone-then choke it out of me. But when one morning Mr. Anderson wrote four simple words on his blackboard-candy, bubble, box, and stream-and assigned his students to write a story about one of those subjects, little did he know what path that would lead shy little Kirby Jonas down. I wrote a story called "The Stream," about three horses, a cowboy, a young Indian brave and an old chief. Mr. Anderson accepted that story with enthusiasm and insisted on reading it aloud to the class. As I listened to my written words come out of someone else's mouth and saw the way the class listened, seemingly enthralled, I knew I had to write again.

Not long after, I sat at home one evening, bored out of my skull, as sixth grade boys often seem to be. I decided I was going to write a full-length book, and I lay down on my bunk and brain-stormed over ideas for a title. Those titles are all lost to time-all except one.

I took my long list of book titles to my daddy and asked him which one he liked, and he made his choice with little pause: The Tumbleweed. Daddy was my editor, my inspiration and my idol. He instilled in me a love for all things Western and all things natural from a very young age, and the light I saw in his eyes as he read my chapters was enough to cement in me the desire to continue writing forever.

With Daddy in mind, and a little of the egotist at heart (Debbie would say way too blasted much of the egotist), I modeled the main character on the cover of the book after Daddy and myself. That is my tribute to the man of whom I hold so many fond memories.

Sometimes I feel Daddy watching over my shoulder even now, reading even as I write. His spirit lives on in the words.

Forward
by James Drury

I first met Kirby Jonas at a western film festival in Laughlin, Nevada. He presented me with a copy of his western novel, Death of an Eagle. I was flattered and amazed to read on the "About the Author" page that The Virginian television series had been an inspiration to Kirby in his life and work.

Then I read his book.

I judge what I read by goose bumps, and there certainly were a lot of them in Death of an Eagle. I called Kirby on Christmas morning and told him how much I had enjoyed his book. I mentioned that I believed it would make a great audio book and that I would love to record it. We are now working on an arrangement to record Death of an Eagle, and his other novels as well, including Legend of the Tumbleweed.

Shortly after our initial conversation, Kirby provided me with copies of his other works and asked if I would write a forward for Legend of the Tumbleweed, his latest novel.

It has been many years since I have been so impressed with a new author. And I hope, dear reader, that you will make a point of reading Kirby's other books, Death of an Eagle, Dansing Star and Season of the Vigilante (presently in two volumes, soon to be combined into one book).

Kirby Jonas writes originals. It is not that we have not seen elements of some of these stories before, because of course we have. It is the characters that he develops before our eyes that give his works that first time quality that is so admirable. In Legend of the Tumbleweed, it is fair to say that Kirby's skill and passion have been honed and polished to a high gloss. His dialogue is moving into areas of acute recognition on the part of the reader.

The scene where Tom McLean warns Tye Sandoe about imminent trouble with Slug Holch and JoAnna Walker has a living, breathing, steaming, heartfelt, razor-sharp ring of truth as to how worried folks think and talk in a real crisis.

Many of Kirby Jonas' heroes are outlaws, and many of his outlaws are heroes. That is, after all, what makes up the human condition. Kirby has the gift of taking the reader right inside his characters, into their innermost spaces. It is said that everyone has a public life, a private life and a secret life. In Legend of the Tumbleweed, we get to see all three lives with our principal characters. When you ride the outlaw trail with Tom McLean you will smell his fear and taste the acid bile of his courage. And as in all of his books, Kirby pays great attention to detail in his descriptive passages about the country, the horsemanship and gunmanship.

Legend of the Tumbleweed is told in the first person, and that for me lent an immediacy to the story that was irresistible. As the story unfolds, you will meet some amazing characters, good and bad, and the richness of the names and the cultures and origins they reveal are a constant source of interest.

Goose bumps are a measuring stick. As a lifelong actor, I, of course, look at all the fiction I read from a dramatic or cinematic point of view. Every one of Kirby Jonas' books I have read so far would make a wonderful motion picture. If a piece of fiction gives an actor goose bumps when they read it, it's a good bet it will give them goose bumps when they play the role and give the audience goose bumps when they see it. If an actor can give you goose bumps in a performance, you can pay them no higher compliment. Kirby Jonas makes us laugh and cry and feel the sorrow. He moves us emotionally and viscerally, and you can pay an author no higher compliment.

I believe we all have far too little fiction in our lives. The pressures and realities of everyday living put fiction way down on our list of priorities. This is a shame, for by losing ourselves in the troubles, travails and triumphs of fictional characters we inflame our imaginations and inform and validate our hearts in a way that will let us live and appreciate our own lives more fully and richly. It is also wonderful to let ourselves go subjectively and give our objectivity a rest.

Tom McLean is an outlaw. He is also a hero...for a thread of responsibility as old as time itself runs through the fabric that is Tom McLean; first for Tyrone Sandoe and then for JoAnna Walker, and it lifts Tom McLean to grand places. Woven in the fabric as well is an almost invisible thread of conscience that proves to be his strongest weapon and the only thing that brings him peace.

All characters, even the lesser of importance, are beautifully and individually drawn. Kirby, I am sure, with pen in hand, could take off with any one of them and have a great book. Legend of the Tumbleweed made me laugh, it gave me chills-not once, but many times. And...ahhh...dear...it made me bawl like a baby.

I don't know what else you could ask from a book.

James Drury
Cypress, Texas
1999

To Daddy, who inspired me, and to the Shelley High School Class of '83, who played a part in a twelve-year-old's drama.

"Killin' don't make a boy a man—it just makes him a killer."
— *Tom McLean*

KIRBY JONAS

Chapter One
Wanted Man

The Outlaws: Tom McLean

I had killed another man. Where his bloody hands had smeared it, my sleeve was hardly dry. Reckon I'd been better off dead myself, and I almost wished I was.

As the first bright stars of evening began to wink in the twilight sky, I rode the tangled bank of Clear Creek, letting my horse pick his way. Times like this, I was mighty thankful for Sheriff—that's what I called the gray. The name started out as a joke. But there was no joke to the way Sheriff watched out for me. He was cagey enough to keep me out of trouble when my mind wasn't on the trail. He knew where I wanted to go—even when I didn't.

Right now my own mind was far away.

It seemed like days ago, but the cigar-tainted air inside the bank and the black powder smell of my Remington still stung my nostrils. And the odors of the old man—the stink of early morning breath before a meal, and of night sweat. And in his face the look of hate, then desperation, and finally resignation. It was all there as he looked into my eyes and slid slowly to the floor, at last relinquishing his grip on my wrist.

I rammed my eyes shut and shook my head. It did me no good to relive the memory. The old man was dead. I'd seen his pupils get big and sort of dull. His life was gone; I had taken it. Now I had to make time, or I'd pay for his death with mine. Justice is a dandy idea—long as it's only dished out to other folks.

A breath of wood smoke reached me over the smells of sage and cottonwood. It drew my thoughts to a fire, a meal, and fresh water. The trace of a trail slipped over the dusty edge of the bench, and Sheriff took it. He'd smelled the wood smoke, too, and certainly a long time before I had. He'd been smelling the waters of Clear Creek, too, and the two scents must have meant camp to him.

At the bottom of the trail, we leveled out into a dry creek bed paved with water-rounded stones and littered with fallen limbs from the trees along its banks. Clear Creek had once run here, and maybe it still did, in kinder years. But some act of nature had changed the creek's course, or the water was low enough with the drought that it couldn't wander here. There was a cluster of tumbleweeds all heaped in one cove along the bank. I sort of gave them a nod as we passed. The tumbleweed and me, we were both drifters, both outsiders. I'd started to think of us as kin. They say the tumbleweed came in with grain seed Russian farmers brought all the way across the ocean. Me, I only came from as far as Ozark, Missouri. But we were outsiders all the same.

Sheriff picked his way, then paused in the middle of the wash. He perked his ears, listening into the darkness, beyond the rattling of the creek. Among the shadows above the creekbed, I picked out an old cottonwood, half-dead yet impressive in its massiveness. Its trunk prodded into the bank, and crooked arms bent upward and knitted themselves into the twilight, their dry leaves rustling like sheaves of paper. Its roots writhed over the lip of the creek bank, holding great stones prisoner behind a living cage. I rode closer and pulled Sheriff in with a tug on the reins. Peering at the furrowed trunk, I found the sign I already knew was there. A depression was hacked out of the bark—the sign of a cross.

Patting the gray's neck, I spoke softly into the dark: "Not far now, boy." His answer was a nicker and a chain-tinkling shake of his head.

Again, a momentary waft of wood smoke on a swirl of wind. A welcoming fragrance, yet acrid in comparison to the scents of the night range. It eased my memory of the bank in Buffalo. The gray flared his nostrils, pricking his ears forward and stamping his foot. After a moment, he nickered with apparent anticipation. At the touch of my spurs, he scrambled up out of the creek bed, adding the cool, musty smell of the dust to the other smells of the night. Head up and ears shot forward, he walked along through the drought-stunted grass.

Again the wood smoke, still stronger. Sheriff stopped to test the air. I keened my ears but heard nothing beyond the rustling creek. Still, I knew where we were. Ahead, the creek would cut across the dry wash, and in the triangular patch of grass at the junction I'd find camp.

With gladness I swung out of the saddle, favoring my right leg. It was always stiff around this time of night. A .38 caliber bullet had left me a scar as a souvenir below that knee as I pushed a herd of stolen shorthorns across one last cattle range in the Blue Mountains of eastern Oregon, back in eighty-three.

Less than fifty yards farther on, the glow of a campfire winked at me from a hollow beneath the black hulks of trees. I stopped and watched until I made out the dim features of a man seated by the fire. He peered into the night, revolver fisted, his eyes cutting into the shadows. The rest of the clearing was quiet except for the music of the crickets and the creek.

My voice rose with the long-practiced call of a great-horned owl. The near-as-perfect imitation of a nighthawk's scratchy cry answered from camp. My partner, Tyrone Sandoe, was as good as me at the sounds of the range.

I spoke soft into the night. "Tye, I'm comin' in."

A pause, while Tye got over being startled. "Come on, Tom. Spotted pup's hot."

I smiled at the thought of filling my belly and laying my head down to sleep. But before I'd let myself relax, I had to tend to Sheriff. The first thing I looked to was his wound. He'd taken a bullet in the hip, and it had come out, leaving a nasty hole. I dug a silver flask of whisky from a saddlebag and poured some on the wound, which the horse didn't like one bit. Other than that, there wasn't much I could do. I'd read about some government animal doctor in the Bighorn Sentinel, but it was obvious I couldn't chance looking for him.

I watered Sheriff at the creek. Then I brushed him down with twigs and grass, being mighty careful around his wound, and staked him out by Tyrone Sandoe's bay. As I worked, I enjoyed the smell of his hot skin, his dusty hair and sweat. Those were smells of home. Smells of a hard day plowing fields. This was quiet time I tried to grab at the end of a long haul, time the horse and me enjoyed. We'd been together four years now. Longest I'd ever owned a horse—perhaps the longest *any* wanted man had—maybe one for the record books. We were true amigos.

Sheriff and the bay whickered back and forth a couple times, then both went to cropping that curled-up grass in earnest. Wasn't much of it that year, but they made the most of it.

I walked to the edge of the firelight, smelling fry bread and the "spotted pup" Tye spoke of. That was his pet dish: rice, canned milk, and sugar, dotted all over with raisins and stewed to perfection. Tye sat near the fire, leaned against the rotted stump of a cottonwood. He set his plate aside as I came in, standing up and wiping his hands on his pants. Stepping forward, he pumped my hand.

Tye was nineteen years old, with green-blue eyes like evening sky and jet black hair hanging over his ears and three inches past his collar. A soft mustache of the same deep black rode his lip like a spring caterpillar. On his chin, a scar half-hidden by a two-inch tuft of black beard rescued his face from being what some might've called perfect, but it never seemed to bother the women we came across. He had a white-toothed smile and clean-featured face that made them forget about the scar and the fact that he appeared to be no more than a saddle bum.

Tye was taller than me but slighter across the chest and shoulders—and stomach, too, I'd noticed of late. He wore a cross-draw holster and Smith and Wesson Schofield on his left hip. Tyrone Sandoe was about as naturally handsome a man as I'd ever laid eyes on, but he was no dandy. He could use that .45.

As for me, Thomas Jefferson McLean, I wasn't an overly tall man, not by any stretch of truth. But trudging after a plow and a crock-headed mule from childhood, wrestling cows and pounding spikes alongside the Chinamen on the Union Pacific had given my upper body its share of beef. And the rough places the rails took me had taught me a skill at rough and tumble I'd not have learned in an easier life. I lacked three inches of standing eye to eye with Tyrone Sandoe. He lacked twenty years of standing toe to toe with me.

Letting loose my hand, Tye grinned and pulled a sack of coins from inside his vest, holding it out. "Well, I guess you lost Bennett, or you wouldn't be standin' here. We pulled it off!" He threw the sack up in the air and let it land with a jingle in his hand, a grin cutting his face in two.

"We sure pulled it off, all right. Bennett's chasin' his tail." I allowed myself to smile back, though I was more the cynic and sensed our escape was far from secure. But we'd come away from Buffalo with more money than Tye Sandoe had ever laid eyes on. And some of his excitement was catching.

"Tye, why don't you be a pard and throw some of that spotted pup and bread on a plate? This old man's about had all the liftin' he can do today, outside o' maybe a fork."

He laughed. "Anything you say, gran'pap."

I sprawled out on my side by the fire and ate what Tye fixed for me. Spreading a saddle blanket on the ground, he began counting bills and gold coins from two bags into piles. In twenty minutes, he sat back and smiled at me, flashing those perfect white teeth and crossing his hands.

He seemed to have put the money he'd lost totally out of his mind now, and I was glad. It'd been eating at him. "Three thousand six hundred and forty dollars," he said. "An extra three hundred twenty each for spending money. Won't the girls be happy to see us now!"

"Me, maybe. Them girls ain't pinin' fer a 'spotted pup' like you." I chuckled, but Tye already knew well enough I was joking. Any woman drawn towards this pair of drifters wasn't there for *my* whiskered jowls.

"Hey, don't feel bad," was Tye's answer. "If I get too many to handle, I c'n sure enough find a blind one an' send her hobblin' yer way." He let out a roar of laughter, then spit between his teeth into the fire.

"Laugh now, kid. Soon enough you'll see women ain't all they're cracked up to be. They'll be neck and neck with you, sowin' your wild oats right alongside you, and spendin' your money, too. You ain't nothin' but fresh meat to the calicos we're liable to bump into."

"Yeah, yer just a stick-in-the-mud. One o' these days I need to teach you how to have a little fun."

I nodded, only half listening. Sometimes I envied Tye Sandoe and his easy-going, live-for-the-day outlook. He didn't seem to have a care past what he'd eat that day, where he might sleep or what girl he might kiss. But he was young. The cares would come soon enough. He'd get old like me and watch the women forsake him.

As for Tye, I sort of thought he envied me, too, at least just a little. After all, I could use a gun, and I could plan a bank robbery. And when we chose to ride with other men, it was true enough they tended to lend an ear to what I had to say. Likely because I'd been in the game a long time. And an outlaw had to have more than mere luck to survive long as I had.

Sometimes I felt a twinge of regret for leading Tye off on the owl-hoot trail. But he was a wild kid when we met over in Idaho City, and someone, if not me, would've led him astray—or he'd have gone alone. I needed a partner, and he'd took to the outlaw life like a bear to a beehive.

Sandoe's voice suddenly broke into my ponderings. "I just wish I could go back. I'd like to hang onto the rest of that loot better." A bitter regret had come into his voice.

"Dang it, Tye. I told you before. Stop worryin'. Leastways we saved my half." When he didn't laugh at my attempted humor, I stopped grinning. "We all make mistakes, kid. Your biggest mistake was ridin' out with me in the first place—not droppin' them bags."

Sandoe looked at me, then finally let himself smile again. "I can see 'em now, chasin' their tail around the prairie. Bet they're goin' crazy lookin' for us. Two men against an entire town!"

I chuckled, despite myself, and my thoughts took a trail of their own—back to Buffalo...

Chapter Two
Buffalo, Wyoming Territory, 1886

We'd heard the town was there, nestled down in the valley un-der the shadow of the Bighorns. Even so, it surprised us. We topped out at the crest of the road, and Buffalo sat below, just a dot among the gray and rolling sagebrush hills. Two rows of log and clapboard-sided businesses lined the long, winding main street, and a scatter-ing of residences hemmed them all in. Midway, cottonwoods traced the path of Clear Creek, which cut across the street, splitting it neatly in two.

As we rode down the street, the smells of the creek way mingled with those of the town—of wood smoke, food cooking, and of stables and stock pens. Flies hummed about the street, frequenting animal dung and the occasional household waste.

We rode past a number of saloons, most on the west side of the street; a number of eating establishments; a drug store; furniture store (which was also the undertaker's); and two hardware stores, one of them displaying the brand-new, bright green John Deere plow out front, and a three-foot stack of Glidden bobwire rolls. We counted three livery stables, a grocery store and two banks, the big-gest being the First National. Clear Creek bubbled sweet and clear out of the Bighorns and held tight to its free-flowing charm as it rambled through town. Here it was over thirty feet wide, and our horses' hooves made hollow clopping sounds crossing its sturdy log and lumber bridge. We passed the Occidental Hotel, the court-house soon after.

The main street was busy as I imagined it ever could be on a Wednesday evening, when most of the residents would be resting up from a day's labors. In spite of any imagined importance as the seat of Johnson County, Buffalo couldn't have been home to more than a thousand people that year. Many of those were ranchers and cowboys who had better things to do than roam the town streets at six o'clock in the evening, mid-week. Still, in the short time it took me and Tye to ride Main Street from one end of town to the other, we must have seen a good forty people, one place or other along the way. Some were obviously businessmen, some were women on the last-minute errand. Some were idle loungers. But all of them watched us like we were the most curious couple of drifters they'd ever seen.

We picked out one more element in Buffalo: the wolfers. They'd come from miles around, hoping to cash in on the wolf bounty put up by the Wyoming Stockgrowers Association. If the look of these men hadn't made them stand out like a second nose, their stench did. Between the animal rot and sweat and dog pee, I couldn't figure which was worse. They used the dog pee to mask their scent around traps.

It was a prime country for wolves, too. They had gathered from miles around that spring. They had feasted heavily after the death of so many cattle from hard snows and lack of grass going into winter. Wyoming's cattle ranges were in a hell of a bind.

"Looks just like the bunch that finished off the buffalo three years ago," I said. Other than an occasional solitary straggler, the year of eighty-three had seen the last of the northern herd—the last of the American buffalo.

Tye turned and looked at me, shaking his head with a half-puzzled grin. "Yeah? Buffalo, hell! They name a town after somethin', an' then everybody an' his baby sister come along and wiped the critter off the face o' the earth!"

I laughed. "It was a fever, Tye. Some boys were at it for years. All the way across the plains, Texas and Kansas. Finally here. They didn't know any other way. Then there was those that *did* know it was a dyin' way of life, and they just wanted a piece of it to tell their grandkids. The way they tell it the town wasn't named after the animal anyway. It got its name from some homesick settler comin' out here from New York. We had a Buffalo in Missouri, probably from the same thing."

"I guess it didn't matter then. Kill all the fuzzy critters!" Tye said jokingly and slapped his leg, looking brazenly at the huddle of wolfers at Charlie Chapin's Saloon. "Bet them wolfers are retired buffalo hunters theirselves. Wiped out the cows, now they're here to kill the dogs. Personally, I'll be glad when they're gone. Them gents could draw blow flies off a bloated carcass."

When me and Tye had rode the length of the street and casually glanced over the two banks and the looming red brick courthouse, we turned around and rode back the other way. Just before the Clear Creek bridge, we reined in at the Occidental, a big two-story log hotel. It was cool and dark inside, a single kerosene lamp glowing directly above a mirror behind the front desk. Any other light was provided by the two windows in front. Down a long hallway back of the desk we could hear the rattle of plates and silverware from the dining area. And to the right, beyond a set of doors, came the clack and buzz of a billiard room.

"How you set for rooms, friend?" I asked an elderly man seated behind the desk.

The fellow pushed his glasses farther down his nose and looked over them at us. He glanced several times back and forth between us, and his eyes narrowed noticeably. "Well...I have one for two dollars—only one bed in it, though. Are you two friends?"

"Yeah." I glanced at Tye, who grinned broadly.

The old man cast an unfavorable glance at Tye, his eyes sliding over the shoulder-length hair. Long hair had fallen into disfavor with the general public in the last decade. Sign of a rebel. "Just so's you know m' mind, I run a quiet place here," he said. "I like to keep it that way."

I lifted my hands away from my body in a gesture of surrender. "I don't plan on giving you any trouble, friend. We're not drovers in for a bender, if that's what you're thinkin'. Just travelers lookin' for a place to light."

"Where you hail from?"

"Just around," I said after a pause. His brazen curiosity annoyed me.

The old man nodded nervously and dismissed the exchange. "Room's two dollars a night."

I nodded and placed three silver dollars on the counter, then backed away, letting Tye pick up the key.

"Room's at the head of the stairs," the old man added.

We stepped out onto the porch to the horses. Here we leaned across our saddles and reviewed what we'd seen of the town. There were at least a dozen saloons; I made note of those things. My memory ticked off five—the Senate, the Cowboy, the Minnehaha, Kennedy's, and Charlie Chapin's. As we passed, Kennedy's and Chapin's had been the only two with any sign of life. Kennedy's seemed to be where cowboys hung out, and at Chapin's the wolfers had been lounging. There were at least three livery stables, the Fetterman, the Pioneer and Billy Hunt's. But we'd paid a room at the Occidental, and it boasted its own stable. We untied our horses and walked them around to it. A boy took them from us, leaving us free to walk the streets.

I knew from research the sheriff of Johnson County was Van Bennett. I knew the man—only by sight and reputation—from my days in Oregon. He'd retired from a whaling ship after fourteen years of hell and had been working for a freight outfit out of Baker City.

We spotted Bennett early on during our rounds of the town. He stood at the corner of the Senate Saloon, glaring through eyes like tarnished silver coins from under the over-wide brim of a sweat-stained hat. Physically, he was all I'd heard tell, towering at least nine inches over my head and nearly as broad through his chest from front to back as I was from side to side. The late afternoon sun splashed over his stone-like features, made twisting flames of the curls of his full beard. He took in everyone and everything with a keen eye while seeming to dwell on nobody.

We walked past the lawman and into the Senate Saloon. We looked the part of work-hunting cowpokes down on our luck, both dressed in ragged range clothes and riding boots. Tye wore a natural-colored Boss of the Plains Stetson, and I wore my Montana peak with board-straight brim, a common style of north plains buckaroos those days. Tye carried his Schofield, and I had a Remington Frontier. They were in sight, but we carried them like cowboys, tight in the holster and high on the hip. Other than Tye's uncommon looks and long hair, there wasn't anything about us that should have drawn anyone's attention to us. But everyone watched us anyway, and there was suspicion in their eyes.

We drank light and slow in the Senate. Wanting to play out our part, we asked about work, found none. Acting appropriately disappointed, we moved on to Kennedy's, then to the Cowboy. Thanks to the drought and the scarcity of grass, people were scared. No work anywhere, and we were glad. It would have been pure hell if someone had took pity and offered us a job.

In every place we stopped, folks sized us up carefully before giving any response at all. Like I said, the town was scared, and it was more than just the drought. I'd heard tell of the war shaping up in Wyoming Territory between the big eastern and foreign ranchers and the homesteaders. The way folks were looking at us, I was beginning to take serious notice.

Last stop was Germania House Restaurant and Beer Depot, where they advertised lager beer on tap, straight from the Buffalo Brewery. After our customary query about work, we ordered a meal of steak and fried potatoes. Before we got our grub, an old man happened in, and when he saw us sitting there he stopped. His eyes peered at us from a shaggy, grizzled face. He was nowhere near secret about his suspicions. Finally, he just up and invited himself to sit at our table.

"Where you gents from?"

"South of here, most recently," I said.

"Oh?" The shrewd look in his eyes sharpened. "South, eh? Cheyenne, maybe?"

"We were there."

"What doin'?"

I chuckled, half-amused at his lack of tact. "Same as here, old feller. Huntin' a job."

He gave three deliberate nods of his head. "Didn't find it, eh? Let me see yer hands."

Taken by surprise, I turned my left hand over on the tabletop. I kept the right in my lap, closer to my gun. He peered at my hand, then nodded again. "Workin' hand, all right. Maybe you are a-huntin' work." He skewered Tye with his eyes. "But he ain't got no workin' hands."

"You'll have to pardon Tye. He's my cousin, up from California. Worked in a bank but wanted to be a cowboy." Of course it was all a lie. First place, he was from Idaho.

The old man seemed to relax after that. He placed an order of black coffee when the waitress came by. Then he glanced back and forth from me to Tye again.

"Well, gents, I hope you'll pardon my curiosity. If I read you two right you are what you say you are. But we're keerful in Buffalo. This place is on the verge of all-out war," he told us with a knowing nod. "Now, mark my words. Them rich Cheyenne Club boys, they're pushin' their weight around the entire territory—even beyond, where they figger it'll do 'em some good. When you said you come through Cheyenne, well…" The suspicion returned for a moment, but he seemed to shrug it off. "You boys don't look the part, but they's a rumor the big ranchers are hirin' help—gun help. Already got a couple range detectives shovin' folks around."

Like I said, I'd heard a bit of news about this war. But I didn't let on. "My pardner an' me've been long on hoofin' an' short on hearin'. We didn't stick in Cheyenne long enough to catch the gossip. What's caused all the ruckus?"

The old man scoffed, but his eyes lit up with obvious pleasure that we hadn't heard. "They don't like the small folks that's been movin' in here an' tryin' just to live. Tell you this, gents: Any man don't have proof he's workin' for a Association brand is quick becomin' fair game all acrost the territ'ry. Them Easterners—an' worse yet the fureigners—they've bought up as much of this country as they can. An' the rest they *act* like's theirs. It's a gold mine fer them what's got the means. They're tryin' to run off the little ranchers—homesteaders, too. They want it all. Callin' ever'one else rustlers. So beware. Johnson's a good county—a small man's county yet. But it's gittin' so's yer only middlin' safe here. You go out of this county, best watch yerself an' don't trust nobody. You see a group of riders, best avoid 'em if you can. Like I say, they're callin' anyone they don't know rustlers, an' they're mad 'nough to bite rocks—an' spoilin' for a shootin'. They won't let nothin' come 'tween 'em an' their money—nothin'. I g'arantee you, it's comin' fast onto some killin'."

I started to respond when I saw the five wolfers we'd watched earlier stumble through the door, loud and hungry-eyed. They leered about the room, one of them guffawing seemingly at nothing. Even across the room, we already smelled their stench.

A wiry Mexican with a thin blade of mustache sat on a stool, sipping a beer with his hat lying on the counter nearby. I'd seen the man when we first walked in, and he'd nodded politely as we passed. Quiet curiosity was in his eyes, but he quickly looked away. His somber skin was made darker by the sun, and although he didn't appear to be much past twenty-five, thin white wrinkles creased the corners of his eyes. He wore the simple clothing of a cowboy.

The wolfers swaggered toward him, one of them sweeping the Mexican's plainsman hat up off the bar and holding it at arm's length to eye it with a sneer. "Whad'ya call *that*? Greaser, that ain't no hat!" The man flung the hat across the room, where it thudded against the wall and rocked to a stop on the floor.

The wolfer was a big man, the largest of the five. Blond beard hung in oily snarls, hiding his throat, and hair made dark by grease, smoke and dirt hung limp against the shoulders of a wear-shined buckskin jacket. He glared at the Mexican.

The Mexican's eyes ticked over the group. He stood up and took his glass of beer, starting to step away. The wolfers waited expectantly, watching the Mexican and their henchman.

"Where you goin', greaser?" growled the blond wolfer. "No one steps away from Lige Swofford without he invites 'em to. Now set yer carcass back down there."

I glanced over warily at Tye. He'd never said as much, and I'd never asked, but he was dark enough to have Mexican in him. He sat there outwardly calm. But his eyes burned, and his fingers turned white against the arm of his chair.

"That's Poco Vidales," the old man whispered. "He's a game little banty rooster. If that feller was alone, I bet he c'd fix his wagon."

Vidales stood still. Resignation shone in his eyes as they rolled over the group. He looked at his hat on the floor, and in swinging back his glance touched on me and Tye and the old man. At last, he settled his gaze on Swofford.

"Señor, I don't wish no trouble with you, please. I am here for a drink only."

"*Señor, I don't wish no trouble with you, please.*" Swofford scoffed. "Yer not only a chili eater, yer a yella back. Well, you got trouble. I had a great uncle or some such kin 'twas butchered down in San Antone. At the Alamo. I swore I'd beat hell outta ever' greaser I saw the rest o' my life. An' you shore fit the bill."

Vidales wore a belt gun, but he didn't have time to use it. Swofford's big fist came up and struck him across the cheek, laying him and his stool both out on the floor.

The Mexican sat up slowly, putting his hand to his cheekbone. I could see Tye was getting edgy in his seat, so I spoke his name soft. When he looked my way, I shook my head. "Ain't our fight, Tye. Let it go, or you'll disappoint me."

Tye didn't get out of his seat, but he didn't like sitting. I figured part of the reason he sat was the other four wolfers standing there spoiling for a fight of their own. It was obvious they were a brutal lot. They'd be merciless in a fight.

"Now get up, greaser!" Swofford bellowed. "Get up an' hit me back—chili eater. How you even call yerself a man?"

Poco Vidales pushed to his feet, careful to keep his hand away from his gun. He glanced toward his hat then looked back at Swofford, waiting. I noticed his hands were shaking at his sides, but I didn't think it was for fear.

When Swofford came in it was with killing rage in his eyes. He swung at Vidales, but the little man ducked out of his way and planted a hook in the big man's midsection. He landed three blows before stepping away.

Swofford roared with rage and tried to grapple, but the Mexican was too quick and whirled aside, scoring two more solid blows that should have hurt Swofford but only seemed to anger him more.

The Mexican's tactics impressed me, but he could only do so much alone. When two of the wolfers stepped in and grabbed his arms, I knew it was over for him. And me and Tye, with our plans of laying low, couldn't afford to take a hand.

Swofford's blows were sickeningly loud in the room, but Vidales took them without a groan. I cursed, wishing I could be elsewhere. I knew what some folks thought of Mexicans, but they were just people. Most of them didn't have anything to do with the Alamo, no more than I had to do with driving the Injuns off their homelands. Besides, Vidales was a game man. He deserved a fair chance.

A big shadow loomed in through the front door, and before I realized what was about there were two wolfers on the floor by the bar. My glance showed big Van Bennett lumbering toward Swofford and the other two, and he swung with the same gun that had laid out the first two. The barrel struck Swofford alongside his head once, then again. He dropped to his knees with a groan.

The bore of the gun now swung back and forth between the other two wolfers, who had let Vidales slide to the floor. For a moment, I thought he'd shoot them both. His eyes glared fire at them, and his mouth twitched in his beard.

There was a barely audible scrape behind Bennett, and I glanced that way. One of the downed wolfers had managed to come to his knees, and he started to pull an old Dragoon revolver from his holster.

Without me thinking, my Remington was fisted, and I spoke quickly to catch his attention. "Mister! I'll kill you if you do." My sights lined on his throat. From the corner of my eye I saw Van Bennett whirl, and his gun turned on me.

Chapter Three
First National Bank

I didn't have time to regret drawing my gun. All I had time to do was cringe and wait for Bennett's shot. I was still aiming at the wolfer, and I didn't even know why I'd drawn. There hadn't been time for a sensible decision. Had there been, I think my pistol would still have been in the holster.

Bennett glared at me, his bared teeth showing behind his beard. I could see the tension go out of him slowly, and he looked over where my gun was aimed, at the first man he'd knocked down. The man still knelt there, his hand froze with the Dragoon half out of its holster.

Three big strides brought Bennett to the wolfer. His boot drove out viciously and the bottom of its heel caught the man in the mouth, sprawling him backwards. He landed on his back but rolled over quickly. With terrified eyes, he came again to his knees. His torn upper lip bled down through his beard.

"Mister, I quit!" he yelled. "I'm out of it."

I thought Bennett was going to kick him again, and maybe he was. But instead, he just pointed his gun at the man's face. "Drop that gun or I won't mind takin' your head off." The wolfer did as told. "Now get over with your friends." Bennett motioned with his revolver barrel toward Swofford and the other two.

The man looked puzzled, but he stumbled to his feet, squinching his eyes to clear his vision. He scrambled over by his partners.

Bennett again walked close to the two who had pinned the Mexican's arms. He looked at them for a long moment. I could see a move being tossed back and forth inside his brain. His face settled, and his gun barrel swung out, taking one man above the ear. As the man dropped, Bennett advanced on the other with equally vicious intent.

"No!" The man's plea was frantic as he backed up, covering his head with his arms. "I'm done, I'm done! I'm beggin' you!"

The cries infuriated Bennett. He struck at the wolfer several times, battering his forearms. At last, a blow slipped through to the crown of the man's head, dropping him to his knees. Bennett's kick to the man's face knocked him onto his back, and he lay still, his arms sheltering his face. I figured him for a fake, but I couldn't blame him for playing unconscious.

Bennett's eyes were wild when he looked over at me. His mouth twitched. I didn't know what to expect, but he nodded as he holstered his weapon. I took that as thanks.

In spite of his wild-eyed appearance, Bennett treated Poco Vidales like a loving father as he helped him to his feet. Tye and me both stared at them, wondering at the obvious affection as the big sheriff brushed sawdust off the back of the Mexican's vest.

"You all right?"

Vidales just nodded. "They didn' give me much chance, but hell, I recover quick. Quicker than they will."

Vidales looked over at me and Tye. Wiping a sleeve across his cheek, he walked to us. He wasn't smiling, but there was a look of gratitude mixed with curiosity in his eyes and the twist of his open mouth.

"I don' know you, *amigos,* but I have to say *gracias.* Thank you—for the Sheriff."

The Mexican held out his hand, and it wasn't until then I realized my Remington still dangled along my thigh. Embarrassed, I stuffed it in the holster and shook his hand, nodding.

"My name is Enrique Vidales." He smiled and dabbed at his bleeding lips with two fingers. "Everyone just calls me Poco."

"McLean," I replied with a nod. I was instantly cursing myself. I'd not meant to use my name, but Bennett looking on must have made me nervous. It had slipped out.

Bennett walked to us with a swinging gait that made him look like one leg was too long. He had the ominous appearance of a gnarled red ponderosa that would one day topple and crush someone to death. "I'm the law in Johnson County. Bennett's the name. I appreciate the stepping in there. Too bad you couldn't have done it a touch sooner. Before Poco got trompled." One eye squeezed shut a little as he looked from me to Tye. Belying his words, I saw no gratitude in his eyes. Only cold calculation.

After the place had been cleared, Tye and the old man and me sank back in our chairs, and Tye and me looked at each other. I sighed.

The old man glanced back and forth between us, then spoke for the first time since the fight broke out. "That Mex—Poco—he an' the sheriff're friends, if you couldn't tell. Poco's papa sorta partnered up with Bennett in the War Twixt the States. Saved his life a couple times, they say. Then got hisself killed the last time he tried to save it—at Chambersburg."

I nodded, recalling the fury in Bennett's eyes. "Bennett would be a good man to make a friend of."

The old man chuckled. "Right enough, he would. He's sorta like a big dog with sharp teeth an' a lotta brute force. Loyal to the end— to his friends. But prob'ly the worst enemy a man could ever make."

After leaving Germania House, we walked north a ways until we came across a building whose sign read GEO. L. HOLT and CO. DRUGGISTS. I went in there with Tye on my heel and bought me a newspaper. I wasn't much of a reader, but I'd learned to muddle my way through a paper or two in my time. If I had a hard time of it, I'd have Tye read it. He was a natural-born reader.

On our way back to the Occidental, after the sun set, we stopped to gawk at Buffalo's red brick courthouse. It towered on a grassy hill just off Main Street. Johnson County's lawmen had a pretty nice setup. I hoped we wouldn't have to rely on their hospitality before our business here was done. We went on and turned in at the stable to collect our personal gear, then went into the hotel carrying our rifles.

There was music playing back in the barroom, and the soft voice of a woman singing. They'd advertised nightly music at the Occidental, and I'd've liked to go, but right then I had other things on my mind.

A woman I assumed to be the owner's wife, a smiling old girl of sixty-odd years, lit a lamp and led us up the stairs. She even turned the key and opened the door for us. She walked inside and lit a lamp on a table next to the bed.

"You get cold, there's another blanket under the bed with the chamber pot," she said.

"Oh, we'll keep each other warm," Tye said, grinning and winking at me. I had to chuckle. I was too old to get embarrassed.

Smiling impishly, the old woman shook her head. "I'll start frying eggs at five. I stop at eight."

"Don't expect us," I replied politely. "We'll prob'ly sleep in a little."

After she left, I sat down at the head of the bed and tried to work through some of my copy of The Bighorn Sentinel. I was amazed to see them still talking about Custer's massacre, which had been over for ten years that month. Another one talked about how long-horned cows were no good and had to go. Guess they figured the wolfers would take care of all the wolves soon enough, and them cows wouldn't need the protection of their horns. They wrote of a big flood down in New Mexico Territory, and how Laramie City had just put in electric lighting, which made me shake my head in amazement. I read that to Tye, and he seemed to take it all in stride. Being younger, I reckon he could accept more change.

Calf roundup on Crazy Woman Creek was over, and they claimed to have a heavy crop, which surprised me after that winter's die-up. And new towns were still cropping up and making the newspaper: a place called Douglas had just been named, over east of Fort Fetterman. A little town called Sheridan seemed to be prospering, or at least they claimed one store in that town was the most complete establishment of its kind in the country.

And then a story that really caught my eye: the Bighorn Sentinel was arguing against an article that had appeared in the Yellowstone Journal claiming ninety per cent of the cows around Buffalo were dead, due to the hard winter and lack of grass. The Sentinel claimed the ranges around there had never been in finer condition, but on that count I knew they were lying. Sandoe and me had seen the bones of dead, skinned cattle all the way from Cheyenne, where the skinners had been hard at work the previous April. Wyoming just didn't want to admit their losses to the world because so many people had their money tied up there.

They were talking about General Nelson Miles' inability to capture "General Geronimo," down in Arizona; rioting in Belfast, Ireland; how a feller by the name of King Ludwig had recently been *deposed from*—I figured that meant kicked off—the Bavarian throne and then committed suicide by drowning. They claimed his doctor had drowned trying to save him.

But the story that most caught my eye was one about a feller name of Lampasas Jake. Its title, in great big letters, said, LAMMING SINNERS AND RAPING THE ENGLISH LANGUAGE. That second part could've been about me, but as for lamming sinners, they were talking about somebody else. I'd heard of lamming *season*, but I wasn't guilty of anything to do with sheep, in spite of whatever that feller up in Oregon said.

But never mind about that. About Lampasas Jake—the article went like this (and I read it out loud to Tye before I realized how close to home it really hit): "Lampasas Jake", the cowboy evangelist who is holding revivals in New Mexico, can beat Sam Jones as a vernacular preacher. Here is an extract from one of his sermons: "How many of you's ready to die with your boots on? Where'd you be to breakfast? Don't any of you drunken, swearin', fightin', blasphemin', thievin', tinhorn, coffin paint exterminating galoots look at me ugly, because I knows ye. I've been through the drive. You're all in your sins. You know a fat, well fed, well cared for, thoroughly branded steer when you see one, and you can tell whose it is and where it belongs. There's a man that owns it. There's a place for it to go. There's a law to protect it. But the maverick—whose is that? You're all mavericks and worse. The maverick has no brand on him. He goes bellowing about until somebody takes him in and claps the branding iron on him. But you whelps, you've got the devil's brand on you. You've got his lariat about you. He lets you have rope now, but he'll haul you in when he wants firewood."

We laughed about that quite a bit, but me, I was laughing only because Tye expected me to. Inside, I felt like them words were printed just for me, and it gave me a cold feeling down deep. Lampasas Jake had sure enough read my brand.

After Tye had drifted off, I lay there staring at the ceiling, with sleep far from me. I couldn't get them words out of my head. I just kept thinking I ought to get out of the outlaw life while I still could—*if* I still could. Maybe it was already too late.

I rolled over and dug around in my saddlebag until I came up with an old tintype. Turning onto my back again, for several minutes I studied that picture. It was a pathetically marred portrait of my daddy, Jedediah McLean, with his arm around Mama.

Memories of my folks were good. I smiled when I looked at them, as I often did of a sleepless night, even though they'd both been dead more than twenty years.

Outside of a coating of trail dust and five days of whiskers I toted now, I favored Daddy in most ways. I had his rough-hacked face, his short-cropped brown hair, tinged lightly with red. His had been streaked with gray at the hairline, I recalled. And last time I looked in a mirror mine was going that way, too. Like Daddy, my low-hung eyebrows shaded blue-gray eyes flanked by crow tracks. The wrinkles that slashed my forehead and the sides of my mouth gave me eight or ten years I didn't feel I'd lived. I guess they spoke of the worry and troubles my life had seen. People used to tell me I looked meaner than God had intended me to because I seemed so easy-going. Most of those folks hadn't seen me with my back up.

In the morning, I woke with a backache. It wasn't that the bed was bad. In fact, it was pretty soft, and that was the problem. For a man used to sleeping on the ground with a saddle for a pillow it was *too* soft. And don't let some soft-headed city boy tell you using a saddle for a pillow isn't done. A man gets mighty dizzy lying with his head on the ground. I've tried it and hated the feeling. I've even laid my head on the heel of a boot once, and another time on a holstered gun, when a saddle wasn't to be had—I'd try anything short of a rock to lift my head off the ground. Take it from a trail rider—the saddle's preferable.

The sun was up, and the street was abustle with activity long before me and Tye stepped into it. Rigs and saddle horses crowded the main thoroughfare, and somewhere along it we heard the cussing of a deep-voiced man. A half-interested glance showed me he was a freighter, upset at a wayward horse. He was only speaking the common rough language of his kind. The rest of his train, five wagons and ten teams long, made every other outfit on the street seem small.

We didn't see Sheriff Bennett around, but before long two riders, one on a stocky sorrel and one on a red roan, caught my eye. The man on the sorrel wasn't much above average height, perhaps an inch or two taller than me. A silver star clung to his vest above one pocket. His lips were pursed beneath a well-kept moustache, but as they passed us he smiled and nodded. The corners of his blue eyes crinkled up under the slightly curved gray brim of his hat.

The other man was younger, his face thin and his eyes nervous. He wore his gun a little too low on his hip.

Tye and me glanced at each other. This answered one of our questions: what if Bennett had deputies? He did, leastways today.

I shrugged and shook my head. "Don't worry 'bout it, Tye. They won't know what hit 'em. I promise. I've hit a hunnerd banks in towns livelier than this." I was lying through my black teeth there. I'd robbed five banks and a few stagecoaches in my lifetime, and a handful of establishments that didn't amount to much. Most of my work had been stealing horses and cows. But it didn't hurt to give Tye a little confidence.

Tye pulled his eyes away from the riders and looked at me, a grin breaking over his face. "Who's worried? I know you ain't lived this long for nothin'."

Just then, I caught a change in the riders' movement out of the corner of my eye and turned to see the both of them turning around and riding back towards us. They climbed down and walked over, the older one smiling amiably, the other just watching.

"You must be the pair that saved the sheriff's bacon yesterday," the older one said. "My name's Anthony Ribervo, and this is Lucius Bird. We help the sheriff out a little."

"Good to know you," I said, not volunteering our names.

Ribervo's eyes flickered back and forth between the two of us. "Well, I just thought I'd say hello. Van—the sheriff—is a gruff fellow, but he's a good man. I appreciate you keeping him around a while longer."

"My pleasure," I said with a smile. I looked at Lucius Bird, and he was staring at me like I'd kicked his horse. He just nodded as the two of them turned away.

"That younger one looks like somebody stepped on his nose this mornin'," said Tye as we walked along the boardwalk.

I laughed and stopped at Germania House. "Let's drop in for some breakfast."

We killed that day "job hunting", crossing our fingers again in hopes of no success. Toward mid-afternoon, I paid the First National Bank a visit to tack up a notice to the effect that two experienced punchers were looking for ranch work. Inside, there was a long mahogany counter cut in half. The section near the door had a sign that read TELLER, and the other advertised ACCOUNTANT. I tried as casually as I could to look over the two men beneath the signs. The accountant, a black-haired fellow with spider-like limbs, was speaking rudely to an older customer. It was plain he had the old man flustered, and he kept pushing him—not enough to gain notice from the teller, but enough to anger me, even when it was none of my affair. It was plain he was enjoying his self-importance. Holding my irritation in, I left the building.

The bank closed at five o'clock. I left Tye in the room again and went to the street. Figured I'd be less noticeable to passersby alone than with a young man of Tye's looks and charm. He drew people—especially women—like hobos to a money tree. Me, I was just a drifter, nothing more. Couldn't even spare a dime for a shave.

I wandered like my only goal was killing time. I soon found myself near a shed behind the bank at a little run-down corral. Leaning up against the top rail, I rolled a cigarette and watched a rangy pinto bully his corral mate, a Spanish burro, until the littler fellow gave him a solid kick to the jaw. The fight, such as it was, ended with that, and I watched the burro wander to a trough and soak his muzzle as if nothing had happened. The pinto cut him a wide swath.

I glanced at the sun, then reached into a vest pocket and drew out a scratched silver watch. Ten minutes past five. And still no sign of the bankers.

Sudden voices from the back door of the bank drew my attention. I looked over casually. The two bank clerks stood there twenty yards away. The older one spoke to the tall one as he bent and wiggled a key into a hole and turned it with a sound click. Then his partner did the same on a lock above the first. Two locks—two separate keys. I cursed under my breath. A man had to work like hell to make a honest living anymore.

The black-haired man's legs climbed at least halfway up his back. He was little *but* legs, in fact. As I followed him from the bank, trying to be nonchalant, he set a pace my shorter legs were hard-pressed to keep. Fortunately, he didn't walk far.

He went three hundred yards up the slope behind the bank to a white house with a picket fence, then up the walk and through the front door. I walked on to a point of cover where I could watch the house. I wanted to make sure Longlegs wouldn't come out. There was a chance he could just have been visiting, though he surely seemed to be at home there.

I gave Longlegs an hour then slipped from the bushes where I'd been concealed. I took a moment to brush ants and other assorted wildlife from my clothes, then ambled downhill toward the Occidental. A simple plan formed as I walked, and by the time I reached the hotel porch it was set in my mind. Barring the unexpected, me and Tye would be some richer by tomorrow at that time. I smiled and pushed through the hotel door.

I hashed my idea over with Tye until both of us were satisfied with its details, such as they were. No—more than satisfied. We were dead sure we knew it forward and back.

Five minutes after I doused the lamp, Tye was softly snoring. As for me, I couldn't stop going over the plan in my head. You know how it is, when you really want something to work. I was only a bank robber—an occasional one at that. But I couldn't do a sloppy job. If ever I was found out, at least I wanted them to know they'd had a task doing it. Thinking about that made me think back to giving my name away in front of Sheriff Van Bennett, and I cursed myself for that. I hoped his memory for names was as bad as mine.

Somewhere around midnight I drifted off. When I blinked open my eyes again it was still full dark. Outside our window flickering pinpoints of fire filled the sky. I pulled my watch and lit a match. Four o'clock. I lay down and stared at the dim blackness of the ceiling, listening to Tye's breathing. Another half-hour, I told myself. No more. And that half-hour galloped by quick as a cabbage full of slugs.

Out among the houses, a dog barked, startling me awake. I cursed myself for dozing off. Looking at my watch, I saw only twenty minutes had passed since I lay back down. I stretched and sat up on the edge of the bed, rubbing my eyes. I groped for my hat on the floor, found it and shoved it on. Then I shook the bed lightly and whispered, "Tye. Get up, boy. It's time."

I was disappointed at the time it took Tye to revive himself. Every day I tried to teach him the art of catnapping, but he couldn't get it into his head. Guess he had the notion men needed sleep to survive. I worried that someday if I wasn't there to watch out for him that foolish idea was going to cost him his life.

I threw the covers off on the floor and cuffed his head lightly. "You're gonna get us killed, Rip VanWinkle," I said.

"Stop it."

He spoke too loudly for the thin-walled hotel, and I grasped his arm in a grip that came from years of holding a plow and swinging a nine-pound hammer.

"Keep it down," I whispered harshly. "And get your butt out of bed now or stay here."

My words and tone of voice somehow reached Tye's brain, and he sat up when I let go of his arm. "Bruised my arm," he said, half in fun.

"Good. Remember it tomorrow. Now get dressed."

There was quiet in the room. Only the rustling of trousers, the tinkle of a gunbelt buckle, metallic clicks as we put our weapons on half cock and checked for six full loads. (We carried a round under the hammer on days we expected trouble.)

Except for the long, curved brace under the barrel, and the little pin of a front sight, my 1875 Remington Frontier was a careful mimic of Colt's Peacemaker but chambered for Remington's own .44 cartridge. When I had checked its loads, I dropped it into the Mexican double-loop holster and drew it out again even as it settled. I repeated the exercise a dozen times. Tye did the same with his Schofield then finally holstered it, and I patted his shoulder.

"Keep at it, Tye," I encouraged. "You got the touch. By dang if you ain't another Hickock."

Picking up our saddlebags and rifles, we stepped to the door and eased it open. In the hallway, all was dark except for the dim starlight coming through the window in the front. We crept down the stairs and out the front door. Remaining motionless for several moments in the shadows of the porch, we listened to the talking of Clear Creek, hurrying by on its night rounds.

Once certain there was no one about, we walked around to the barn. Used to operating in the dark, we found the oat bin. Tye struck a match so he could search the gear on the wall, and seeing the nosebags he brought two of them down.

As Tye set about the feeding, I threw saddles on and cinched them down. When impatience overtook us, we removed the nosebags, slipped on bridles, and shoved the Winchesters into their boots.

I patted Sheriff's neck and let him rub his head up against my chest, nudging me backward. "Okay, boy. Just hold on, an' we'll be movin'," I said softly.

I rested my hand on Tye's shoulder and tried to focus on his eyes in the dark. "Remember, when I've been in that bank five minutes, take 'em to the creek and let 'em drink. But not much. I'll be comin' on the run. Be ready."

"All right."

"Let's go."

In the shadows, we crept toward Longlegs' residence. In five minutes we were inside the picket fence, and Tye stepped around the side of the house to look for a back door.

The front door was unlocked—most folks didn't worry about burglars back then, leastways not in the West. I eased it open and left it ajar as I stood listening into the shadows. The rustling of blankets told me someone was awake.

Taking a deep breath, in four strides I was at the bedroom door. I'd no sooner reached it than Tye made his entrance. Well, leave it to Tye to do things in a big way. Don't just humiliate them—make them really despise you. Around the corner he came with his .45 in one hand and a brightly glowing lantern in the other, throwing the room into full light. The man and his wife were huddled close together, their bare shoulders showing over the top edge of the blankets.

The man recovered first and sat up, making the covers fall away from both of their unclothed torsos. He reached frantically for his nightclothes on the floor beside him but overbalanced and fell off the bed on his face, pulling half the covers with him. The woman's mouth dropped open like her jaw had dissolved. Whipping her arms up to cover herself she sat staring for some seconds while Tye gaped at her hesitantly.

I lunged to where Longlegs, on his hands and knees, was clawing for his clothing. I jammed my boot heel down hard on the back of his hand. He cried out in pain and anger, glaring up at me and my Remington.

"If either of you move or yell out, you'll both die." I wasn't that hungry for blood, but I said it with a tone that left no room for doubt. I tried to look the same way.

Must've been my voice that brought the woman out of her trance. She suddenly whipped the quilts up to her neck and sat staring at me like I'd just crawled out of a rotted apple. "What are you doing in my house?" she snapped.

"Shut up, Martha!" yelped Longlegs, his hand still pinned under my boot.

"Good advice, ma'am. Mister?" I looked at the banker with my deadliest glare. "Cover your ugly body an' get your shoes on. We're goin' for a walk to your partner's house." I stepped back and let him rub his hand for a couple of seconds before I spoke again, gun barrel riveted on his head. "Now."

Once Longlegs had made up his mind, he climbed into his clothes rather nimbly, considering the two armed robbers surveying his every move. Tye covered Martha the whole time with his revolver, and she hadn't opened her mouth or moved since the first time. Tears of terror rolled silently down her face, but I forced all sympathy out of my gaze. I wished I could force it out of my heart.

"I'm takin' this gent to his pard's house, then to the bank," I told Tye. "If you hear shootin' or a commotion of any kind, kill her an' go for the horses."

Tye wouldn't kill a woman, and I didn't expect him to. I wouldn't have either. I gave the order only as a scare tactic. The plan was for him just to tie her up and gag her, then leave her on the bed. I guess Longlegs really did care for his wife, because his eyes widened even farther at my words. "Please don't hurt her—I'm begging you. Please. She's going to have a baby. I'll do anything you want if you won't harm her."

With my hardest stare, I shoved Longlegs for the door and growled, "Just do what I say. Maybe there'll be someone besides an orphan living here when this is all over."

Me and Longlegs reached his partner's house without event and without seeing another soul. We walked in, lit a lamp, and pulled the groggy older man from bed, my pistol at his temple.

"Where's your key to the bank, mister? Fetch it now."

It took no time for the older man to find his senses when he looked down the barrel of my gun. He went right to a dresser, opened one of its drawers and withdrew a key. I took it and thrust it toward Longlegs. "Is that the right key?"

He nodded vigorously and looked at the older man. "Thank you so much, Henry. They've got Martha at the house."

The older man looked at me with fire in his eye and took a menacing step toward me, stopping only when he heard the click of the Remington's hammer. "That's my daughter up there," he said, shaking a finger at me. "If you hurt her, so help me…"

"What?" I waited, but he didn't finish his thought. "Come on and get dressed, mister. You're goin' to the bank with us, where I can watch you."

The bank was gray in the quiet chill of the dawn. The clicking of the keys in their locks sounded unnaturally loud. I dared a glance toward the water trough in the corral across the way, and there in its shadow crouched Tye. I didn't want them to know he was there, for then they'd know we no longer had a hostage. I smiled and raised my hand in signal once the bankers had turned their backs on me and stepped inside the building. Tye returned my signal by raising his pistol above his head, and I saw starlight flicker off its nickel-plated barrel.

Old Henry didn't seem to have any will to fight, knowing we had his daughter. Once inside the bank, with quick, deft turns he spun the dial on a huge safe and clicked open its door. Thirty or forty plump bags were stacked on its floor.

"Open one," I said. "I'd like to see what you're payin' for your daughter's life."

Henry undid the string on one of the bags and laid it open for me to see. Gold coin, all of it. Twenty-dollar double eagles.

"We'll take one bag of those," I said. "But I want the rest in cash—big bills. You—" I turned to Longlegs. "—as soon as your pardner gets a bag full, tie it up."

Henry turned to his shelves, where crisp new bills were stacked in banded bundles.

"Twenties and above," I said. "And show 'em to me first. I don't trust you any more than you do me."

Henry went to work quickly, showing me each bundle before he dropped it into the sack.

He had ten bags sitting on the floor before I stopped him. I was letting my greed carry me away. I didn't know where we'd even carry that much money. At the time, I guessed there was close to eight thousand dollars on the floor.

"All right, gents, your chore is almost done. Now, take four canvas bags and divide them little ones evenly in 'em. Move." And move they did, nervously, as if expecting me at any moment to shoot them down in cold blood.

Just as they finished, I heard a horse nicker outside the back door. I turned involuntarily toward the sound, and in that fleeting second I heard metal scrape on wood, and I wheeled back toward the bankers. I lunged to my right a half-second before a huge Colt Walker revolver exploded in the hands of old Henry, its bullet missing me by inches. In that next second, when he swung the barrel on me and laid a thumb to the hammer again, I shot him in the chest, then again.

Longlegs' gumption surprised me as he swung a foot to kick the gun out of my hand. He missed, but I didn't. I leaped forward and buffaloed him alongside the skull with the Remington. He spun into the counter and dropped like a dry goods dummy.

Old Henry was leaning against the wall, trying to bring the massive revolver to bear again. But its four pounds was too much for him. Blood trickled from both corners of his mouth, and with a sickening realization I knew I'd killed him.

I reached over and pried the uncocked weapon from his stubborn fingers, throwing it over near the counter. His hate-filled eyes glared at me. He was close enough I could smell his breath, his body smell...his hate. I wished I could put my weapon to his head and end it all quickly for him, but it wasn't in me. The urgency of the moment was gone. The old man reached up suddenly and grabbed a hold of my wrist with his bloody hand. I don't know why, but I didn't try to pull away. He slowly sank to the floor and finally just let go of my wrist.

I whirled around, Remington cocked, as the door swung open. No one was there, but a voice hissed from around the corner. "Tom?"

"I'm okay, kid. Let's go!"

Tye rushed through the door and jolted to a halt. He stared with wide eyes at the fallen bankers, frozen for several seconds. Then, with fear in his face, he turned to the heavy canvas sacks, and with one hand grabbed two of them. As I picked up the other two, my eyes were forced back to Henry and Longlegs. Longlegs lay unconscious, but Henry continued to stare at me, his eyes accusing. What life was left in them—and it was little—drilled me with reproach. It was a sight I could never forget. And then the sight began to fade from his eyes.

As I looked down on him I heard the first voices from close outside. "—shots from the bank!" were the first words I heard. "If it's robbers, kill 'em all. Hey!" A handful of shots rang out. And they couldn't be Tye's. He had his hands full of stolen money.

Chapter Four
The Getaway

The town looked like a stomped anthill. Voices called back and forth, and lights flickered to life to brighten the streets in sickly rectangular patches. I looked toward the water trough to see Tye and his dark horse, lit up eerily by bouncing lanterns. Even as I looked, Tye's arm came up and spurts of orange light speared out as if from the tips of his fingers. Two hollow reports crashed along the street. A rifle answered, then several handguns. Tye screamed like a madman and fired again, snapping a glance toward me.

Cursing, I shoved the two bags of cash under one arm without thinking. I should have just left it. I thrust my Remington into its holster, clawed the big Walker off the floor and charged out the door into the line of fire.

A Colt Walker makes an awesome sound in the dark of dawn. I snapped a shot into the gathering group. With two gunmen against them now, people scattered, only one of them finding the nerve to fire back. At a sprint, I reached Sheriff, and I daresay he'd've left me if Tye hadn't been holding on to his McCarty so tight. He was pitching around like he had a far better place to be and a strong urge to get there. I still can't say how, but I managed to drop the bags of money into the nearest saddlebag, though I didn't get it buckled. A shot zipped past me, and I turned and answered it without trying to hit anything. That time I shot twice, and somebody swore angrily and dropped a lantern.

I stuffed the Walker hastily inside the front of my gunbelt and went for the saddle. At the same time I reached for my saddle horn a gun cracked, and the top of the horn exploded into leather fragments even as I touched it. A bit of lead stung my palm, making me forget jumping aboard.

"Let go of him, Tye!" I yelled. He did so as I grabbed the horn, reached over the saddle skirt and got hold of two saddle strings, taking a wrap around my hand. The second I kicked my foot into the stirrup, Sheriff bolted forward. He nearly ripped horn and leather strings both from my grasp.

I cursed as I felt my foot slip out of the stirrup. I was dangling!

Sheriff, even off balance, made for all the speed he could muster. He was after Tye's horse, and as for me, it was my lookout to stay with him. A hoof slammed me in the shin. Felt like it shattered the bone. I gritted my teeth and held on, trying to pull myself forward and up. Shots like fireworks rattled behind me. My feet slammed against the ground every few yards, jerking me around. It was only by desperation I held on. Where was Tye's horse? I couldn't hear it anymore. I only heard my own heart crashing and the frantic gallop of Sheriff's hooves. I hoped Tye was close ahead. He was my only hope now.

Behind me people were shouting, and lights were still flickering on along our path. It felt like we ran forever. But it couldn't have been more than seventy yards. Gunfire shook the night. Once, Sheriff screamed out, veering wildly to one side. I prepared to go down. Yet somehow he ran on, straight ahead into the night and past the courthouse that loomed like a castle in the dark.

I started yelling at Sheriff. I must have sounded like a maniac, but I'd nearly lost all hope. At that speed, without a stirrup hold I couldn't climb up. And I couldn't hold on much longer. The gray faltered in his step, but he'd got the urge to run. I couldn't penetrate the excitement in his brain long enough to make him stop. I felt my hand slipping on the horn. I gritted my teeth and squeezed harder, but my palm had already slipped away from the leather. Only my fingers and thumb held my left hand there, and it was a precarious hold. Then, like in a nightmare, my hand slid free. It seemed like I held on forever with my right hand alone. For a moment, my body weight made the saddle strings draw tighter around my fingers, so tight it hurt. But it must have been mere seconds before Sheriff's hoof caught me in the leg, and I let go.

Like I'd been rolled in some giant carpet, then had it ripped out from under me, I careened across the ground. The world spun around me until I couldn't tell where I was. I felt my face and hands tear against gravel, my mouth fill up with dust. I landed on my back, my wind gone, my head ringing. Panicking, I shoved up to a kneeling position, trying to force myself to take a breath. When it came it was with a tremendous gasp, filling my lungs with air and dust. I doubled over coughing. I could see more lanterns bobbing along the street. And now I heard people yelling behind me and to the sides.

A rifle sang out, spraying dust at me. I couldn't tell where it came from, but it was too close. Another cracked and made the wind move along my cheek. I clawed for the big Colt Walker. It was miraculously still in my belt. Jerking it free, I snapped off a shot towards the bobbing lanterns.

I fired another.

They wavered as I heard a horse bearing down on me from behind—no, two horses. I threw myself sideways, landing on a shoulder. A rider was nearly on top of me as I leveled the gun and pulled the trigger.

The hammer clicked on an empty chamber.

I cursed and threw the Walker, reaching for the Remington. But a voice drove through my panic. I looked up and saw the pale face of the rider I'd tried to shoot. I heard his voice screaming at me to take my horse.

It was Tye!

Summoning strength from somewhere, I lurched to my feet and almost fell into Sheriff, cursing him but overwhelmed with joy to see him. This time when I grabbed hold of the horn and cantle it was with the devil's own determination. I urged the gray to a run, going alongside, Injun-style. When I got the rhythm I swung up. It had never felt better to have a saddle pound my backside. I never intended to get down again.

Tye galloped along behind me. I could hear him swearing vehemently about something and yelling my name, but I didn't dare look back. As we passed the north edge of town I laid eyes on big Van Bennett, his face a snarl of desperation and hate.

When I heard him yell "Stop!" I ducked low in the saddle, and a bullet flew past me, not close enough to feel but enough to hear its breath.

The gray gave his urge to run to Tye's bay, and we thundered at full speed along the road. The bay was a good horse, but he fell back in spite of the excitement. More shots crashed behind us, but they were firing blind. In the darkness none found their mark.

Then, dead ahead, a horse charged into our path, wheeling broadside. Its rider held a rifle on us and at seventy yards he roared, "Halt!" I spurred the gray harder and drew my Remington. I wasted two shots on this fearless, stupid man who refused to give us the road. He was so far out of town he couldn't even have known who we were and if we were fugitives! He was a fool to try and stop two total strangers, judging only by circumstances. But fool or not, he was right about us.

Tye was firing past me. I cursed as the other man's first shot echoed down the road. When he fired again something burned along my ribs. I almost dropped the pistol. We were only twenty yards away when he decided to move, and my next shot—the last one in my pistol—dumped him from his saddle. Even as he fell, recognition flashed across my fevered mind. It was one of the deputies we had met the day before—Lucius Bird! His mount backed up, then turned and bolted.

We were clear of Buffalo except for a scattering of ranches that hid out there in the dark. Our horses splashed through a narrow creek and started up the gentle rise beyond. We let them run until completely out of sight of the last lights and the vengeful chatter of Buffalo. A mile out I had to slow down and wait for Tye to catch up. Like I said, he had a good horse under him—we'd picked it together. But I didn't keep old Sheriff for nothing. There were few horses that could best him on a flat stretch.

After several more minutes of running, I eased Sheriff to a walk while I checked the wound in my side. The bullet had just nicked me, cutting through my shirt and vest. I got down and felt around until I found warm wetness at the point of Sheriff's right hip. He shied a little when I felt it, and his skin quivered, but he waited to see what I'd do. The bullet had sunk in at an angle but had come back out, leaving a nasty hole. There wasn't anything I *could* do.

Stepping around him, I moved one of the moneybags to the opposite saddlebag, relieving the strain being off balance had put on the horse and on the saddle strings. Taking this chance to catch our breath, I walked the gray, renewing the loads in my Remington as I rode. As we went along, I could see by Tye's face he was upset. After a while, I asked him why.

He looked over at me, a sick expression on his face. After a moment's hesitation, he said, "Tom, I…I had them bags. I had 'em tight! But when they started shootin'… I … Tom! Damnit!" I thought he was going to break into tears. "I couldn't get 'em in my saddlebags. All that shootin'… You still inside. I lost the bags when they started shootin', Tom. I lost 'em. All that money!"

I was suddenly sick. All that for nothing. Nearly getting killed. *Scared* to death if not shot outright. In my head I called him a dozen names. Damn that worthless boy!

We rode in silence for a long time. I didn't look over at Tye, and *all* he did was look at me. Finally, I let a long sigh escape my lips. There was nothing for it now. The money was gone. Anyone could have lost it, especially someone like Tye, on his first job and all. I'd done worse things myself. And why be greedy? We still had

LEGEND OF THE TUMBLEWEED

half—several years' wages, to a cowboy. More than anything, I felt sorry for Tye. I knew he was cursing himself without mercy.

"Don't worry about the money, Tye," I finally said with a crooked smile. "At least you only lost your half."

When he looked at me with shocked eyes, I just laughed and put spurs to the gray. We turned off the road and headed toward the Bighorns.

The going became irritatingly slow. Washes slashed the land, and along hilltops we had to skirt low stands of mahogany or struggle through them when forced to it. The sun crawled into the sky, and I couldn't help but be glad for its guiding light. Unfortunately, it was on Bennett's side, too, and by now I knew a posse would be on its way. He didn't seem like a man to putter. But we had a plan of escape. We'd planned that before anything else. With that in mind, I turned south.

It was nine o'clock when we rode to the west of the place where we'd make camp that evening. In-between, we could see the buildings of Fort McKinney, on the north bank of Clear Creek. That meant we were due west of Buffalo now, and not very far away. We'd camp just a mile east of Fort McKinney after the wild goose chase I planned to take the posse on all day long. No robber would be fool enough to hide near the fort. That's what I counted on them thinking, at least.

Circling to the south of the fort, we turned along the creek and rode toward Buffalo, glancing cautiously around for troopers. We knew the chances we were taking, but I planned on going back to draw off the posse long before they reached this point. They'd be led far away from here by nightfall, and Sandoe'd be alone.

We found the cottonwood where someone had carved a cross a foot long and wide. I turned to Tye, who was watching me. I jerked a thumb in the direction we'd come.

"You get down in there somewhere and hole up, Tye. Watch your hoss. Keep 'im from makin' noise if anybody gets close. That posse's close enough, I'm sure. But I won't let 'em find you. When I get done with 'em, they'll figger we're headed south—to Cheyenne or someplace. Then we can circle around and head north. They'll be chasin' their tails 'fore we're through."

Tye glanced along our back trail. "What'll you do if they catch up?"

"Lose 'em. Or die tryin'. But there's one thing I need you to do. While you're layin' low, you find a likely place to hide this loot. Just have a place ready, a place we can cover it up with brush and rocks. If it gets tight, we'll leave it here and come back another time."

I jumped down and reached into a saddlebag to tug out the sack. I handed it and the other in turn up to Tye. He looked at me with a heap of gratitude in his eyes, so much gratitude he didn't say a word. But I could feel it, and that was enough. He'd lost half our take, but I still trusted him.

"Don't bed down till after dark. Wait back in the trees an' watch. They won't be expectin' us to come here, so I'd say around dark you can build up a little fire. And don't worry, Tye. I ain't lived this long for nothin'. I'll use a few old Injun tricks—throw 'em off the trail."

I left Tye there with the loot at that cottonwood tree. He just sat his saddle and looked at me thoughtfully as I touched my hat and rode away. Tye could ride anywhere he wanted to now and be a wealthy man—at least for a while. He had all the money. And as much as I liked Tyrone Sandoe, I'd probably let him go, if that was his choice. I wouldn't have the heart to hunt him down.

As I rode, I thought about what some folks might say I'd done to Tye. I'd led him on his first big robbery. By the time I returned to camp, if Tye hadn't buried the money I knew he'd have counted every dollar, maybe several times. I'd helped convince him the outlaw trail was the way to go. And under my guidance, Tyrone Sandoe, a man of only nineteen, was bound never to turn back from a lawless path. At that moment, with the old banker fresh in my memory, the thought made me sick.

I rode north, and on the horizon I spotted a thin veil of dust only minutes after leaving Tye. If that was the posse, they were way too close, and I was afraid they could catch Tye if they split up and tracked us both. But the problem was about to be remedied, even if I had to get my tail scorched in the process. Hopefully I wouldn't get it caught in a crack.

I rode straight for the dust cloud that grew more and more distinct above the dry grass. In half an hour, I reined in and sat the saddle, rolling and lighting a quirly. I watched the dust and knew the posse was close. Close and keeping their horses to a healthy trot. They'd found our trail, and they weren't sparing their animals, from the looks of it. I guess they figured they'd catch me before long.

Five minutes later, the first rider's head appeared over the top of the hill. He saw me instantly, and as his horse came into view he hopped to a halt. Even at four hundred yards I could see it was the little Mexican, Poco Vidales. He pointed toward me and looked back at someone on his left. When the other man showed himself there was no mistaking the fiery beard of Van Bennett. A couple more seconds, and my tally came to more than ten men.

With a show of nonchalance, I pulled the cigarette from between my teeth, crushed it on the saddle horn, and dropped the dead butt into the grass. Sucking in a deep breath, I turned the gray, rolled my spurs across his sides, and took off like a rabbit at a beagle show.

Rifle shots rang out behind me, and the race was on.

Chapter Five
Beauty Among Beasts

Ever ride a fast horse? I mean a horse so fast he takes your breath clean away from you? Sheriff was a horse like that. Putting rocks and critter holes out of my head, I let that gray stretch out and pull across the sage for all he was worth. Once, a flock of sage hens drummed up from under our feet, pounding away in all directions. It seemed only to make Sheriff go faster, even to fly like the birds. It certainly made my heart go faster.

We were still in rolling hill country, but it was rising. Sheriff reached out, pulled back, bunched and reached again. With his ears flat against his head and nostrils flared, he made for the mountains. His sides heaved between my knees as he made a sound like a strong, clean steam engine chugging. He stumbled once, grunting, but I grabbed for the old apple and held on, keeping myself centered. To fall here would be certain death for me. If the fall didn't do it, Van Bennett sure would.

I'd no doubt I'd left the posse behind after we'd gone a couple of miles and were climbing into the foothills. But when I turned to look, there was that Mexican! I couldn't believe what I was seeing. At first I thought it must be some wandering cowboy. But sure enough, Poco Vidales was behind me—and gaining. And there was another man back of him. Two of them, not two hundred yards away, but not another soul in sight.

Vidales I already knew was a small man, at least fifty pounds lighter than me. The other man didn't look much larger. They had that advantage. Even the best horse in the world can't win a race with a fifty-pound handicap. And we were starting into hill country now, too. Sheriff was a good horse anywhere, and clear-footed as a horse can be. But he was at his worst in steep country, where a horse had to have a lot of meat on his hindquarters to keep him going steady.

There was no time to plan. And no time to waste. I either made a different move now, or I was dead. I'd made the mistake of not accounting for my weight, and it would cost me. I reached down and whipped my Winchester from the saddle boot. Even before coming to a complete stop I swung out of the saddle, counting on the McCarty tucked under my belt to keep Sheriff with me. He dug in his hooves and stopped when he felt me leave the saddle. Whirling, I sat down hard on a pile of rocks, drawing my knees up. Sheriff leaned his head over me.

The man down there behind Vidales veered suddenly sideways and flew from his horse. But the Mexican either didn't see me or didn't trust my marksmanship at that range, for he came on. Yet it wasn't the men who were my targets. They were far too small at two hundred yards.

Centering the sights on his horse's lower lip, I squeezed off a round. The Winchester drove against my shoulder, and I jacked in another shell. The report of the first was almost startling on that quiet hillside, a barking, echoing cry that hung forever around me as I waited. Suddenly, the Mexican's horse went straight up. It seemed to hover there for a second or two, with Vidales stuck to it like a fly to a wall. Then they both went down.

I didn't have a chance to see the Mexican land. Dirt kicked up near me, followed by the flat report of a rifle. I looked over to see the other man prone across his horse's neck. His horse was flattened out in the sagebrush, lying perfectly still. I squeezed off a shot in return but couldn't see where it hit. I tried another and saw a faint puff of rock-dust near the horse's head.

I guess that was too close, for the little man lunged up, and then up came his horse. At a stumbling run, he led the animal into a cluster of bushes in the bottom of the draw, and I didn't shoot again. I didn't want to kill anybody else. I just wanted them to back off.

Returning my attention to where Vidales had been, I couldn't see him. His horse had regained its feet and now stood fidgeting around on the flat, but the rider was gone. Casting a look farther down the valley, I saw a heavy cloud of dust. The rest of the posse was coming on—too close. Jumping up, I threw myself onto Sheriff's back and tickled his ribs with my spurs. He had his second or third—or *fourth* wind now—I didn't know which. But he was ready to go.

Like I said, Sheriff was built to run. And for a flatland horse he didn't do bad. He put himself to a lope, and nothing could stop him. The sage flew by, and I looked back to see the posse's dust growing fainter already.

Once I knew I had a good lead on the posse, I took to riding along a table-top ridge and stuck to it for a quarter mile or so. At last, I rode to its edge, finding myself neatly silhouetted against the sky. Below, the flank of the ridge plummeted to a churning creek edged by cottonwood and tangled bushes.

Climbing down to tighten my cinches, I stepped back into the saddle and patted Sheriff's neck. He knew instinctively we were going down that steep slope. When I patted him he just started down.

It was a chore staying back in that slick fork saddle, trying to push the stirrups past Sheriff's nose. But either I kept my seat or it was a long way to the ground, followed by the unpleasant sensation of four steel shoes dancing along my body.

It was a long two hundred feet to the bottom, but we made it there still attached. I kept riding until we dropped off an embankment and into the fast water of a two- or three-foot-wide creek.

We turned north, walking sometimes in the current, now and then on the bank, trying to leave plenty of obvious sign. I wanted the posse to be dead certain I'd headed this direction and had only accidentally left any tracks at all. We went a quarter mile down the creek in the *opposite* direction from our rendezvous spot with Tye. I kept Sheriff at the fastest walk I could without risking our necks on the slippery creek bottom.

I knew I was taking a gamble risking the time it took to make that distance. The posse might've come upon me still in the creek, where I'd have been helpless. But I had to risk that. Tye was too vulnerable, and now so was I. Even the gray couldn't run forever.

At last I turned around, and we traveled back up the creek, more than a half mile past where we'd first gone in. It was tough. Sheriff didn't like that water rushing at his feet or those slick, moss-covered rocks. I fought him all the way to keep him in center-stream. He wanted on firm soil again. And maybe more than that he didn't like to walk. He still quivered with the urge to go all-out across the range.

When we left the water, I turned south and kept Sheriff to a fast walk for a mile or so. All I needed now was to send up a funnel of dust like a smoke signal into the sky, spoiling my careful strategy and calling Bennett and his posse right to me.

It was after ten o'clock by then. I touched spurs to the gray's flanks, held him to a trot, and headed into the mountains. I prayed the posse didn't double back to Tye's trail, and I prayed I could find my way back to that cottonwood before the sun went down.

Late that afternoon, the sun was working its way down the sky. I sat in the shadows of the Bighorns, Sheriff standing over me. Up here the country was steep, and the cows hadn't got to the grass, at least not yet. So it wasn't dusty up here. The grass was two feet long, and green as pine needles. There was a fresh smell to the air that seemed missing on the range down below. And as I had sat there for the last hour, it was plain to see why. A man couldn't look anywhere out there without seeing cows. Red spots, white spots, black spots—every color of cow brute polka-dotted the landscape. Along with piles of bleaching bones. Some claimed the winter of eighty-five had killed fifty percent of the cows on the range.

The rich men who came from back East and from across the Atlantic to invest in the "sure thing," as cattle were touted, had thrown every animal they could afford out on this open range. Horace Greeley himself claimed it cost no more to raise a cow here than it did a chicken. The fools that listened to him were killing the grass—and their cows. Any man who'd ever lived with the land could see that. But they didn't care. They only cared about their money. Some of their money—a measly amount—sat in Tye's camp waiting for me now.

I'd seen the posse once during the day. From high on a hill, among a stand of ponderosas, I'd watched them following my trail doggedly. It must have taken a while, but they'd figured out my trick in the creek. They were back on my trail again. But that trail led south, and since then I'd turned sharply north and ridden another three or four miles to try and line myself up due west of Fort McKinney. I was somewhere above where Clear Creek got its beginnings. It would be a long while yet before the posse reached the point where I'd turned north. They probably wouldn't reach it at all until the next day. And by then me and Tye would be miles away.

I climbed onto Sheriff again and started down the steep slope. I'd waited too long already. If I didn't make it back to Tye by dark, I might not make it at all…

The Posse: Poco Vidales

Deputy Antonio Ribervo was Señor Bennett's *segundo*. His true name was Anthony, but I preferred the much prettier name as my people say it—Antonio. Riding his *caballo rojo* in front of us, Antonio stopped at the bottom of the ridge where the *bandido* went up. It was I who followed tracks for Señor Bennett. Myself and a man who called himself Señor Storrie—Cale Storrie. But we had a rough time and were resting. This bank robber had shoot my *caballo*.

He still carried the bullet in the heavy part of his chest. But he was good caballo, and still he went on.

We rode along a plateau above the French Creek. At last, we follow the tracks to the north and saw where the bandido went down. Most the other men were owners of banks or *mercados;* they were not *charros*. And also it already was a very long day. But the men were not cowards, and they very much wanted this bandido. They wanted to get back the *dinero* that belonged to them.

Antonio was first man to go down to the creek. He made it without nothing bad happen to him. The next to go was Cedroe, then Dunaven, then Storrie, then Burlen, then McCabe, and then Flagg, the hombre who come for writing the newspaper in Buffalo.

Señor Spencer, he was a younger man, and he was the first to fall down. But he got back up quick and laughed about his fall, taking his pistol out and knocking the dust from it.

I have always been proud to be called a *"charro excelente"*. We *Mexicanos*, we are proud people. Maybe so *too* proud sometimes. So I had to show those others by letting Chico run down the slope. Chico—that was the name of my caballo rojo. No one tried to do like me. Señores Bell and Chantry were no charros, but they did good going down, and they showed much courage.

Then only was left *mi amigo*, Señor Bennett—and a hombre who call himself Señor Buck Auburn. Señor Auburn was a man who did not care what he looked like. He never seem to shave or keep his hair clean. He had teeth growing all different ways in his mouth, making his lips poke out, some sharp like teeth of a dog. His eyes, they poked out anyway, but now they seem to be half out of his head with his fear. The Sheriff Bennett looked down at him with a look that said he knew he was a coward.

"You have a problem, Auburn?"

Señor Auburn sit back farther in his saddle. "I cain't go. This hoss won't make that. I'm goin' back to town."

Señor Bennett was not a man many would argue against. "You promised me you'd keep up, mister. Now there's no backing out."

He made his caballo *bayo* go forward, and he forced it into Señor Auburn's horse. Señor Auburn made a scared cry, and his little caballo went over the side. The caballo was scared, and it was not ready. It could feel the fear of its rider. It lost its feet and fell on its side. It made a grunt of pain. Señor Auburn rolled out of the way, and both them slid for a ways. Then his caballo, he leave him and come down to us, and Señor Auburn had to walk to him. He looked up the bank and saw Señor Bennett. Señor Bennett had a little smile on his face, and I could see Señor Auburn wanted to say something, but he said nothing. I picked up the reins of Señor Auburn's horse and handed them to him. He did not even have the courtesy to say *gracias*. He just take the reins from me and get on his horse.

The others gave little laughs about what happen, but when Señor Bennett and his horse came down everyone stopped laughing. Then they only wanted to get out of the way.

Señor Bennett was a smart man, smart like a good shepherd dog. He had track enough men to know this one would probably stay in the water as much as he could to lead us off his trail. He divide his force in two groups. He send six of them one way with Antonio and took six of us with him.

"Yell out if you find his sign, Tone. If you get too far to yell, fire a shot." With this last order, Señor Bennett rode down the stream.

Señor Cale Storrie, like myself, was a pretty good tracker. He was a blond hombre, his skin light. He had what some would call a handsome face, but handsome like a boy, not a man. Señor Storrie had spent some of his life on the reservation of the Crow Indians. He was the only *hijo* of the Indian agent. To tell the truth, he was probably the best man there at reading the sign, even better than myself. Señor Storrie went with Antonio, so I knew one of us would find this bandido's tracks. Pretty soon I saw them.

"There he is, Sheriff." I pointed.

Señor Bennett leaned over the side of his caballo and looked at the tracks that went back to the water five yards farther. It was like the bandido had never meant to leave the stream. Señor Bennett pulled a *pistola* and fired it once in the air. Then, without waiting for the other riders to catch up, he led us all on. There was no more need for me to track for him. The sides of this arroyo were very steep. The bandido would have to have wings to leave it.

Señor Bennett pushed as hard as he dared on the slippery bank. He looked close at the rocks, brush, and little trees ahead. The bandido would be foolish to stop, but with a bandido, *¿quien sabe?* Who could know? Antonio and the six men with him caught up with us, and we all rode quiet behind the sheriff.

It was half an hour later the Sheriff Bennett came to a stop very sudden. Across the trail and across the water was a large dead tree. His caballo could go no farther. Señor Cedroe, a man with a gray beard and not so much hair on top his head, stopped his caballo next to the sheriff. He stared ahead, and all of us came to stop behind them.

The Sheriff Bennett called me and Cale Storrie to him. We rode near him and stopped when we were by Señor Cedroe. I looked at the dead tree. It stretched out from one tangled bunch of cherry bush on one side of the water to the other side, where many big rocks were together.

I look over at my friend, not knowing what to say to him. Señor Bennett stopped looking at the tree and turned to look at me.

"Could a good horseman get over that?" Señor Bennett asked.

"The good horseman, maybe yes." Then I shook my finger from side to side to show how important were my next words. "The caballo, I do not think so. Myself, I would not try it."

Señor Bennett's eyes looked over all the group, but he didn't seem to really look at any of us. He made a shrugging gesture with his hands that rested on the saddle horn. "He out-foxed us then. I didn't see any tracks leaving the creek, and I've watched all the way."

I gave a little nod. "I also."

Señor Storrie spoke in his soft voice. "I think I know what he did, Sheriff. He didn't come this way at all. He rode this way just long enough to make us think we were on the right trail. That's why his horse kept steppin' out on the bank. It was a-purpose. He wanted us to see them tracks. Then he turned back in the crick and rode the other way. He knew we'd come this way after seein' his tracks. I think he headed into the mountains. That's why we ain't seen no more tracks in a while."

"I suspected," Señor Bennett said in an angry voice. "Well, we got him pegged now. Turn it around! And push like the Devil's behind you. Because I sure as hell am."

The Outlaws: Tom McLean

That's how it went, and that's how Tye an' me met up again. I figured the posse was still headed south. We rode out of camp not long after the moon had slipped beyond the Bighorns. Instead of hiding the money like more prudent men might've done we brought it along. The horses had rested and eaten their fill, and their bellies were full of water. We kept to an easy walk, lined up with the North Star as much as possible and moving in the shadow of the Bighorns. The going became touchy now and then, sometimes downright aggravating when we'd run into thickets of brush in the dark.

As we traveled, I led the way back toward the road, down out of the mountains. The stars began to fade along the paling eastern horizon as we dropped into the lower foothills and made our way to the valley.

The Bozeman Trail crawled up the bottom of the valley in some places, along ridgetops in others—it was the same road that became the main street of Buffalo south of us. Some miles north of that town, and not far ahead, lay the roadside rest spot of Cherry Valley. I'd set up a tentative rendezvous there with an old friend of mine from Oregon country. He'd be around for a very brief, quiet stay. So secret was his stay that he'd made me promise not to tell Tye anything about him and the bunch he was with before he'd let me know when and where we could meet.

A stiff wind picked up, and it had been daylight for a while when it pushed the rain clouds in. A sky that had promised sunshine now quickly gloomed over, and black cloud bellies shifted and rolled with the wind, soon blocking out any blue overhead and filling up the air with the scent of rain. Tye kept looking back along the road, and then he'd glance at me to see if I'd noticed him. Finally, he turned, sighing with forced nonchalance.

"How far is it now, Tom? I mean, we're right on the road. You think it might rain and knock our tracks down?"

I turned and looked at Tye, noticed his hand resting on the .45 on his left hip. "Ease up, Tye. We're settin' perty for a while. I don't know how far it is—five miles, maybe. As soon as we meet this fella we'll leave the road, with him or without. As for the rain..." I glanced upward at the lowering blackness, and I could feel dampness in the wind beating at my cheeks. In the mountains we'd just left, gloomy gray curtains sifted out of the clouds, dusting the land. "I'd be surprised if we don't get a good downpour even in the valley, judgin' by those rain buckets up there. An' as for where we just come from, it's already began. So ease up, boy, 'fore you spring a nerve."

Tye laughed and seemed to settle down some. But now and then I caught him looking off toward Buffalo, squinting his eyes and chewing his mustache. It was only ten more minutes or so before a fine drizzle began, and not long after that we were drowned.

Cherry Valley was a bare bones frontier settlement sitting in the middle of the sage. The road shot through its center with no intentions of slowing down for such a ramshackle sprawl of civilization. A scattering of houses, corrals and outbuildings sprinkled its borders, its entire business section consisting of a saloon and trading post.

The two business establishments, constructed of rough-hewn

logs, sat side-by-side, squat and ugly in the slanting dark rain. Three horses at one hitching rail in front of the saloon and a lone bay by another stood ducking their heads and tucking their tails against the downpour.

Tye and me tied our mounts at the side of the trading post under a lean-to. We shucked our rifles and brought them inside, comforted by the cold wood and metal against our palms.

Inside, the light was dim. We stood dripping just inside the door, water running in rivulets down our yellow "Fish" slickers. In the center of the room squatted a dully-glowing pot-belly stove, its pipe running the length of the ceiling to exit from a side wall. Varied goods were stacked about with no apparent order, and there was a disagreeable dank odor about the place that dug far back into my nostrils to nest. The rain dripping in two corners didn't help any. Tye brushed at the rain on his Fish, then ambled toward a row of shirts and trousers. I walked straight up to the counter, which was a pair of planks stretched across three barrels.

A half-breed boy of sixteen or seventeen with long hair in braids that ran down to his chest stood there and nodded at me, his eyes dropping to the pistol I wore. "You want to see my father, or can I help you?" he asked politely.

I shrugged. "All the same to me."

Before he could make his reply, an old man with flowing white hair and beard stepped from behind a partition at the back of the room. At his chin his beard was split in half, both halves tied with little bits of leather. Following him was an Indian woman and two girls under the age of twelve.

"*Bonjour.* I'm called Philipe DuPres." The old man smiled, revealing several gaps between tobacco-browned teeth. "This is my woman, Long Morning—she is Crow. This is my son, and these my daughters. There is *café* in the back, if you like. I am sorry—*coffee.*"

"Considerin' the weather, I'll take the offer, friend." I turned and nodded at the woman and girls, pulling off my hat self-consciously.

DuPres quickly waved his hand back and forth several times in front of him. "No, no, no. It is not necessary, *monsieur*. It is cold. *S'il vous plaît*—cover your head. My woman is only Injun. She will bring your *café*."

He turned and in the Crow tongue ordered the woman away with a wave of his hand. Then his attention returned to me, after favoring Tye with a brief glance. "And what is it I can do for you, *mes amis?*"

"We came here to meet a man who calls himself 'Lonely Wolf'."
The old man pooched out his lower lip as if thinking, then slapped a hand on the counter top. "Ah, *oui*! *L'homme noir*! The dark man?" I grinned and nodded. "Yeah. Negro with sad-dog eyes. Is he here?"

"*Ici? Oui*, he is here." He limped around the counter, and putting a hand on my shoulder he steered me back toward the door. There he stopped and pointed to a little run-down cabin sitting out all by itself in the sage. "*La-bas*. He stays there."

"Thanks, friend." I touched my hat. "Would you keep that coffee hot for me? And no sugar." At that moment I smelled a snatch of the homey odor from the back of the building.

When I caught Tye looking my way expectantly, I held up a hand, palm forward, signaling him to stay put. I stepped out the open doorway and took five steps into the road, my boots squishing in the mud. I twisted my neck so the hat brim caught the brunt of the rain. Watching the lonely cabin for a moment, I threw back my head, cupped my hands to my mouth, and in my deepest, smoothest voice let out a long, mournful howl. It was a poor imitation of the wolves I'd spent a winter listening to in the Blue Mountains of eastern Oregon.

The sound had no sooner left my throat than a Negro man appeared in the cabin doorway fifty yards away. He was a sad-eyed man with a bushy mustache, whiskered face sporting one long scar down its left cheek, and kinky hair cut close to his head. He wore suspenders, a butcher knife on his left side, and a short-barreled Colt Peacemaker on the right.

His name was Duke Rainey.

He ran a few yards out from the cabin, laughing delightedly. He threw back his head like I'd done and performed his own rendition of the wolf call. Mine would pass in a pinch, but Duke sounded like the real thing.

When he'd finished his call, he trotted toward me, his run-down boots splashing in the mud. I walked out to meet him. As he got close, he jarred to a stop and faced me dead-on, his hands out.

"Hey, Thomas!" He grinned as he grabbed my shoulders.

"Duke, you haven't changed a bit. Dang it, boy, it's good to lay eyes on you. "

Duke laughed again. "Yessir, and you too, Thomas. You too, an' thass a fact." He released my shoulders then cupped them again gruffly in his big hands.

I caught a sudden questioning look in Duke's eyes as he dropped his hands, and I followed his gaze to where Tye leaned in the door-way behind me. I slapped a hand on Duke's shoulder and aimed him toward the door of the trading post. "Come and meet my pardner, Duke—Tyrone Sandoe. He's a good man."

We halted in front of the door, and the two looked each other over briefly. "Duke Rainey, Tyrone Sandoe." I smiled.

Over scalding cups of coffee in the trading post we spoke in low tones. There was no mention of why we'd met Duke here, where we were going or what we might do there. This was talk of old times. Duke Rainey had once been a carefree boy, much like Tye in personality, in spite of the way some folks felt about his skin color. It didn't take me long to see he'd changed.

"You do it?" he queried. "The bank in Buffalo?"

"Keep it down," I shushed him. "Yeah, we took it." I swallowed and glanced away. "But we had to kill a couple men doin' it."

Duke's eyes fell, and he shook his head. "Now that's shore a shame, Thomas. Sorry t' hear 'bout that." His regret for me was sincere. "I kilt another man, too. Back in Ore-gone. I didn't want to, but he's tryin' t' kill ole Slug."

"Yeah, I heard about that," I admitted. "I've seen your jughead on a poster or two. Yer makin' a name for yourself. That's not what I taught you."

Duke laughed, and it was sort of a lonesome sound. "No, it ain't. I musta not learnt too good, I guess. They's rewards on me in Ore-gone, Washin'ton, Californie. In Wyomin', too, I think. Better'n fifteen hunnerd dollar, twixt the lot of 'em."

The black man's glance instantly flashed to Tye, and he searched his face for several seconds. It took me a moment, but I put a name to the look in those eyes. He was challenging Tye to try and collect the reward. He didn't trust my partner. But I couldn't say as I blamed him. When a man has a price on his head, trust is a hard thing to come by, and friends can be harder to find than lawyers in Heaven. I found myself wondering if Duke even fully trusted me anymore. For that matter, could I still trust *him?*

After stocking up on supplies, the three of us left town together in another rainstorm. Hunched over in our fishes, we rode almost due west, toward the Bighorns. After a night's camp in the shelter of some massive ponderosas, we rode on, climbing ever higher into the shadows of the mountains. The rains had ceased, but now we were hidden by heavy timber. It wasn't the dry, open forest of ponderosas, but deep, moist Doug fir woods—the firs with their massive, furrowed trunks and some others that pointed up, tall and sharp as pencils. I watched an eagle float out over the mountainside and imagined what it would be like to fly. Problem was my imagination kept ramming me headlong into the side of a tree or a cliff.

I had time to think as we rode, and I kept mulling over this life I led. How I hated it, and how I wanted out! It was a trail for young men, and I was no longer young. I'd be forty years old by early next month. An old-timer long ago for a profession of stealing and killing.

I hadn't always been an outlaw. I'd started out that way after the last of my family died. But later I'd tried to be good and given it a fair shot. I'd been a cowpuncher, a prospector, a railroad worker, a timber jack. But something always happened to drive me back to a lawless life. Seemed there wasn't a place fit for me on either side.

And then there was the men I'd killed. Two, before Buffalo. Two lousy souls! Hardly a record for a hardened criminal. Then the old man had died—I'd killed him in self-defense, of course, but that excuse was like trying to carry water in a bandanna. If I hadn't been breaking the law, he'd have had no reason to pull down on me, and I'd have had no reason for killing him. And then the horseman in the street—Lucius Bird. I didn't even know if he was dead. I was just assuming. And I assumed he was, for if I was going to whip myself for my mistakes, I'd best make it good.

Tye had managed somehow to keep his curiosity in check for the entire ride through the mountains and kept any questions to himself. I was proud of him for that but expected the questions to come any time now. He didn't let me down. "So where we headed?" He directed the question at Duke.

Surprised, Duke looked over and grinned, flashing straight but yellowed teeth. "Done well t' keep silent so long, boy. Wondered when that question was gon' come. Happens we'll be there in another half-hour. Then you c'n see for yo'self. I will say, though, it's a rough bunch up here, but one of 'em you might take a cotton to." Duke turned and winked mischievously at me. He'd mentioned something about a woman to me when we'd talked two weeks back. He'd also mentioned she had a beau in camp.

We heard the cattle, then smelled them, before we saw the herd. From the sound and odor, there was a bunch of them, and to a Missouri farm boy like me the smells and sounds were good. They reminded me of bringing in the cows back home. They reminded me of Daddy.

Duke led us around a rocky side-hill bare of trees, then down a cattle trail that crossed a timbered gulch. On the other side, the land leveled out, and I caught the scent of streamside growth. When we were halfway through the trees we saw the first of the cattle. Two heavy-bodied black cows and a bull started at our appearance and stared at us mistrustfully, ready to run at the slightest excuse. They were good-looking animals, fat and healthy. Scottish Anguses. Nothing like the rangy, giraffe-legged Longhorns out of Texas, but animals that packed real meat on top of their shoulders and all around, down to relatively short legs.

By the calculating look in Tye's eyes, I had the feeling he realized just what kind of people we were about to meet. He began to scan the trees, his hand near his gun and his eyes filled with anticipation.

We came upon the water, a stream about two feet wide with muddy, hoof-churned banks. Duke motioned for us to rein in, and he stopped at the water's edge. Throwing back his head, he let loose with his wolf howl, and if I hadn't been there and seen it I'd have sworn old Lobo himself was calling at the sky.

Several seconds passed, and then, from somewhere in the trees up ahead, the call came back. But the quality of that sound was different—not completely unlike a wolf, and obviously practiced, but higher in pitch.

As the call faded off, cattle began to bawl nervously and move about in the brush all around us. A few of them crept out of hiding in the streamside bushes to have a peek. The call came again, even higher, and Duke sent it back then turned to give me a wink.

Jerking his head as a signal for us to follow, he splashed his chestnut across the stream, and we rode behind. We weaved through a dense patch of firs to arrive at the edge of the clearing, and there lay the camp. We slid down out of our saddles to lead the horses on in.

The camp was no grand affair but carried a look of semi-permanence. Four lean-tos bordered it, two on either side, roofs thatched with pine boughs. A pole had been set up, and three saddles balanced across it. Two more saddles rode a pair of bay horses tied to another pole lashed between two pines. Beyond the campsite, I saw at least six more horses watching us and heard more of them moving about in the trees. Odds and ends of gear littered the clearing. More gear loosely surrounded the small, guarded fire in the center of camp. Two over-sized pots of coffee brewed there, and coals loosely hid a Dutch oven.

Three men sat or lay beside the fire. One was an older man, one a Mexican perhaps twenty-five, and one a blond not much older than Tye. And Tye could've been considered a kid in any place but the wide-open West. As it was, he was quick becoming a seasoned veteran. I was surprised to note none of men moved when they saw us with Duke. But each of them had a revolver lying near to hand. They looked casually from Duke to Tye to me, and finally the older man's smile broke a heavy-whiskered face into creases.

"Light 'n' set, boys."

He pushed to his feet, holding onto a plate of beans with his right hand, and thrust a Smith and Wesson Russian .44 into a holster on his left hip. The man didn't look the part of a rustler, if a man can be judged by looks. His strong Ozark accent and ragged appearance put me in mind of farmers back home. He was probably forty-five years old, with a floppy gray hat clamped over a shaggy mop of sandy hair that hung past his ears. He wore a long john shirt, button fly Levi's rolled up at the bottom, and gallowses across his bony shoulders to hold them up. Belt loops and trouser belts were a rarity in those days, but most cowboys wore tight enough trousers so they didn't have to stoop to wearing gallowses.

"This is Thomas McLean, my ole pardner," Duke said around a chaw of tobacco. Then he jerked a thumb. "This here's his new pardner, Tyrone Sandoe."

Duke introduced the man as Barlow Tanner, and I shook his hand. I found the grip warm and strong, just as I'd expected if the fellow was a Missouri man like his accent indicated. Tye followed my lead, and just as quickly he dropped his hand, and his young eyes scanned the camp.

The other two men were now standing with guns holstered, watching us without expression. Tanner indicated the Mexican with his thumb, a man slightly shorter than me, well built, and clean-shaven but for the slender wisp of a moustache. He looked at me with narrow eyes that held no hint of trust.

"This is Tovías Ruiz," Tanner said, "and that's Key Bachelor."

Bachelor was short, Injun dog-thin, with an unkempt head of blond hair. Both him and Ruiz wore two short-barreled Colt Peacemakers in holsters with the tops carefully cut away. This revealed more iron than a prudent man would've let show. A careful man generally wanted all the gun leather he could get to keep his guns clean and safe from falling out on a pounding horse ride.

We shook hands all around and exchanged greetings. Ruiz had a limp handshake, like a clump of moldy leaves, and Bachelor's wasn't much firmer. I formed a hasty opinion of the two of them and looked back questioningly toward Duke Rainey. Two people were missing, one who I knew, and the other one who I was sure had answered the wolf call. The number of saddles told me they were on foot and wouldn't be far off.

Before I could ask, I heard brush crunch beneath heavy boots, and another man, a blond fellow about three inches taller than me whose white undershirt accentuated the powerful chest and arms beneath, stepped into the clearing. His was a rock-hard, merciless looking face, its upper lip hidden by a big dark mustache, his jaw shaded by a week's growth of beard. But there was nothing unfriendly about the grin that broke over his face.

"Tom McLean. If you ain't a dang sight older."

I chuckled and strode toward him, holding out my hand. When we met, he grasped my hand in a firm but gentle grip and clapped me on the shoulder, keeping his hand there while he looked me over.

"You're no baby pig yourself, Slug," I said with a laugh. "An old hog, more like. Smell like one, too."

He laughed and gripped my hand a touch harder, slapping my shoulder. His big jaw muscles bulged out as he chewed a couple times and spit a stream of tobacco into the brush.

He looked behind me, and his blue eyes picked out Tye. Letting go of my hand, he motioned me over to the others. We walked over to them, and Slug looked Tye up and down. His eyes narrowed and his jaw flexed when his gaze stopped on Tye's blue-green eyes.

"Tyrone Sandoe," I made introduction, "this is Noel Holch. Everybody calls him Slug—and not only because he's slow," I gibed. "He tells me 'Noel' is French for Christmas, an' that was just too nice for him. We call 'im Slug because he likes to hit things—and people."

They shook hands, and without warning Slug turned and feinted, as if to punch me in the stomach. I flinched, and of course he laughed. "Slow, huh? I'm only gettin' faster in my old age, Tom. Looks to me like you've slowed down, though."

"May be." I smiled. I couldn't do more than smile because the truth hurt too much to laugh.

I turned back to Duke Rainey and gave a little shrug, as if to question him about the woman. He grinned and winked. I was suddenly aware of another presence in the camp. I was aware of it mostly because I looked over at Tye, and he was staring off behind me with sudden alertness, but trying not to show his full interest, kind of like the sly old cat watching the master's pet bird. I turned to catch the object of his attention, and it stopped me dead in my tracks.

I was never a ladies' man, not by any stretch of imagination. God gave me five or six feet of extra tongue, and whenever I even tried to speak to a pretty woman I walked all over it and spent the rest of the day picking debris out of my teeth. That's a mite exaggerated, but put plainly I made my best efforts to avoid the delicate sex. Now here I was, the closest one to the edge of the clearing, staring at the prettiest thing I'd seen in some time. Her beauty set me back on my heels.

"Tom McLean, Tyrone Sandoe," said Slug Holch. "Meet my friend, JoAnna Walker. The boys call her Jo."

Chapter Six
Bringing Out the Herd

I stared at Jo Walker, trying to get over my surprise. When Duke had told me a woman rode with them, I naturally assumed she'd be some mean-eyed hag with a fry pan for a face and paws for hands, a woman who could stand up to most any man in a brawl. I hadn't seen many outlaw women, but that seemed like a fitting picture for one.

That wasn't Jo Walker.

A flat-crowned, narrow-brimmed hat shaded the woman's deep brown eyes, kept the sun from rich black hair that flowed brazenly over her shoulders and onto a tan canvas vest and blue riding blouse. Her oval-shaped face with its dark undertones was sun-burned, but that didn't take away from her beauty, just gave it a roguish charm. And her full pink lips, cracked by the Wyoming sun and wind, melted against the wind-whipped background of her clean jawline and chin.

But despite all her good looks, I didn't need to look at her too-large canvas britches to know that Miss Walker was a hopeless Tomboy. It was in those dark, devil-may-care eyes, in the challenging way she held back her shoulders, and in the cocky little smile on her face as she looked me and Sandoe over. And it was in the Colt revolver on her right hip, the prairie belt of rifle shells slung across her left breast, and the Winchester dangling from the fingers of her gloved right hand.

Duke Rainey pivoted his body around to spit a long stream of brown juice the other way. He turned back with a grin beneath his ragged moustache and nudged me in the shoulder. "She's pertier than she is feisty, but not by more'n a hair."

I was at a loss for words, but that had no effect on Miss Walker. She switched the rifle to her left hand and took off her glove. Then she moved forward, with a slight swagger to her walk—I wondered how much that was exaggerated to look the part of a rugged rustler. She thrust her hand straight out at me. I was taken aback once more, but I shook the hand and found it unnervingly soft and small in my palm. I guess I held it longer than I'd meant to, stunned at how delicate it seemed. She finally tugged it away, giving me a look of veiled appraisal.

"So how do you do, Mr. McLean?"

"Just fine, ma'am," was the only response I could summon.

I wasn't surprised to see that when she went to Sandoe her walk seemed to alter ever so slightly—maybe only because I expected it to. She even allowed herself a smile, and a nod. The gentleman that he was, Sandoe bent at the waist in a slight bow, and instead of shaking Miss Walker's hand, he lifted and kissed it! I could've kicked him for embarrassing me. What was he, blind? Couldn't he see she wasn't the kind that wanted to be treated like a lady? I waited for her to cut him down with her tongue like a willow.

Instead, she turned red and looked up at him in surprise, letting her hand flop to her side. And then she was the one who couldn't find her tongue, and I was angry with Sandoe for his lady-killing charm and laughing inside at the woman's confusion all at once. I made up my mind to call her "Walker," like I'd use any other man's last name if I didn't know him well.

Later, Slug, Duke and me were sprawled about the fire, rehashing old times, laughing and enjoying each other's company. I saw Barlow Tanner, Bachelor and Ruiz approaching us from outside camp. Tye and JoAnna Walker came along a couple yards behind, and I looked across at Slug to see if he noticed them together. Slug had been lying down on his side, propped up on an elbow. But now he was sitting, and his pale blue eyes watched Tye and the woman with an intensity that almost scared me. I'd seen the same look in the eyes of wolves.

The five of them stopped at the fire, and Tanner, who more or less ran the outfit, bent and poured himself a steaming cup of coffee. He looked up at us, let his eyes run the ring of faces, then blew his coffee and took a tentative sip. Again he looked around.

At last, he cleared his throat and spit into the fire, then rested his eyes on me. "McLean, yer partner tells me yer headin' north t' Montan'. He also said yuh had some trouble with the law in Buffalo."

I glanced quickly up at Tye, my instincts telling me he'd spilled the beans about the bank holdup and the few years' worth of "cowboy pay" in our saddlebags.

Tanner waited several moments to judge my reaction, then went on. "Whatever trouble yuh had with the law before now is none o' my business. There's not a one of us here who ain't ridin' among the willers, so to speak. Yuh look like a couple o' rannies, an' I'm guessin' there's mebbe a bit o' curly wolf in yuh, too. That's all I care about. I don't need a man that can't do a job. If yuh think yuh've outran any posse yuh mighta had on yer tail, I'd be mighty pleased t' have the two o' you along with us—we're headin' north, too, an' we could stand a couple more guns—just in case."

Watching Tanner whip his hands and move around as he talked, I couldn't help but smile. But I didn't respond just yet and, with a shrug, Tanner went on. "Let me cut the deck a little deeper, McLean. Slug an' Duke tell me yer hell on wheels with a gun an' a good man with cattle. I could use another hand like that—for a spell, at least. An' yuh can count on bein' paid healthy, too. You seen the cattle out there. They're from down Cheyenne way, an' prime breeders, they say. Leastwise, there's a man as is willin' t' pay us fifty a head if we c'n push 'em another twenty miles north, t' the Flyin' B ranch."

"Fifty a head? They must be droppin' gold pies."

Tanner chuckled and shifted his cud inside his lip. "Don't know about that. They're some new breeds, blooded stuff. You seen 'em— Herefords and Aberdeen Anguses. Durhams. Some others. I'm told a first year Hereford heifer will bring twenty-five bucks, even when there's cows dyin' all around us."

I returned to the question at hand. "Twenty miles isn't far. Why you need me so bad?"

"Well, like I said, I hear yer good. Don't git me wrong—I ain't beggin'. If yuh wanna tag along yer welcome—'n' yuh'll earn yer money. You hang around a while, yuh'll see one of'Jo's meals is worth a week at a cafe, too. 'Sides, McLean, if yuh ain't heard, this Territ'ry's on the ragged edge o' war. The big fureign an' eastern interests is pushin' like hell t' git the little uns plumb outta the country. In Wyomin', yuh work either fer the big outfits—an' sell yer soul—er yuh work fer the small ones an' stick yer neck out on a choppin' block. Whether yer rustlin' er not, they'll say yuh are, an' they'll make it stick, 'cause the law's in their pockets. They've drove us t' this, McLean. An' I'm proud t' say I don't steal nothin' but Association cows. Fact is, if'n I wasn't stealin' 'em fer gold, chances are I'd go outta my way t' eat a Association cow. Er kill it an' jus' leave it."

Tanner's normally restless hands were still, nursing his cup of coffee as he concentrated on his words. "Yuh cain't tell it now, but once yuh been around some yer gonna see this here ain't no penny-ante rustling operation. We're in big business. We deliver only the best stuff at the highest prices. We're workin' through a member o' the Association, from Cheyenne. In the past year there's not a one of us here ain't made at least a hunnerd in a month. An' no one's been touched—by the law er anyone else. We got us a network— least that's what our boss called it.

"The Easterners, an' the English an' Scots're takin' over the cattle business in this country, McLean, an' them's the ones declared the war. We may's well take advantage whilst it's easy pickin's. 'Course, the easy pickin's could change quicker'n spittin' on a stump. An' that's why I wouldn't mind havin' you an' Tye along. Heck, it's fer yer own good as much as ours. Kind of a mutual protection deal. We watch out fer each other. So wha' d' yuh say? Yer pardner's already decided t' stay."

My eyes flickered to Tye. He reddened and shrugged an apology, averting his eyes. I glanced at Duke, then Slug. Neither spoke, but both watched me expectantly.

Tanner broke the silence again. "At least ride with us fer the next few days. Take a look-see what this is all about. The man we're workin' with, he'll be up there at the Flyin' B, 'n' you c'n meet 'im 'n' talk to 'im. He'll make no bones about it. He'll tell yuh all 'bout the Association 'n' the crap they're doin'. We won't be there fer a couple days, but if the law's on yer tail, yuh'll be safe along with us. There's not a amateur here—'n' that includes Jo." He jerked a thumb at the woman. "You ride with us four days, then don't like it, we'll send yuh on yer way with a little extra pocket money—say twenty-five dollars. What say?"

I could see if I rode on I rode without a partner. And I'd miss Tye. If I stayed, on the other hand, I knew sooner or later I'd find myself in the middle of more than one kind of fight—Tye and Slug came to mind offhand. But I liked to wander, and new partners and adventures intrigued me. Besides, I liked working with cattle—it'd been an honest (although dirt-poor) way of making a living for five years in Oregon, and a dishonest way for many after that. And what better way to hide my back trail than mixing in with a herd? That posse was looking for two horsemen, not a herd of cattle. So I shrugged and gave a half-grin, and like the fool I've always been, I threw in.

"Sure, Tanner. Count me in—for a few days. I'd like to see how this deal works."

"Yuh'll see," Tanner said with a smile, and he pumped my hand then stood up. "We're just one big, happy family."

I don't know why, but I glanced over at JoAnna Walker then and caught her eyes on me. In an act of seeming defiance, she stared me down for the few seconds I continued to look at her. I was first to drop my gaze, and she turned back to Tye.

Right after breakfast next morning—an early breakfast in the chill before dawn—we began bringing the herd in out of the bushes. I was riding a dun I'd borrowed to rest the gray, and he knew his work. No cow was tricky enough to lose him, no bull fast enough to run him down. I was glad for the use of him, for of all the things Sheriff was, he was no cowhorse.

By the time the sun came up over the plains, and every one of us had a shirt full of twigs and leaves and what-all, not to mention bruised or missing knee caps from barking them on every tree in the woods, Barlow Tanner had tallied the herd at close to two hundred. He, Bachelor, Ruiz and Walker rode around them slowly, keeping them in line.

As the last of us rode to the herd, pushing the stragglers before us, Tanner called us together. Only Ruiz, singing loudly but in a fine Spanish trill, continued to circle the herd while they milled in confusion.

I listened to Tanner while I wiped aspen dust out of my eyes and massaged my bruised knees. "This is all breedin' stock," he said, directing his speech to me and Tye. "This man's payin' for numbers, not condition. Push 'em hard. Don't fret 'bout keepin' the weight on 'em.

"Jo. Slug," he went on. "Drop back 'n' pack up, then bring the horses along half a mile er so behind us. 'N' keep an eye on yer back trail," he added emphatically.

We moved out at a good pace, as Tanner had advised us. Not the pace of a market drive but of desperate men pushing toward a destination before anyone could catch up to them. Roundups were still being conducted all around this country, and even though the one for this section was done, it was likely the ranches would send out prowlers to find anything they'd missed. So we had to keep our eyes open for strange horses, on top of watching ourselves so we didn't wind up de-saddled and broke up by a tree limb. It was harsh work, even for these experienced cowhorses, all of which had scrapes and cuts all over their hides. They were used to working out in the rolling hills. But here on the steep, timbered mountainsides one wrong step could cost them dearly. They seemed aware of the danger and acted accordingly.

We bunched the herd in the late afternoon and made a dry camp on the levelest ground we could find, surrounded by heavy-barked gray fir trees with the girth of a two-hole privy. Squirrels peered at us from around tree trunks, and birds flitted through the branches as we threw down our bedrolls. I sacked out on top of mine, too bushed to even take off my boots.

All day I had kept my eye on Tye, who in turn kept both of his on Walker. At that moment, Slug Holch glared with deadly intent at them both. I was relieved when Tanner sent me and Tye off to gather firewood. Tye gave him a half-disgusted look but stood up, brushing off the back of his California plaid wool trousers. He looked over and waited for me to come alongside him before he started off at a good pace into the forest.

No sooner had we left earshot of the camp than Tye whirled toward me. "Did you get a good look at that woman?" he burst out. "What a charmer she is!"

"Yeah, that's just what she is," I replied sarcastically, pretending to look about in earnest for fire-sized branches.

Ignoring my tone of voice, Tye smiled on. "She's a beauty, all right. Wonder what she's doin' out here with that bunch of hardcases."

Casually, I picked up an arm-length club of wood. "Don't jump the gun, Tye. She may be a hardcase herself." As I said it, I straightened up, and our eyes met in shocking collision.

"What do you mean by that?"

"Don't get your back up, kid. Remember, the woman's runnin' with a bunch of cow thieves. She ain't no schoolmarm. Besides, in case you ain't noticed, she sort o' cottons to Slug Holch—an' he does to her. Women can't help likin' when a man like you notices 'em. Just remember that. But she's spoke for an' knows it."

Tye continued to stare at me for a moment, jaws flexing. Finally, he turned his eyes away and chuckled, sweeping his hand down to catch up a log by one branch and swing it up into the crook of his arm. "How old you think she is, Tom?"

I had to laugh at the boy. He retreated from a cause as easy as a kicked bull. "I wouldn't guess she's under twenty-five," I replied. "An' that'd make her…what? Six years older than you?"

"I'm almost twenty," Tye countered. He raised his unburdened hand and scratched his whiskered jaw. "You really think there's something between her an' Holch? I mean, she doesn't seem like the type to hang around with an outlaw."

This time I swore in humored disbelief. "Open your eyes, Tye!

The woman *is* an outlaw!"

"Well, you know what I mean."

"Sure, I know what you mean. But I've seen the two of 'em watchin' each other. They may not be readyin' to tie the knot, but there's an understandin' between 'em. An' there'd best soon be one between you an' Slug."

Tye shot me a glance almost challenging in its intensity. "I ain't scared o' him. You act like I ain't never been in a fight before."

I stopped and squared myself to the boy—for he was hardly more than that. "Yeah, Tye. You been in fights. But you never been in a fight with Slug Holch." Tye stared at me, taken aback. I continued on. "You don't even know what a fight is yet. An' when you find out, you better hope yer on the watchin' side."

Tye forced a laugh. He pursed his lips and jerked his head sideways, trying to pop his neck. "I've seen *you* in fights, Tom, an' you're good enough. You ain't scared of Holch, are you?"

"He's my friend. I hope I don't have reason to be. I reckon if I felt I had reason, I'd fight him—an' I'd lose. But if you aim to keep ruttin' around that woman, you best have you an edge, because the fight's comin'. An' if you go down, take my advice and stay down—you can live with the joshin' you might get from the boys. Slug's not a man to kick someone who stays down the first time. But I've seen him kill one man an' maim some others who got up."

Tye swallowed audibly, searching my eyes. He wiped at his mouth and glanced away, then back at me. "If it got to that point, I'd shoot him."

"Sure you would. In case you didn't notice, he's wearin' a gun too. An' he's skinned it a time or two."

Nodding soberly, my young partner looked away. We wandered for a while, gathering more fuel, and it wasn't until we started back to camp again that he looked over at me. "You really do expect a fight, don't you?"

"I'm not whistlin' Dixie. I know Slug."

Tye prodded on. "You an' him were perty good friends, I take it. If there was a fight, how would you side?"

"I'd rather not have to. But I'd side with you, Tye. I always side with the loser."

Tye chuckled, although he looked on with mock reproach. "Good. With any luck, the old horse an' the banty rooster'll whip the bull this time."

"They just might," I rejoined. "They sure shoot enough of it."

The Posse: Anthony Ribervo

We rode into the little settlement of Cherry Valley in the late afternoon. Rain had drenched us for part of the day, but now the sun broke from dirty-looking clouds and slanted across the late afternoon sky. It had been a long day, a hard day. Riding with Van Bennett could drive less-determined men than us to the ground. But most of us were out here either because we had interest in what had been taken from the bank or because we knew the men who'd been killed in the robbery. We wanted justice, and we wanted revenge.

Van stopped, and we stopped with him. We climbed from our saddles in front of Philipe DuPres' trading post.

I walked through the door of the trading post with Van while the rest of the boys stayed outside, most of them slouching onto the porch, exhausted.

Philipe DuPres sat on a stool behind his counter. He smiled at me but just looked blandly at Van. "What can I do for you, Messieur Le Sheriff?" I felt like the tone of his voice was sort of mocking, but Van didn't seem to notice or didn't care.

"We're looking for a couple of bank robbers, DuPres," he said flatly. "One's a brown-haired man riding a gray horse, and his partner has long black hair and rides a bay. You'd remember the gray, if you saw it. There aren't many better than that one for runnin' a race."

DuPres cleared his throat and looked at Van. "*Oui,* they were here. They came earlier today. There was an *homme noir*—a Negro here, a man who called himself 'Howling Wolf'. They left together, headed for the mountains. They didn't stay here long."

"All right." That was Van's only reply. No thanks, no goodbye. Van was like that. He just turned and stepped outside. After hearing his boots on the porch, I turned to DuPres, who was smiling again.

"Thanks for the help, Mr. DuPres," I said. "The sheriff isn't one for formalities. I'll have to apologize for him."

DuPres waved a hand in dismissal. "Do not worry, *mon ami.* You are polite enough for both. *Ça va.* There is no problem. These two men, I did not know they were robbers. I wish I could be of more help."

I thanked the Frenchman again and went outside, where Van was talking to the others. Now, Sheriff Van Bennett was probably one

of the hardest men born for a man to get to know. Other than myself, I'd never met a man who got comfortable enough to call him
by his first name, and that included Poco Vidales. I figured I knew
him better than most, and that still wasn't good. I liked him, and I
called him a friend. But he was distant. Very much so. Distant, but
I never met anyone who was more of a man. It was just too bad he
could never relax.

"If he's headed up into the mountains," Van was saying, "there's
no point in going on tonight. It's pretty late. I'd be satisfied just
finding a track—something to go by come morning. Poco?" He
turned to the little Mexican. "If you could find a track I'd appreciate it. Same goes for you, Storrie. If not, we'll see what mornin'
brings."

Neither of the little trackers responded, but both stepped off the
porch wordlessly and went about their job. In the gathering dusk,
and after the slashing rains, the trail was hard to find. It wasn't till
just after dark that the little trouble hunter, Cale Storrie, stubbornly
prowling the sagebrush with a lantern held aloft, found the faint
hoofprint sheltered by a big sage. Van nodded with satisfaction when
Storrie told him what he'd found. His gaze went to the rim of the
mountains as he nodded his big, shaggy head calculatingly.

"We'll roll out right here and catch a night's sleep. Tomorrow's
already close. Be ready."

In the foothills, a coyote yapped its lonesome trills. We laid our
beds in the sagebrush without any argument and settled in for the
night. Sheriff Bennett was right. Morning would come too soon.

Chapter Seven
The Sale

The Outlaws: Tom McLean

I never liked to gamble. With my luck, I might as well have sat on a cliff and spun coins over the edge. Would've been a heap more fun—and maybe more profitable. A man could never tell when he might knock some passing jehu out with the tossed coin and find a gold shipment in the stage boot. More likely for me, I'd've clunked some Cheyenne chief's mother on the head with a nickel and ended with the whole Cheyenne nation breathing down my neck.

But that night we sat around the fire with nothing to do, so when Duke Rainey plopped down across from me and dug out a dog-eared deck, I reluctantly agreed to try a hand. He called it a friendly game, but in my experience those were few and far-between.

It wasn't long before everyone wanted to join the fun. Taking turns in the game to avoid a seven-player circus, we gambled our piles of rock chips and fir cones. But when even the loss of rocks and cones started to ruffle feathers, I fell gladly out of the game. Slug left when I did, and Barlow Tanner was already sitting back in the shadows smoking a quirly.

We gathered at the giant fir whose furrowed gray trunk served as the straw boss' backrest, and he passed out the makings. Slug was still rolling his when he spoke, his fingers performing their age-old chore as his eyes met mine.

"Yer boy likes JoAnna."

I held my finished cigarette between thumb and forefinger and chuckled. "He ain't my boy, Slug. An', yeah, he likes her. He's just a kid, an' she's perty. You jealous?"

Slug considered this a moment, rolling a quid of burley tobacco around against his gums before at last spitting it in a wad to the needle-strewn forest floor. He shrugged carelessly. "I don't like men botherin' the woman. She knows her own mind, but he makes her nervous."

"Come on, Slug. Let it ride. He's just a kid."

Slug jerked a thumbnail across the tip of a match, and it flared and lit up his square face and pale blue eyes. He raised the match, and sucking in at the cheeks he brought the tip of his quirly to life. "Yeah, you said that before, Tom. He's just a kid. A *randy* kid— that's what's eatin' at me."

"If she's bothered, don't you think she'll tell 'im? Seems like she c'n handle herself."

Slug blew a smoke ring and shrugged. He flung the dead match at his feet. "Maybe you oughtta think about tellin' him, too. He's yer bunkie."

I nodded and glanced uneasily toward Tye. He was watching the woman. "I'll talk to him, Slug. But you said Walker knows her own mind. Why don't you let her handle it?"

Slug straightened up. "What'd you call 'er that for?"

I looked at him mildly, pinning the still-unlit cigarette between my teeth. "Mostly 'cause that's her name. Far as I'm concerned, she's just another one o' the boys."

Slug studied me for a moment, his eyes dancing back and forth between mine. At length, his eyes smiled at me. "Too bad yer friend don't have the same attitude."

Barlow Tanner cut in. "Shoot, Slug! He's just a young buck. He's lucky t' have Jo even talk to 'im. Do like McLean says 'n' let it ride. You know damn well yer only one she goes with. Well—" He started to say something more, but suddenly he glanced over at me, then dropped his eyes. I looked at Slug, and he, too, was looking at the ground. An uncomfortable silence ran on for several moments, leaving me puzzled by the wordless exchange.

Then Tanner stirred, and he pushed himself up on stiff legs and slapped the seat of his pants, making needles fall. "Reckon I'll push inta the game fer a while—see if I c'n lose some rocks too. Either o' you back in?"

I looked at Slug, with no intention of playing another hand. The big man sighed and struggled to his feet. He shot a look toward the game, glanced down at me meaningfully, then turned and followed Tanner.

In a few moments, I saw the Mexican, Tovías Ruiz, leave the game and wander off in the dark on the inevitable errand. JoAnna Walker was next to leave the game, and she came over near the tree and stood above me, resting a hand on the trunk.

Our eyes met, and then she dropped hers indifferently to my cigarette. "You got the makin's?"

I looked at her mildly. "The makin's of what?" I asked sardonically.

Walker grunted. "The makin's of a man," she said with a shrug, glancing away with exaggerated boredom. I looked up at her, unsmiling, and my eyes followed her as she hunkered down. "The makin's of a quirly," she said. "Figgered you spoke range talk."

"How long you been smokin' these things?" I pulled my cigarette out and looked at its unlit tip. "Don't seem ladylike."

Walker humphed. "Most folks don't accuse me of bein' a lady." She tried to stare me down like she was in the habit of doing, but this time she swung her eyes away with an irritated sigh. She gathered her wits and looked back. "I'd guess I've been smokin' 'em longer than you. You ain't even figgered out how to light it."

I shrugged, pulling the quirly from between my lips with my index and middle fingers. I studied it, then reached into my vest pocket and dug out a match with thumb and forefinger, holding them both out to her. "There you go, ma'am. Take mine. But it don't suit yuh."

Her eyes dropped to the cigarette and match, studied them a moment, then looked away deliberately. "Keep 'em." She slumped back to the ground, tugging a pair of tan leather gloves out of her vest pocket and pulling them on. She looked around uncomfortably as she folded her arms and shivered, avoiding my eyes. But by the look in hers I knew she was aware I was watching her. I thought of offering to get a blanket for her but quickly shrugged the thought aside. She was just as much a man as I was. She wore boots and pants and a pistol. She could fetch her own blankets. Chances were she wouldn't take the offer anyway.

Feeling suddenly ill at ease, I got up and walked off to where the horses were staked out in a clearing. I gathered up Sheriff and the dun and led them back to a spot between two stout trees where Duke Rainey had loosely stretched a rope. Drawing butterfly knots up into two places along the rope, I tied the animals off to them and brushed them down. Then I threw a blanket and saddle on Sheriff, cinching it loose enough so he could breathe easy through the night.

I heard duff crunching behind me and turned to see the woman walk up on me, a rifle swinging free along her thigh. She stopped and looked into my face. The full moon shone down enough to see the whites of her eyes.

"Perty horse," she said abruptly.

I turned and glanced at Sheriff, then back at her, puzzling. "Gets me through the country."

Walker gave me a square, frank glance. "I'm sorry you don't like me, Mr. McLean. If I said somethin' to offend you, I didn't mean to." Her voice was gruff, but only halfway hid the embarrassment near its surface.

Taken by surprise, I just looked at her, then shrugged. "Never said I didn't like you."

"But I'm not blind."

"I don't even know you," I offered lamely. "But this outfit ain't no place for a woman."

Walker speared me with her eyes. "Well, yer right. You don't know me." With that, she turned and walked back toward camp.

I stood out in the darkness listening to the sounds of the cattle back in the trees, and of Key Bachelor's toneless singing as he rode around them. It was a still night, and crisp with high country snows. Stars sparkled like ice chips across the sky, blurred by their own brightness, glittering between the black tree limbs.

I sat on a downed tree trunk near my horses, listening to the others grazing across the meadow, watching their lazy movements. I thought of JoAnna Walker. What brought a woman out here to this? A hard, ragged woman, maybe I could understand. But Walker was young, and she was pretty—no, she was beautiful. It wasn't just Tye who noticed—I wasn't dead myself. But a woman like that had to've shook a stone loose in her fence to be out there rustling cattle, stretching her neck across the Association's chopping block. And I guess the whole bunch of us had shook a lot of stones loose in our own fences. We weren't any smarter than her.

I thought of the old banker back in Buffalo, and the sickness seeped again into my stomach. There was a good chance I'd killed Lucius Bird, too, but the old man in the bank had been closer, and I'd had to look right in his eyes. The feeling wouldn't ever go away.

Some time in the morning darkness Barlow Tanner shook me awake. I woke with my pistol palmed. I came half up from my blankets, but I was accustomed to waking up in a hurry. The moment I recognized the voice, I took a deep breath and lay back down, relaxing the pistol to my side on the blankets.

"Bachelor's been ridin' herd out there since we circled 'em last night, McLean," said Tanner in a low voice. "An' Duke went out after you went t' bed. I wondered if I might persuade yuh t' relieve one of 'em. I'll send Jo along, too."

Well, when a man asked like that, so polite and all, I couldn't hardly refuse. Besides, even though it was a little cold, it was a pretty night. A nice night for thinking.

I took Sheriff, since he was already saddled, and climbed into that icy-cold leather. I wished I had chaps to fight off the cold, like most of the others did. The other horses whickered softly as I crossed the clearing, and soon I was into the trees and could hear the rustling of cattle.

I heard Duke Rainey singing long before I reached him. He didn't have much of a voice for the pursuit, but he was definitely exuberant at the strains of "Dem Golden Slippers." Personally, it didn't seem to me like it would soothe an animal, but they weren't stampeding, so I guess it worked.

I called out before I reached the Negro, and he answered me shortly. He was still singing, in a lower voice, when I rode up to him.

"Howdy, Thomas." Duke's smile almost gleamed in the dark. "Iss a bright evenin'—an' mighty friendly out here, too. Hope a Nigger's singin' don't rile you none."

I laughed. "Not yers, Duke. Sounds like old times."

Duke was quiet for a moment. Then I heard the sandpaper scrape of his fingers scratching his jaw. "Yessuh. I wisht it *was* old times. I wisht we was back bein' cowhan's again."

I nodded my agreement, but there was no use in a reply. We'd both gone far beyond that point. "Tanner said to come an' send you back to camp. You an' the boy, wherever he is."

"Bachelor?" Duke grunted. "Hell, he ain't no boy, Thomas. He's done kilt 'im six men."

I swallowed, a little surprised at that revelation. "Killin' don't make a boy a man—it just makes him a killer. He's still a boy t' you an' me."

Two hours passed, and I hadn't made it through a full song yet. Fact was, I didn't know any songs, to speak of. "Shenandoah" was my favorite, but to me it was mostly a violin piece. Same with most of them. My family'd been ones for enjoying the music of others, for if ever we took to singing the howling of the dogs would drown us out.

I saw Walker's silhouette coming toward me through the timber, barely visible in the star-shadows. She called out, and out of courtesy I returned the call. She rode her horse up to mine and stopped it, facing me. The horses stood and blew their greetings, touching noses, switching their tails and shaking their bit chains.

"Lots of stars," I said, only to break the silence.

"Yeah. And they're so bright up here. They weren't this bright back home."

"Where's that?"

Walker looked over at me, brushing her hair back over one shoulder. "Kansas. Lawrence, Kansas, the doorway to hell. How about you?"

"I was born in Missouri."

Walker gave me full attention. "Missouri, huh? Then I expect our families prob'ly killed each other." She laughed after she said it, but I sensed bitterness in her voice. And truthfully, I couldn't blame her.

"The war's long done, ma'am. Long done, an' I had no part in any war in Kansas. Don't recollect as I ever been to Lawrence. I rode farther east to do my fightin', so I wouldn't be so likely to be killin' neighbors."

Walker nodded, but she didn't speak.

"What makes you stay out here? In Wyoming, I mean?"

"Just this." Walker waved a hand. "The stars. The trees. The mountains. And my father's buried here," she said after a nervous pause. "He died with Captain Fetterman, back in '66."

"Yeah. December twenty-first," I added immediately. "I know. I had a cousin that died there. Red Cloud and Crazy Hoss: two names I guess both of us'll always remember."

We talked of that infamous battle for a few minutes—of fierce Sioux warriors, of foolish cavalry commanders. We were awfully close at that moment to where it all happened. And then the conversation went on to other things. Some of the woman's observations proved to be blunt.

"They say you're hell on wheels with that Remington."

My eyes dropped to the pistol in my belt, and I had to chuckle. "Yeah. Tanner said the same thing. An' it ain't true. First place, this thing has a eight-inch barrel. It wasn't made for speed. I'm no gunman, where speed might count. I reckon I can shoot alongside most, but give me a shotgun and some double-ought buck any day. Nine hunks o' lead for every pull o' the trigger—that's more to my likin'."

She laughed. "Well, that's honest. And smart, too. None of us here are gunmen, I guess. Except for Key Bachelor. He's supposed to've killed seven men."

I grunted in derision. "That's the second time I've heard that tonight. 'Cept he killed one more since I talked to Duke. Where'd you hear that?"

"Him."

"Well, there you have it." I chuckled humorlessly. "A real man don't kill if he has a choice. An' he sure don't go braggin' it up if he does. There's nothin' to be proud of there. His braggin' starts me to wonder if it really happened or if he dreamed it."

We talked about the stars. We talked about the trees. She surprised me by knowing all their names, and all the little pictures in the stars, too. We talked about the fresh smell off sage and buckbrush and of meadows we'd seen that day, so full of wildflowers it nearly hid the grass and dazzled the eyes. In spite of seeming uneducated in the way she talked and the like, JoAnna knew an awful lot about nature. We talked a lot and laughed a little. And JoAnna Walker and me came to understand each other some that night. Or so I thought.

"So how far t' this Flyin' B Ranch?" I asked.

The woman's gaze fell away from me. She cleared her throat and looked back up with a shrug. "We'll be there sometime tomorrow." Her voice had taken on a different tone. The humor was gone, along with the wistfulness. Some other emotion took its place, and what it was I really couldn't say. I just knew it wasn't gladness.

"You don't sound happy to get there."

The woman sipped a deep breath, and just when I thought she was about to answer me, she took a look through the trees. "I prob'ly better get to the other side of the herd before they get up an' wander off. We been here a while."

Confused, I nodded. "Yeah, guess yer right. Thanks for the palaver."

Walker nodded. "Yeah, sure. Maybe another time."

With that, she put heels to her horse, moving past me and off along the edge of the herd. And I was left to wonder about this woman. It was like I said: she must have shook a rock loose from her fence somewhere along the way. She sure was abrupt in her ways.

It made me think back to my talk with Slug and Tanner. The way they'd acted when Tanner made the comment about Walker "only going with Slug." There was something odd here. My hunch was I'd find out what it was when we reached the Flying B.

Around noon the next day, we started working our way down through the timber, and I was glad at the thought of being out of it. There were cattle and game trails up here, but some of them were mighty dim, and most times a man couldn't dictate where he rode when chousing cows. You just went where they went and prayed

you didn't bark your kneecaps off on some tree trunk or poke an
eye or an eardrum out with a branch. Fortunately, this bunch had
been recently trailed, and they didn't have any calves to look after.
They stayed with us most of the time and didn't make a nuisance
of theirselves trying to cut from the herd. They seemed content to
wander along before us, needing only an occasional guiding hand.

I happened to glance over at JoAnna Walker once, and she looked
pale, even in the shadow of her hat. Pale, even ill. She glanced about
her nervously as she rode, and her eyes kept searching out Slug
Holch, then resting on him. But the big man seemed to keep his
eyes away from her a-purpose. I guessed they'd had a fight sometime that day, and I shrugged it off as such.

We were following a creek that brimmed with snow water. It
must've been somewhere after one or two o'clock. The trees began to thin, and then the mountain fell away before us into a wide
valley sparsely shaded by groves of new-leafed aspen. Sagebrush
and thousands of wildflowers filled most of the valley, and cattle
dotted it here and there. On the far side was a stout house made of
logs, and from its stone chimney curled a dirty ribbon of smoke.

As soon as we paused to survey the valley, the herd strung out along
the creek, spraddled their legs and bowed their heads to the water.
Barlow Tanner cantered up to me and Tye, breaking a path before him
through the milling herd. "This is it, boys—the Flyin' B."

"Nice place," Tye said, looking around.

Duke sat his horse close by, and he grinned broadly. "Boss ain't
even tellin' you all. This is on'y a line camp. Big house is another
ten mile t'ward Sheridan—northeast."

I looked at the Negro, then glanced in the direction he'd indicated. "How far's Sheridan?"

"Still another fifteen miles," Tanner cut in. "But we'll steer clear
o' there an' maybe rest up fer a while at some line camp—maybe
this one."

"It's a good spot," I said musingly. "No law for miles."

Tanner chuckled. "That's no lie! Hey, why don't you an' Sandoe
come on up t' the house? Man that ramrods this outfit should be
there, an' it'd be a good time t' meet 'im. If yuh decide t' throw in
with us, he may be yer boss fer a spell."

Walker sat a buckskin horse fifty yards away, and over the din
of cattle bawling Tanner called to her. It seemed to me she was well
within hearing range, but she didn't look up. Her horse was drinking from the creek, and she seemed to be concentrating on the back
of his head with an awful lot of interest. Again, Tanner called out,

and again Walker seemed not to hear. At last, Key Bachelor, who was even farther away than the woman, pushed his horse through the cattle and rode up near her, saying something. Haltingly, she looked toward us.

Tanner jerked his head sideways, indicating for her to follow us. It was a straightforward gesture, yet she hesitated. She glanced around, her eyes stopping on Slug Holch. He sat his black as far from her as he could get. His eyes were turned the other way, and he didn't look over.

I looked puzzledly at Barlow Tanner. The look on his face was one of frustration. When I glanced back at Walker, she was just returning her eyes to us, and Slug still looked off the other way. Again, I followed the line made by his eyes. What in tarnation was so fascinating to him? There wasn't even a cow over there to draw his attention.

Something seemed to fall in JoAnna Walker's face, and her shoulders slumped with the same resignation as her eyes. I shot a sideways glance of wonder at Tye to see if he was as bewildered as I was. Then we both watched her start to thread her way toward us.

As the four of us rode toward the little shack, I glanced back, and Slug Holch was watching after us. He jerked his horse's head around and rode away when he saw me looking.

We rode at a trot down the swale, our horses' hooves clipping through lush grass and flowers that gave no hint of the drought farther down the mountains. I glanced over at Walker, expecting her to be looking at the flowers with appreciation. Instead, she was staring straight-ahead, gripping her reins in one hand and the saddle horn in the other. I had seen Walker ride. She didn't need support, but she was shakin' hands with grandma just the same, her knuckles turning white.

We rode into the yard and drew up with little puffs of dust erupting around our horses' hooves from the newly rain-speckled earth. A couple of camp robbers called raucously from a nearby fir, taunting us. A short man with a watch chain hanging from the pocket of his vest stepped from the doorway of the shack, his shotgun chaps brushing together as he walked out toward us, a Winchester cradled under his arm. Soon, a second man, one with a drooping mustache, appeared from the shack, looking over his shoulder before turning to eye us with suspicious reserve. He too held a lever action rifle.

Keeping my eyes on the two men, I heard Barlow Tanner say, "Howdy, fellas. Reckon yer boss is in?" he spoke conversationally.

The words had no more than left Tanner's mouth when a broad-chested, bearded man with grass-thin black hair ducked his head to come through the doorway of the wooden structure. He held a double-barrel shotgun along his leg. With his left hand, he drew a cheroot from between chapped lips and looked at us boldly. He seemed about to speak when another man came out of the house behind him, nudging him gently so he could pass.

The second man was strikingly handsome, with violet-blue eyes, straight nose, a square jaw and flawlessly groomed mustache. He wore a brushed suit coat tailored around broad, sloping shoulders, a neckerchief knotted just so at his throat and two steer's head ivory-handled pistols buckled around lean hips. His boots, at a glance, I judged to be of the highest custom specifications, and he wore them outside his pants, showing off intricate stitching and new-fangled deep-cut V tops.

"Hello, gentlemen," the second man spoke, his voice a soft deep purr. He smiled, and tiny crows' feet crinkled the edges of his eyes, grooves creased the freshly shaved space beneath his cheekbones. "I'm glad to see you made it through safely. Did you have any trouble this trip?"

"Went good," Tanner replied, his voice startlingly harsh against the other man's. He turned in his saddle and glanced at me, then Tye. "Jason Shilo, meet a couple o' friends we picked up along the way. This here's Tom McLean 'n' Tye Sandoe. They're good men—real workers—friends o' Slug 'n' Duke."

Shilo's eyes met mine, and his glance was pleasant. He raised his hand and tapped the brim of his hat with two fingers, smiling amiably. He gave Tye the same favorable glance, looking him up and down. "Good to meet you boys. Any friends of Slug's and Duke's, I'll consider friends of my own."

Then Shilo turned his level gaze on JoAnna, and mine followed. Although it seemed she tried to meet his gaze, her eyes fell away. "And JoAnna," he said with an openly admiring look. "You become more beautiful every time I see you, dear."

Walker blushed quickly and looked up. "Thanks," she said. Again, her glance flickered and fell away, and she forced a cough.

"Well, boys, by all means, come on in the house. It's not much, but I've a bottle of champagne that's been cooling in the stream, waiting for you. It would be my pleasure if you'd join me for a glass."

Before any of us could step out of our saddles, he took four long strides, causing Tanner's horse to sidle nervously, and came to a stop beside Walker. "Allow me, JoAnna. It's good to see you again.

You just don't know how good."

Before swinging off Sheriff, my eyes were drawn back to Walker's face. That look was still there—the look of fear. It was in her uncertain movements as she allowed herself to be supported down from the saddle, it was in the pinched look around her eyes and the tight set of her mouth. And all this was disturbing, almost shocking, to me because it was a side of the woman I hadn't seen—a side I hadn't really thought she had in her.

Faintly bothered by what I'd seen, I stepped from the saddle and turned curiously to look at Tye. He was watching me, searching my face for some sign of understanding. Even young as he was, he too had caught the tension in the air.

Jason Shilo was standing with his hand resting confidently on the woman's shoulder as me and Tye stepped around our horses. Tanner glanced about the yard, shuffling his feet. He never even looked at Walker.

"Will you boys do me a favor and take these horses for the folks? They've had a long ride." Shilo's words broke several seconds of uncomfortable silence, and the two hands we'd first seen obeyed and led our horses away.

Shilo then turned to the burly black-haired man. "I present to you Mister Marlin Boyington. Most people call him 'Swiss'. And Swiss, this is Barlow Tanner. He runs the show for me, and a fine job he does of it." He turned to me. "And this was...Tom McLean, right? And Tye Sandoe. But I guess you heard. And this..." He turned with a broad, fond smile and dropped his arm around JoAnna's jacketed waist, pulling her close to him. "This is my little sweetheart, JoAnna Walker. I trust she'll be spending the night here with us."

Tye's eyes flickered to mine, and I gave a barely discernible shrug. His face red, Tye turned away, making a point of studying the terrain around the shack. Tanner glanced about and forced a close-mouthed smile when Jason Shilo looked at him.

"Well, Barlow, let's go inside, shall we? There are settlements to make, of course. And a bill of sale to be drawn up. Come in, gentlemen. The bubbly is bubbling." He laughed at his own humor.

The camp robbers were still making their racket in the tree, and at the doorway Shilo paused. He looked up at them, then around at us. One side of his mouth tilted up in a wry smile. "Those cursed birds never rest." I noticed his hand raise to the butt of one of his Colts, but it lowered again, and he shook his head and walked on inside.

Inside, the cabin was homey. Strangely out-of-place, the floor was puncheon, rather than dirt, and draped by a generous buffalo hide and two large black bear skins. The table was hand-crafted, and there were two windows in the place, or window *openings,* anyway. Neither one had glass in it and didn't look like they ever had. There was a wooden bench along one wall, three chairs, and a shoddy waist-high cabinet that provided counter space. I had the feeling Swiss Boyington spent a good share of his time here at this shack. I doubted he would provide so much furniture for his hired help.

Me and Tye, we sat on the bench, and Boyington sat down on a log end. JoAnna Walker and Tanner and Shilo each took chairs. Walker's, I noticed, Shilo drew very near his own before he waved her into it. From that point on he managed to keep a hand on her throughout most of our visit—either on her shoulder, if his entire arm wasn't draped there, or on her waist, her thigh or her hand.

For her part, Walker stared dully about the room, meeting no one's gaze. Her shoulders were rigid, her hands held tightly to her canvas-clad thighs. Looking close, I detected tiny beads of sweat glistening at her temples.

I admit I didn't know what to make of what I was seeing. In the first place, what was going on between Shilo and the woman? They obviously shared a relationship, but it seemed a little one-sided, even to someone with the curse of man-dust in his eyes like me. Perhaps stranger still were the woman's actions. Was this the same JoAnna Walker I'd become accustomed to the last miles, and last night in camp? Was this the same tough, self-confident woman cattle rustler who could exchange biting comments with the hardest of men? It hardly seemed so. What I saw before me seemed oddly like a…a lady. And somewhat like a frightened child. The woman could do nothing to resurrect her former image with me. She was no longer "Walker." She had transformed at this meeting to "JoAnna."

Shilo and Boyington had settled on forty dollars a head, cows and bulls alike; a good deal for Shilo, who had paid nothing, and a good deal for Boyington, who would have paid more than that for good breeding cattle on the legal market. It came to a total of seventy-four hundred dollars when one of the hands came in to return the total tally of one hundred and eighty-five animals. And Swiss Boyington didn't even flinch. He just opened up a desk drawer and counted out the sum in greenbacks onto the table before them, taking the bill of sale Shilo had forged for him. And then came the inevitable.

"Well, Barlow?" Shilo turned to the older man with a smile. "I think Mr. Boyington's a little anxious to get a good look at his purchases." He glanced at me and Tye, then back. "Do you think the three of you could take him out and show him the herd?"

Tanner cleared his throat quietly, and his eyes flickered to JoAnna, then jumped nervously away. He wiped a hand across his mouth, and his Adam's apple bobbed when he swallowed. "Uh, sure, Mr. Shilo. Anythin' you say."

"Thank you." Shilo nodded and blinked his approval with his eyes. Then he looked again at me and Tye and gave another nod. "It was good to meet you boys. Really. I hope you'll decide to stay on with the outfit."

I nodded at Shilo, and I felt Tye look uncertainly at me as Tanner slid back his chair and he and Boyington pushed to their feet. I stood up and held my hat in my hands for a moment, eyeing Shilo uncertainly. There were words on the tip of my tongue I had intended to say, but I just didn't feel like speaking to Jason Shilo at the moment. In spite of an initially favorable impression, I didn't like the man.

I turned to go, tugging on my hat, and as I did my eyes passed over JoAnna's face. Her eyes were downcast, fixed on the hands folded in her lap. Shilo had stood up, but the woman made no move to. Then her eyes jumped upward, and they caught mine. There was a plea in them, I thought, but she must not have intended it, for she looked away even as our eyes met.

Outside, I turned and looked at Barlow Tanner, who glanced nervously away. I was fairly boiling over with curiosity, and by the pressing look in Tye's eyes I could see he was, too. Even the boy wasn't naïve enough not to know why Jason Shilo had wanted to be left alone with JoAnna. But the question was why had she stayed? My irritation was made worse by the never-ending chatter of the camp robbers, setting my nerves on a dangerous edge.

We walked around to our horses while Boyington gathered a big bay from the corral behind the house. Everyone else climbed aboard, so I did, too. But my heart was pounding with guilt, and my head rang with dissatisfaction. Why was JoAnna still inside that house? What was the story? Why didn't she fight? It was obvious she didn't want to stay.

I felt Tye watching me, and that made me feel even guiltier. I spoke before I really thought it through. But once the words had left me, I wasn't sorry.

"Tanner, I was just thinkin'. I don't wanna seem like a weak-ling, but it's been a long road for me. You prob'ly don't need us all just to look at the herd. If you don't mind, I think I'll just hang back here an' try to catch a catnap."

From the corner of my eye, I caught the pivot of Tye's head as he turned to look at Tanner. Both Tanner and Boyington had raised their eyes to stare at me.

"Uh, McLean," started Tanner hesitantly. "I think you prob'ly oughtta go with us. I mean, well, we might need all hands in case…in case Mr. Boyington wants us t' move the herd er somethin'."

Boyington snapped his eyes back to me. "Yes, that's a good idea. Maybe we *should* move the herd back in the trees, just in case some-one should ride by here in the next few days. Yer boss is right. I'd appreciate you going with us."

I held Boyington's eyes for a moment, then shifted my glance abruptly to Tye, to the house, then back to Tanner. I watched Tan-ner, but my words were for Boyington. "Well, I'm sure you boys c'n handle it. It's only a couple hundred cows. Like I said, I'm tuck-ered. An' Tanner's not my boss. I'm only ridin' along, not workin' with the outfit." My eyes swung from Tanner at last and settled on Boyington. "If it's all the same to you, I'll stay here an' rest up."

Boyington didn't speak for several seconds. His face turned a deeper shade of red, and he stared at me. His eyes flattened out as he studied my face, every inch of it. "I think Mister Shilo would be happy if you went. Very happy. We could use all hands."

I stared back at him and finally shrugged. I didn't like being pushed. "Well, if it's that important we're all there, I'll ride along." I could almost hear Barlow Tanner sigh with relief—until I went on. "But if you need all hands, we best fetch Shilo an' the woman, too."

A new voice broke into the building confrontation—the deep, mellow voice of Jason Shilo. "You're right, of course, Mr. McLean. You're absolutely right." JoAnna had just walked up beside him in the shadow of the awning. She made a point of avoiding our eyes. "Let me bring my horse up, and we'll leave JoAnna here. She can start preparing a meal for you boys—I'm sure you're hungry after pushing a herd that far. I apologize for being so inconsiderate."

Shilo's eyes caught mine, and he smiled. But it wasn't a lingering smile. It disappeared even as he was turning away for the corral.

I dared a look toward the house when I sensed no one else was watching, and I caught JoAnna's eyes on me. She wasn't smiling, but her face had the drained, happy look of great relief. I knew then she'd been watching me to see if I'd look her way, and now she raised a hand in thank you. Just a tiny wave, and then she turned and disappeared inside the shack as Shilo led his horse around the corner.

Although a spacious line shack, the place couldn't hold all of us. And it promised to be a clear, beautiful night with a heaven full of stars. So we made three fires out in the yard, picketing the horses around where there was enough graze, and threw our blankets out on the ground.

As inevitably happens in any camp, sooner or later each of us gravitated to a favorite fireside. Tye and me ended up at one with Duke Rainey and Slug Holch. Tovías Ruiz and Key Bachelor stayed at another, just the two of them. And at the last one sat Barlow Tanner, Swiss Boyington, Jason Shilo, and, of course, JoAnna Walker. Tanner kept looking our way, trying to hide a longing look—a lonely look. JoAnna stared silently into the fire. I had a feeling, except for some strange brand of social obligation, our circle would have contained another two bodies.

We had ridden some gnarled timber that day, along with thickets of dusty brush. So each of us pulled out our weapons and unloaded them, blowing them free of dust and debris. Our occupation had no tolerance for carelessness.

As I opened the loading gate and slid the round-nose .44 Remingtons into my palm, I couldn't help but think of another revolver I'd recently fired. It was an object that haunted me, wriggling back into my consciousness from where it always rested too near the surface: the Colt Walker I had pried from old Henry's hands at the First National Bank. But of course it wasn't the Walker I thought of for long. It was the man. His accusing eyes, the blood on his lips.

I cursed under my breath, shaking my head agonizingly.

Without needing to think about it, I put the Remington on half cock, pulled the cylinder pin, and let the cylinder drop into my palm. I placed a thumb inside the pistol frame and held the weapon up to the light, looking down the barrel at the firelight that flickered off my thumbnail. In this way, I could see every bit of grit along those steel lands and grooves. And there was very little; standard gun leather in those days was built to keep a weapon clean, not necessarily to draw one from its grip in a hurry.

I stared down that barrel, and the old man's accusing face appeared there in place of my thumbnail. I found myself cursing him, cursing his foolishness. He should have known he couldn't beat me! What was so important to risk his life for? And what was so important to force me into sending another soul to eternity?

With a throbbing heart, I slid the Remington back into its holster and allowed myself momentarily to engage in the owl-hoot taboo of staring into the fire. There again I saw the face of the old man and smelled the rush of wind-swirled wood smoke that turned to gunsmoke.

I looked up, and my eyes fell on Slug Holch. He, too, gazed at the fire. His jaw was flexed, and his hands clenched in his lap. Nobody at our fire seemed talkative. The only noise there came from the popping of pitch pockets exploding with heat, and of an occasional angry hiss of steam.

Slug continued looking at the flames. Their light danced brightly on his cheeks and forehead, glistened in gilded slivers off his whiskered jaw. He had hardly moved in fifteen minutes, sitting like a statue chipped from a cold block of stone.

I wondered what his thoughts were. I would have bet money JoAnna was in them, but what secrets would they reveal if I could read them? Why did this woman he'd passed off as his sweetheart sit at one campfire with another man's hand on her knee while the mighty Slug Holch sat in brooding silence over here? Was this Jason Shilo so powerful as to captivate his followers with total fear? Or, on another hand, so charismatic as to inspire complete loyalty to him, no matter the cost? That hardly seemed likely. This was Slug Holch. He kowtowed to no one.

Or at least he hadn't in his younger days.

All of a sudden, Slug Holch lunged to his feet, his big hands quivering in the firelight. His pale eyes flickered with reflections; the fire colored his face like that of a demon. I felt myself rise up a little from the ground, and a glance toward JoAnna showed what I judged as a new look of hope in her eyes. Looking back at Slug, I saw he was settling the gunbelt about his waist, and I didn't believe by his face he knew all eyes were on him.

Then, just as suddenly as he had risen, he turned and walked off into the dark. Five minutes later the pounding sound of a galloping horse echoed back to the yard.

Duke Rainey blinked his eyes deliberately and stared into the fire. "Fool man gonna kill hisself, runnin' in the dark."

I glanced around at Tye, and at those beside the other fires. Everyone was silent now, sitting still or sipping gingerly at steaming tin cups.

Five minutes later, I happened to look over at Jason Shilo as he tapped Swiss Boyington's shoulder and stood up. The bigger man lumbered to his feet, and together they disappeared inside the house. Moments later, a lamp illuminated the inside of the little house.

I glanced over at JoAnna, relieved she was still there. I hadn't expected her to stay beside that fire when Shilo left. I don't know why I even cared, except that like I had told Tye, I fought for the loser, and in this case she seemed to be it. Curse Shilo! Curse the woman! Curse every bit of the air in camp that night! They had no right to place me, a total stranger, into that boiling pot.

JoAnna stared into the fire, but once in a while she would look up toward the house then suddenly fold her arms tighter around her up-curved knees. I caught myself following her nervous glance toward the house.

With no warning, Barlow Tanner stood up from the fire and traipsed off into the dark. We watched him go, and then Duke Rainey instinctively turned his eyes to glance at me. I looked at him questioningly, but he only shrugged and looked away. Still, I knew he was well aware what was going on. I only wished someone had let me and Tye in on it.

I heard Tovías Ruiz and Key Bachelor speak to each other in low tones, and then they got up and walked toward the horse corral. That left me and Tye at the fire with Duke and JoAnna at the other one by herself.

She looked so lonely and lost over there. I was not a completely hardened man, though most people I knew might not have believed it offhand. But the truth was, I felt sorry for the girl—she didn't seem like a woman at the moment. Just what was the story here? Why did Jason Shilo control this camp? Why did only Duke Rainey remain here with me and Tye? I sensed something was about to happen.

The door to the house opened, and I heard Swiss Boyington's booming laugh. I looked over to see him slap Shilo on the shoulder as they stepped off the porch. I heard his faint words, "No problem. What are friends for?"

Shilo only laughed in response as the pair approached JoAnna's fire. The woman watched them coming, and this time she didn't look away. Slowly, JoAnna rose to her feet, standing there waiting for them. When they reached her fire, Boyington picked up three good-sized logs and threw them onto the flames. With a heavy grunt, he plopped himself down in the orange glow.

In the firelight, Jason Shilo's handsome face gleamed and looked wolfish, the light flickering dimly off his teeth when he smiled. He took JoAnna by both shoulders and looked into her eyes. Then he raised one of his hands and laid it alongside her cheek. The woman didn't move into it, but she didn't move away either.

Silently, I begged for JoAnna to say something, to make some plea. I longed to understand this bizarre situation. Perhaps she wanted to go with Shilo. I couldn't know for certain. After all, she was smiling at him now too, though it was a weak smile. JoAnna said nothing in protest. She didn't even look our way. And when Shilo placed his arm across her shoulders and led her toward the house, she went unhesitatingly.

Tye and Duke stared at the fire, but I couldn't help looking after Shilo and the woman. Jason Shilo, with his broad shoulders, his narrow hips, his perfect form; he towered over the now seemingly tiny frame of JoAnna Walker, made her seem almost of no account.

They disappeared inside the little house, and the shutting of the door was a flat, awful sound in the night. Only the popping of the fires broke the dead stillness of the dark.

And no one would meet my eyes.

Chapter Eight
Two Hearts Revealed

No one moved for an hour. We shifted our weight now and then—perhaps changed from one side to the other, but we didn't get up and leave the fires. We didn't go to our blankets, either, with one exception: Swiss Boyington had crawled into Shilo's bedroll and now lay snoring. Tanner, Ruiz, and Bachelor had returned, and they sat in silence at the center fire, now and then building up its flames without really seeming to think about it.

A cougar snarled up in the trees, startling us all enough to make us look around. Unlike wolves or coyotes, the big catamount didn't use its voice much. It cried again, this time louder, sounding like a gruff-voiced woman screaming in pain. It made the hair prickle up on the back of my neck.

In a moment, we heard plodding hoofbeats. There was no moon, but I saw a large shadow that matched the sounds loom past and lumber to the corral. Several minutes later Slug Holch strode into camp. He glanced toward the fire where JoAnna had sat, and where Boyington now lay stretched out alone. He quickly looked away, running his tongue around the inside of his lower lip. Then he let his eyes raise and rest on the house.

After several moments, Slug came over to our fire. He must have known he was being watched, but he didn't look at anybody. He slumped to his backside, leaning back. He drew up one knee and rested his weight on his elbow. With the other hand, he reached up and tugged his hat a little lower over his eyes.

Finally, he looked up at Duke Rainey. "Did he force her?" he asked. His voice was low, defeated.

Duke knew Slug, and so did I, for we had ridden with him. But Tye Sandoe hadn't. When Duke only shrugged, Tye cleared his throat. "She went quiet an' easy. An' not a damn person tried to stop her goin'."

A warning bell rang in my head, and I glanced quickly from Tye back to Slug. The bigger man was watching Tye intently now, and he raised up almost imperceptibly on his elbow. The fire was back in his eyes. "Boy. I hope you don't mean anything by that."

Tye rolled over and sat up. He stared into the fire, then finally looked up at Slug. The big man was still watching him.

"Well? Yer awful quiet of a sudden."

Tye shrugged, glancing at me. "Nothin' to say, I guess."

Pushing himself up from his elbow to his backside, Slug curled his feet inward, Injun-style. "Well, now, you sure had somethin' to say a bit ago."

"I only said no one tried to stop her goin'."

"Meanin' me."

"Well, you left, yeah," Tye said lamely. "She's s'posed to be yer woman, ain't she? She prob'ly coulda used you."

Slug emitted a noise—half grunt, half laugh. Slowly, deliberately, he pushed himself erect, looking down with almost glowing eyes at the younger, slighter man. "Yeah, they say she was s'posed to be my woman. But you obviously didn't notice that 'til just now. You been tryin' to start somethin' up with her yerself since you boys rode in."

I looked over at Tye, trying to decide what he was thinking, what his next move might be. He was sometimes an impetuous man— or *boy,* depending on how I wanted to think of him that day. I hoped this time he'd be smart enough to hold his tongue—if it wasn't already too late. He just stared silently up at Slug, defiantly meeting his eyes.

"Don't have much to say, do you, Nancy boy? Why so quiet of a sudden?"

Tye glanced quickly over at me again. Caution tightened the skin around his eyes, paled his face. But when he looked at me, realizing I was watching for his reaction, his expression changed. He swallowed hard and wiped a hand across his mustache. He looked back up at Slug and slowly climbed to his own feet, standing eye to eye with Slug but forty pounds lighter. He knew I was watching him, and the rest was for me.

"I'm quiet because I don't have much to say," Tye said, a slight quiver to his voice. "I just think you should've stuck by yer woman a little closer. I don't know what's goin' on here, but it ain't right." I noticed his right hand was curled up tightly into a fist, but the left was still open, drawn into claw formation near his gun butt. To anyone paying attention to that, especially someone who knew for a fact the boy was right-handed, that would look pretty strange. That holster was on the left hip, sure, but set for a cross draw. If Tye was setting himself up to draw, why wasn't that right hand ready?

"When it comes to my woman, you don't say what's wrong or right, pretty boy." Slug started to undo his gunbelt.

Tye followed suit, using only his left hand to do it. He stooped to lay his holstered Smith and Wesson near me. Straightening back up, he stared into Slug's fiery eyes. "I'd be ashamed to call myself a man tonight, if I was standin' in yer boots."

At that insult, Slug started across the close space, and as Tye's right hand came up it flung open, showering Slug's face with dust. I silently congratulated him for remembering what I said about having an edge if he ever fought Slug.

Tye charged the bigger man, leaping right over the fire. He rammed his head into Slug's chest with all his force, knocking him to his back. In the process, Tye stumbled and went down, and they came up together.

Slug, trying to clear his eyes of dirt, shook his head and spit mud, pawing at his face like an angry bear. Before he could recover, wiry Tye plowed into him again and knocked him back, but this time Slug had braced his legs. He didn't go down.

Tye took advantage of Slug's blindness and hammered him with blows to the abdomen and face. The last one shook Slug again, almost putting him down. But I'd seen Slug Holch fight through hits that should have killed him.

Groping, Slug leaped forward and caught the front of Tye's shirt. Tye was quick and tried to leap away, but there was no escaping the bigger man's claw-like grip. He pulled Tye into him, at the same time ducking forward with his head. Slug still wore his hat, and it cushioned the blow. Its brim struck Tye's chest, and its crown his nose. Pinned there for a moment, when their heads parted the hat fell off and landed in the dust.

When Slug tried the head butt again, Tye was ready. The first blow had shaken him, but now he brought his hands up to protect his face. Angered, Slug ripped at Tye's shirt, tearing the front of it off. Stumbling away, Tye grabbed at the remains of the shirt, pulling the material away and throwing it to earth. Revealed were lithe, long muscles and a flat, rippling belly under a dusting of black hair.

Unfortunately for Tye, while he took the time to pull off his shirt, Slug recovered from the dust in his eyes. He was ready for the fight, and Tye's only chance was to stay out of his reach. But Tye's pride wouldn't let him do that.

They met toe to toe. Arms pumped madly. Fists thudded into flesh. Tye was the faster of the two, by only a fraction, but he couldn't withstand Slug's power. The bigger man had fought many such battles, and Tye's punches hadn't even begun to affect him, far as I could see. Tye became more haphazard with his blows. He weakened steadily, while the source of Slug's power had scarcely been tapped.

Finally, Slug laid Tye across a bedroll with a solid right cross to the forehead. The rest of us were on our feet, and I grimaced, looking at my partner. His face was a bloody mess. He opened one eye, turning his head groggily, and his vision fell upon me. His open eye started to roll back in his head, and he closed it.

When he opened the eye again, I knew he'd get back up, in spite of what I'd told him. I growled at him as he started to roll over. "Stay down!"

He was on his hands and knees now, with blood dripping off his nose and chin. He came to his knees, and I ran to his side to subdue him. Arms grabbed me from behind and shoved me aside. As I turned around, Slug struck me in the cheek, and the pain of the blow drove me to a knee. As I pushed back up, Tye had just reached his feet, standing hunched over like an old man.

"Slug, he's through!" I yelled angrily. But I knew no one could penetrate the thunderheads of Slug's brain once a foe stood back up.

The big man stepped forward, and before Tye could move he struck out with his booted foot. Since he was hunched over, the kick took Tye in the chest and nearly lifted him off the ground. If he'd been bent double, it probably would have. Instead, he stumbled and went down flat on his back. His lungs made a horrible whooshing sound, and he rolled onto his side and vomited.

But Slug wasn't finished. Waiting only for the younger man's retching to subside, he stalked forward and kicked him viciously in the ribs. And then I knew I could no longer be neutral. Slug's guilt would drive him to kill Tye.

I put a hand to the throbbing place on my cheek. Only a gentle reminder: I couldn't fight Slug Holch with my bare hands. Picking up my Winchester, I stepped forward and swung, laying the barrel across the back of his head. He stopped in his tracks, and his entire body tensed mightily. He stood there pressing his eyes shut, growling in pain. Then he went to his knees.

I could show no mercy. I'd seen Slug recover from too many potentially crippling injuries. I kicked him in the side, then kicked him in the back, knocking him on his face. I kicked him again while he lay there, and all the time I held the Winchester and hoped I didn't have to use it again.

Slug struggled to rise, but his breath and his strength were gone. He came almost to his hands and knees, so I kicked him again. He fell heavily onto his side, and then he lay still. I stood over him, looking down, breathing hard with the exertion. I wanted desperately to kick him again, and again. I had to keep him down. But it wasn't in me now. I had to consider the fight finished. I couldn't bear it any other way.

Tye was groaning, and I went to his side and knelt, gently touching his arm. "Tye—you all right, boy?"

He only grunted, spitting blood. I flinched at the sight of his once-handsome face. It would never be the same after tonight.

I turned to Duke, who knelt beside Slug. "Leave him there, Duke. You sure don't want 'im wakin' up anymore than I do—not in *his* mood. Come on—help me get Tye over to the pump. He's hurt bad."

Duke looked back down at Slug, his hand resting on the heaving, muscle-rippled back. At last, he turned toward me. "Yeah, sure, Thomas. I know you right." He stood up and walked to Tye's side, shaking his head regretfully as he looked at the young man's face. "He's no perty boy no more. No—for shore, he ain't."

We pulled Tye to his feet with very little help from him, and practically dragged him to the pump. While I held him there, Duke fetched me a piece of his shirt for a rag, and then he worked the pump handle to bring up an ice-cold gush. I wet the rag and sponged Tye's face. And I was proud of the way he just crouched there and took it, showing no pain.

It had looked like a herd of buffalo ran over Tye's face, but when I was through I saw it wasn't as bad as I'd thought. It didn't look like the work of anything more than a herd of horses.

While he sank back against the water trough, I used the rag to sponge my own face. I tried to be the man Tye had been, but it hurt a lot worse washing my face than it had his. When I was finished, I helped Tye struggle to his feet. He stood there swaying, bent over and looking up at me through that one eye. I turned with him and stopped.

There was Slug Holch.

Only four yards away, the big man stood with his legs spread wide and his fists clenched. He had buckled his pistol about his waist. And he was grinning like a lop-eared mutt with a mouth full of feathers.

The big man stepped forward and stopped within four feet of us, peering out of swollen eyes. He held out his hand to me. I shook it and grinned. I just couldn't hold it back. What the heck? We were friends.

Tye stood there staring, but when Slug held his hand out he, too, shook it. He started to grin, but he cringed in pain and put a hand to his mouth. Slug smiled, oblivious to pain, and slapped Tye roughly on his bare shoulder, nearly toppling him.

"Yer a marked fighter now, boy. An' let me say you put on one hell of a good fight."

I smiled, then laughed out loud. Slug Holch was back. Or so I thought.

Long after the fires had died, I blinked my eyes open, realizing everyone was asleep—or at least bedded down. The moon splashed soft light across the yard, revealing mounds of blankets and sleeping forms. I sat up and looked around, blinking my eyes. What had woke me? Restlessness? Strange noises? Maybe the cougar again.

My eyes traveled unbidden to JoAnna Walker's empty bedroll. I wondered why she had even unrolled it. It seemed obvious she hadn't expected to be able to use it.

A strange feeling of guilt clutched the pit of my stomach as I thought of the woman. I huffed it away with a gust of breath, but it returned. Had I done everything I should have? Had I done *any-thing*? The answer was of course a flat no. No one had done any-thing. But then, why should *I* have? JoAnna wasn't *my* problem. In fact, I hadn't a thing to do with her. But still, something in her face throughout that day haunted me. She had gone with Shilo to the cabin, and she had gone without a fight. But why? There had been no desire in her eyes in spite of the forced smile on her lips. Only fear and resignation.

I sat there for a moment more, contemplating my state of sleep-lessness. When at length I realized sleep had flown, I reached out for my hat and slid it over badly tousled hair. I picked up my boots and shook them, then drew them under the covers to tug them on. I listened to hobbled horses cropping grass. My eyes delved into the dark, and I could make out some of their forms.

I caught a faint nicker from the horse corral, then restless move-ment. Nervous, since that was where Sheriff and several of our other horses were, I buckled on my gunbelt and picked up the Remington. I climbed from the blankets and crept toward the house and the corral beyond it.

As I snuck along the side of the house, nearing the corral, I heard a soft voice in the darkness. I stopped and strained my ears. A horse nickered again, then another. And then I heard the voice, this time louder.

It was JoAnna.

Slipping an eye past the corner of the house, I peered into the shadows. Through the bars of the corral, I could see her standing there, brushing back the forelock of mane from a horse's head. The horse was Sheriff.

"You're so perty," the soft voice was saying. "He takes perty good care of you, handsome man. He must love you very much." She patted his neck and leaned her face close so it almost touched his.

Suddenly, the gray's nostrils flared, and he jerked away, his head and ears coming up. He glanced around, as if searching for something, and I knew I'd been detected.

"What's wrong, handsome man?" JoAnna whispered soothingly. "No one's gonna hurt you here. Your daddy cares about you—he won't let anyone touch you. You're okay."

Surprised at the soft voice, speaking so caringly, I slowly slid the revolver back into my holster. This didn't sound like the tough tomboy I knew as JoAnna Walker. Did the moonlight bring this out in her, or just the innocence of the horse?

I wanted to listen longer, but Sheriff was staring my way. I stepped away from the house, and the gray saw me the same instant. He had already recognized me by smell, and he nickered loudly, prancing toward me. I couldn't see the woman's eyes, but her hands flew to her mouth as if to stifle a yelp. She made no other move.

I walked forward, making no sound in the dust. I bent to step between the corral bars. At that point, I didn't know if JoAnna had recognized me yet, or if she thought I was Shilo coming to find her. I spoke to her softly, like she had to the gray. "It's all right, ma'am. It's just me, McLean."

JoAnna dropped her hands from her face and hurriedly folded them across the front of her nightshirt. She said nothing.

I walked up close and stopped, patting Sheriff on the shoulder as he nuzzled me. JoAnna was hatless, and the moon gleamed in soft blue waves off her curving tresses of black hair, shone dimly on her slender neck. Her feet were white against the dark dust of the corral.

"He likes you," I said quietly, stroking the gray's neck. He bowed into the pleasant sensation, his silence attesting to his enjoyment.

JoAnna wasn't looking at me, but at the horse. I searched for words to set her at ease. "My coat's near that post over there," I offered. "You must be cold."

She shrugged, and I saw a little shiver pass up through her torso and neck. "No," she said in her husky voice. "I'm fine. I…I hope you don't mind me touchin' your horse. I couldn't sleep. I came out here to think."

I smiled, glancing at her disheveled hair, her rumpled clothing, the broken spirit that, even in darkness, shone like mist from her eyes.

"What happened to your face?" she asked.

The question took me by surprise, and I reached up and touched my cheek unconsciously. I cleared my throat. "We had a ruckus." I chuckled uncomfortably. "Slug an' me—an' Tye."

One hand darted upward, and the fingers brushed her lips. "Oh. Is he all right? Your friend, I mean?"

I smiled to myself, so slightly she probably didn't see it. She knew Slug enough not to even ask about him.

"He's in rough shape, ma'am. But he'll pull through. He's too proud to stay down."

JoAnna's voice became huskier. "That bruise on your cheek— that's from Noel?"

I paused, thrown off guard by the use of Slug's Christian name. "Uh, yes, ma'am."

"Why did he stop there?" She sounded oddly disappointed.

"Because he was still busy with my pardner."

"And you just let them fight?"

"Well, not exactly, ma'am. I sorta stepped in an' ended it—diplomatically."

She searched my eyes for a moment, then again dropped her hand and wriggled it back into the crook of her other arm, shivering.

"Ma'am, I'll fetch that coat," I said. She protested, but I had already started across the corral, and I ignored her. I untied the coat from my saddle and walked back to her with it, holding it out wordlessly.

JoAnna paused, looking at the coat, not me. At last, she reached and accepted it, putting it around her shoulders. She smiled, but it quickly flickered away.

"So…you beat Noel in a fight? To protect your friend?"

I chuckled softly. "Yeah, well, I guess you could say that."

"I can't believe it." She shook her head, watching me with a look I'd never seen in her eyes, at least not for me. "I've never seen him beaten. I just can't believe it was you."

I chuckled, taking no offense. "It's surprising the edge a rifle barrel c'n give a man."

The woman looked past me, her thoughts suddenly elsewhere. I stared at her, my heart thudding in my chest. I had to ask her something, and I opened my mouth to begin.

"What woke you?" she asked suddenly, cutting me off.

"I don't know. The horses, maybe."

"I'm sorry. What were you sayin'?"

I cocked my head. "Pardon?"

"I cut you off," she reminded me, although I didn't need it.

"Oh! No, ma'am, I had nothin' to say. Except…well, it ain't none o' my business."

She laughed, not a pleasant laugh, but a bitter one. "Since when does a man care what's his business? Men make everything their business, unless it's somethin' they wanna ignore."

I didn't answer. I just looked at her, wishing I could read her mind.

"I hope yer friend's all right," she said suddenly. "Noel can be a hard man. But he can be a coward, too."

I nodded in silent agreement. "Ma'am, did he hurt you?" I blurted out.

"Hurt me? Noel?"

I shook my head, embarrassed. "No, ma'am. Not Noel. That fellow, Shilo. It's none of my business—I know. But, are you okay?"

She stared at me for a long moment, her lips parted. For the first time, I saw moonlight glitter along a wet trail on her cheek. Dropping her arms, she laughed, again that sound of forced-back bitterness in her throat. In her huskiest voice, she said, "Why would you care? Why would any man care how I feel?"

Although flustered, I bulled on. "You're a woman—no matter how you act. A tough one—I'll give you that. But still a woman, an' Jason Shilo's a tougher man—obviously in more ways than I understand. Don't try to fight me, ma'am. I may just be the only friend you have."

Pursing her lips, she looked down, and I saw a teardrop slip from her jaw. I stepped toward her instinctively, and she backed away. I held up my hands. "I'm not gonna hurt you, ma'am. You been hurt enough."

She laughed again. "You're a man, just like the rest. How can you tell me how I hurt?"

I just looked at her. How *could* I tell her? I'd known physical pain, but what she was going through I could only try to understand and maybe help her. As far as I could see, I was the only one in this camp who would. I was ashamed to admit that—ashamed for the others.

And of a sudden I realized that no matter how much I might despise Jason Shilo, I'd stay on with Tanner and the boys. Maybe it was foolish, but I didn't have the heart to walk away from JoAnna

Walker. Maybe if I stayed to help her I could regain some of my-self—perhaps a part of whatever I'd lost when I killed the old man.

I ignored her question. I couldn't answer it. "Why don't you leave here?" I asked. "Get yourself away from this bunch. You weren't meant to be an outlaw."

With a disgusted sneer on her lips, she stared at me. "And be *what?* A whore?"

The moment the words left her, she stopped and stared at me with a look of pure hatred. A ragged sob broke from her throat, and before I even had time to feel bad for her she stepped forward and swung a fist at me. I ducked sideways, or it would have caught me square in the face. Missing made her angry. She tried again. That time, I caught her arm and pushed her away.

She came back fiercely, making an angry growling noise that was almost scary, putting me in mind of the cougar. She swung with both fists, and one struck my wounded cheek. She sobbed openly now and flailed with uncontrolled fury. I grabbed desper-ately and pinned her arms against her sides, holding onto her and once even lifting her clear of the ground as she kicked and struggled to free herself. But she did little damage with her bare feet. She cursed me desperately and growled in her throat like a demon until I was almost ready to fling her away from me.

Tears ran down her face, and she started to weaken. My feet and shins stung from her kicking, but I had successfully protected my vital parts and still held her arms pinioned beyond her strength to escape.

"Why didn't you stop him?" she sobbed. "Why did you let him—take me? Why? Why did you all…all just sit and watch? Why is it always that way?"

As if she had passed out, her body went suddenly limp, and she leaned against me, exhausted. I loosened my hold on her, but I didn't let go. With one hand, I reached up to the back of her head, draw-ing her face against my wool shirt.

She didn't cry like an animal anymore, but like a little girl. She worked her arms free of mine, and they closed around my back and held on, crushing her shuddering body against me, stirring me in a way that was far beyond physical. I held her and patted her back, allowing her tears to wash away the violence inside her.

I marveled at the spot I'd got into. And I wondered when and if I'd ever know the entire story here. I wondered if *she* even knew the story. All I knew was Jason Shilo would never touch JoAnna Walker again. I'd make certain of that.

Chapter Nine
The Challenge

In the pre-dawn stillness, I was first to rise. No wind moved, and the only sound was from songbirds twittering in the evergreens. Last night's chill clung stubbornly to my cheeks, and the sky was colored like old gunmetal. In the west, it silhouetted a great-horned owl perched in the crown of a fir. I watched him pivot his head, surveying his domain.

I took care of Sheriff, number one priority to a wanted man. I led him to the creek, and he sipped the water disinterestedly. I drank some myself and understood his lack of taste for it: cold as frozen metal, it numbed the throat on contact. But it was clear as new glass.

When I turned to lead the gray back toward the line shack, JoAnna was standing on the porch watching me. Over her white nightshirt she wore a denim jacket, and her arms were folded across her breasts. She was seventy yards away, and light was dim, but I could see her tousled black hair and the shadows of her eyes.

Not knowing if the sensations of last night's encounter had left her, I approached carefully. I hadn't made it to the house before several of the others, hearing Sheriff's muffled hooffalls, sat up and looked around them warily. Prudently, I went to the corral instead of the house, and tied the gray to the top rail by his horse hair McCarty.

Walking back to my fire of the night before, I sifted through the ashes with a stick until I found dim-glowing red on the end of a branch. With shivering fingers I formed a fire nest of grass and carefully placed the coal down into it. I coaxed the coal to life with long breaths, then rebuilt the fire until it crackled in lively time. Soon, others were crouched over their fires, and those also began to flicker to life. Before long, three pots of coffee were brewing over the flames.

JoAnna hunkered near the farthest fire. Her cheeks were red, and blue tinged her lips. She rubbed her hands together and held them toward the fire, her gaze never wandering near me. She didn't seem ashamed of her attire. It didn't matter anyway—the men avoided her like a riled porcupine. She stared into the fire, watching steam lift tentatively from the coffee pot spout.

Duke Rainey sat in his blankets and gazed into the flames. Sleep hadn't yet left his eyes, but his frizzy hair looked just as it had before he went to bed. Slug and Tye still lay rolled in their bedding, and I wondered how their faces would look today. In spite of Tye's apparent quick recovery, I knew he wouldn't feel so spry now that the stiffness and pain had time to sink in.

I sat Injun-style at my fire and again wished for my old pair of shotgun chaps to wear against the chill. I had noticed that most of the others had gone over to the new style of chaps they called batwings. They'd come out in the last few years and grown quickly popular for their ability to be donned without removing boots and spurs. But they weren't near as warm as shotguns. Myself, I'd always wondered how chaps made of wolf or bear skin would work— or even sheepskin. If I'd had time, I might have pursued the idea. It was a cinch someone would some day.

I tugged on my boots, the spurs still attached to them from the night before. I wrapped my bandanna tighter around my throat, then waited for the coffee to boil.

JoAnna continued to act aloof. She didn't look at anyone—it wasn't only me. She worked quietly at shifting bacon and cornmeal cakes around a greasy cast iron skillet and appeared to give only fleeting notice when Barlow Tanner and Swiss Boyington walked to the house, talking in low voices.

When I stood up I glanced over at the woman. She caught my movement and looked my way. When our eyes met she leveled her gaze at me and nodded, blinking deliberately. Reaching up with one hand, she lifted a stray wisp of hair and pushed it behind her ear, and then she smiled, bringing up tiny wrinkles at the corners of her eyes that made my heart skip a beat. The same moment the smile tilted her lips upward, her eyes fell away. She started to turn the bacon—needlessly, for it was still raw on both sides. She stared at the bottom of the pan. It was obvious the woman knew I was watching her, so I returned my attention to my own breakfast.

As the gray in the east took on a yellowish cast, I began to pick out little birds hopping about in the trees, swapping places. Some were grayish brown, some white and gray with black-topped heads. I watched them and listened to their soft music. That and the pine-bitten air made the morning worthwhile, even after last night's violence and regret.

It soon became obvious the sky wasn't going to get much lighter. Clouds along the horizon began to darken, then to hover lower, and soon pools of mist could be seen drifting among the trees and in the canyons. Moisture filled the air, turning me colder than I'd been all night. Again I looked at JoAnna, and she was shivering. But I wouldn't let on that I cared.

I fished into my blankets and came up with the holstered Remington, strapping it around my hips. A smear of blood across the leather brought back keen memories of the night's events, and I reached up gingerly to touch my face. My cheek was swollen, and mighty sore where my fingers touched it. They didn't call the boy Slug for no reason. He sure packed a wallop.

At about the same time Slug sat up and I noticed his bruised face, the cabin door opened. I looked that way and saw Jason Shilo step onto the porch, hat in hand. As the day before, he was freshly shaved, and his hair was pressed perfectly into place. He wore a horse hide coat with the winter hair on. Its black folds hung to his knees.

Seeming at ease with the world, Shilo glanced about the yard and drew deeply of the misty, pine-bitten air. He settled his hat just right on his head and stepped off the porch with such perfect grace it made me envious, in spite of my hatred for him. His walk was smooth, long-strided, casual. His face was a perfect mask of calm.

Crouched by my fire, I slipped the Remington from its holster and idly opened the loading gate. I put the hammer on half cock and spun the cylinder, not looking over directly at Shilo but seeing him just the same. When he stopped at the farthest fire, JoAnna didn't look up. But I noticed her start to stir the bacon round and round the pan.

I glanced up, and my eyes met Shilo's and held. His gaze dropped almost imperceptibly to the pistol I held, then returned to my face. I couldn't remember ever seeing a more self-confident expression. The corners of his mouth were turned up slightly, his eyes almost friendly, not challenging. With the slightest of movements, he casually lifted the right side of his coat and laid it back behind the ivory steer's head butt of his gun.

Shilo nodded at me ever so slightly. The corners of his eyes crinkled up, and to anyone watching it would have seemed a friendly face. He looked down at my Remington again, and there his eyes rested for several seconds. My fingers stilled on the cylinder without me even thinking about it. I wanted to look away, or at least to smile, to show my calm. But I wasn't calm. In his way, Shilo was challenging me. And somehow I knew he could kill me if he chose. At least he was awful confident he could. Too confident.

When I holstered the Remington, still looking up at him, the creases around his eyes deepened, and he looked away. Up in the fir tree near the house, two camp robbers had begun again to make their chatter. Shilo looked up at them with a frown.

My eyes fell upon Slug Holch as I stood up. I couldn't feel the cold anymore, for I was warmed by a fire inside. Slug sat there tugging on his boots, and I saw him wince in pain as he leaned forward. When he started to put on his hat, he grimaced and changed his mind. As he climbed gingerly to his feet, Shilo watched him with an appraising look. Slug didn't look up at him, even as Shilo spoke, his eyes shrewdly taking in his face.

"Morning, Slug. Are you going to be ready for the trail?"

Slug still didn't look at the man, but his face settled into determined lines. With his jaw muscles bunched, he reached up and pressed the hat firmly on his head. Aside from a slight widening, then narrowing of his eyes as the pain hit, you'd not have known I'd laid the barrel of my rifle along the back of his head.

"I'm ready now," Slug said quietly, looking at the fire. He hooked his thumb in his gunbelt, deliberately near the buckle, away from his holster.

Shilo just nodded. "Well, you boys can all rest easy for a day or two. You've had a long push of it." He looked down at Tye, then back at Slug. Finally, his eyes went to Barlow Tanner. "Take it easy on these fellows, Barlow. They'll need to be fit for riding."

Tanner laughed nervously. "They're dog-tired, Mr. Shilo. I think they'll relax a while."

"Good. I'll be gone for a time. Mr. Boyington says you can all stay here, and I think it'd be a good idea. I have some folks to see down in the valley. When I get back, be ready to ride. I may even go with you this time."

I was relieved thinking Shilo would be gone for a while. But then he changed my relief to sick dread. He turned to JoAnna, with that cool look on his face unchanged. He smiled his perfect smile. "JoAnna, honey, I'd like you to ride with me down below. Get your things together. And Barlow, do me a favor and saddle her a horse."

I glanced involuntarily at Slug, but he was still looking down as if he hadn't heard. When I looked at JoAnna, her eyes were on Shilo, but they flickered quickly to me, and I saw them fill with tears just before they dropped. She crouched and started to roll her blankets, unused from the night before.

Tanner walked off toward the horse corral, his shoulders slumped even more than usual. I didn't see him look back. Duke Rainey was fidgeting with his breakfast, but his mind seemed elsewhere. And still Slug Holch made no sound.

When I looked over at Tyrone Sandoe, he was sitting up in his blankets and watching me through his one good eye.

The young man's face had been destroyed, or so it seemed. It was swollen almost past recognition, with blood caked on it here and there where wounds had broken open during the night. But there was enough emotion in that one half-open eye for me to read my young friend's mind. He was watching for my move, and whatever he thought of his partner from this time forth would depend on the next few minutes.

But I never cared to be the boy's hero. Damn it all if I'd get myself killed over JoAnna Walker! Sure, I'd sort of made myself a promise the night before that Jason Shilo wouldn't touch JoAnna again. But that was in the night. I'd had time to think about it since then. And look at the woman, after all. Without a second's hesitation she was rolling her blankets as if she couldn't wait to roll them out later for Shilo. She hadn't even raised a protest. Who was I to buck the odds anyway? I was just a man, and there was sure some reason everyone around here bowed to Shilo every time he passed.

It was obvious there was a pecking order established long before my arrival. Barlow Tanner gave Slug Holch orders, but it was plain who the cock of the walk was when they were on the trail together. Slug might not have been much of a planner when it came to stealing cattle or such, but he was the man people would turn to in a fight. And I had seen that on the trail JoAnna listened to his every word, no matter how tough she liked to act.

But here in camp with Shilo things were different. Here, the real leader stood out like a thoroughbred in a corral full of donkeys. Jason Shilo was made to lead men, and for whatever reason, they followed him like sheep. He had a power over them—charisma, manliness, reputation. I didn't know what it was, but whatever he had, it made him top dog. There was no getting around that fact. And it wouldn't do to upset the ladder now.

But then I saw the teardrop roll down JoAnna's cheek. Her finger swept it away, but not soon enough.

I closed my eyes resignedly and pulled my Remington out again, resting it along my thigh as if I wasn't even aware I'd done it. My heart pounded in my throat, and in my mouth I tasted blood. I must have bit the inside of my cheek. I swallowed and looked at JoAnna, then almost immediately at Shilo as I spoke.

"Miss Walker, I know yer tired from the ridin'. You don't have to go if you don't feel like it. I think Mister Shilo would understand." Even as I said it—*Mister* Shilo—it turned my stomach. But there was something about the man that was undeniable—a power, a demand for respect. I hated the man for the fear he caused, but for some reason I still succumbed to his spell. *Mister* Shilo. What made him deserve to carry a title?

He was watching me now, as I'd known he would be. As any man would be who'd been challenged that way. In fact, I felt all of them watching me. But I couldn't afford to look at anyone but him. His square jaw was bunched at its bend. His lips, though still turned up in that fixed smile, were pinched together. He watched me carefully, glancing at the gun against my leg, then at my eyes. Once, his eyes flickered to JoAnna. Her hands were frozen in motion, as if she was afraid to move again.

The camp robbers fairly screamed in their tree, but all sound was muffled with the glowering black cloud bellies pressing down over us and the tongues of smoky mist snaking through the trees. Horses stamped and blew in the corral, and Barlow Tanner returned without a mount. His hands hung at his sides as his eyes swung over the gathering.

For a long moment Shilo's eyes rested on my gun. Last, he looked down at JoAnna and gave his most caring smile. "I'm sorry, JoAnn. I wasn't thinking. I guess you have been in the saddle quite a bit lately. No need to push yourself. Mister McLean is right. He seems to be right quite often." He looked back at me, his face perfectly composed. He nodded and smiled. "Thanks for keeping an eye on the girl, Mister McLean. I don't know where my mind was."

I shrugged, not missing the fact that he had called me "mister" twice. "Don't mention it," I said. My voice came out louder than I wanted. "I just figgered she was beat. We all are."

Feeling a bit foolish, I casually slid my revolver back in the holster. It had only settled when Shilo moved. His hand was a blur. It shot to his holster while I watched, helpless. I started to raise my hand to grab my gun again, but there was no time. Shilo's Colt cleared the holster, and he whirled. With two shots closely spaced, he shattered the morning's quiet and filled the air with gunfire and feathers. At twenty yards, the two camp robbers exploded from their branch and flopped down through the foliage to the ground, landing lifeless in the grass and needles at the foot of the tree.

"Damn noisy birds." Shilo thumbed two shells from cartridge

loops on his belt and replaced the emptied cartridges in his Colt. Without turning back, he holstered the gun and walked off toward the horse corral.

Chapter Ten
Call of the Law

The Posse: Augustin Flagg

The tangled curls of beard lay against Sheriff Van Bennett's shirt like rusted shreds of steel wool. Standing beneath the shelter of the blacksmith's awning in Big Horn City, he turned an ear to the clanging of a hammer on strap iron, but his mind seemed elsewhere. His eyes were, anyway. They stared fixedly into space. I frowned at my words. *Stared fixedly into space...* Was that a fitting portrayal of the man who would soon win the respect of the entire United States?

I had tried in my head to come up with a description of Sheriff Van Bennett. I'd jotted words down in my notes, but none of them seemed to do him justice. Yet I absolutely had to come up with something that would inspire awe in readers everywhere. I had no doubt this story, or at least parts thereof, would be published not only in the Buffalo *Echo*, but also in other papers across the West, and even on the Pacific coast and back East. This story could make my career as a newspaper correspondent. In fact, there was even a chance I could make a book of it all, in the end. And that would surely bring me fame. *Augustin Flagg, the new James Fenimore Cooper, the new Charles Dickens, the new Mark Twain.* I could see it all now, and it looked fine.

It had been my extreme good fortune to be in Buffalo the fateful day of the bank robbery. I'd struck up a friendship with Mister T.V. McCandish, you see—through mail correspondence. Mr. McCandish was the editor for the Buffalo *Echo*. I'd been visiting, just arrived on the stage coach two days previous, in fact. I'd come from San Francisco to meet Mister McCandish, and to do a story on the Wyoming Stock Growers Association. But I'd stumbled onto something of much more import. Something fantastically large. This was the type of story that brought fame to a young writer like myself. T.V. McCandish had been strapped with a deadline on the next issue of the *Echo*, or he would have been on this trip himself. It was a tremendous stroke of good fortune for me. Only twenty-five years old, I had blundered into the story of a lifetime.

The blacksmith in Big Horn City, a short stocky man wearing a flowery white bandanna around his head, stood with braced legs at his anvil, swinging the four-pound hammer with short, sure strokes. The cold steel struck the red-hot horseshoe, shaping it to replace a shoe Sheriff Bennett's horse had thrown. Paper-thin flakes of metal fell away, disappearing among chips and shavings scattered across the earth. The smith's hands were thick and powerful-looking though cracked from use. Sweat ran down his forehead and neck, glistening in oily beads on his cheeks.

Beside Van Bennett his trusted companion, Poco Vidales, sucked on a ragged toothpick. True to his nickname, Spanish for "Little," Vidales was a small, wiry vaquero. I wasn't sure I'd ever heard his real Christian name. Vidales was reputed to be deadly in a one-on-one fight of almost any fashion, and fiercely loyal to Bennett. The sheriff, repaying Poco's father for giving his own life to save him in the Civil War, had nearly supported the Vidales family in Poco's younger days. Poco Vidales could never forget that, it seemed. He followed Sheriff Bennett's every word like a loyal dog. It was touching, yet sometimes almost embarrassing.

Deputy Anthony Ribervo—the sheriff referred to him by the nickname Tone—lounged against the wall nearby, slapping vigorously at the mosquitoes that buzzed his head and neck, whining near his ears. Away from the heat and nostril-assaulting coal stench of the forge, the insects swarmed in droves. The rest of us stretched about the yard, all of us fighting the same losing battle as Ribervo. The only four who seemed to show any intelligence at all had gone two hundred yards down the street to the Oriental Hotel for their habitual draught. And the fearless mosquitoes even invaded the Oriental, I had noticed, though in lesser numbers.

Not far away, cottonwoods rustled along the banks of Jackson Creek, and among them and the willows swarmed hordes of the winged insects. Dragonflies cruised the air there, also, darting this way and that to capture their hapless prey. But this afternoon a chilly breeze cut down out of the Bighorns, promising a change in the weather. If the temperature plummeted as it promised to, the mosquitoes would suffer. That fact caused great distress among us and the horses, for as one might well imagine we had grown quite fond of the little beasts' constant companionship.

Anthony Ribervo slapped a big mosquito on his neck, leaving a bright red spot. "I hate to say it again, Van. I know you're sick of hearin' it. But they have to've headed over the top, gone east. We would've seen or heard something by now, and no one seems to've seen them. They didn't come this way."

Sheriff Bennett skewered his deputy with a look of irritation and spat a stream of tobacco juice against the wall of the blacksmith shop. He wiped a hand across his beard. "I guess I was just hoping. Just hoping. Hell of a note, boys, when the two best trackers in the country can't even cut a track." His eyes flicked to his faithful companion, Vidales.

The little Mexican straightened up, his eyes studying the lawman coolly. A smirk tugged up one corner of his mouth. "Sorry, Sheriff," he spoke in his appealing Mexican accent. "These eyes, they can only see so much. The rain…you know. Up here in this country, I'm surprised it did not even wash the beard off your face."

Sheriff Bennett grunted, but the affection in his eyes for the little Mexican was not well hidden. "Soon's they get that shoe on, we've a decision to make. Best the rest of you decide. If it's up to me, I'll just keep going. 'Tain't just the robbery—weren't *my* money. It's old Henry. And Lucius Bird—that idiot shouldn't have mixed into something he didn't know anything about. But that fella killed both him and old Henry without blinking an eye. The man's cold-blooded. He'd best be stopped. I don't want to face the folks back in town if I don't give this a fair shot."

Anthony Ribervo looked thoughtful. He squinted toward the sun, then turned and took in the mountains, lit up brightly against the backdrop of a storm. Black clouds hunched together behind the unruly ridge of mountains, with sheets of moisture plummeting down in isolated patches. "Somebody somewhere'll run them down," he said. "That gray horse alone'll give them away. A man can't hide forever. It ain't the old days when a fella could just disappear. Personally, I think I'll cast in my two bits for doubling back. It was passable cold last night, and it's fixing to get worse yet, looking at that sky," Ribervo spoke in his typical western drawl.

"Yes, that sky." Sheriff Bennett let his gaze follow his deputy's. The tree-clad mountains, cast in gold light, looked unnatural against the storm, like two different scenes pasted together. But some of their rocky tops were obscured even now by the descending mist. "Rain's comin', down here. Rain, then…maybe snow, up there. That's a cold bank o' cloud."

Poco Vidales took out papers and tobacco for the hand-rolled cigarettes his people favored and passed them around. They would warm the fingers. He rolled his with the deftness of a practiced expert and held a match to its tip as he squinted down the street toward the Oriental Hotel. "I think, Sheriff—you don't mind, I will come with you. Nothing to do in town now 'cept wait for a war anyhow."

Sheriff Bennett looked at his little companion through eyes like gunmetal. The sheriff wasn't an emotional man, but it was plain he had a special liking for the little Mexican. They understood each other. And not many men would have promised support without first knowing if there would be others. Poco Vidales was a fearless little man.

Hooves clattered echoes down the narrow street. Sheriff Bennett, Poco Vidales, and Anthony Ribervo straightened, and the others sat up, looking toward the sound. We saw a lone cowboy as he rounded the corner, head pivoting left and right. His eyes stopped immediately upon seeing us at the blacksmith shop. A look of relief washed over his face.

Easing up his horse, the man leaped out of the saddle and came toward us, holding his reins. "They told me you might be here, Sheriff," he said nervously. Van Bennett had an uncanny way of making men ill at ease. "I was afraid yuh mighta gone on."

Sheriff Bennett glanced the young man over. Only a tuft of golden down grew on his upper lip, but he wore a Smith and Wesson pistol stuffed inside his vest, behind a cartridge belt. "Speak your mind, son. I hope you got good reason for dogging your hoss that way."

"Yessir. They sent me up from Buffalo to tell you Mister George Holt, who's the president of the Wyoming Land and Cattle company, just came in from Cheyenne and wanted to see you about some rustlers. But— "

"Well, he'll have to wait." Sheriff Bennett plainly had no great love for the large cattlemen who congregated in the Territorial Capitol. He felt they tended to do things their own way, and they didn't seem to care whether it was within the laws of the land or not. To their way of thinking, they *were* the law.

"Well, sir, that ain't truly what I come to tell yuh." The young cowpuncher shifted his eyes back and forth. "Somebody brung word they seen the rustlers up this way, pushin' a mess o' cows. An' then our outside man saw 'em, while he was on his way back to the ranch from roundup. There's a man there on a nice-lookin' big gray. Thoroughbred kind o' hoss. Could that be one o' the fellas that robbed the bank?"

"Where was this bunch?"

The cowboy swiped at his mouth. "They gone onto Flyin' B grass, sir. Swiss Boyington's place. Nobody's seen 'em since."

Sheriff Bennett swung his eyes on Ribervo. "This might be our lead. Could be it's them—that's a remarkable hoss." He spun on the blacksmith. "How long till you're done?"

Looking up from his work, the blacksmith wiped a sleeve across his sweaty brow. He raised a nail hammer and the hot shoe, held with tongs, toward Bennett. "This is it."

He walked to the horse, hefted its rear foot up between his legs, and placed the shoe against the shaved hoof. From the hoof curled a cloud of acrid smoke, and the horse cranked its head around and rolled its eyes. A smell like burning hair filled the air, and Poco Vidales grinned. "Smells like the branding," he claimed to no one in particular.

After searing the hoof with the shoe to give it a tighter fit and seal the surface, the smith cooled the shoe in water and returned to nail it with confident strokes to the hoof. He clipped the nail points from the outer edge of the hoof with the tongs, then picked up his farrier's file. After a couple dozen strokes, he dropped the leg and gave the horse a slap on the rump, causing it to fidget and step forward. "There you are, Sheriff."

By now, the rest of us had caught the drift of what was about to happen. We looked around at one another, aware our rest might soon be over. Some of the men stood up and dusted off their trousers, taking time from their busy schedule of swatting mosquitoes.

We were reunited at the saloon. Cale Storrie, Ted Burlen, Cory McCabe and Buck Auburn had several drinks under their belts by that time, and it was plain they were ready to go home and forget the pursuit. But Sheriff Van Bennett could be a persuasive force. After several minutes of heated discussion, we decided to camp in Big Horn City that night, then take up the trail again around five the next morning. Sheriff Bennett wanted to leave right then, but Anthony Ribervo's cool head prevailed, saving us for a time: there was no sense getting someone hurt trying to ride in the dark, and dark was altogether too near.

But in the morning, five o'clock found us saddled and gone. And the Bighorn Mountains loomed close overhead.

The Outlaws: Thomas McLean

I sat on the ground and mindlessly rubbed my thumb back and forth over a hole in the sole of my boot. For a "successful" bank robber, it was funny I couldn't keep myself in a decent pair of boots. But who had time to have them repaired when someone was always riding behind you, wanting those boot toes forever pointed skyward?

A man named Dudley Griggs had made the boots for me over two years ago in Baker, Oregon. They were seal brown and nearly knee-high, with red geometrics stitched into calf hide tops to sturdy them up. They had the old fashioned stove pipe tops, not the V-cut of modern ones. Those were made for men who might choose at times to walk, was my guess. Me, I wouldn't walk if I had any other choice. But there were new elements in boots I liked, for the same reason. I'd chose the new style of taller, slanted heel preferred by horsemen, and the new style of toes, no longer square but rounded to slip easily in and out of stirrups. Seemed strange someone hadn't come up with such improvements years ago.

I talk of boots, but boots weren't what held my thoughts. I was pondering on how I might've been dead if Shilo hadn't been satisfied demonstrating his gunmanship on the birds instead of me. I didn't know if his prowess with a handgun was the reason everyone there kowtowed to him, but if it was I would've understood. Shilo was impressive. I knew the man could kill me, and I doubted he'd feel any remorse for it. It wouldn't have took a lot to convince me Jason Shilo had little in the way of a heart, and I knew he'd killed before.

But surely it wasn't just the man's gun speed that had them all buffaloed. He had a winning way with people, for a fact. And most men follow charisma and power, whether they like to admit they do or not. Most men are just plain followers. But I never was. I was always a rebel, a trouble-maker. Some would probably say I hated taking orders, and I'd never grown up. That could have been true, but the fact was even though I'd gained a new respect for Shilo I still didn't like him. And no matter how fast he was, he couldn't win against a load of buckshot in the back. Me, I didn't intend to die in a face to face gunfight if another choice was to be had. I also didn't intend to listen to his orders any longer than it took to get my carcass to Montana. After that, if JoAnna chose to stay with him, that was her own lookout. Same for Tye. Me, I'd be gone. I'd heard good things spoke of Montana, and I had me a ranch there, somewhere. All I had to do was find and claim it. I was done with this god-forsaken outlaw life.

The sudden sound of a horse galloping in along the trail made me jerk my head around and put my hand to my gun. Out of the haze came a sorrel bearing a man in range gear. In spite of the cold, the horse's shoulders and neck were lathered, and spouts of steam gushed from its nostrils with every breath, only to be whisked away by the swirl of wind it made. The horse skidded to a halt, scattering gravel and dust over us. The rider leaped from the saddle, making a grab for a rein but losing it. He swore as the disgruntled horse cantered off for the corrals.

The puncher flipped a greasy shock of hair out of his eyes and spoke excitedly to the group. "Where's Swiss Boyington?"

"Inside," Barlow Tanner replied. "What's the hurry?"

Instead of answering, the man turned and jogged for the cabin, slamming through the door without an invite. In less than a minute, out he and the rancher came. Boyington looked around with a tight-drawn face. He was barefoot and shirtless, except for long johns. He made a quick effort at buttoning the fly of his pants as he sought out Shilo.

Shilo'd been saddling his horse, and now he brought it around to the front of the house, looking expectantly from the newly arrived cowboy to Boyington.

"I thought your boys were careful," the rancher said with a groan. "We got a heap of trouble, Mr. Shilo."

"What's the problem?" Shilo's eyes turned cautious.

"There's fourteen men headed our way, and Van Bennett's in the lead. He's the sheriff of Johnson County!"

Shilo cursed. "I know who he is. I don't know what happened. Somebody must've tipped him off. But whatever happens, you don't know me, Swiss. Just play it cool, and no gunplay. Have your boys drive the cows off in the timber and scatter them. Swiss, I always repay a man who looks out for me. I can be your best friend. Don't let me down."

Swiss Boyington seemed a smart man. By his look, I could tell he caught the veiled warning in those words, and so did I. *I can be your best friend.* Hidden behind the seeming comfort of those words was a cold warning: he could also be his worst enemy.

"I need to return this way," Shilo said. "I can't let a little draw-back affect business. What's the best bet to lay low for a few days?"

"I'd go southwest," said Boyington. "They followed you from

the south and wouldn't expect you to go back the same way. They'll be looking for you to the north." He turned and pointed almost due southwest. The mountains there were very green, and heavy patches of timber climbed their flanks. "You can't see it from here, but back of those mountains are some peaks that'd take you up to the sky, if that's where you wanted to go. You head up into that country and you c'n lose yourself forever, then come down at your will. And prettier country you won't find, as long as it don't start to storm. Then you'll think you'd went straight to hell."

Boyington glanced at his messenger, then back down the trail he'd just ridden. "Jim says the posse's still five miles back, comin' from Big Horn City. That'll give us all time, if we start now. Sorry about all this, Mr. Shilo."

I stood dumbfounded. Boyington was apologizing to Shilo! Only moments ago he'd almost accused him of leading the posse there! I couldn't deny the queer power Jason Shilo had over people. It was almost scary, to a man with wits about him.

The camp came alive, with the others trying to rope out horses all at once and roll up their gear. JoAnna Walker had gone with the others to the corral, but I stayed at the fire. My first concern was Tyrone Sandoe.

Going to him, I crouched, putting a calm mask over my face. "They're five miles back, Tye," I said softly. "This bunch is riled over nothin'. That posse won't find us, not by the look of the country we're headin' into."

I helped Tye to his feet, doing the best I could to hide my bleak thoughts. Of course, he could see only out of one eye, and even that one was a slit. But sometimes a body senses things that don't show through the eyes.

"Am I that bad off?"

His question startled me. "What?" He frowned then, and my eyes dropped away. I forced them to return. "Bad off? You look like ground meat. But you're a man to reckon with. That's one thing you can count on. These boys look at you with new eyes, Tye."

He nodded, trying to slip his arm into his extra shirt—now his *only* shirt. "And…what about …what about her?"

"It's not her I'd worry about, kid. She'll still admire you. Other women might look at you different. But JoAnna, if anything she'll like you more. It was her you fought over, remember? And the rest of the women? Well, I've known quite a few that liked the look of a rugged man. It tells 'em you been around. Maybe seen the elephant a time or two—maybe heard the owl hoot."

Tye tried to smile. I smiled with him, and we walked to the horse corral. "Get one o' these boys to ketch your horse. I'll start rollin' up our stuff." Even as I spoke, I looked up and saw Duke and motioned him over. "Tye needs help ketchin' his horse. Could you—"

"You don't even got tuh ask, Thomas. Not after last night. This here boy's a man now. I'm proud tuh help."

I'll give Jason Shilo this: he waited longer than I'd figured. After all, he'd had his horse already saddled for his trip down to the flats. He could have skinned out quicker and it wouldn't have surprised me. I expected it. But he hung around for five minutes or so, drawing deep breaths through a long, slender cigar. To outward appearances, he seemed cool, looking around at the birds, the clouds, the urgent activity going on around him. But his eyes now and then wandered back down the trail, and his puffs on that cigar were coming faster by the moment.

He turned to Tanner. "I'll head as directly southwest as I can, Barlow. Up this drainage. If I get somewhere where it looks like you might lose me, I'll wait, but otherwise just head into the mountains, and we'll meet. If we don't, come back here in one week. I'll be here to see you."

With that, Shilo climbed onto his horse, offering no excuse for leaving before us. With one glance toward JoAnna, who was occupied saddling her own horse, he went up the hill at a long-legged trot. He set so perfect in the saddle and looked so straight and over-broad of shoulder you couldn't help but admire the look of the man. But he was a devil.

It wasn't long before Tanner, Bachelor, and Ruiz had their horses saddled and their gear loaded on. They set quickly to hitching the packs on a couple of extra horses, while JoAnna finished cinching up her saddle on a little bay. Slug, in the meantime, had managed to slap his tree on his own horse and was threading the latigo carefully through the cinch ring when I glanced over at him. He was a tough man, and not one to complain, but by the bunching of his jaw muscles I knew he was in pain. I could still see the clotted blood in his hair where I'd hit him with my rifle. His hat hung from a chin strap at his throat; he'd probably choose not to wear it for a while.

Duke Rainey was good with a rope; throwing the hooley-ann, he quickly had not only a roan roped out for himself but a stout-looking sorrel for Tye. He saddled them and tied them with McCartys at the corral. Tanner could see the progress being made, but he kept looking off down the trail, then nervously back to the others. He already sat his horse at the corner of the house, with Bachelor and Ruiz beside him. They'd managed to load the gear on the packhorses and were only waiting for us.

Picking up Tye's stuff and my own, I hurried toward the corral, knowing I was holding up the bunch. Slug had finished saddling his horse, and Duke, JoAnna and him waited beside their mounts.

Tanner cleared his throat. "Hey, McLean. We're gonna head up the trail 'n' try to ketch up to Mr. Shilo. I'd hate tuh lose him complete. When we ketch 'im, we'll string folks back along the trail so's you c'n foller us. Why don't you keep Slug, too? He's the cause o' you bein' so slow." He chuckled nervously, but Slug scowled at him.

"Hell with you, Barlow," Slug said. "I'm glad to stay back where the men ride."

Tanner grunted, the humor running out of his eyes. "Come on, Jo. You too, Duke. No sense hangin' back here." He started to turn, then hesitated, waiting for the girl and Duke. But neither moved. Duke, he didn't say anything, just looked nervous. JoAnna glanced toward Slug.

"I'll stay with them," she said. "They might need help."

Tanner looked at her with confused eyes and again seemed about to turn and go. Yet he hesitated, scratching his jaw. "Come on, now. Both of you come on. They won't be fur behind."

JoAnna just looked away. Duke shrugged and turned his eyes to me. Tanner cursed and gigged his horse with the spurs, and him and the Mexican and Bachelor followed Shilo at a stiff canter up the slope.

I walked wordlessly to the corral and dropped the gear I was packing. I looked at the others, all gathered around with Tye leaning against the corral. "Me an' Tye were alone before. Don't feel obligated to stay. We'll catch up. If we don't, it prob'ly don't matter."

"Damnit, let's go," Slug growled. "I ain't leavin' you behind. I ain't in any mood to catch up to Tanner right now anyway."

"Suit yourself." I called Sheriff to me and let him out of the enclosure, throwing my blanket and saddle on. I bridled him and wrapped his McCarty loose around the saddle horn. Lashing my saddlebags on, I was ready to ride.

Tye looked at me through his one good eye. I could see desperation in his face, and I knew he was wondering if he could ride. I wondered too. But the boy never squawked. He just hobbled over, holding his ribs, and gamely let me help him into his saddle. He tried to sit up straight, probably for the woman. But he was a horrible sight, and I didn't figure she'd be looking at him for his beauty. I wished he'd just slouch over and make himself feel better, but I wouldn't say it. At least he had his pride intact.

I tucked his McCarty under his belt, so he could keep hold of the horse if he fell off. Then I climbed up and did the same for me, and we started into the mountains. If I'd known what waited ahead, I'd have rode the other way.

Chapter Eleven
He Stoled His Last Cow

Swiss Boyington

I rode back to the cabin just before noon. I'd managed to move the stolen herd far back in the trees, and I'd left my hands to push them along even farther, then scatter them. I didn't want evidence anywhere that a posse could arrest me for—or shoot me for. You never knew about posses. I rode down into the meadow, trying to whistle "Oh, Susanna" through my dry lips. I wouldn't have told anyone, but I was worried. I'd never had a posse on me so quick before.

I studied the ground around the cabin, hoping to see tracks that showed the posse had already gone by. No such tracks were there, only tracks of Tanner's bunch. That didn't make sense to me. The posse'd been reported to be only five miles back. They should have been by already.

I'd no sooner thought this than horses began to show up in the trees across the meadow. The dark shapes of the riders and their horses showed plain against the brightness of the wildflowers in the grass. I reached to touch my pistol, and it was there. But its cold, wet grip wasn't much comfort. There was a passel of men in that posse. The butt of my rifle jutted up from its scabbard under my stirrup leather, but damnation, there were over ten riders coming at me, and I was alone.

One of them riders was a huge man, and the horse he rode made him look even bigger. I was a big man myself, but not like that fellow. The top of his hat was a good six inches higher than any other rider there. That would have to be Sheriff Bennett. I'd seen him once at a hanging in Big Horn City, but he was a ways away, and I never realized how big the man was. I wasn't any coward, but that lawman was downright scary.

I took a deep breath and tried to relax my shoulders as they came close enough through the mist for me to see Bennett's famous red beard, made dark and sort of hanging down by the rain. I nudged my horse forward and stopped in front of the cabin. The posse also came to a halt, ten yards away from me.

Sheriff Bennett pried off his hat, causing a shower of water from its crown. He wiped at his forehead, smoothing the hair to one side. He spit and rolled his huge shoulders inside a ragged buffalo coat.

"You the owner of this ranch?" he asked.

"I'm Boyington."

"Van Bennett. I need to talk with you. Let's go inside."

I swallowed past a lump in my throat and scanned the group carefully. I knew some of them. A couple of them were ranchers, members of the Association, and some were businessmen. But some were hard looking toughs I hadn't seen before. One of them, a blond gent, stared at me through eyes as pale as the sky of a winter evening. Real cold, almost dead looking. It was downright eerie.

I motioned toward the house and invited Bennett in, like I had a choice. I got off my horse and led it to the corral. I spoke over my shoulder, trying to sound calm as I could. "Make yourself at home in there. If you don't mind, I'll put up my horse."

With the horse unsaddled and loosed with the rest of them, I went past the dismounted deputies and inside the house. Bennett and a clean-cut deputy waited for me inside.

I pushed the door shut behind me and shrugged out of my coat, throwing it on the table. When I removed my hat, I felt a rush of cold air across the top of my head. My hair wasn't as thick as in my younger days. "What can I do for you, gentlemen?"

Bennett's voice was low and gravelly. "We're following a cow herd, Boyington. And it appears they came by here. Being pushed by rustlers."

I tried to look casual. "There was a herd of cows here this morning. My boys brought in a bunch of fresh-branded stuff and headed 'em back up into the high country to graze. But that's the only stuff that's been by here."

Bennett's face seemed to stiffen. He looked slowly around the room, as if searching for something. At last, he looked back at me and met my eyes square-on. "Then it's possible a fellow with a Thoroughbred-looking gray and a black-haired kid with a stocky bay joined up with your hands. Those two robbed the First National Bank and killed two men doin' it. Did you notice if your bunch had somebody new with them?"

So that was it. The posse had just stumbled into the herd! They weren't after rustled cattle at all. It was the two newcomers, McLean and Sandoe, Bennett was after. Bank robbers! If I came out of this one, old Shilo was sure going to hear about it. They led the law right to my door, careless fools. But for now, I knew I had to lie and lie good.

"I didn't notice, no. But I wasn't looking real close, either. If they were with 'em when they came, they didn't stop for any grub. And if *I* was on the run, I'd stop an' eat where I could." I knew the story sounded lame. I just hoped I was more convincing to them than I was to myself.

Van Bennett nodded and looked around the room again. I watched him without saying anything.

"Well, thanks for your help," Bennett said. He looked over at his deputy and motioned him toward the door. "Come on, Tone. Let's get back on the trail."

The Posse: Cale Storrie

Bennett and Ribervo had been inside alone with Boyington for a while when they stepped out on the porch together and found me and that greaser, Poco Vidales, there waiting for them.

"Sheriff, I wan' talk to you," the Mexican said. "*Solo.*"

Bennett just looked at the greaser for a moment, then walked off with him to the side of the house. The greaser'd said he wanted to talk alone, but I dogged 'em anyhow. I seen him studying the horses out in the corral, and I was curious to see what he discovered that I didn't. The greaser pointed toward the corral, ignoring mc bcing there.

"See that horse in the corral over there? That bay? His feet match the one we been following. Is that the horse you saw in town?"

Bennett walked over to the corral and leaned on the top rail, looking close at the bay. After a few seconds he nodded, and his eyes narrowed down. "That's the one, Poco. Good job."

We walked back around the house and climbed onto our horses without Bennett saying a word to Boyington. As we rode out of the yard, one or two of the posse, members of the Association, lifted a hand to the rancher, but Bennett seemed to make a point of not looking at him. I could tell he was ready to explode.

At the back of the house, away from windows, Bennett reined in his horse, and I stopped beside him. He waited for the others to gather 'round him. He looked over the group until he spotted big ol' Ted Burlen. Burlen was over six feet tall and built like a ram.

He had wide shoulders, thick hands covered with scars, a broken nose and black hair that curled down over his collar. To anyone but Bennett, he was an impressive feller, a fighter. I didn't like to admit it, and I'd fight if anyone said it out loud, but I was a small man. I'd always cursed my luck. I had no doubt Burlen could beat the hell out of me if he took a notion. Good thing he was a friend.

"Burlen," said Bennett, "I want you to split off here and ride up into the trees where they pushed them cows. If you see any but Boyington's brand, catch up quick and let me know. I think he's lyin' to us. And take your partners with you in case you run into trouble."

By "partners" we all knew who Bennett meant. Burlen had hung close to his group of pards since the beginning of the chase, and I was one of them. The four of us sort of stayed away from the group of stuffed shirts and that damn little newspaper reporter the best we could. The rest of the posse was made up of "respectable" members of the community. The four of us were misfits, and we liked it that way. I had no hankering to fit into a crowd of pencil pushers like them. Even the ones who owned ranches didn't seem to do much on them. It was men like me doing all their work, and them getting the money for it.

Buck Auburn was a scrawny man with a battered hat and large, crooked teeth that grew everywhere but straight. Cory McCabe was a man with blue eyes so light they almost made him look dead. He was a pard, but I didn't know how much I really liked him. He gave a man the willies. Almost like the story about that Count Dracula feller. After riding beside McCabe the last couple days, I was ready to get shut of him for good. I mean, I liked a fight, but he was set to kill somebody some day—if he hadn't already.

Without having to speak a word, the four of us broke from the posse and went off through the trees, pushing branches aside with our sleeves. The two of us lucky enough to own yellow fish, them long coats made of yellow "rubberized" cotton, were the only two that could be seen in them dark trees. Burlen and Auburn, they both wore linen dusters that was soaked with rain now. They blended in pretty good with the timber and became invisible.

It wasn't long before I spotted a lone cow, a Hereford, off in the trees. I motioned to the others, and we all moved toward her. Once the cow realized we'd spotted her, she tried to slip off through the mist, but I cut around her, and between the four of us we surrounded her. I was the only real cowboy there, so it was up to me to catch the brute, and I dabbed a loop on her head. Then, of all the fool things, I had to let Burlen hold the rope while I borrowed a beat-up lasso from Auburn and heeled that cow. We stretched her out until she just sort of fell over, and McCabe got down to look closer at the big brand on her left hip. It was a Diamond L, and she carried a double underbit crop on her left ear. That was Vince Leonard's marks, if I recalled correct. His spread was down somewhere near Laramie.

McCabe looked up through his narrow eyes at Burlen and nodded with satisfaction. There was a look almost of humor in them pale eyes, but not humor of a pleasant sort. It made a chill run up my spine, and I started wondering right then what would happen. Burlen was sort of the boss among us, if there was one. He met McCabe's eyes for a moment, then wiped a hand across the back of his neck. He glanced at me and Buck Auburn.

"Well, it don't belong here. What say we go back an' teach that old boy a lesson 'bout thievin' cows?"

I grinned, and so did Auburn, after looking at me to catch my reaction. He was a dumb old boy, not much brainier than the cow we had down. I figured the Lord had poured in his brains with a teaspoon, and somebody had joggled his arm while he was pouring. The fool couldn't even grin without checking with someone else. That gap-tooth grin didn't pretty up his heavy-whiskered jowls any either. He was still ugly as a pig's caboose. "Let's go," Auburn said with a chuckle.

We arrived back at Boyington's little cabin less than a half-hour later. We were now far back of the rest of the posse. We tied our hosses at the side of the house, then looked about the yard carefully. By the hosses in the corral, no one seemed to have arrived since our earlier visit. So it was just Boyington alone here. Burlen walked up on the porch, and we followed. He picked up a piece of wrought iron and started clanging it about inside a rusted triangle that hung from the corner of the cabin.

Pretty soon the door flung open. It was Swiss Boyington, mad about the noise. When he spotted us, the look of anger turned right quick to a confused sort of stare. "What the—"

Before he could finish, McCabe put his fist on his chest and shoved him back inside the room. Burlen, Auburn, and me followed them inside, and Auburn slammed the door. For a bit, the only sound was the rain sluicing off them cedar shakes to cut its trench along the cabin wall. That and the scared breathing of Boyington. At last, he started talking. "Where's the sheriff?"

Burlen laughed, and his voice was full of meanness. "He went on ahead. You don't think he'd waste time here when he's busy chasin' that bank robber, do you? He sent us up to check your stock."

Boyington's eyes jumped back and forth between us. "Oh? I don't suppose you saw any."

"We saw one." It was me that spoke. I had a soft kind of smooth voice that matched a boyish face. I hated knowing that, but I'd been told it a hundred times, and I tried to make my voice sound hard as I could. "We saw a cow with Leonard markings on it. The Diamond L. How d'you explain that?"

"I have no idea. If you read it right, it must've been missed during roundup."

Burlen laughed, and we joined him for a couple seconds, all except McCabe. He had pulled his pistol out and was slapping it against his thigh. I looked over with a warning at Burlen, but he was watching the rancher.

"Yeah, it wandered clear up here from Laramie. You're a liar, Boyington," Burlen said. "An' we caught you with the goods."

"I'm not lying. The only cows on this place right now should be mine. As far as I know."

Burlen smiled, showing his tobacco-stained teeth. "Yeah, they *should* be. But they're not." He spit a stream of brown juice onto the scarred top of Boyington's desk. A light was glowing in his eyes, and his fists balled up as he started going at the rancher.

I spoke quick and stepped in. I used my hardest voice, hoping to distract Burlen at least for a bit. "What we want, Mr. Boyington, is this bank robber. He killed two people in town. We could rough you up, too, but we might be able to help each other."

Boyington looked at me. "Help each other how?"

"Well, somethin' like this." My mind churned as I slapped my soggy gloves against the palm of my left hand, coming up with a plan in my head. "We want that killer. And you can tell us if we're really on his trail or not. That'd be a start. But of course, to keep us from talkin' to Bennett, fifteen or twenty dollars each would sure go a long ways to keepin' us quieted. So, uh, we'll help you by not lettin' on to Bennett what we found out about the cows, and you help us by tellin' us if that killer was with the men who brought the cows. And then the money, of course. Sound fair?"

Boyington swallowed and started to object. He clamped his mouth shut again and looked at each of us. His eyes only touched for a second on McCabe. I could tell he was scared of him, and with every right to be. Even I was. McCabe was still slapping the gun against his wet slicker, but his eyes weren't even on the rancher.

He was studying the room like he was only a casual observer killing time.

"I told you, I don't know about that cow," Boyington said at last. "What makes you—" Without any warning, Burlen's boot swung out and took Boyington's legs out from under him. The rancher landed with a grunt on his left hip and swore. As he started to get up, Burlen's boot toe caught him in the teeth. Boyington fell on his face with a groan of pain. Again, Burlen kicked him, this time in the back. Then he tromped down on the back of his neck with his muddy boot. I'd knowed this was coming, I guess. Burlen loved to beat people. He had ever since I'd knowed him. And I normally had fun at it, too, but today, with Cory McCabe standing there, I was out of the mood.

"Now, Mr. Boyington, we been friendly up till now. So you best be helpin' us out." Burlen's voice was harsh, but he smiled over at us because Boyington couldn't see him. That sort of set my mind at ease like maybe he didn't intend to hurt the man too awful bad. Then again, I didn't know that it really mattered. He was a thief, after all. Maybe he *should* be beat. But I didn't want to have anything to do with a killing. Roughing up was my limit. "Now tell us the truth so we can ride on out of here with peace of mind," Burlen said. "An' get ready to lighten your pockets a tad. You got more than you can spend honest anyways."

His mouth battered, and pressed hard to the floor, Boyington mumbled something we couldn't nohow understand. Burlen let his boot up from his neck. "What's that you say?"

Boyington rolled onto his back, looking up like he expected to be hit again. His mouth was covered with blood. "I said I'll do it. Just let me up."

With them two big meat hooks he called hands, Burlen reached down and took Boyington by the shirt, jerking him to his feet. "Start talkin' then."

"It was him—that man on the gray. The fella's name was Tom McLean, an' he rode with a partner name of Sandoe." The rancher pressed a sleeve to his bleeding mouth and winced, spitting blood to one side. "And they're well ahead of you now."

"Good," I spoke up. "Now how 'bout the money? Where is it?" That's what I really wanted. It'd pay for a hell of a bender when we got back to old Riley Smith's Minnehaha Saloon.

"How do I know you'll leave when I pay it?"

"We ever lied to you?" I asked, trying to look surprised that he'd question us. Auburn laughed stupidly, his big round eyes full up with excitement. The little weasel was sure embarrassing.

Boyington just grunted. "The money's over here. Let me get it."
He went to his desk and walked behind it. He started to slide
open a drawer, but the click of McCabe's pistol stopped him cold.
My heart jumped. I shore expected McCabe to shoot him down.
"I'll get it," McCabe growled. "Maybe you should just step away
from there."

Very slow, Boyington raised his hands and got away from the
desk. Before McCabe could move, Burlen sidled around the desk
and jerked the drawer open farther.

"Well, lookee here," Burlen said with a mirthless grin. "Now I
wonder, did you plan on grabbin' that cash…or somethin' else?"
He reached down and picked up a wad of greenbacks, flopping it
carelessly on the desktop. Then, looking at McCabe and me, he
pulled out a pistol and plunked it beside the bunch of bills. "I think
you wanted to pull down on us, didn't yuh?"

The rancher met his eyes but soon broke off the look, glancing
down at the floor. "I was only after the money. You think I'm stupid enough to fight all four of you?"

"Well, I don't know." Burlen picked up the weapon and started
toward Boyington, who backed away. "Just hold it there," Burlen
growled. "Take another step and I'll shoot you."

Boyington stopped. Burlen reached him and walked beside him,
then behind, while Boyington tried to follow him with his eyes.
Sucking in his breath quick-like, Burlen raised the pistol and brought
it down hard on the rancher's neck. Boyington cringed and fell to
his knees, and Auburn laughed his crazy laugh. Burlen reached
down and grabbed the rancher by the left hand, jerking it to the
side and laying it across a nearby chair. Before Boyington could
react, Burlen brought the barrel of the pistol down on the rancher's
fingers. The sound of crunching bone was drowned out by
Boyington's scream. It was sort of a nauseating sound even to me,
and I'd heard a few bones get broke before.

"You'll learn to try tricks on us," Burlen said as Boyington sat
on the floor, holding his broken hand. "You'll sure learn."

With that, the big man picked up the wad of cash and slid it inside his vest, then made as if to throw the pistol into a corner.

"Wait!" Cory McCabe's voice drew him up. McCabe had holstered
his pistol. "Give me that iron."

Burlen looked down at the Colt, then handed it over with a shrug.
"You'd think you had enough guns already." He stepped past Boyington
to form a little group with the rest of us. "Let's go. We got a lotta ground

to make up 'fore nightfall. I doubt the old man's slowed his pace any."

Me and Auburn turned with Burlen, after one last look at Boyington. He just kind of sat shamelessly groaning and holding his hand in the crotch of his arm. I don't know what made me turn, but at the last second I paused at the door and looked back at McCabe. He stood there staring down at the rancher, and he had a big smirk on his face. Without no more emotion than a man would swat a fly, he plunked that pistol into Boyington's lap. Then he drew his Colt.

With a smile, he shot Boyington twice in the gut.

Burlen and Auburn whipped around, gawking from McCabe to Boyington. The rancher laid on his side, cussing us all. Without batting an eye, McCabe finished him with one last bullet.

"I guess he stoled his last cow." McCabe gave a little smile with his mouth shut and holstered his gun, walking past the rest of us and out the door.

Chapter Twelve
The Handshake

The Outlaws: Tom McLean

We rode for a ways up the mountain, and the trail was easy to follow on the moist ground. But I was back of Tye, and he lagged farther and farther behind the others. They would glance back now and then, see him, and pause to wait for us. I let them do that several times before objecting. "You move on ahead. Trail's a little rough, but we'll get there. It's not doin' anybody any good to wait on us."

JoAnna looked over at Slug with a question in her eyes, as if he had to make up her mind for her. That took me back a little. Was she still looking to him for guidance, after what had happened? I'd thought she'd be disappointed in him, but if she was her face didn't show it.

Slug glanced at me, then gave a long look at Tye. Last, he turned and gazed after the others, who were far out of sight. Finally, he sighed. "Well, it ain't like it'll be hard to find 'em. They're leavin' a trail like a herd o' buffalo." He looked back at Tye and frowned. "Yeah. My horse don't like this pace much. I think I will ride on, if you don't mind."

I motioned him on, expecting the others to go with him. JoAnna looked at his retreating back, and I saw her mind churn with indecision. But Slug never looked back at her. At last, she turned and smiled at Tye, and I could see the decision come into her eyes. "My horse don't mind the pace," she said.

Duke hadn't said a word. He just turned his horse and struck out up the trail, but not near as fast as Slug. He held in on the reins and stayed just ahead of us.

Some time later, we came to a place where we could ride two by two. I pulled alongside Duke, whose sad-dog eyes were scanning the trail ahead. He glanced at me, sadder looking than normal, but quickly returned his eyes to the trail.

"What's eatin' you, Duke?" I asked.

"Oh, just Slug. Figgered he'd stay. Just up an' left without hardly a word. Didn't even look back to see if any of us followed 'im."

I nodded, sharing Duke's glum look as I tugged at a wisp of Sheriff's mane. "I think he's hurtin' some. A rifle barrel can't do a man's head much good. Besides," —I glanced back toward JoAnna— "I guess he feels poorly about the situation. He perty much left JoAnna cold."

Duke turned nervously but saw the woman and Tye forty yards down the trail. He spoke in a low tone. "Thomas, I ain't done right. I never tolt you much about what goes on here. I 'spect I better so's you won't feel too bad 'bout ol' Slug. Jo, there, she come with Mr. Shilo when she joined up with us. She ain't really Slug's. Least she weren't at first. They just sorta took a likin' to each other, an' we thought maybe Slug would take her away from Mr. Shilo."

Ignoring the revelation for a moment, I spoke irritably, "I never knew you were in the habit of callin' people 'mister'. Everybody here seems to have the same ailment."

Duke looked sheepish. "Well, I don't know what it is, Thomas. He just sorta calls for a mister in front o' his name. Fits. I never thought 'bout callin' 'im nothin' else."

"I have."

Duke got a good chuckle out of that. But after several moments his face went serious. "Mr. Shilo's been real good tuh us, Thomas. I know you an' him was havin' your differences back there. Everybody could see that. But there ain't none o' us has no complaints 'bout him, most times. He even called *me* 'sir' once. Imagine that! A rich white man callin' a Nigger 'sir'!"

We rode for a ways, and I mulled over the new information. So JoAnna had been Shilo's before Slug showed up. I wouldn't have guessed it, but it made everything fall into place. Yet she obviously didn't want to be with him any longer. Why was that? He'd made no move to beat her. Hadn't even spoke down to her that I'd heard. So what was wrong? In spite of her tough front, I got the feeling she liked people taking charge of her actions. And there wasn't a man who took charge more fully than Jason Shilo.

But something was wrong, and I wasn't the only one who'd seen it. Everyone in that camp had been nervous as cats in a doghouse when Shilo came to take JoAnna with him. Was it only because of Slug? Had they thought there'd be a fight? As quiet as everyone kept about it, I couldn't tell. But two things were sure: JoAnna wasn't happy, and

Slug Holch wasn't man enough to do a thing about it.

"I wouldn't trust Shilo."

The words left my mouth so sudden-like I didn't have time to think about them. Duke looked over and spit to the side. He chewed on my words for a moment, then spoke. "What makes yuh say a thing like that?"

"A hunch," I said. "He gives me a bad feeling in the guts. I know he's treated you good. I saw myself how smooth he is. But he'll cut you from behind the moment he thinks it'll save his own hide. Mark my words."

We rode up into the clouds, our horses' hooves slipping in the greasy mud of the trail. We threaded through stands of scattered fir trees and lodgepole, their tops showing blurry through the mist. Several had toppled along our way, and we had to skirt them. As we climbed, the clouds became steadily wetter, and soon a fine rain was drifting down. But not enough to hide our tracks.

I had fallen back behind Tye to make sure he stayed in the saddle. He was in rough shape—about as bad as I'd expected. I figured only the pain was keeping him awake at times. Duke rode in the lead, JoAnna close behind him.

Soon, spruce started to show up among the fir and lodgepole. The rain was still falling, and the timber grouped around us like silent ghosts. Outstretched limbs brushed at me now and then, dumping their loads of moisture on my hat, down my collar, down my boots. I finally stopped and pulled my pants to the outside of my boot tops, then caught up with the others. My socks were already soaked.

The trail was still easy to follow, but some of the hoofprints were starting to hold water. I didn't like the idea of getting wet clean through, but I hoped it'd rain enough to cover our trail. I wasn't in the mood for a fight with any posse. I didn't want to have to kill again—or to get killed myself, for that matter.

We were in meadow country now, and wildflowers made a fascinating multi-colored carpet like nothing I'd seen in years. Every color a man could dream of was there, almost thicker than the grass. Only the dead metallic sky dulled the show of color. Ahead, the mountains were leaden haystack shapes in the gloom. I kept my head down most of the time, letting the rain sluice off the front of my hat brim and down Sheriff's neck—I have no doubt he appreciated my consideration. Nothing like cold water down the neck to refresh a body. I learned that myself more times than I could count that day.

As we rode higher the wind came up, a cold hard wind. Then snow began to fall, and here it was the end of June! It drove sideways, plastering the northern sides of tree trunks, making a white ocean of the meadow grass. It stung my face, left it feeling raw. I tied my bandanna over my hat and under my chin, then pulled my collar up against the biting wind.

Tye was wide awake now. I judged that by the way he hunched in his saddle, fighting with his hat and coat collar. The wind shook out the horses' tails, stringing them almost straight out to the side. It tangled their manes and moaned along the crust of freezing snow that hid the grass. Snow built on the horses' rumps and necks, stung their eyes so they walked with them almost shut, twisting their heads to one side or looking at the ground like animals walking dead.

I was glad for the snow because it hid our trail from the posse, or whoever it was who followed us. But on the other hand, none of us were prepared for the weather, and it was going to kill us all if we didn't find shelter soon. A single layer of cowhide don't make for winter gloves. I could hardly feel my fingers anymore, and I'd been stuffing them now and then in my armpits to warm them up. My feet didn't have that luxury. My boots were worn thin on the soles, and my feet were long since numb.

Clouds surrounded us, and sometimes I could scarcely see Duke and JoAnna, only sixty feet or so in front. Masses of cloud hung in the trees, spewing waves of snow. It was miserable, but I was betting—or maybe just hoping—the posse would call it quits and turn back. There was no point in all of them dying, even to try and catch a couple of killers. I guess I shouldn't say a "couple." I was the trash that actually cashed in my six-shooter at the bank and done the killings. Sandoe was only along for the ride.

At last, when I had started to become indifferent to the cold, we passed into a heavy stand of evergreens and found Slug Holch and Tovías Ruiz waiting for us. I was glad, because the trail was becoming nigh impossible to follow. Tanner had been considerate enough to leave them back to make sure we found the way.

"Cold enough for you?" Holch yelled above the shrieking wind. "You'd think it was the middle o' December."

I only nodded, not interested in breaking my lips with useless talk. I glanced over at Tye. He was huddled in his saddle at the side of the trail with his good eye half shut and hidden back in the folds of his coat. JoAnna clawed at her hair, tugging out bits of ice. Duke just stared at Slug and Ruiz expectantly.

"Barlow says he'll make a camp not far ahead, even if he don't find Shilo," Tovías Ruiz offered. "He's sick of this *mierda*. We all are. Looks like we'll be hid in the trees for a time now. That's one good thing."

Slug nodded agreement and slapped his gloved hands together. It made a dull thumping sound quickly whipped away by the wind. "Come on," he yelled. "If we don't catch 'em in a mile or so, we'll make our own camp. This weather's enough to make a man glad to go to hell!"

The snow started to break before we'd gone another mile. And with it the wind died down. But even though it couldn't have been later than three or four o'clock a twilight glow surrounded us. Clouds drifted through the trees in long, thick herds, obscuring from sight the same timber that had kept the wind from freezing the marrow in our bones.

We smelled the smoke before we made it to the meadow. It brought with it all the imaginary odors that come with that welcome scent: meat roasting, coffee boiling, wet wool steaming, leather boots set too close to flame. It also brought to mind the comfort of sitting there with my back to a log, letting the warmth soak into my muscles. The comfort of bacon and beans and fried cornbread stewing inside my paunch. It's a wonder what one smell can do to a man. It even made me think of home, memories that were often on the edge of being dead.

The trees became thicker long before they grew thinner, and we had to get off and lead our horses just to keep from taking a fall. The walk worked to get some of the feeling back in frozen limbs.

At last, the timber thinned, then ended, and we were standing at the edge of a long, bare meadow where blades of grass and wild-flowers struggled up through the snow. On the other side of the meadow the trees seemed to crowd together even thicker than on our side, and their shaggy tops pricked into a ceiling of metal-colored clouds.

There a collection of seven tepees crowded the trees, and shad-bellied Injun horses huddled on their leeward side, heads down. Only two of them looked toward us. The others seemed not to care what went on around them. The day was too full of gloom.

Two hundred yards to the right of the tepees, and closer to us, a couple of tents stood stark against the ghost-blue of the timber. Large fires in front turned them orange, and the white smoke, like that filtering out of the tepees, puffed and swirled, struggling to rise against the wind. It never made it any farther than the treetops.

"Them's gotta be Crow tepees," Duke observed. "But I thought they was all stuck to the reservations."

"May be, but would you stay there if you could go somewhere else?" asked Slug. "I can take or leave a Injun, but I'll call the man a liar that says them Crows're treated good up there in Montana. After they helped wipe out the last of the Sioux, we kinda forgot 'em. They did their part, just like good dogs. Then they weren't needed."

"Red Niggers is all they are," said Tovías Ruiz. "They don't deserve no better. They don't belong here. They're lucky they weren't all shot."

We all turned in surprise, and no one spoke for a moment. Duke Rainey just stared at the Mexican but at last found his tongue. "They're red Niggers, and I'm a brown one. Maybe both of us should be shot, since we don't neither of us belong. But neither does a chili-eatin' greaser—not in a white man's world."

Ruiz stared at Duke, his face turned sour. "Who the hell you calling a greaser?"

"You, is who. You wanna talk 'bout Niggers, you best be ready to hear the names what white folks has made for you. Me, I'd like us all to be the same color, if the Lord would let it be. But until then, I shore try my best to act like we is."

The Mexican's hand slowly slid away from his holster, and he gave his horse's head a savage jerk. "*Ándale!*" He spurred down into the meadow snow, loping toward the twin tents.

"I didn't like that look in his eyes, Duke," I said. "How well you know that man?"

"Not much, but I ain't lettin' 'im talk like that while I'm sittin' right here."

"I've heard you call yourself a Nigger," I said.

"Yeah, well that's different, whitey. We's allowed!"

I rode behind Tye as we walked our horses on into camp. He was swaying in the saddle, pale as the snow. He barely hung on. The moment we stopped I jumped down and hurried to his side, just in time to steady him as he nearly fell off his horse. JoAnna came over, and together we walked him to one of the fires, setting him down between it and the tent.

Tanner stood there with a cup of Arbuckle's in his hand, watching Tye doubtfully. "Here, take my coffee, McLean." He handed it to me, and I gave him a grateful look. I gently put the rim of the cup to Tye's lips, and he took a sip and shuddered. I slipped my fingers under the front of his hat brim, and his skin was cold and moist.

"Get me a blanket, JoAnna. He's chillin' now, but it'll be fever next if we don't do the warmin' ourselves."

Jason Shilo stood beside Tanner, his hand in his coat pocket and his own cup of coffee gripped by the gloved fingers of his left hand. I was surprised he had his coat drawn over his pistol and didn't seem ready as the man I'd come to know.

"How'd the boy do, McLean?"

I was taken by surprise, then remembered Shilo's cordial front. "Fine, considerin'."

Shilo nodded, and he glanced back across the meadow the way we'd come. "See anybody back there?"

"Just the trees, when they weren't covered by clouds." I tried to keep my voice civil. But even though I'm a hard man to rile, I can hold a grudge forever. I suspected Shilo could sense my dislike for him.

Tanner sensed it too. "Bunch o' Crows camped across there." He motioned loosely with a new cup he'd poured. "Menfolks all gone off huntin', I reckon. Oldest boy there's no more'n fourteen."

I nodded absently and crouched down by Tye, giving him another sip of coffee before I took one myself. "Maybe we can mix our tracks with theirs on our way out," I suggested.

"Not unless they're goin' back toward Big Horn City," Shilo said. "We'll be picking up another herd over that way. We have to trail it up toward Billings."

I looked at Tye, and I was thinking I wouldn't be in on that job. If I could get Tye healed up and talk JoAnna into leaving, I thought we might push on across the mountains into western Wyoming and then north to Montana by our own route, far away from Shilo.

As I stood up, Shilo's hand came out of his pocket, and it held a pistol. Casually, without letting his eyes meet mine, he parted his coat and slid the gun into its holster. He'd been waiting to see if I'd make a move. So much for him not being prepared.

That night we all huddled around the fires rather than go to the cold of the tent. JoAnna, Tye, Slug, Duke and me sat at one fire while Shilo and Tanner had Tovías Ruiz and Key Bachelor for company. Ruiz and Bachelor seemed to just go wherever there was room for them. They didn't talk much to anyone, I'd noticed, except to each other. They seemed disgruntled all the time, probably about traveling with a group that reeked of indifference toward their prowess with guns. Myself, I'd never have pictured them riding with this group. And I didn't imagine they would be for long.

Tye was propped against a log, asleep. The blanket we'd wrapped about him had slumped down around his waist, and I left it there, for I could see he was full of fever. Beads of sweat hung on his face like vapor collecting over a boiling pot, and his cheeks and forehead were scarlet. JoAnna kept watching him, then looking down at her hands. I supposed she felt the same helpless way I did.

The rest of us sat and sipped endless cups of coffee. When the pot emptied, we boiled another with the same grounds. Holding the tin cups close to our bodies was like holding our own lifeblood, afraid it might slip away. It and the fires were our only comforts.

"It's your turn to fetch wood, Tom." I heard Slug speak, and for a moment his words didn't register. When they did, I got up without a word, picked up the double-bit axe with its chipped edges, and eased off into the trees toward a giant dead spruce we'd found.

The bit rang as it ate into the hard, barkless wood of a limb bigger around than my arm. The sound died quickly against the cushion of snow, and I paused, looking around me. I glanced back toward camp and thought of JoAnna. I'd been thinking I'd take her with me when I left here. But why would she go? Sure, I'd spoken up for her a couple times, but it sounded to me like she was Shilo's. And it looked like it, too. Shilo's or Slug's, one. Who was I, anyway? Just a no-account. Shilo could shoot me down if he wanted to, and Slug could pulverize me with his fists. Wasn't the woman safer with them?

I struck at the log again, this time harder. The limb cracked where it met the trunk, and another blow drove it into the snow, but not before sending the axe ricocheting back to almost hit my leg. I swore and took a deep breath of icy air that near made me cough. I looked back toward camp, seeing only the backs of the tents. Cold firelight glowed off the undersides of trees and dimly through the dirty canvas. When the wind whipped a certain way, I could smell the pungent scent of smoke, and mixed with it the coffee and the roasted venison of a deer one of the others had killed. Otherwise, I felt completely removed from the camp, as if studying it from a great distance. My partner was there, JoAnna was there, and two old friends were there. But did I really know any of them? Had I ever had to place all my trust in one of them? I couldn't swear they'd stick beside me if it came to a question of life or death.

A man's life shouldn't be that way. It should be full of comforts, and of family. He should be surrounded by a wife, brothers and sisters, children—folks he knew he could trust. Parents, too, if he was young enough they should still be alive. But here I was with a bunch of outlaws who might leave me at any time, if I got in a bad way. Even Tye. He'd not really been tested yet, and JoAnna either. And why even consider the woman? I didn't know her. Not like I'd known Slug or Duke or Tye. She'd likely be the first to leave me when I was down. I was nothing to her, no more than perhaps a temporary savior, and I wasn't sure she even wanted me for that. I was a fool to even think of her.

Clenching my teeth, I began to swing the axe in earnest. Even when it bounced and came near chopping my boot tops, I kept on battering at the aged wood. I didn't want to think anymore. I just wanted to work, to use my muscles, to drive unpleasant thoughts from my head.

When I had a healthy armload of three-foot limbs, I started back toward camp, this time leaving the axe near the tree. I paused at the edge of the timber and watched the seven tepees. I could see the glow of fire through their thin, patched walls. And even in the moonless night I could see smoke lifting from their flaps and rising until caught and scattered by the breeze. The scrawny horses grazed outside, pawing at the snow, but there were no dogs. They must've taken them inside, for I couldn't imagine an Injun camp without dogs around.

I wondered what these people were like. Poor, like most Injuns of that day and age. There was little question of that. But who were they? Renegades, up here to steal horses or cows, or whatever they could get? To murder travelers, if the odds were in their favor? Or were they peaceful family people? That was my guess. There were women there, and little kids. They probably had the Army looking for them right then, for they were supposed to stay on their allotted land. But even so, they were probably better off than me.

I returned to camp and let the load of branches roll off my arms with clunking sounds onto what was left of our earlier pile. I picked two up and added them to the fire, then sat back down on my saddle. I folded my arms across my knees and dropped my chin against my chest, closing my eyes.

"Duke, could you spare a couple of those logs?" I heard Shilo say. I thought nothing of it for a moment. I was too tired. But when it registered, it angered me. Who the hell was he, taking wood I'd just spent my energy cutting for our own fire? It angered me even more when Duke took it to him, placing it over his fire.

"Well, thanks, Duke," Shilo said amiably. "I would have come and picked it up."

I shook my head unconsciously. *The hell,* I thought. *You expected it.* When Duke sat back down, I looked over at him. "Ain't come very far from your roots, have you, Duke?" I don't know what caused me to say that, for Duke was a friend. But I was so tired I didn't think before I spoke. Duke didn't answer me, at least not with words. He just leveled a long, hurt look my way, then returned his eyes to the fire.

I felt someone else watching me for several moments before I heard Shilo's voice again. There was a certain tone in it that let me know before he even said my name he was talking to me. "May I talk to you for a minute, McLean?"

I looked at him, and my heart began to beat faster, which irritated me. Who was Jason Shilo, to cause my insides any kind of change? Just another crook that'd be dead soon enough.

I got up, and when I did Shilo stood up, too. He walked past me and off toward the Injun tepees, stopping fifty yards from camp and drawing the makings from inside his horsehide coat. He held them out to me, but I just shook my head. He proceeded to roll himself one, and when it was finished, he again held it out to me, retaining the makings.

Some men might have softened, but I'd done that too many times in my life. I'd long since told myself I would no more, at least not with a man I should hate. "Keep your smoke."

Shilo held my eyes for a moment. His gaze was cool and calculating, but not angry. At last, he shrugged and stuck the end of the quirly between his lips, returning the tobacco and attached book of papers to the inside of his coat. He drew a match from the same place and struck it on a thumbnail, cupping it and the cigarette in the palm of his hand, out of the wind. When the end of the cigarette began to glow, he flicked the match off into the snow and took a couple of long puffs while he squinted against the smoke and studied my face.

"What was that comment you made back there?" he asked bluntly.

"What? To Rainey? I just wondered why he was actin' like a slave."

Shilo took another puff, hollowing his cheeks as he sucked it deep into his lungs. Suddenly, he laughed, not an angry laugh, like I might have expected, but one genuinely amused. "McLean, you and I have spent way too much time at each other's throats. But I want to tell you something. I don't expect the feeling to be mutual, but I like you. You're the most man in this outfit. And I'd like you on my side. Truth is, after watching you I wouldn't care if half this crew dropped away. Not as long as you stayed."

I was stunned, and my silence must have showed it. Shilo laughed again, a friendly laugh, and even in his eyes I could read no malice.

"I'm sorry this has surprised you. I know you expect me to hate you over this thing with the girl. But I don't. The fact is JoAnna and I have grown away from each other. She needs to move on, and so do I. But whatever happens with her and me, I want you to stay on. I need a man I can count on. And I think you know as well as I do Tanner's no real leader of men. He's just a blackballed nester, trying to get back at the Stockman's Association."

While Shilo spoke, I had time to think. He talked so much, and so fluidly, it was easy to think. My first thoughts were angry ones, but they gave way again to dismay, and then to caution. I wanted in a way to thwart the man, but I decided to just tell him the truth. If I angered him, and he wanted to, he could kill me. And I was too close to freedom to get killed now.

"Well, you surprised me, that's for sure. I appreciate you tellin' me how you feel. But the truth is I want out o' the outlaw life. My plans were to head for Montana an' lose myself. Figgered I'd get a ranch an' settle down."

Shilo looked at me appraisingly, his gaze shifting from eye to eye. "A lot of men talk about that, McLean, but once you've gone the way you have, it's too late. You can't go back. Not really. There's always that feeling someone's after you. Besides, what are you going to buy a ranch with? The days of squatting on free range are over. Look at me. I inherited a good place from my father, and I intended to be a huge success. But they came from back east, from Scotland, from England, from all over. They came with all their money, and they bought the land and all the cattle and pushed us off the range. Even me, and I was one who folks thought was set. Sure, I have enough to live comfortably, but it's not like before. Believe me, until we break these rich landgrabbers and push them back home, we'll be wandering with nowhere to go."

"So that's your reason for doin' all this? To break the big ranchers?"

Shilo chuckled. "Can you think of a better reason?"

"You don't really think it can be done, do you? They have money enough to keep buying. They'll replace every head you make off with. But in Montana they say the little man is welcome. I can find a place there." Shilo'd shaken my confidence, but I wouldn't let him know.

"Look around you!" Shilo raised his voice a touch. "You've seen the ranges. Don't be fooled. This country's been overstocked for years. Most of these ranch owners have seen their places once a year if they're lucky. They throw fifteen thousand cows out and expect the grass to always be there. But it won't. It isn't even now.

And it's the same in Montana. They're all hiding their heads in the sand. Really, they've broken themselves. If we have a winter anywhere near as hard as the last, it'll finish them off. I'm only pushing the process along. You might say I'm sort of an impatient man."

I'd come to understand Jason Shilo better now that I knew what drove him. But I still didn't like him. I didn't like the way he treated JoAnna as his property and how he expected everyone to kneel and kiss his feet wherever he went—like now. Maybe he had his reasons for what he did. I could sort of see that. But I had my own plans, and after I made the Montana border, none of my plans included Jason Shilo.

"I 'preciate yer interest, Mr. Shilo." I almost shuddered after I realized I'd called him 'mister'. "But I really think I c'n make a go of ranchin'," I said. "'Specially if what you say is true. It won't be long before some place c'n be had cheap."

"Maybe, but that could be years. What will you do between now and then?"

"Stay alive," I said flatly.

Shilo gazed at me a while, then shook his head resignedly and shrugged. "Well, I wish you luck, McLean. You'll sure need it."

He held his hand out to me, and after a moment I took it. I had to admit, I never thought I'd shake his hand, not after the first day we met.

Chapter Thirteen
The Truth About JoAnna

In the morning, the sky had lifted. In place of clouds lurking in the trees, a yellow sun poured its blinding light out across the fresh layer of white on the peaks. Frost that was grained up on the grass and wildflowers sparkled like a million diamonds in the meadow. But already it and the snow had begun to melt. Sheets of snow tipped and fell from water-logged tree trunks or slid down them in slushy chunks.

All of us had crowded into the two tents, with me against a wall and Tye under the same blanket next to me. I hadn't minded the cold outside, for Tye, with his fever, was like sleeping next to the fire. JoAnna had also taken advantage. She was still snuggled up with her back next to his when I pulled on my boots and stepped outside.

From a pile of logs, two-foot flames waved like little flags in front of our tent. Slug Holch and Duke Rainey stood with their hands outstretched, their fingers spread to catch every ray of heat.

"Mornin', Thomas," Duke greeted with a smile.

Slug also offered one, and I returned it. My respect for the man had plunged, but I still couldn't help but like him and be glad he was my friend.

Duke's dark face was heavy with little clots of whiskers. He'd never been one for shaving. But Slug had. He took pride in his appearance, for the most part, and I noticed for the first time that he hadn't shaved in the last couple days himself. After greeting me, he stared into the fire, his blue eyes reflecting the flames yet taking on no warmth in the process. It was a lost look Slug had, a forlorn, solemn gaze that made me sad for him. He'd always been a scrapper, punching his way through any ruckus. But this time he'd lost. His own weakness had taken JoAnna away from him. And now, far as I could see, she didn't belong to anybody. She was just one of the crowd.

At that moment, the flap of Shilo's tent edged open, and his familiar black glove thrust through, holding his hat. Then his head slipped out, his eyes surveying the outside. After he'd looked at Slug and Duke, then at me, he stepped out, sticking a forty-five back in its holster and shifting his black horse hide coat to cover it up. His spurs made soft jingling sounds as he moved to the fire's warmth, and he snugged the hat down low as he stopped at the fire.

"What a miserable night." Shilo blinked swollen eyes and wiped his lips with his gloved fingers, rubbing dried-up spit from them. He glanced irritably toward our tent, then at me. The other two caught the glance and followed it. When Shilo said nothing, they turned warning looks to me. I was kind of smug about the attention. I had spent the night with JoAnna in a tent, and *Mister* Jason Shilo had spent his night with Barlow Tanner. It was only fitting.

I knuckled my eyes and looked down at the fire, my stomach starting to growl. There was no particular need to speak, but the silence grew heavy. "Maybe summer'll come back now." I glanced around at the sun. It sat cupped over a twin-peaked mountain, flinging a fierce but cold light down the slope.

"I hope so," Duke said. "Nights like that put this Nigger in mind o' Arkansas. Never got so cold there."

No one answered. I guess we'd all thought a little of other places through that long night. Other places and other times. Me, I'd dreamed of lying in a bed listening to the tick of a clock, with no fear of being hunted on my mind. Some lop-eared hound might sleep at the foot of my bed, keeping my feet warm, and maybe a frisky colt or two would make a ruckus outside. I had simple dreams, and lately they'd had a woman in them. A woman sleeping in the same bed as me, with her breath warm on my cheek. Mostly, that woman had the face of JoAnna Walker. Yep, I was an old fool.

The camp livened up when Barlow Tanner stumbled out of Shilo's tent. He buckled his gunbelt around his hips, then went off into the woods—he said to check the frost on the grass. Duke jokingly figured he meant to melt a sight of it.

Tovías Ruiz was up next, and then Key Bachelor, and they stepped lively into the undergrowth, too. Guess I hadn't drunk enough myself to have the urge. I stayed at the fire and was there when JoAnna came out.

By the look of her eyes, she'd been awake a while. She'd used her ivory-handled brush on her hair, too, for she didn't have the windblown look the rest of us had covered up with our hats. There was a smudge of dirt on one cheek, but it didn't hurt her looks any. Either did the dirty canvas trousers or rumpled blue shirt and blanket-lined denim coat with a middle button gone and one pocket hanging half off. Her hair hung loose across her shoulders, made darker against the light blue of her coat. Her nose and cheeks were chilled a bright pink.

Jason Shilo smiled at her as if nothing had changed between them. "Morning, honey. You look prettier than that sun coming up. You know what I'm hungry for? Some of your biscuits. If one of the boys finds the oven, do you think you could do us the little favor of biscuits and gravy? It'd make a pretty day even better."

Shilo's talk was smooth, and his face was bright. He was the same man I'd met the first day, and yet he made no move toward her. His casual glance slid past me, and I had a feeling he was just checking to make sure I'd noticed.

"Anything I can help you with?" he asked.

JoAnna forced a smile, bringing pale blotches to the red of her cheeks. She quickly dropped her eyes away from Shilo's glance and shoved her hands in her pants pockets, drawing her shoulders up against her neck.

"If you c'n get out the makin's an' the oven, I'll make the biscuits," she agreed. "Guess one of these boys can clear a place for coals."

Before she'd even finished talking, Slug bent to the task, not looking at her or saying anything. Duke looked at him, then over at me with a sad smile. Then something pulled his eyes beyond me. "Looks like the Injuns is wakin' up too."

I turned and glanced toward the Injun camp. It still lay in the shade of the mountains and trees, but they'd started a fire in a central pit, and several were standing around it with blankets snugged about their shoulders. Even from this distance, I could see the gaunt of the horses. The grass wasn't bad up this high, but they'd come off the reservation not too awful long ago. The horses appeared to've been rode hard and not had a chance to catch up.

A boy who looked to be about fifteen stooped out of one of the tepees and straightened up, looking our way. He wore a battered black hat with a low, flat crown and what appeared to be a trade blanket made into a coat.

"Livin' rough," I said. "Looks like they're in need of their menfolks comin' back with grub. If they got menfolks."

"Let's you and me go visit with them," suggested Jason Shilo, taking me off guard.

I turned and looked at him, feeling everyone's eyes on me. They probably wondered what had happened to the fight brewing between me and him. Maybe it was still coming. I promised myself not to let him get behind me till I had a better notion of how the wind blew with him.

I shrugged and looked back at the camp. "Sure you wanna leave the sunshine? Looks a lot colder over there."

Shilo smiled his friendly smile. "Sure. The walk will loosen up the blood. Besides, they might be able to tell us something about this country. I like to know where I am."

Again I shrugged and looked over questioningly at Duke. I'd have liked his company along. But Shilo caught my look. "Why don't you go gather some more wood, Duke? I'll bet JoAnna would give you an extra biscuit or two."

Duke Rainey didn't argue. He just looked at me apologetically and started slipping on his gloves. "Sure thing, Mr. Shilo."

As Shilo and me walked toward the Injun camp, the dogs I'd missed seeing the night before came out to greet us. When they drew near, they came barking and stomping challengingly on their forefeet. Most of them were gray and brown mongrels with scattered spots. Two were big, looking to have wolf blood. One had pale eyes with tiny pupils. He had the heaviest bark of them all and came toward us walking high-legged and proud, his back bristled up and his tail held straight out behind, like a rudder.

That big wolf dog was nearer Shilo than me, and he was closing warily but with no fear. Shilo just walked and outwardly ignored him until the last possible moment. Then he looked down and stared the animal straight in the face. The dog kept barking for a while, then at last turned around and paralleled us as we finished our walk to the Injuns' fire. He never looked directly at Shilo again.

By now, the remainder of the camp had turned out to watch us walk in. No one had spoken, that we heard, and they made no move to quiet the dogs. They just watched with solemn curiosity, and maybe a touch of fear. There were three old men, one of them with hair that matched the new snow and flowed down, ever-thinning, to his waist. It was parted down the middle and carried no feather or ornament of any kind.

All the people held blankets about them, but some of the blankets were near to falling apart. Some of them you could see patches of clothes right through. There was one woman in her late thirties, handsome but stooped of frame. Her face was gaunt, with sharp cheekbones begging the padding of flesh. Her eyes were large against the thin of her cheeks and the pencil-straight bridge of her nose.

I noticed a younger woman, too, no older than twenty. She had the same features as the older one, only fuller, prettier. I figured her for the woman's daughter. I guessed the boy we'd seen earlier as a son. He stood with them and watched us, eyes shifting back and forth with half-hidden worry. Of a sudden, he put an arm around his mother's shoulders and a hand to the head of a five- or six-year-old boy that stood in front of him.

"We come to you in peace," Shilo said in greeting. "Do any of you speak English?"

Silence for a time, then the teenage boy spoke. "Yes. I learn English at the agency. I speak good."

The older people looked at him. They eyed each other, then waited. As an afterthought, the boy turned to them to translate, speaking the guttural words of his native language.

"We would like to camp here in this meadow for a few days, if you would not be disturbed," Shilo went on. "We have one man who is very sick, and our horses are tired."

The boy talked to his elders for a few minutes, and they nodded back and forth and spoke in low tones. All that time I was thinking how if they said no it wasn't going to change Shilo's mind anyway. He was used to having what he wanted. But the Crows seemed to loosen up as they spoke, and they kept looking over at us. Some of them smiled.

"You are welcome to stay here," the boy said at last. "We also are strangers here. My fathers wish to apologize for not being more friendly. They thought maybe you were soldiers from the fort coming to take us back."

Shilo laughed. "No, no. That's the last thing we would want to do. We just want to rest here peacefully, the same as you. But you were here first, and we thank you for your hospitality—your kindness. If we find meat, we will bring some to you."

The boy smiled happily. "I am a hunter, too. I have a long gun."

"Good," said Shilo. "What's your name?"

"The soldiers at the agency call me Toy. My name is Paint Horses."

Shilo and me both smiled at the soldier moniker. Shilo introduced us, and Toy spoke both names back to us haltingly. He could speak English better than some white boys I'd known, but our names were foreign to him. Still, he probably spoke as good as I did. I never was strong on good speaking, not like Shilo was. Seemed he was good at lots of things.

Toy told us the names of a few of his elders and of his mother and sister and little brother. His mother was Long Grass, and his sister, Yellow Grass. Long Grass just looked at us and nodded gravely. She didn't look unfriendly, yet not quite trusting either. And I didn't blame her. Yellow Grass, on the other hand, had a pretty smile for us, even though she bowed her head shyly when she offered it. When she raised her eyes again, they were set on Shilo, and he was smiling back with all the confidence of a full-bellied tomcat.

Our camps quickly became friendly, once the Crows understood we had no notion of taking them back to the reservation. They intended to go back, in time, but before they did they had to get some meat laid by. That's what their menfolks were at now. They had thirteen braves over seventeen years old, Toy informed us.

The Crows weren't any different from most tribes around that time. In spite of the help they gave our army during the Sioux wars they were treated almost as prisoners now, confined to their dry reservation in southeast Montana. The reservation contained the same piece of blood-stained grass where George Custer and his bunch hung up their spurs for good, along with a handful of white-friendly Crow scouts. Like the Sioux, Cheyenne, and Arapaho they'd helped to conquer, and the Shoshone and Bannock they'd warred with before, the Crows were now starving on their little token plots of land. The government promised provisions, but they never came to much. A bit of beef now and then, and no accounting for whether it was rotted or not. Some grain and other staples, a few blankets. What it amounted to was hardly enough to live on. Just enough to give them the strength and will to go out and look for more the first chance they had to make tracks without being caught. But not all of them took their chances. Those who had seen the U.S. Army at work up close were sometimes so afraid they'd rather starve plumb to death than walk off the reservation.

We returned to our own camp, where JoAnna and Duke filled up our bellies with venison and onion stew and biscuits and gravy. Soon as we'd ate, and the sun had melted most of the snow off the grass, Shilo pulled out a deck of cards and told us he was going over to pass the time gambling with the Crows. Most Injuns, if they'd been around whites at all, knew how to play cards. It was just a variation of the methods of gambling they'd been practicing themselves since before any of them could recall. Barlow Tanner and Key Bachelor went along with him, and Tovías Ruiz did, too, though he showed no real taste for it. Duke and Slug followed not long after, leaving me with Tye still asleep in the tent.

And, of course, JoAnna.

I checked on Tye after my breakfast was gone. He still ran a fever, though not so bad as before. Sweat was beaded up in tiny drops on his forehead. His brow was furrowed, like he was in distress, and his mouth was open like he wanted to say something. Yet he slept and didn't move around much. The boy'd taken a pounding. I wondered if there wasn't something inside him that ailed him more than outside, but I recalled a time or two getting hurt myself in fights when I was sick for a couple days. Just not so sick as Tye.

There wasn't a lot I could do, so I went outside and built the fire back up and sat beside it while JoAnna sewed a mismatched button back on her coat and fixed her loose-hanging pocket. The snow was gone in the meadow, but it was chilly. A breeze pushed cold down off the slopes, where snow still shone whiter than the clouds. The breeze came at us colder than spring water, nipping bare flesh, and numbing if we didn't move around some. The fire felt good.

JoAnna sat across the flames from me, the smoke blowing into her face more often than not. She would screw up her eyes and cringe, looking down until the wind shifted to give her relief. She'd fixed her hair, but loose pieces that hadn't been braided in would lift and fall under the flat-crowned hat, tickling her cheeks. She'd brush them away and start to look up at me, but then her eyes would swing past me or back to her work.

I'd lived among rough men all my life, been in the most brutal crowds a man can imagine and seen men killed just for their boots or spurs. I'd not only seen the elephant, I'd bit his tail off. But I just couldn't speak right when I wanted to say something to JoAnna. Half the time I couldn't speak at all. I just wasn't used to seeing a woman—especially one as pretty as Joanna—who'd made herself an outlaw. I sat there looking at the fire, at the mountains, the trees, the black earth coming up loose and rich and fresh-smelling at the grinding of my boots' heels. I'd sucked a few blades of grass and repaired a fraying horse hair hatband before I could dig up the nerve to say something meaningful to that blasted woman who didn't mean a thing to me.

"If I was to ask you a private sort of question, would it bother you?" At my words, JoAnna looked up, and I tried to look casual and meet her eyes.

She shrugged and summoned her huskiest voice. "Reckon it wouldn't bother me none, but I might not answer it."

"What made you go to be an outlaw?"

JoAnna blinked her eyes and looked at me for a moment before dropping her gaze. Finally, she lifted her hands in a kind of shrug, the needle glinting between her thumb and finger. "It's not somethin' I planned," she said. "I never had a choice, because of my pa bein' friends with Mr. Shilo."

Puzzled, I studied her eyes.

"Do you think whoever was following will find us here?" she asked before I could form another question.

"Anything's possible, if they stuck out the snow. Our tracks will still be there, once it melts off. A hard rain woulda done us more good."

I looked down at my hands, fidgeting. Uncomfortably, I drew my gloves on, turned my hands over to look absently at the scarred palms, then pulled them off again. I looked up and no more than started to speak when JoAnna stood, shrugging into her coat.

"I'm gonna walk over with the others for a while. Wanna come?"

Feeling defeated and puzzled, I just shook my head. "No, I'll stay here with Tye. He might wake up and want somethin'."

After she was gone, I picked my gloves up off the ground again and whipped them against my leg. I sat and breathed in the smoke, the smell of loamy soil and wet grass and trees. Now and then the musty smell of the tents drifted to me, mixing with the stench of my utter failure to learn a thing about why a woman like JoAnna would run with a bunch of outlaws.

It was true she wasn't a refined woman. She talked pretty much the same as the rest of us, and she played the part of a man the best she could. She wore a handgun and carried a rifle and threw a wide loop with the best. She even smoked, when I wasn't looking, and I swore I'd seen her take a chaw of tobacco from Duke once. But what she was now wasn't what I was curious about. Why she had become it was my question. And it was plain she didn't care to tell me. *Her pa was friends with Shilo.* Now what did that mean? Didn't seem much of a reason. And on top of that it didn't seem possible, since she'd told me her pa was a soldier with Captain Fetterman when his troop got wiped out back in sixty-six. What would he have had to do with Shilo? Unless Shilo'd been in the army then, too. That was possible. After all, twenty years had gone by. A lot could've happened since.

Twenty years. The number bounced around in my cavernous head, making questions come together as it broke loose little thoughts. Twenty years! What had JoAnna been doing all that time? Training to be an outlaw? Had she lived with Shilo as a girl? She couldn't have been very old when her pa went under. No more than four, if I guessed at her age correct. What could've held her to him for so long, if she hadn't stayed willingly?

I made up my mind to one thing. Shilo'd used us a-plenty. He made a habit of using people, while making it look like he was helping them. For once, maybe I'd use him. Maybe, if I could get him alone, I'd use him to find out more about JoAnna. He seemed willing to talk to me now. Maybe he'd give me a clue why she was what she was.

When I took a bowl of gravy and bits of venison to Tye a couple hours later, he was awake. He just lay there staring up at the ceiling, and his bad eye had healed enough he could see out both of them.

"Tom!" He greeted me with a weak, lopsided smile. "Where'd we get to?"

"A long ways up in the mountains. One o' the pertiest meadows you ever saw, right up in the flowers and trees and green grass. Yeah, they actually have grass here. You'll see."

"Not like the Wyomin' desert down below, eh?" He chuckled and looked at the plate I held. "Well, did you come to feed me or just torture me? That dish don't make much of a decoration—let me have it."

I grinned and thrust the plate toward him as he pushed to a sitting position, his long black hair poking every which way and not mattering to me one bit. Tyrone Sandoe was back with me.

Shilo was willing enough to ride with me when I asked. He'd worn the Crows down at gambling and figured they could use a rest. So I took Sheriff, and he took the little bay colt Duke'd been riding, and we rode the edge of the meadow till we crossed into timber again.

It was dark and cool under the shadows of the big trees. With the new moisture and the sun beating down on it, the smells came at us so powerful we couldn't help but just suck them in time and again through our noses. It was like medicine for the soul. It smelled of fir and spruce and moss and loamy ground and dead needles and buckbrush, all tinged by an occasional dose of musky horse and leather and saddle soap. It was a fine day to be alive.

We didn't talk about anything I'd come to talk about, not for a while. The world was too alive. Shilo knew the names of wildflowers, and of birds and animals and trees. Not just names me and others called them, but their real names, and some Latin ones, too. I wouldn't have much use for such knowledge, but I was impressed all the same. Like the bird I called a camp robber—he called it a Clark's nutcracker. Made me wonder if he was thinking over its Latin handle while he was blasting two of the unlucky critters out of their tree.

He pointed out a fisher to me, crouched up on a limb. It watched us through little black eyes, thinking itself hid. There were hummingbirds about, among the robins, warblers, tanagers and orioles. To me they were just perty birds. To Shilo, they all had a different name. He could even tell them by their songs. I had a feeling JoAnna had hung around this man more than I'd ever guessed. She'd got all that knowledge from somewhere, and I figured now I knew where.

Shilo talked about the trees, calling them Englemann spruce and Douglas fir, subalpine fir and limber pine. He pointed out flowers like lupine and Indian paintbrush and American bistort until I'd've never had any idea what was what and didn't really care to know, either. To me, they were just blue and red and white flowers, making that mountain world pretty as a calico dress on a fine-figured woman.

We'd ridden for upwards of four miles before my mind came back around to JoAnna. I waited for Shilo to run out of new names to tell me, and then, before I could say anything, he turned his dark eyes on me, a little smile at the corners of his mouth.

"Now. What did you ask me on this ride for? I judge you give little damn for the trees and flowers and things of nature."

I gave a short laugh, caught off guard. Reaching up, I tipped back my hat a little. "I was curious about JoAnna, to tell you the truth. She's a perty woman. She could find her a man an' settle if she was inclined to. So why's she here?"

"Ah…" He studied me appraisingly. "Thinking maybe you'll run off with the girl, is that it?"

I shook my head and looked at him with some annoyance. "She's way too young for me. I'm just curious."

"Well, it's a fair question. I'll give you a fair answer. But maybe you should talk to her."

"I tried. That's when she left and went over to the Injun camp."

Shilo laughed. "Well, some people are secretive. And maybe it isn't my place to tell you either. Do me a favor and don't tell her we spoke of her."

I only nodded.

"When JoAnna was sixteen years old, back in seventy-eight, I was running a big operation down by Laramie. I had the world by the tail, and my neighbors mostly up a tree. As far as anything that happened within a hundred miles, I gave the final word. I was king. JoAnna's father came and squatted on my land. It was on the very edge, but mine all the same. I paid him and JoAnna a visit—they lived alone since JoAnna's mother was killed in one of Quantrill's raids. I told Walker how things were. I felt generous, and I told him he could stay there. I didn't mind having someone there to watch my herd on that side of the range. But he began stealing from me. And he was caught at it."

I rode stiff in the saddle, expecting him to tell me next that he'd killed her father. I was also running some recollections around in my thick head, of what JoAnna had told me, and what I was discovering made me sick to my stomach. If Shilo wasn't lying to me— which with the detail he was providing I doubted he was—then the woman had.

"In those days, it was mostly Americans here, McLean. The English and Scots and all of them hadn't discovered us yet. So Dirty Zach Walker was stealing American beef, and he knew it. He knew he was stealing from a man who'd given him a chance, too. In my book that was a crime worth hanging for."

"So you hung JoAnna's father?"

"No. I didn't. But I could have. I didn't even turn him over to the law, which would have landed him in prison. No. With JoAnna young like she was, young and helpless, I didn't want to cause her any grief because of what her father had done. So I made a bargain with him. I had her come to work for me—as a maid and a cook— in order to pay off his debts. She's been with me eight years now."

"And her father? Where's he? Still on your place?"

"No." Shilo shook his head and returned his eyes to the trail. "He was killed six years ago—dragged by a horse up in the hills. JoAnna doesn't have any family left."

As we rode back toward camp, neither of us spoke. I was quiet because my stomach churned with the sick feeling of being taken in by a lying woman. JoAnna had told me her father died fighting under Captain William Fetterman in sixty-six. She'd lied. I was convinced of that because Shilo had no reason to lie—not about that, anyway. Not that it was any great crime, that kind of a lie. Maybe she just didn't want to talk about the truth because she was ashamed. She didn't want me to find out her father had been a thief. But if she'd lied about one thing, what else had she lied about? The woman couldn't be trusted, and I didn't know that I wanted any more truck with her. I made up my mind to ride clear of her.

JoAnna Walker was a liar.

Chapter Fourteen
Fresh Meat

Back at camp, Tye was awake. He'd fixed himself a pot of coffee and sat at a roaring fire sipping it, with his gray wool blanket wrapped around his shoulders. No coffee was leaking out any of the holes Slug had put in his face, so I figured he was healing up all right. He smiled at me when I rode in and climbed off Sheriff to pause at the fire.

"Smilin' now without it hurtin'?" I asked.

Tye laughed. "Never said it didn't hurt. Where you been?"

My face turned serious, and I looked away. "Me an' Shilo went for a ride."

Tye was silent for a moment, giving me a searching gaze. Finally, he took a sip of his coffee and looked down at the fire. "Never thought I'd see the day."

I shrugged again and reached out to tug the bridle over Sheriff's ears and let him walk away to better graze. I forced myself to mull over my ride with Shilo and not speak to Tye too soon, before I found the right words. I leaned down and picked up the coffee pot and my bent white porcelain cup, pouring it full and putting the pot back over the coals. The palm of my hand and my fingers ached from the heat of the thin handle.

I stood spraddle-legged across the fire from Tye and looked at him squarely. "I know what you mean. I never thought I'd trade words with Shilo myself. But I figgered he'd have some answers I was lookin' for. About JoAnna."

Tye raised his eyebrows and sighed, looking down again. "So what'd you find out?"

"The woman's been lyin'. She lied to me about her pa. An' she's hidin' other stuff. I don't know as she can be trusted about anything."

Tye grunted and stared at me, frowning. "You believe Shilo, but not JoAnna?"

"I can't figger why he'd lie to me about the things he said. She had more reason. Besides, she tried to avoid telling me anything at all. That was my first clue."

"Well…maybe you oughtta ask her. She's over at the Injun camp. I guess he is too. But maybe you don't wanna buck him. Maybe you don't want 'im to know you question what he said." Tye's gaze was challenging, and it rankled me. He was too young to be looking at me that way and acting like he knew so much.

After I'd unsaddled the gray and brushed the sweaty kinks out of his hair the best I could, I let him loose to graze wearing rawhide hobbles. Tye was untalkative, so I wandered back to the Injun camp and stood a while watching the poker game. It was Shilo now against a couple of Crows, Slug Holch and Key Bachelor.

Yellow Grass, the young Crow woman, stood nearby. At first glance she appeared to be intent on the game. But a closer look showed she was watching Shilo. Trying not to be noticed, I studied her, as she did him. She watched his hands, his face. Sometimes she smiled to herself. But mostly she had that half-scared, half-hopeful look, the look a young person gets when they think they're in the presence of someone exciting. It made me sad for this girl, Yellow Grass.

Suddenly, Key Bachelor swore vehemently, reaching out to grab the hand of one of the old men in the circle who had gone to sweep in a round of bets with his arm.

"What's the matter, Bachelor?" asked Shilo, half smiling. "Looked like he won it fair and square to me. Come on, now. Let go of his hand."

Bachelor didn't look at Shilo. Instead, he lunged to his feet, jerking on the old man's arm to drag him up with him. It was a move that took only one or two seconds, and already Bachelor was dropping the Injun's hand and going for his gun.

Before anyone else could move, Shilo came off the ground like a spring and caught Bachelor's gun hand coming up. The gun exploded, sending a round into the coins, tobacco, and trinkets piled on the blanket between the card players. A forceful yank by Shilo brought Bachelor to his knees. Shilo leaned over him, his face set. With his right hand, he backhanded Bachelor across the cheek, keeping hold of his hand.

Bachelor cringed in pain, partially because of the blow, but mostly because of the crushing grip Shilo held on his hand. It kept him virtually pinned to the ground on his knees. Shilo hit him again and again, and just for a moment I saw a wild look in his eyes. But it burned out, and then the man of total calm returned. He yanked back, seeming almost casual, and slammed Bachelor to his face in the dust. Then he stepped down on the back of the man's neck before Bachelor could react in any way except for a grunt of scared pain.

"Key Bachelor," Shilo said, filling his voice with disdain. He looked down coolly at the helpless gunman. "Key Bachelor, the man killer. You should have let go when I suggested it, mister. I'll shoot your heart out next time."

He stepped back and left his hands hanging at his sides, his face the usual picture of total confidence. "Get up."

Bachelor eased himself erect, spitting grass out of his teeth and brushing dust off his cheek. His face was bright red, and he didn't look Shilo in the eyes.

"Go get a horse and take a ride, mister. Take a long ride and cool off. Then remember, you work for me. And while you do, you do what I say."

Later, while our camp was asleep, Paint Horses, known to us as Toy, came over and invited me to hunt elk with him. I was the only one awake. He had an old needle gun, its cracked stock repaired with rawhide. He'd tried to doll it up some with brass tacks and with beadwork glued with pitch to the fore end. But it was a sorry looking piece.

I accepted his invite, and when I came out of the tent carrying my Winchester I also held Tye's. Toy questioned me with his glance.

"For you to use," I said simply. "My friend's asleep. He won't be usin' it."

Toy smiled happily and took the rifle. I reached into my pocket and withdrew a handful of .44-40 shells, holding them out to him. I made to show him how to load them, but he held up his hand to stop me. "I know," he said. "My father has a long gun like this."

Toy had seen elk not far from camp, which was what prompted him to go hunting. Their warriors hadn't returned, and he said they'd been gone three days. Those in camp wanted some meat to jerk, and some hides to begin tanning. They were tired of being idle.

I fetched Sheriff so we'd have a packhorse in case we were successful. When I climbed on, Toy looked up at me, then off toward his camp and the scrawny horses that grazed there.

"Climb up," I suggested. "We'll walk back. One horse is enough, ain't it?"

He grinned, and without need of further persuasion he took my outstretched hand and swung on behind.

We rode for a quarter-mile through the trees before bright sunlight began to show from another meadow ahead. Toy dropped off the side of the horse and motioned me to do the same. In a moment, I saw a cow elk grazing out in the center of the meadow, blending into her surroundings. Moving slowly, Toy pointed in the direction of the elk but closer. My feeble white eyes began to see other animals among the timber, most of them bedded.

Using the horse as a shield, we walked forward. Almost immediately, one old cow spotted us. Her head spun, and her ears pricked forward. She pushed off the ground, first with her hind legs, making her look like she was praying, then all the way up. She turned to face us dead on. She seemed ready to run but didn't know what to make of the gray. Chances were she'd never seen a man before, but even if she had the gray "elk body" and all the legs below threw her off.

She put her nose skyward and laid back her ears without warning, trotting a few steps into the meadow. When the others didn't follow her lead, she stopped broadside to us and stood, eyes bulged out. Slowly, the others got up and eased into the meadow, glancing back nervously at us.

Being early summer, there were young calves, their spots still sparkling bright as they trotted on ungainly legs, head-high, out into the long green grass. I hated to shoot that big cow. She was a matron if ever I'd seen one. It was almost certain she had a calf. But she was the biggest one out of the nine I counted, and the Injuns needed meat. I had to be realistic and take the most meat I could with each shot.

Pushing our luck, I kept Sheriff walking for another fifty yards. The elk seemed curious enough to wait for this big gray stranger to come out in the sunlight. But at one hundred yards I stopped, not wanting to ruin our chances. I eased the gray around so his right side was toward the herd.

I turned to Toy and pointed toward the big cow, then tapped my chest. He, in turn, pointed to a younger cow who stood off by herself, half-hidden by a pine. I nodded and raised my Winchester, resting it across the saddle. Soothingly, I patted Sheriff's barrel, making sure he was ready. He'd been shot off many times, but being a man who never liked surprises myself, I figured to save him the shock of a sudden shot.

Toy crept under Sheriff's neck, knelt down, and rested his barrel along the trunk of a tree. Before I could squeeze off my shot, Toy's gun boomed, and the young cow jumped straight up in surprise. I fired at the big cow, and her step faltered, but she took off running across the meadow. I fired again, aiming at the base of her neck.

The young cow was on her knees, and the rest of them ran every which way. There was one lighter animal with small knobs of velvet protruding from his head. Far as I could see, he was the only bull there. I leveled on him and led him by a few feet, and me and Toy fired as one. The bull stumbled and sprawled forward, rolling onto its side.

Then the meadow was quiet. All I could hear was a ringing in my ears, Sheriff's breathing, and the muffled crashing of the rest of the elk making their way through the thick timber on the other side of the meadow. All that was left was the young cow and the bull, which slowly ceased to struggle and lay still. Smoke curled among the tree trunks, and Sheriff shifted nervously around, looking toward the silent, sun-gilded grass.

I slapped Toy on the shoulder, and we stalked forward, watching the two downed elk. Neither of them moved, and when at last we stood over them we could see both had died quick. If the big cow was only wounded, she'd lie down and stiffen up. Then she wouldn't be able to run as far when we found her again. So we decided to wait on trailing her. We went to work gutting out the other two.

Finally, we set out after the big cow, and on the other side of a blowdown we found her lying dead. My first shot had taken her through the heart. It looked like the second had missed.

After we'd gutted the cow and propped her open to cool, we sat down on the dead log and caught a breather. As we worked, the sun had oozed down the sky until blue shadows crept across the meadow grass, shadows much longer than the trees that made them. We sat there in the cool air and breathed deep of the smells of the forest. Toy smiled over at me, and on a sudden whim he reached into a pouch hanging from his belt. Fishing around, he withdrew a tiny object and held his closed hand out to me, palm down. Smiling curiously, I put out my bloody hand, and a shiny bit of gold rolled into it. Surprised, I looked up at Toy, and his grin widened.

"Yellow Grass and I, we found it in the little water—a—a *creek*. Yes. A creek. Over the mountain, there." He motioned toward the north. "That is what the white man always looks for, yes? It is the yellow stone—gold."

"Yes, it is," I said after a moment. As far as volume goes, the nugget wasn't a huge thing. But it was probably worth ten dollars. "Could you find that place again?" I asked. I didn't entertain much hope for it. It was a big country. But Indians were famously observant. And by the rough look of the gold, it hadn't traveled far, over rocks that would have worn it smooth. It wouldn't surprise me to find a vein nearby.

Toy smiled confidently. "I bet I can. I bet I can find any place again."

I laughed. "I bet you can. How far is it?"

"One day. One day, if you travel slow. But you could not find it. It is not for a white man to find. Only a Injun could find such a place two times."

My heart fell, and it must have showed in my face. Not so much because I thought he was right as the fact I could see he wasn't going to tell me where to look. But then Toy smiled. "You wait, friend. I have more. And Yellow Grass, too." Before I could answer, he untied the pouch from his belt and motioned for me to hold out my hands. I did, and he emptied the pouch into my palms. I figured I was looking at two or three hundred dollars, all told.

"For this long gun and your horse, I will give you all of this," he said with a hopeful smile, glancing at the gray with admiring eyes.

I laughed, giddy with the gold in my hands but knowing I couldn't sell Sheriff, not to anyone. "That's a big offer, Toy. A good trade for us. But this horse, he is my friend. He is like a war horse to your people. We've been together four harvests, as your people say."

"Then you keep your horse," the boy replied quickly. "You have helped my family get much meat to dry and to feast on. You give me the rifle, and you can have all this gold."

It would be like taking advantage of a child. But I wasn't going to let a deal like that slip by. I couldn't afford to. Not if I had any hopes of getting myself a ranch. And Toy had said himself he could find the gold again. So let him. He wouldn't have to go without. Freezing my feet off standing in a creek wasn't my idea of gainful employment anyway.

"I'll trade you a rifle," I said. "Only thing is, I'll have to give you mine. That one belongs to my friend. It's not mine to give."

Toy nodded and studied my rifle. Then he nodded. "Your rifle is good, too. I will trade."

The sun sank by the time we returned to camp. There we recruited help and hauled the elk carcasses back in the dark. We skinned, quartered and hung them in the trees. Then we sat around a huge bonfire while Toy bragged on his exploits and mine. We were heroes that night. Long Grass' eyes shone as she gazed at her son, her nearly grown-up man. He pranced in the firelight, his lean young body almost seeming to glow. He spoke in his own language, but most of it was talk anyone could understand, if they followed his actions.

When he came to showing off my Winchester, I was glad he

was speaking Crow, not English. It was plain the others thought me a fool for the gift. But it was easier for me to pretend to be a fool than to have them know it had been a trade, and what I'd received in exchange. There weren't many of them I'd have trusted with knowledge of the gold—to say nothing of the money from the bank. I didn't even intend to tell Tye about the gold. He was too fond of JoAnna Walker, and young men tend to talk to impress women. I didn't need him impressing that lying woman at my expense.

Jason Shilo didn't stay long before excusing himself and walking back to camp. He didn't look tired—he never did—and I wondered what would send him off to bed so early. Ten minutes later I saw Yellow Grass sneak away, and I had my answer. I guessed they'd become acquainted while Toy and me were hunting. Shilo sure didn't waste time.

We sat and chewed on chunks of bloody elk meat, wiping at the juice that ran down our chins. JoAnna sat across from me, and a couple of times she smiled, but I quickly looked away. I didn't have the heart to smile back, after learning how she'd lied. Before long, she seemed to understand something was wrong, and I could see she was hurt. I tried to pretend I didn't notice when she got up and headed back to our camp, where Shilo and the Indian girl had also gone.

Far as liquor went, this was mostly a dry camp. I didn't mind it that way. I'd seen too many Injuns turn mean on whisky. Too many white men, too, for that matter. I suspected Shilo kept a supply in his saddle bags. And Tovías Ruiz had a silver flask he took a pull from now and then, but he never offered it to anyone else, even to Key Bachelor. As for me, my flask was riding empty, ornamenting the inside of a saddlebag.

What the rest of us drank and made believe was something stronger was biting cold spring water and the warm juices of the elk meat. That was good enough, and it let us keep our senses. We ate and talked and laughed, and one by one everyone dropped off, stretched beside the fire that those of us who stayed up kept blazing.

In time, only a few of us were left awake. Me, Slug and Tanner. All the Injuns had gone to their tepees or laid down by the muttering fires. Flickering thoughts kept drawing my mind back to JoAnna, and I couldn't help but think of Tanner. Something nagged at me. Far back in my thoughts I kept hoping JoAnna hadn't lied to me, even though I knew she had. Something told me Tanner could set the story straight.

I stood up, stretching my arms. The motion drew the others' eyes, but mine were on Tanner. I jerked my head to the side, my look asking him to walk with me. He stood up and followed me to the edge of camp, looking over curiously when I stopped.

"Somethin' on yer mind?"

I wasn't in the mood to be tactful. I'd had a bellyful of tactful people in my life, and even if I wanted to I was too short of sleep to waste time on words. "Tell me about JoAnna. Either she's been lyin' to me, or Shilo…or both. I'm not gonna tell you what's been said. I only wanna hear what you know."

Tanner was taken by surprise, and his pause showed it. At last, he sighed. "S'pose it's time you knew, McLean. We're all wanted here, else I wouldn't tell yuh nothin'. But I don't 'spect yuh'd go to the law. Yer neck'd be in a noose sure as ours. An' still, the only reason I tell yuh is 'cause yuh've stuck by Jo like a real man, 'n' that's more'n the rest of us c'n say."

Now that he'd built my curiosity to boiling over, Tanner turned and started to walk along the meadow. I was forced to follow.

"I met Mister Shilo nine years ago. Met 'im by squattin' on his land. A lotta men woulda run me off, 'n' maybe rightly so. Some woulda kilt me. But Shilo, you know what he did? He tolt me I could stay. He let me stay on his land 'cause he wanted someone there to watch the cows on that side of his range. He knew I was smalltime, 'n' he give me a chance."

Tanner cleared his throat and stopped, turning to face me square on. His face was almost completely shadowed by the starlight and that of the sliver of moon striking down on his hat. "Jo's pap had the same chance I did, McLean. He squatted on the land, too, 'n' Mister Shilo give 'im a break. Tolt 'im he could stay on there, long as he kep' an eye on things 'n' he'ped out when called on. 'Twas only ten or so acres of Shilo's land anyhow. Rest was public domain. But Dirty Zach Walker went t' stealin' from Mister Shilo's place. Squattin' on his land weren't enough. Went to stealin', 'n' he got caught. I know. I done the ketchin'."

That didn't surprise me. It only explained all the more the seemingly endless trust Shilo had in Tanner.

"Mister Shilo coulda kilt Dirty Zach right then. 'N' bin justified. Fact is, I'd a he'ped 'im do the stringin' up, if it come t' that. Dirty Zach'd bin trusted, then turned ag'in the very hand what he'ped 'im in his fix. Ain't no worse dog'n that. But what's worse, he'd beat Jo up, time to time. We never knowed fer a fact, but she was allus bruised, it seemed like, 'n' they allus had some fool story fer how it happened. Mister Shilo, he never believed the stories. I could tell. He was allus too smart fer that. But he never done nothin'. Never *said* nothin' about it even.

"It wasn't till he caught Zach stealin' from 'im that he done somethin'. He tolt him if he wanted t' keep his life he'd let Jo go live with 'im, an' Zach'd never say a word t' nobody 'bout the arrangement. Was only me 'n' two other hands that knowed what happened, 'n' we weren't about t' tell. We knew Jo was better off with Mister Shilo, 'n' she liked 'im. All females like 'im," he said with a chuckle. "So that was it. Jo went to live with Mister Shilo. He *took* her. An' she's bin with 'im ever since."

"What about Walker?" I asked. "Shilo told me—" I stopped. "Well, never mind what Shilo told me just yet. What happened to Walker?"

Tanner cleared his throat uncomfortably. "Well, that's the bad part. Range law took care o' Dirty Zach, 'n' Jo still don't know it. I caught 'im stealin' ag'in, McLean. Drivin' a herd o' Mister Shilo's cows offa the range. Mister Shilo, he never even acted mad when I tolt 'im. He jus' had us tie Zach up by his feet, tie the rope to a mustang's tail, an' let 'em go, in the badlands. In time, the rope broke. Zach Walker was found in the hills. Bin dragged by his horse. Dragged t' death."

I stood silent, thinking. Shilo hadn't lied to me. He'd sashayed around the truth, sure enough, but he hadn't lied. He told me Walker was dragged by a horse. Sure enough he was. Shilo'd only left out how he came to be attached to the horse in the first place. Much as I'd hoped against it, it still came down to one fact. JoAnna had lied to me, and Shilo hadn't. But I could sure see why the girl didn't want me to know about her father. He'd been worthless. Not a heritage a body might want to brag on, sure and certain.

Long about five o'clock in the morning I was the only one left awake, sitting there by the fire in the Injun camp. It was a sure bet I wasn't going to sleep, not with all the jumbled thoughts that filled my mind. I got thinking about Jason Shilo and Yellow Grass. I was dead tired and don't know why they even came to mind. But I realized they'd never come back from our camp. And as much as I didn't want to think about it, JoAnna had never come back from there either.

I was comfortable, with a belly full of meat and water. But blood that'd been running warm inside me suddenly grew cold. I looked down at my pistol in my belt. I drew a deep breath. For what seemed like many long minutes I stayed there, trying to calm my nerves and will away the feeling of doom that crept up in me. If Shilo and Yellow Grass were back in one of the tents together, I couldn't believe JoAnna would've stayed there of her own will, though she might've gone to sleep in the other tent. Yet something nagged at my mind, something I couldn't put a finger on. I stood and started to walk with heavy feet and a thundering heart back toward our own camp.

Something was wrong. Very wrong.

Chapter Fifteen
Lady Killer

I reached camp with my heart in my throat. I'd stopped thirty yards away and tugged off my boots, and I walked now in my holey socks. But even in socks each step seemed to me like a crack of thunder. I held my Remington in my hand, not cocked, but with my thumb on the hammer. My grip on it was too tight, but I couldn't relax. I'd tried.

I was listening so hard to the night that my ears rang with the effort. What I heard, over my own slow-paced footsteps and the waking birds, was nothing. *Nothing.* I should have heard horse sounds—munching grass, crunching hoof falls. I heard silence.

And then, as if called up by me, I heard the muffled sound of hooves beating on soil. I waited and watched, my eyes strained. The pale shape of Sheriff appeared from beyond camp, trotting through the timber and out into the open. He blew harsh through his nostrils and shook his head, slowing down as he came within sight of the tents. Something had happened, I knew for a fact then. Sheriff had been hobbled, and there was no way he could've ran like he did now with the hobbles still on his feet.

Behind him came another horse, then another, more heard than seen. Most of them were chosen because their darkness made them less noticeable when trying to escape a posse at night.

Sheriff recognized my smell, and his keen eyes picked me out. He came trotting to me, dipping his head up and down as if in greeting. The fact that Sheriff wore no hobbles told me one thing: someone had let him loose. Someone had let all of them loose. But why? When I found out what had become of Shilo, I knew I'd find the answer.

It came to me as I crept toward the first tent that the Crow men might well have returned and stole all the horses. Maybe Sheriff and the others had escaped and returned. Maybe the Crows had killed Shilo and JoAnna in the process. But common sense put the lie to that. If they'd killed Shilo and JoAnna and stole our horses, they'd have come to their camp and killed the rest of us. Whatever else they might be, they weren't stupid. They wouldn't have waited for us to wake up and fight back.

I paused at the first tent, gun still palmed. What did I do now? I wouldn't be able to see anything inside the tent. What if someone, Shilo or a Crow, was lying in wait for me? They'd see me silhouetted, I'd see nothing. And I'd be dead. I couldn't light a lantern—that would be even worse for me.

And then there was always the possibility that I'd stumble into something else, something awfully embarrassing for a shy sort of man. But even if all I found was Shilo and Yellow Grass in bed, they'd surely be sleeping at that time of morning.

Because the tents had no floors, I decided to go under it, rather than through the front door. I crept to the back, with Sheriff dogging my heels. I didn't like the noise of his hooves but hoped it at least covered my own movements. Going to my belly, I took hold of the musty canvas and started to lift. At first, it wouldn't move. Something was resting on it, weighting it down. I tried again, and with great effort it slowly gave way.

Her half naked body lay curled there at the edge of the shelter.

For a long moment, I only stared. I knew by the dress it was Yellow Grass. Its soft yellow cotton showed bright in the light of the moon. And I knew without putting a hand to her skin she was dead.

But because I had to be sure, I reached to feel for a pulse at her throat. What I found was a gash, sticky with drying blood. Appalled, I jerked my hand away. I'd seen many dead men, back in the war. I'd seen men, and pieces of men, piled up on each other, not only by their comrades for burying, but by falling in the thick of battle. The ranks were so thick at times they couldn't even fall after a while but would die leaning against a pile of their comrades. Some of them were young, like me. I was only seventeen and eighteen years old when I was forced to see those goings-on. And I'd once taken a thirteen year old drummer boy under my wing, then watched his head taken off by an exploding mortar shell. Blood and killing like that had to do fearsome things to a kid's mind. Like make him a criminal.

But this was different. This wasn't war. Death was unexpected here. We'd all been at peace only hours before. And it was a girl, to boot. Yellow Grass. She'd never see her seventeenth year. But one thing this death proved to me without waiting for further evidence. The Crows hadn't come back. This had been the work of Jason Shilo. But where was JoAnna? Could she have had anything to do with the killing?

I pushed to a sitting position, then just stayed there, immobile. I held my Remington, and Sheriff stood over me, bowing his head to touch my shoulder with his bristly lip. His breath was warm against the side of my face. Funny as it sounds, it was a comfort to have the big critter by me, maybe more of a comfort than any person could've been.

JoAnna, where are you? I thought. *Don't be any part of this murder.* It sounds callous to think I'd believe she had anything to do with it. She didn't seem like the murdering type. But then she'd fooled me over other things. And yet, I would've felt it if she'd been a killer. Wouldn't I? I would have seen that in her. No, she wasn't a killer. But from what I'd seen so far, she'd run off with one. She was still under Shilo's spell, after all.

I no longer had any doubt Shilo was gone, and almost certainly with JoAnna. I had no idea why he'd killed Yellow Grass, but he had. Had he discovered her gold?

Shilo had run off the horses in leaving, knowing we'd come after him. Or else he hoped the Crows would return before we could escape, and thinking we'd killed their daughter they'd take their revenge on us, letting the real culprit and his girl run free. Whatever Shilo figured, he'd removed the horses' hobbles and chased them off, and only by chance had three of them returned.

Getting to my feet, my mind numb, I holstered the pistol and moved around to the fire. There was usually a lantern left around the fire circle somewhere. I found it by the starlight reflecting off its glass chimney.

As I lit the wick and watched the light melt the darkness for several yards around me, I realized how cold it was. My head throbbed with the cold. My cheeks were drawn tight with it. Well, partly with the cold, partly with fear. I'd admit that only to myself.

As I walked back toward the front of the tent where Yellow Grass lay, I kicked something that made a loud *tink*, then rolled across the ground and into the grass. I looked down at a dark, empty liquor bottle. Shilo's, no doubt. As much as I disliked him, I had a hard time believing the sober Shilo would've killed the girl like he had.

I didn't want to go back in the tent, but I had to set the scene straight in my head. I wanted to figure out what'd happened, see if maybe there was a clue left behind as to Shilo's reason for the murder. I eased open the tent door, and even before the lantern light touched inside, I could see the second body, there inside the door. It was in dark shadow, cast by the lantern light on the outside of the door. But it was enough to know.

It was a woman.

I backed away from the door and let go of it, wanting to be sick. I swore at Shilo out loud. I cursed him, throwing all my hate at him. I slumped onto the ground, carelessly setting the lantern beside me. Then I leaned forward and put my hands over my face, sitting there still and cold in the dawn. Somewhere far down the mountains now Shilo rode free. He'd killed two women, and now he was making his escape. And because my own freedom wasn't yet sure, I couldn't even go after him, much as I wanted to.

I rubbed vigorously at my eyes, then drew a palm slow and harsh down my face, blinking to clear my vision. What would I do now? How would I tell the Crows about Yellow Grass? How would I tell the others about JoAnna?

But was JoAnna dead? At that sudden thought, I sipped a deep breath of cold air. I couldn't know if she was dead! She could've been unconscious. I hadn't seen her close enough to be sure.

Taking a deep breath, I eased forward and groped a hand around inside the tent door. I didn't want to see her. Even as much as JoAnna's lies had disappointed me, it unnerved me to think of seeing her dead. She was too young and beautiful and gentle to just be crushed and broken like a hunted deer. I only needed to feel for body heat. That would be enough to tell me.

And then I laid a hand on her. First, her hip. Embarrassed, and feeling foolish because of it, I slid my hand away until it touched on her bare arm. It was as cold as the night around me. Cold and unbending. I knew, because I tried.

Shocked, I looked slowly about me, hardly feeling Sheriff's nearness. But he hung by me, somehow sensing my distress. While the other horses grazed not far away, Sheriff stood faithful at my back.

I stood up with sudden resolve and started across the meadow. But my step wasn't quick. I didn't want to arrive too soon. I walked to where I'd seen Slug Holch, because I knew he was the first one I must tell. As I reached him he rolled over and came up holding a pistol on me.

"Tom! Don't be walkin' up on a man like that!" For a moment more, he held the gun. Then it dropped loosely to his lap. "What's wrong?"

A laugh escaped me, a short, helpless laugh that told my fear of speaking what I must. I don't know why I laughed, perhaps because even in the half-light Slug had read my face.

"Slug. Slug, pardner." I put out a hand and clutched his shoulder, probably a little too hard. "JoAnna's dead. Yellow Grass, too."

I heard a fierce rustling of blankets beside me and a man lunged to its feet. As I turned, hands clutched my arm, and Barlow Tanner's voice spoke with shocked disbelief. "What the hell'd you say?"

Slug suddenly found his tongue and pawed Tanner out of the way. He not only made Tanner lose his grip on my arm, he about knocked the both of us over. "This is some kind of stupid joke, Tom!" he spoke insistently, almost angrily.

The boys were stirring all around us, trying to figure out what the disturbance was. Slug started to say something else, and I growled at him. "Just shut up! Shut up till everybody's up. We all best know what happened right now, at least as much as we can."

Because I'd known about the murders longer than anyone I was partially over the shock, and I was able to relate the story while the others looked on in dismay. When I looked at Tye, I thought he was about to pass out.

Without warning, Slug shouldered through the gathering and headed across the meadow. Its frosty grass and sagebrush were well lit now from the gathering light in the east. The rest of us followed, almost running to catch up to him.

As he came to the tent, Slug took the door and ripped it aside, looking down. I came up beside him, and he whirled on me. He stared in my face, his gaze jumping from eye to eye. "Both of 'em was in here?"

I nodded, puzzled.

"Tom, you didn't look close enough. This ain't JoAnna. It's that Injun woman, Yellow Grass' mama."

Unbelieving, I shoved Slug aside and looked down. The others crowded around me, trying to see in. I couldn't believe what I was seeing. I'd been convinced this was JoAnna, mostly because JoAnna had been strong on my mind. I knew she'd gone here the night before. Long Grass I'd thought was back in her tepee. But Slug was right. If I'd looked before I'd've seen it plain enough. JoAnna wasn't here.

"What 'bout the other tent?" I heard Duke ask. "Jo could be in there."

My eyes jumped to him, then to Slug. Slug was already starting across the space between the tents. He reached the other shelter, and with both hands threw the door flaps wide. With a quick glance about, he backed away and turned his eyes on me. "Nothin'."

"What coulda happened then?" It was Tanner, glancing at me and Slug. "Where's Jo?" He didn't ask about Shilo. I reckon no one there was stupid enough to have to ask about him. And I expect Tanner liked

JoAnna so much he didn't want to voice what all of us were thinking. Or else he was afraid of what Slug might do to him if he did. But if that was his thinking he was wrong. Slug was the first to abandon any faith he might have had left in the woman.

"I'll tell you where JoAnna is," Slug growled. "She run off with Shilo like the whore she always was."

Before anyone could respond, we heard hooffalls crossing the meadow and spun around to see two more horses trotting in with severed hobbles flopping at their feet. I was glad the animals showed up when they did. I had a feeling Tye would've taken a swing at Slug for his harsh words. He was close enough, and he had that look in his eyes, the same one he'd had the night of their fight.

Our camp was numb. I reckon that's the best word. Numb. Here we stood with two dead Injun women in one of our tents, our fearless leader vanished—and obviously the murderer—and one of our own comrades gone with him. For me, the worst part was I'd thought JoAnna'd started showing some sense. I thought me standing up for her had showed her a way out of her fix. But maybe she hadn't thought of herself as being in a fix. If that was the case I'd sure read her wrong.

I looked over at Tanner, and he was trying to roll a cigarette and spilling tobacco everywhere. He finally got it rolled, the sorriest looking smoke I'd ever seen, and then dropped two matches before he got it lit.

"So what do you think of your great *Mister* Shilo now?" I said bitterly. "Once a murderer, always one. An' a woman-killer to boot."

Tanner just looked away, his face white in the dim light, even under his whiskers. He rubbed at his cheeks and stared at the door of the empty tent. I could see the whites of his eyes against his cheeks.

"What if he forced JoAnna to go with him?" It was Tye, with his almost-innocent, boyish trust, who made the comment that stopped all our thoughts.

"Yeah, hell, boy—" Slug paused almost as soon as he began. He stared at Tye, then turned to me, his mouth open.

Duke came walking up, carrying a warbag. "Found this in the tent."

We all looked down at it as Duke drew out a handful of its contents. It was JoAnna's stuff, stuff a woman wouldn't willingly go places without. And belongings JoAnna certainly wouldn't leave behind, including a derringer.

When Slug looked at me again, his face had changed. The look there was one of a man who'd taken a blow, and taken it hard and low. He didn't speak a word.

"See!" Tye almost yelled, triumphantly. "She wouldn't leave that. Would she?"

"No. No, boy, she wouldn't," I reassured him, patting his arm. "You were right."

"We gotta go," Duke said urgently. "We gotta go get JoAnn 'fore he kills her, too."

We were moving even as he spoke. I took Sheriff by the mane and walked him to the log where we'd hung the saddles. While the others ran to see what horses had come back and catch them up, I stopped at the saddle pole. At first, my heart jumped, thinking the saddles were all gone. Then I found them lying in the grass, where it was obvious they'd been pushed off.

I grabbed up my blanket, threw it over Sheriff's broad back, then picked up the saddle and threw it on, too. If it hadn't been so dark, and I hadn't been in such a hurry, I'd have seen it then, but I didn't. As I heard one of the others coming up with a horse, I reached under the gray's belly for the latigo but didn't feel it right off. I thought it was caught up under the saddle, so I hurried to the other side to pull it out. It was then I saw it had been cut off at a little less than five inches long. A sharp knife had sawed clean through it.

With a sick feeling, I hustled to another saddle. Its latigo had also been cut. I clawed through all of them, and the same was true to the last. I looked up to see Duke Rainey standing over me, and someone else was walking up behind him. Duke looked at me, puzzled.

"Wha's happened?"

"He cut the latigos, Duke. All of 'em. He's left us for the wolves."

By the slow way Slug walked up to us, I could tell he'd heard. His face was furious, but he couldn't speak, or at least he didn't.

As for me, my resolve to leave the lawless life behind had gone away. Before I could settle down, I had another man to kill. And this time it wouldn't be in the act of robbery. This was for the cause of justice.

Chapter Sixteen
"HELP"

Our first task was to repair the saddles. There was no way that bunch of pampered cowboys was riding out of the mountains without a set of stirrups to push on and a seat to rest against. But how to make the repairs? It wasn't like we could just waltz over to the leather goods store and buy a bunch of cinches.

"What're we gonna do, Tom?" Tye's voice had the same desperate quality I felt.

"How should I know?" I snapped at him without meaning to. I didn't have the presence of mind to apologize.

"*They* got the cinches," Duke Rainey cut in.

I whirled on him; so did everyone else. He was pointing toward the Injun camp. I followed his finger, unsure of his meaning. I turned back to him and started to speak. "They have the—" I stopped. "Hides!"

Duke dropped his arm, nodding vigorously. "That's it, Thomas. Them elk hides. Now we just gotta talk one o' them inta lettin' us have a couple o' chunks."

"When they find out why we're needin' the leather, I think they'll let us have all we want—if they believe our story."

I felt all eyes turn to look at me. "What do you mean, 'if they believe our story'?" asked Slug.

"They might think we're just gettin' away to save ourselves from their braves. They might not believe we're goin' after Shilo at all."

"Then we take what we want." Having spoken those words, Slug started across the meadow, his strides so long I almost couldn't catch up. We reached the camp, and Slug went straight for Toy's tepee. Before he could grab the door, I touched his shoulder, making him jerk around.

"What?" he growled.

"Let me go in. Let me tell 'em."

Without waiting for a reply, I took the door flap and crouched through the hole. I stood for a moment to let my eyes get accustomed to the dark. Finally, I made out the bulk of a sleeping form. Taking a step back, I edged open the door flap to make sure. By the gray light that came in, I could see Toy was asleep under the pile of blankets, his little brother beside him.

I heard the mumble of my partners' voices outside as I tied the door flap back and went to crouch by Toy's side. Taking a deep breath, I reached out and laid my fingers on his shoulder.

With the swiftness of a steel trap, the boy came to a sitting position, staring at me with eyes half-shut by sleep. "It's just me, Toy. Tom."

Toy blinked a couple of times, then raised his hand to rub at his eyes. He pushed himself forward and rested his elbows on his knees.

I was crouched down on my heels, staring at the boy without any words to say. What does a man say to a boy who's just had half his family butchered?

"What is wrong?" Toy asked. "Why do you come here?"

I turned and glanced outside, seeing the legs of Tye and Slug. I looked back, but my eyes couldn't meet the boy's. "Son, I— I don't know quite how to say this. I— Damnit all to hell, boy! It's your mother and Yellow Grass. They— They both— They're both dead. They been killed." I started to raise a hand to cover my eyes, to shade them from his view. But at last I steeled myself, and our gazes met. His face was understandably blank, shocked. His mouth was shut, and he made no sound.

Finally, Toy moved, and the blankets fell away from his bare torso. He glanced sideways at his still-sleeping brother. As he stood up, I rose with him, and we both remained silent for half a minute in the dim light.

"How?" he asked at last.

I closed my eyes and turned my head away. I was wishing I'd never come to this place. "The man who rode with us, Jason Shilo. I think he did it. He took the girl who was with us and rode away last night. We just found the bodies."

Toy slumped to a sitting position on his blankets and started to drop his head in his hands. Then he lunged up. He raised his hand, and I thought he was going to hit me, but he pointed urgently. "You must go. You and all your people. When my father's hunters come back, they will kill all of you."

"Toy, I need your help. I want to go after Jason Shilo for what he did. But when he left, he cut our cinches, and we can't saddle our horses. We need to have some of your elk hides—tanned ones— in trade for the one I shot for you."

Even as I spoke, I realized how pathetic my side of the trade must sound. One raw elk hide, still needing to be fleshed, de-haired and tanned, for one or two of theirs that already had thirty or so hours into them, at least. But if it wasn't fair, it couldn't be helped. We had to have those hides, and now. Not that elk hides would make the best of cinches. In fact, they'd be downright poor. But who were we to be choosy?

Toy was quick enough to give us the hides, one of which still had the hair on. With the dogs barking behind us, some of the village had been aroused. But Toy came with us back to camp, so the rest of the village was left to wonder about the early disturbance.

I stopped with Toy at the tent that held his mother and sister. He looked up at me, and by the look on my face I guess he knew where the bodies were. I didn't have to say anything. It was light enough now that Long Grass' body was well-lit when Toy opened the tent door and squeezed inside. For the sake of time and out of respect, I left the boy alone and went to the saddles.

It took us all of half an hour to carve the necessary cinches out of the elk hide and attach them to our saddles. I was having my doubts about them as I worked, but we had no choice. It was that or ride bareback, and to do that meant to permanently lose the saddles. For everyone but me, those saddles were probably worth more than the horses wearing them.

We left most of our outfit on the mountain—the tents, cooking gear and bedrolls. We took only one blanket for each of us. The rest of the horses had probably followed Shilo, so there was a possibility we'd run into them somewhere down the mountain. But for now there weren't even enough animals for all of us to ride. I'd take Tye with me on Sheriff, and Bachelor would ride with Ruiz. Hoping to find their horses on the way out, both Tye and Bachelor bundled up their saddles and gear into packages they could handle. We'd made cinches for them, too, out of the hide with the hair on. I figured they'd do until we could find something better.

With my heart still sick inside me, hoping JoAnna had been kidnapped and not gone of her own will, I swung onto Sheriff, then helped Tye up behind. It was a struggle. The elk hide gave a lot more than cowhide would've. I had to lean far over to one side at times to keep the saddle from twisting. But until we came to steeper country, it would do. There wasn't time to tighten it every few hundred yards.

Off down the mountain we went, back through the timber. It would've been friendlier country now than during the storm, but my heart wouldn't let me pay it any mind. My only thought was of vengeance and of JoAnna Walker. She might've lied to me, but she didn't deserve being left in the hands of a killer.

We'd gone no more than four miles. All of us had been forced to climb down and tighten our cinches two or three times, but now they seemed to have reached the limits of their stretch. I was riding at the front of the group, with the others strung out behind.

When we rounded a corner, my eyes fell on Sheriff Van Bennett.

His bulk and that of his stocky horse filled the trail before me, not twenty yards away.

I didn't have time to think. I reacted on instinct alone. I'd already been contemplating the narrowness of that trail. I'd imagined running into a party of Crows or being ambushed by Jason Shilo. I knew there was but one thing to do. With a fury I normally saved for men, I drove my spurs against Sheriff's ribs, sending him in a leap that nearly threw Tye off. Lucky he had his arms in a position he could grab onto me, or I'd have lost him.

Before I'd hardly had time to draw a breath, Sheriff slammed straight-on into Bennett's horse. The big lawman hadn't had time to move. His horse was standing still, while mine was in his lunge. Sheriff was a big horse, and combined with my weight and Tye's, and our momentum, we drove Bennett's horse backward and down. The gray humped up and walked all over Bennett's bay while he tried to untangle his legs, and I felt Tye's fingers dig into my ribs as he slipped back and nearly fell. He'd lost his bundled saddle and gear on the first lunge.

I clawed at my pistol and came up with it as Sheriff leaped off Bennett's horse, headlong into another man's. Ducking low, I fired. The other horse screamed, and horse and rider plunged sideways as I came past them. By then, the posse was scattering, trying to clear the way for this crazed horseman. I saw several of them groping for pistol or rifle. But in the confused tangle of man and scrambling horseflesh, me and Tye made it past before any of them had a chance to get off a shot.

I knew I had to damage this bunch some more if I was going to keep them from catching us down the trail. With gritted teeth, I whirled Sheriff as we cleared the posse. I started firing at hazard into the bunch of them. Man and horse, all were targets. I had to hurt them, I had to give the rest of the boys a chance to slip past.

Beyond the posse, some of Tanner's boys were firing now, and a lot of the posse were off their horses, shooting from the cover of trees. That was my signal to leave; a man on horseback is no match trading shots with one on foot. I wheeled my horse, hearing Tye's pistol bark behind me as I did. He grabbed onto me just in time, and I jumped Sheriff into the trees. Several lunges into that thick timber, and we were out of danger. But behind me shots still crackled, and I could hear the neighing of horses and the angry cries of men.

Dodging trees, I stuck to timber long enough to be sure I was well past the shooting. Then I steered Sheriff back to the trail. Now in the clear, I spun the horse sideways, looking back the way we'd come. The shooting had ceased, and soon I heard horses galloping toward us. I paused, not knowing whether to run or stay. Was it my friends who came at me, or some of Bennett's bunch? I dug for shells in my belt and dropped two of them before the Remington was loaded. For a cost of eight or ten cents a shell, I didn't bother to step off and pick them up.

The first horse in sight was Slug's. Even though he was out of the posse's sight, the big man still crouched low over the animal's neck, his gun in his fist. Behind him came Barlow Tanner, and then there were no more.

Suddenly, I heard five closely spaced rifle shots, and I jerked my eyes to Slug. "That's Duke," he yelled. "He went back to make sure they didn't follow. Told us to go on."

Hesitantly at first, because I didn't want to desert my friend, I turned the gray and put him into a trot. Soon we heard a horse coming pell-mell through the timber to our right, and I pulled Sheriff to a stop, jerking my pistol again. The others did likewise behind me. I could feel Tye quivering on the back of my horse. The excitement was like to drive him crazy. He suddenly let go of me and slid off the side of the horse, taking his pistol and running a ways into the trees.

Soon, Tye came trotting back, and behind him rode Tovías Ruiz, with Key Bachelor hanging on tight. Aside from several welts across the face, the Mexican seemed no worse for his side trip, and Bachelor was grinning crazily. But I had seen the look of fear before, and it was strong in Bachelor's eyes and in Tye's. Just two boys, trying to act like men.

I stuck an arm out so Tye could grab it and swing back on behind me. When we heard a lone horse coming at a breakneck run down the trail, we turned and rode. That one man was Duke Rainey. No lone posseman would have dared follow.

In spite of our makeshift cinches, we kept the horses at a hard trot or a canter for an hour after that. It took three times stopping to tighten cinches to make it through that hour of hard riding. No one talked. Tye held tight to me now, and I felt an occasional quiver run through him. He hadn't said one word since my collision with Bennett.

It was around the next bend we found three more of our horses, grazing along the trail. One was the dun I'd rode working cows.

Slug drew in alongside me, looking them up and down, then gave a shrug in reply to my bewildered look. "Decided to break off from Shilo, I guess."

"Guess so." I turned to Tye. "Well, you wanna hug all day, or you want your own hoss?"

Looking sheepish, Tye slid down. I cantered over and caught up the dun, holding it for him while he rigged up a hackamore out of rope and put it on, then swung onto the horse's bare back. I could see he was feeling worthless since even Key Bachelor had held onto his bundled saddle and was now cutting it loose to throw on one of the other horses. Tye hadn't managed to hold onto his, but I couldn't imagine anyone would've, when thrown into the same pile up we were in with Bennett. It was just a good thing his rifle had been in my boot. Otherwise, he'd have lost that too.

"Looks like you'll have the best ride of us, Tye—no cinches to tighten!" I said with a laugh. "Hang on tight." I turned to Duke Rainey. "How'd you fare back there?"

"They ain't gon' be comin'," he said smugly. "Not on hossback, anyways. I shot four o' their hosses."

We made it back to Boyington's cabin long before nightfall. It was unnatural quiet around the place, except for a handful of broncs that trotted to the corral and stuck their heads over, whinnying at us. They stamped around and tossed their manes, happy to have company.

"'Lo the house," Barlow Tanner called out. It was the first I'd heard him speak since the wreck back on the trail. He pulled his hat off and wiped at his sweaty brow, smearing heat-plastered hair to one side. "Swiss Boyington, you here?"

A whisky jack answered him from far back in the trees, then another on the opposite side of the clearing. Made the place seem deathly quiet. Noticing the door of the cabin standing ajar, I looked at Slug and motioned toward it with my chin as I slid out of the saddle. Cautiously, I drew my sixgun. I started toward the house, scanning the surroundings as I went.

I stepped onto the board porch. "Anybody in here?" Eerie silence. "Boyington."

Still no sound. I was standing to the right of the door, the hinge side. I shifted my gun to my left hand and slowly edged open the door, looking around inside. Slug stood at my shoulder with his weapon straight out from his body. Before the door had opened all the way, our eyes were drawn down. Down to a pair of boots with their toes pointed at the ceiling.

Boyington lay on his back, his eyes wide. His face was waxy white, shaded a little to gray. His thin black hair made him look even more sick. His hands were formed like claws, holding onto his gut, where blood had pooled and turned black. But the shot that had finished him wasn't the one in his guts. It was up at the edge of his right eyebrow, no bigger than my middle fingernail—just a dark hole.

I turned and looked at Slug. "Shilo's on a rampage," he said. I just nodded.

We moved on into the room, looking around. Boyington had a Colt Sheriff's Model .44 in his lap. Otherwise, there wasn't much to say he'd made a fight of it. I remembered him stuffing a wad of bills back into a desk drawer after paying us off for the cattle, and I walked around to the drawer. Sure enough, it was open—and empty.

"Shilo got the cash," I said.

But Slug didn't seem to hear me. He was crouched over Boyington, and he looked up as I spoke. "I don't think Shilo killed 'im. He's been dead a while, I'd say. Startin' to stink."

"I'll be— The posse musta done it," I said.

Slug just shrugged, standing up. He'd holstered his own gun and now held the little Sheriff's Model, marked by its snub-nose barrel. He hefted the thing a couple times in his palm, studying it. Then, after checking the loads, he dropped it into a pocket of his coat.

Outside, Duke was crouched in the yard. He looked up at us. "Boyington in there?"

I nodded. "He's in there. Cold as a fish."

Duke's mouth dropped open, and he stood up, looking around at the others. "Well, Mister Shilo's done been here."

"No," Slug and I said in unison. I went on to explain what we'd discovered.

Duke waited till I was finished, then shook his head again. "Well, that may be, but Mister Shilo's been here, all the same. JoAnn, too. These is their tracks. Most o' our'n been wiped out by the rain an' snow. These here's new. That's Mister Shilo's new boots, an' that's JoAnn's little ones."

It took only a glance to see he was right, and to see the two had gone to the house. But they hadn't stayed. They hadn't even traded horses at the corral. They'd simply rode on, headed northeast.

Tovías Ruiz spoke from where he leaned against his saddle, smoking a cigarillo. "You missed this, *compadres.* The woman made this, I bet."

Almost boredly, he pointed with his cigarillo, down by his feet. Even from where I was, I could see the ground had been torn up there. I walked over and looked down, gazing silently with a heavy-thudding heart as the others did the same. There was a word there, scrawled hurriedly with the heel of a boot.

Just one word.

HELP.

Chapter Seventeen
On the Shirttails of a Killer

We rode into Big Horn City late in the evening, worn and sore. We'd spent too much of the day riding off-center and getting on and off our horses, tightening those makeshift cinches. We tied our mounts at the edge of town and left Duke and Ruiz to guard them. No sense taking a Negro and a Mexican into town and rousing up trouble. No telling when a man would run into some galoot who had it in for a man of color or one he thought was Santa Anna's offspring.

The rest of us scattered through the town, trying not to be noticed. Me, the first destination I had in mind was some place that sold cinches, and I took Tye with me. It didn't take long to procure our needs, and for a minimal price. Leather goods came cheap, thanks to the passel of cows that died the winter past. And they were fixing to be a hell of a lot cheaper come next spring if we didn't get a lot more moisture that summer. Fact is even moisture couldn't save those Wyoming ranges, as over-stocked as they were.

After that, we stopped at a little hardware store, where a stocky fellow with slanted, confident eyes and a white lion's mane and beard watched us from behind the counter. "What can I do for you boys?"

"I lost my rifle," I said. "I need a new one, something with some power behind it."

"Single shot? Lever?"

"Lever," I replied. "One I lost was a '73."

He waved toward his rifle rack, over his left shoulder. "Plenty of Winchesters, if you're lookin' for a straight-across replacement. But if you were asking my mind I'd suggest you look at the Marlin. John Marlin put all the best features together in one, and he's a hell of a gun maker, in my opinion. It looks a lot like the Winchesters, but better made."

I shrugged. "Toss me one and I'll look for myself."

The man obliged, and I hefted the solid-feeling weapon, a massive bull of a gun with a twenty-eight inch octagonal barrel and hand-rubbed walnut stock. I put the weapon against my shoulder and sighted down the barrel, not liking the extra four inches over my Winchester, but impressed with the balance. You couldn't beat a Winchester's balance, but Marlin wasn't sucking hind teat there, either.

"It's a forty-five seventy," the man said. "And holds eight in the magazine. You said you want something with some power behind it—well, there it is. Beats your forty-four, hands down."

"Compares to the Eighty-six Winchester?" I asked.

"I would reckon. But I guess that Eighty-six is some gun. I'll admit I haven't played with them much. I've yet to get over my disappointment with the Seventy-six model. But I've shot this one, and you look like you have stout shoulders. You won't be disappointed with Marlin. I'd stake my reputation on that."

"What about barrel length? Anything shorter?"

"They make a twenty-four inch model, but it's a rarity. I think they're trying as hard as possible not to copy Winchester too close. I can also special order them with round barrels and set triggers, and a few other options. But it'll take a while to get it in. You from around here?"

"No," I replied. "That's the tragedy. I'm perty much obliged to take what's on your shelf." I looked down at the Marlin and hefted it. "I think I'll try it," I said.

The rifle, along with its box of reloading tools and a cleaning kit, ran me twenty-eight dollars, and I picked up two boxes of cartridges for three dollars more. It didn't cost much more than one of Toy's gold nuggets for the entire shooting match.

The last place we headed was the Oriental Hotel, a one-story log building not far from the bank of the creek. More important than any of its other assets, they kept food of some kind or other handy for the stage passengers that happened through three times a week. It was hardly what a world traveler might think of as a hotel, but the victuals were all me and Tye cared about. Well, that and one other matter.

"You see a perty woman with black hair come through here recent with a gentleman friend?" I asked a plain-faced little bald man who stopped at our table to bring us bread and meat and pickles.

He squinted at me through thick-lens glasses, then gave a puzzled-looking little smile. I didn't think he was actually puzzled, but just looked that way naturally. Trying to hold up his glasses without the use of his hands, his eyes squinched up like he was in pain. "Well…yes, I did," he replied. "A pretty woman, you say? And young, too?"

I nodded. "She is that. And the man would be a handsome galoot with two fancy guns strapped on. Wears a horse hide coat if it's chillin' out."

"I saw them. They ate here, in fact. Early this afternoon. But they didn't stay."

"Where'd they go?" asked Tye.

"They said they were going to Buffalo. I remember, because he made a point of telling me that—three or four times, in fact. Seemed extra proud to tell me he'd be staying at the Occidental Hotel, and such and all. Liked to talk, he did."

"They ride toward Buffalo when they left, did they?"

"Yes, sir. Rode out real slow, taking their time. He looked back here, like he expected me to be watching him. And I was. A man doesn't see a woman like that around here every day."

The bald man sat down and tried to make small talk for a while, and I tried to be polite. But I was hungrier than a toothless catamount, and Tye the same. We cut off big slices of bread, slathered them with fresh-made mayonnaise and mustard, then draped slabs of roast beef over them. We tried to answer the rest of the fella's questions, but it was hard to understand us around the size of bites we were taking, and he finally found something better to take up his time.

Washing the sandwiches down with warm beer, then warm water, me and Tye left money on the table and made our getaway as quiet as possible. As we were walking out the door, the bald man hollered something after us about coming again, but we didn't even look back. He'd've kept us all day if we'd let him.

In spite of our earlier precautions, Tovías Ruiz had brought his horse into town, and we found him down at the blacksmith's with Barlow Tanner. They both watched the smith work on a loose shoe, intent as vultures on a gutted heifer.

As I walked by, I motioned to Tanner, and he followed me and Tye down the street a ways, where we leaned on a hitch rail and rolled quirlies. Squinting against the smoke that rolled past his eyes, Tanner glanced from Tye to me. "Somethin's eatin' at yuh. What is it?"

"They were here this afternoon. Ate at the Oriental."

Tanner scanned the street like he thought someone might care enough to be listening in on us. He dipped his head and spit, grimacing a little and rolling his bloodshot eyes. "Which way'd they go?"

"They *rode* toward Buffalo," I replied.

Tanner stared at me a moment. "But yuh don't believe the're headed that way."

"They made a point of tellin' the keeper at the hotel they was headed to Buffalo. Told 'im several times. Why would a man do that when he knew he was bein' followed? Shilo ain't no fool—far from it, as we both know. He ain't headed for Buffalo."

"S'posin' yer right. Where's he headed?"

"Don't know," I said with a shrug. "But we need to ride now. Man an' woman ridin' that way, an' JoAnna as perty as she is an' dressin' like she does, like a man—somebody'll remember 'em. Somebody c'n tell us if they turned off. My bet is they circled north."

On my assumption, we rode north as soon as Ruiz had his horse-shoe fixed. We started asking at every place we passed, and it wasn't long before one of them told us they'd seen a couple headed north. The man rode a stout, bright-colored sorrel with two front socks—a horse I remembered. The woman rode a bay with one white splotch on the side of its neck—Tye's horse.

Shilo and the woman had no gear. They hadn't bothered with a packhorse. Shilo, I was sure, just wanted away from us. I knew for a fact he had enough to buy whatever he needed—he'd never settled with the rest of us on the money for the stolen cows. That left him packing about seventy-four hundred bucks, to top off anything he'd had before. So my guess was he'd head for a town. And the only town he'd dare now would have to be the little settlement of Sheridan. I couldn't see him heading south, farther into Wyoming, not when he knew the entire territory would be after him.

We were headed that way anyway, and none of us were trackers of great ability, so we rode and we hoped. As for me, I just wanted to pull JoAnna out of Shilo's claws. And Tye's intent was surely the same. But some of them were more interested in the money.

We rode into Sheridan well after dark. A few lights still glowed, but mostly the town was dead. Wasn't much of a town, just a ram-shackle scatter of rough-hewn buildings with the bark still on and a few shoddy clapboard houses. It nestled along the banks of Goose Creek, a peaceful-looking place full of the smell of sage and woodsmoke.

A couple dogs started barking at us as we went by, but after a kick from Sheriff's hoof barely missed one of their heads they slunk away in disgrace, barking over their shoulders. We stopped at the Bridger Saloon and tied the horses outside. I turned to Duke Rainey and started to speak.

"Yeah, I know." He cut me off before I could start. "Stay an' watch the hosses. I know the game—*massuh*," he said half jok-ingly. But I knew he was riled. Maybe not at me—more likely at a world full of unreasonable hate.

"Duke, if you wanna come in, be my guest. Tye can watch the hosses. In fact, why don't yuh? I'm sure Slug wouldn't mind a good row." I knew there was a good chance our taking a Negro into the saloon would cause a disturbance. It just wasn't proper.

Duke gave me a surly look and started to turn away. Then he turned back and met my eyes. "Yeah?"

"Yeah. Let's get a drink."

It was quiet in the Bridger. The bartender, a dark-haired fellow with a potbelly and a ridiculously thin collar-length beard, stared at us as we walked in. There was a cocky look about him I didn't like right away.

"Strangers?" he said. "Kinda late to be travelin'."

Slug swept his hat off and glanced around. "It sure is." He spit in the sawdust on the floor and smiled broadly, his missing eyetooth looking like a cavern beneath the over-growth of his mustache.

There were five other men in the room, two of them so drunk they could hardly keep their eyes open when they looked at us. Another man was by himself nursing a dark bottle, but his glass was still full. The other two were young enough, with the dirt of the range on their clothes and the crusted stains of years of cowboy sweat seeping up from under their hat bands. Both of them nodded, but they said nothing. One of them kept his hand way too close to a pistol on his hip. The other had a rifle lying at his feet.

The bartender wiped at his mustache, briefly moving its scraggly hair to the side. "What can I do for you boys?"

"Whisky for me." Duke blurted his answer out like he couldn't stand to be second-comer. Guess he knew there wasn't a man in there he couldn't kill. He wanted to be noticed and see what came of it.

Barlow Tanner looked around at the rest of us and sighed as he settled his elbows on top of the bar. "Set 'em all up with what they like. I'm buyin' t'night."

When it came my turn, I swept my eyes across what the others were drinking, trying to remind myself what each of them had ordered. It all came up house whisky, with the exception of Tye's beer. "Got any brandy?"

"No."

"Scotch whisky?"

"Uh-uh."

"Can you mix drinks?" I said it facetiously. It was obvious this wasn't a high-class place, and this gent wasn't making any helpful suggestions.

"Yeah, I can mix 'em. I'll mix you a beer with a whisky, if you want. Might taste like hog pee." He said it with a little smirk under his whiskers, not the "just-funnin'" grin a man might have liked to see of a feller he was about to pay money to.

"Charge for water?" I asked.

"Water? Is that what they drink where you come from?"

"That's what I drink tonight." I couldn't keep the irritation out of my voice.

"We got sherry here." He motioned underneath the bar with a nod of his chin. "Two new bottles some whisky drummer sold us a week ago. Or a local brew of white lightning you'll never forget."

I'd already made up my mind I wasn't paying this man one round coin. "I won't *remember* it, either," I said. "You got me in the mood for water t'night. You should've spoke sooner, you had somethin' else."

He grunted with irritation and poured me a half glass of water from a clay pitcher. He turned to Tanner. "You boys aren't from around here."

"I was thinkin' we rode that ground already."

"Where from then?"

"Down south." Key Bachelor threw in his two cents. "Down Cheyenne way."

"Oh, Cheyenne, huh? I had my s'picions."

I heard a chair scrape on the floor, and the cowboy with the rifle at his feet leaned down to pick it up, sort of casual-like, then stood up and eased over to the end of the long bar, placing the rifle across its top. Its barrel was directed towards us. One of the others had shucked his gun and set it on the table top in front of him. The bartender motioned with his head toward the end of the bar. "Boys, that's Bert Vernon. The skinny one is Rail Dobray, and the one with the bottle is Elias Dunn. They all belong to what folks call the Anti-Association League. Just so's you'll know."

"Don't anybody get itchy," I said when I saw Key Bachelor move his coat away from his gun. Slug and Ruiz were both staring back of the bar, not at anything in particular. But they were tensed. "Our friend there just meant we came up *by way* of Cheyenne," I said to the barkeep. "We ain't *from* there, Association or otherwise. We ain't in on your little war. Just headed for Montana. I hear it's a mite friendlier up there."

"Fact is," Tanner spoke up. "We was s'posed t' meet up with a couple o' friends here on our way t' Montan'. 'Twas a good-lookin' rascal with a young perty gal on his arm. He wears two guns. You boys mighta seen 'em."

No one spoke for a long several seconds. The smirk deepened the lines alongside the bartender's mouth. That's how thin his ridiculous beard was—I could see right through it. "You boys just sunk yourself. Ain't in on the war, eh? But you was comin' to meet up with Jason Shilo?" His smirk flashed away, ruined by a curling lip and lowering eyebrows. "You all better just move along. The Association don't go in this country. You side with them foreigners, you best go get with 'em. Get outta this place. Now." Without any warning, he came up with a sawed-off shotgun, sliding it across the top of the bar so its muzzles pointed at me—square at my middle. His thumb rested on the curled hammers.

I heard the man introduced as Bert Vernon say, "You better go get Utah." Then Elias Dunn, who'd sat alone with his whisky bottle, got up and scooted out.

"You better listen a moment 'fore you move," I spoke softly to the barkeep. I ached inside with the thought that someone was going to die in here. This time maybe me. "Jason Shilo ain't what you boys think. You hate 'im because he belongs to the Association, but we hate 'im, too. He's a hell of a lot worse than just what you know. That girl my friend spoke of, he kidnapped her. They ain't just travelin' together. He already killed two women, an' he'll kill her, too, 'fore he's through."

The barkeep's eyes flickered. "Who you tryin' to kid?"

"It's true. We didn't come here to meet up with Shilo as friends. We came here to get the girl away from him."

There was no point in telling them the two women Shilo killed were Injuns. The Sioux wars weren't so distant that some men didn't still harbor hatred for any man or woman with red skin, even the Crows, some of who gave their lives at Custer's side. Let everyone think it was white women Shilo'd killed. That would stir them up.

Gradually, the barkeep slid the shotgun back from us until it slipped over the edge of the bar, falling to his side. His eyes jumped back and forth between us and the cowboys.

Boots tromped across the porch. I turned, trying to look casual, just in time to see five men come through the door, fanning out across the front wall. One of them was Elias Dunn, who Vernon had sent to "get Utah."

The newcomers, all but one brawny brute of a man in buckskins with a bushy, tan-colored beard, were dressed like drovers. All of them carried pistols high on their hips. Being armed wasn't odd those days. The strange thing was all of them held rifles, except one, a gray-headed fifty- or fifty-five year-old who held a long-barreled scattergun.

A stocky feller in shotgun chaps and patched and faded red wool shirt thumbed his hat back on his head. A shock of flaxen hair flipped down over his forehead, and he let it set. His face was block-shaped, built around slanted eyes and full cheeks that pushed up against them, narrowing them and making them set back deep under his brow. His mustache grew blond like his hair, turning darker down at the sides of his chin.

"What's goin' on, Pitch?" The stranger's eyes scanned our group, lighting momentarily on Slug, then Tanner, but finally settling on me. I could see I'd been singled out again, and I wondered why he didn't pick on Slug Holch. I'd always figured he drew a lot more attention than me.

The bartender replied, "Hey, Ute. This bunch came in claimin' to be on Jason Shilo's trail. Shilo was in town today with some woman. They say he kidnapped her."

The stranger continued to look at me, eyes moving up and down my length. The barrel of his '76 Winchester angled toward my feet. "My name's Utah Chadwick, boys. I'm what you might call the head of the Anti-Association welcoming committee, made up of blackballed cowboys—an' some sure-enough soon-to-be. We oversee goin's-on in Johnson County. If you ain't affiliated with the Association, we're your best friends. But if you are, we ride you out on a rail."

I nodded, wetting my lips against each other. He was still looking at me, so I guessed I was elected to speak. "Well, Utah Chadwick, what the barkeep told you is true. Jason Shilo took this lady friend of ours, and I don't much doubt he plans to kill her before he's done—or worse. He just come from killin' two other women."

"Two *women*? I'll be damned."

"Yeah. The man's crazy. We were headed for Montana, but that girl's with us. Before we leave here we gotta get her back. Then we're outta your hair."

"Well, I'd like nothin' better than to put a round or two in Jason Shilo, Mr..."

"Thomas," I said quickly.

"All right, Thomas. I'd like nothin' better than to kill Shilo, but there've been two or three other men who made the same wish known—more or less. Two of 'em have come up dead. One's never been found. It's a big undertaking, if you ain't aware."

"I've seen 'im at work," I said grimly. "I know."

Chadwick looked over at the barkeep. "What do you think, Pitch? Did you see Shilo with this woman?"

"Yes. Truth is, Ute, that woman seemed perty edgy with 'im. I knew somethin' was wrong. I'd guess they're talkin' the truth."

Chadwick nodded. "Well, Thomas, I ain't much at names, but I'll remember your faces till I die. I hope you're tellin' the truth. See the big fellow there in the buckskins? That's Dale Hepner. That Ballard rifle he's packin' has killed uppards of a hundred wolves in these parts. Some over four hundred yards away. I wouldn't plan to cross him. And the man with the street howitzer, that's Frank Colt—champeen grouse hunter from Vermont before he made the mistake of comin' out here. Flint Drury, there, he shoots sparrows on the wing just for entertainment—with his six-shooter. You better hope you're not steerin' us wrong. It might go bad for yuh."

My eyes fixed on the man named Flint Drury when Chadwick pointed him out. This man was familiar, but I couldn't place him. His name meant nothing. He wasn't a young feller, but not yet my age, either. Thirty, maybe thirty-five. He wore a sweated black planter's hat that shaded his eyes, but not to where I couldn't see him smiling with them. I noticed Drury held his rifle in his left hand, but its butt rested on the floor. And his right hand hung mighty near a Smith and Wesson.

Drury was a handsome man, one it would be hard to forget. It rankled me that I had. He didn't have the memorable face of Tyrone Sandoe, but then that boy was one in a million. Drury was more a simple sort of handsome, not overpowering. He was younger than me, to be sure, maybe no more than five years, or maybe as much as ten. He was clean-shaven but for a prim mustache, and it sat beneath a long, straight nose and those brilliant eyes. He topped his dark hair with a round-crowned hat, its brim turned up slightly at the sides, and his red corduroy shirt and black jeans were as well kept as could be expected, considering the uncertain travel plans of the Anti-Association League.

I had no time to recall where I'd seen Drury. We'd been given our leave to go after Shilo, and I meant to take it. I saw no need to trade veiled threats with Chadwick, and I hoped my cohorts would see it the same. Chadwick was letting us go, and we wouldn't likely see him again. As far as he was concerned, we were just a bunch of drifting cowboys. He didn't know a thing about my past, and that was how I wanted it. I couldn't afford to be known, not in the outlaw world. Men who were known got hunted, and men who got hunted got dead. It was just a matter of time.

"You boys drink your drinks," said Chadwick. "Then I want you gone. If what you're sayin's true, you oughtta be out to catch a man, not here boozin'."

His eyes ran over the entire group of us, then stopped again on me, and he spit on the floor.

"Shilo's right here in town."

Chapter Eighteen
Shilo's Luck

I was taken aback to learn Shilo and JoAnna were still in town. It made sense, for they'd be as wore out as we were. But somehow the thought had never entered my mind that our trail would end so soon. Me and Slug looked at each other, and he nodded almost imperceptibly. The old killing light was in his eyes. Yet I couldn't help but think it must be mixed with fear. I'd seen plenty of the way Shilo ruled over my friend.

When we walked out onto the porch, Tye was still waiting with the horses. I could see by the bright look in his eyes he'd heard the conversation, at least the end of it. He didn't say a word, but his hand was on his gun.

Utah Chadwick pointed down the street. "The long building—the one with the big logs. That's the Royal Hotel. Shilo and the woman got a room there three or four hours ago and went straight to it. He even left his rifle in the livery. Everything but his saddlebags."

I just nodded in reply as I lifted my Remington from its holster and started down the street. Chadwick fell in long step beside me, not saying anything for a moment. The confused trod of many feet told me the boys and Chadwick's Anti-Association League flanked me like a wave, a wave of warm bodies bent on killing. Finally, I glanced over at Chadwick. A grimacing kind of smile flickered beneath his heavy mustache.

"You boys take the front, and we'll take the back," he said. "I hope you didn't expect me to let Shilo get away if I can find somethin' out-and-out lawless I can pin to him."

I chuckled, but it was a forced sound. I knew instinctively that I, not Slug Holch—whose place it should have been—would end up being the first man through that hotel door. The building looked as big as a barn, and I longed to have Frank Colt's shotgun in my hands. A pistol just wasn't enough for Jason Shilo—not with me the one holding it.

We reached the hotel, and on that end of the street all was total blackness. Even the stars and moon hid at a great, unfathomable distance, blurred by clouds—or by my hazy vision. I turned and looked at Slug. He just gave a little nod, shaking the pistol in his fist as if to say he was ready. I had always looked to Slug for support in a battle. But when my eyes dropped to his gunhand I saw how tight it squeezed his Colt. He had no more spine for this than I did.

Tanner's boys and me and Tye stood alone now. Flint Drury with his lightning hands, Dale Hepner with his elephant rifle, Frank Colt with his prize-winning shotgun—all of them, along with Chadwick and the other three, had stepped to the back of the building. I had no doubt Shilo would die before he escaped this place, but who would he take with him? Maybe me. Maybe JoAnna. Maybe half of us. I swallowed and nudged open the door.

The hotel had no lobby, just a little square office and a dark barroom to the left. Leaving the door standing open, I felt my way to the desk and lit a match, searching for the hotel register. I found it, and in doing so also discovered a lantern. But I couldn't stand to completely light this place up. Shilo's eyes had had more time to adjust than mine. As I felt the others crowd around me, I lit another match, scanning to the last name in the book. Jason Shilo. Room number four.

Cautiously pulling off my spurs, I set them on the desk and looked around at the others. I didn't need to say anything. They followed my lead quietly. Then as I moved toward the first room they were more than happy to back me up. They were happy because backing me up meant being behind me.

At the door, I struck another match. I swore under my breath. There was no number. I moved to the next door, the others pausing and looking after me uncertainly. Tye was the only one who followed.

No number on that door, either. And the next was the same. Looking down the corridor, I couldn't see any more than six rooms, all told. We'd just have to check them all.

I backed up to the second door, where the others had waited for me. With no way of knowing the numbering system here, I'd have to check this room first. Common sense said it would be number three or four, if odd numbers were on one side of the hall and even on the other. Not even looking at the others, I stood to the side of the door and eased it open, my gun held chest-high. In the light of the dim stars coming through the window I could see only one person in the bed. I crouched low, scanning the room. Then a quiet snore came from the sleeping one. A man's snore.

Glancing over by the dressing table, I noticed a trunk and an open suitcase—neither of which Shilo had. I turned back to the others and shook my head, motioning them across the hall. At that door, I laid my hand to the knob. My head started to throb. I scratched my thumb across the cross-hatched tip of my pistol hammer. This was going to be it. I could feel Jason Shilo here. And I could feel a bullet in my chest. But if he took me down, I wouldn't go alone. If it took my last breath I meant to kill him. What was my life worth anyway? At near forty years old, I was a relic. I smiled sourly at that thought. I might've only been middle-aged, but killers don't have a right to get old.

I started to look at Slug, but my eyes swung past him to Tyrone. The boy was watching me intently, his lips pursed. He held his gun out before him like a sword. Tye was just a boy, but I knew I could count on him sticking—unless he died. I turned and looked at Duke Rainey. "You make sure that girl stays safe," I whispered.

And I flung open the door.

In the darkness, the door batting against the wall made a sound like coupling train cars. I leveled my gun at the bed, saw nothing, swung the barrel. Dropping to my knees, I spun to point behind the door. Besides the night stand, it was as empty as the rest of the room. Wrong room!

With forced bravery, Duke and Slug crowded into the room behind me. Both of their weapons pivoted back and forth, covering the same ground I already had. While they were at it, I stared at the rumpled bed sheets, lying askew on the bed, half of them dragging to the floor. I had the sudden reassurance this *was* the right room after all. With my gun still drawn, I moved to the bed and felt the bottom sheet. It was cold. As a thought came to me, I crouched down at the bedside and fumbled out another match. I lit it and peered under the bed, and spotting the chamber pot I carefully pulled it out and raised the lid. It, too, had been used.

Except for the nightstand with its water pitcher and wash basin, the bed with its used covers, a little stove and the soiled pot, the room was empty. I heard a screeched whisper out in the hall and spun around, nearly colliding with Slug. We crowded through the doorway and looked toward the sound of voices. Barlow Tanner was talking in a low hiss.

Finally, Tanner, Ruiz and Bachelor came toward us along the hall. Tanner looked from Slug to me, rubbing a hand down his whiskered cheeks with a dull scratching sound. "I…reckon they ain't there? Owner says that's the right room."

I nodded, weary but relieved, in a way. I slid my gun into its holster, missing on the first try. "He got away again. Got away and took her with 'im."

Tye swore. His voice was unnaturally loud, and the hotel owner glared at him. But there was no forthcoming apology. His eyes flashed back to me. "Mr. Shilo's not in there? And the woman?" I shook my head. "Strange. Paid for the night. Couldn't have slept more than two hours."

I just shook my head again. I had nothing to say. I walked in a blind shuffle down the long corridor, lit now by the owner's lantern. At the back door I prudently stood aside and gave it three measured kicks. When no shot blasted through it as I half expected, I pushed it open to see uplifted faces and eyes shining dim in the night. Starlight glinted off bristling gunmetal.

"Gone," I said. "The bed's used, but cold."

Utah Chadwick swore, kicking at the porch. The legs of his shotgun chaps made a harsh sound as they brushed together. "Go check the barn, Rail," he ordered, and skinny Rail Dobray hurried away. "Well, what then?" Chadwick looked up at me. "Is Shilo too cagey for us all?"

I grunted and slanted my eyes away. It felt like they were full of metal shavings. I rubbed at them and shook my head to clear a grogginess that had crept over me like a sudden rain cloud. "We're beat," I said. I thought of the posse behind us, and how if we hadn't made sure enough of putting them down they'd be coming hard on our trail. But we couldn't go on the way we'd traveled that day. "Shilo's already paid for that room," I said. "No sense wastin' it. But in the mornin' we'll be on their trail again. He can't run forever."

"No, but he can run clean to Montana," Frank Colt said.

"So? It ain't like I'm John Law. I cross any border I like."

Colt grinned, spreading his steel-gray handlebar mustache. "I was just checking."

Rail Dobray came back a minute later, while we were all milling on the porch. He told us the sorrel and the bay Shilo and JoAnna had rode were still there. But two others were gone, and so was their gear.

We drew lots for that soft bed in room number four, and I lost— like I lost most of the gambles in my life. Duke Rainey ended up with the place I figured was rightfully mine. But since his bedmate was Barlow Tanner, and neither had took a bath in weeks, I judged myself lucky to lose. I threw my blanket out on the floor between the wall and bed, and Tye crowded along there, too. Bachelor and

Slug slept on the other side, and Tovías Ruiz, who could have taken the foot, went to the stable to sleep near our horses. I appreciated his move. The posse could have been here any time. Ruiz would be our early warning.

I dreamed that night—dreamed of home. Missouri. I was on the farm and Daddy went away, off to fight the War. Mama pressed him to take one of their two blankets, and he took it, but he did it with tears in his eyes. He knew that now, instead of just him, they'd both freeze at night. That part of my dream was a recollection of reality.

Then I dreamed Daddy took me with him, but really he didn't. I dreamed I was there when they killed him. His head was lying on the ground by itself. Not because his head was shot off, but because a shell had exploded his body totally away. Daddy was just a head, but he talked to me. He told me to take care of Mama and Ruth and Hattie and Pete. Daddy always patted us kids on the head, but he never hugged much. In my dream, he said he wanted to hug me now. But he couldn't. And of course I couldn't hug him; his body was gone. I touched his face and saw he was dead.

I woke up with a horrible ache inside my chest and had to fight to get oriented and hold back my tears. When the feeling subsided, I just laid there and stared at the ceiling, listening to Barlow Tanner's snoring drown out the soft sounds of Tye's breath. Poor Tye. Why'd he choose this life? There were better things to be had for a young handsome feller like that. Was it all my fault? I always thought he would've gone with another outlaw if not with me. I hoped I was right.

I didn't like to think of home, but my dream kept drawing me back. Back to home and to my daddy. I thought he was quite a man. We always knew he couldn't read or write, but back then I thought that was only something women did. He was a powerful man, and stubborn as a stump. But kind-hearted. He wouldn't have wanted to kill anybody. Just went off to war because he didn't like bullies telling other folks how to live their lives.

Mama used to open up the Bible at nights. She'd sit by the fire and read, with a ratted shawl around her shoulders. It was a shawl Daddy's ma had give to him, and later he gave it to Mama. Sometimes I'd watch Mama read, and she looked so tired—worn out. I sometimes couldn't tell if she had her eyes open, but she kept reading anyway. I was fifteen years old before I found out she never was reading. Sometimes she really was talking while her eyes were shut, just the way it looked, but it didn't matter, because Mama couldn't read at all. She was telling us those stories from memory, almost always the same, word for word, or at least it seemed like it back then. Since Daddy hadn't ever read to us, I had wondered if maybe it was only women that could read. But when I found out Mama couldn't read either, I decided it was probably only rich folks that could read. I'd always known they had all the best of everything.

Daddy went to war, taking Deke and Adam with him, and I was left to take care of my family, being the oldest one left. I was fifteen. But I couldn't do anything much. Mama and the kids went hungry a lot, and so did I. I took to stealing. Got caught once. Became careful and never got caught again. Those kind of memories were painful. I let my mind slip back to earlier times, to watermelon patches and peach trees, to redbone hounds baying in lantern-lit woods. To learning to swim with Adam, to catching catfish with Deke. They were all dead now. Daddy; Mama; Deke; Adam; Ruth; Hattie; Peter. Wasn't a soul left. Daddy and Deke and Adam had left us to get killed in the War, and I'd left the rest. I wasn't man enough to provide. I went off to the War to kill bluecoats because I couldn't bear to stay and see my family starving.

I came back to Missouri to find a deserted farm. Cholera had took Mama and the kids when they were in a state of starvation and didn't have the strength to fight back.

A man don't cry, but right then I wasn't a man, just a little boy. Tears started streaming down my face, and I had to fight at that lump in my throat just to swallow. I was a sap. A dumb kid—a kid ready to turn forty! I couldn't imagine there was anybody else in this outfit that cried over their past. I felt like an idiot. A man doesn't cry. Not a real man, anyway. I wiped at my eyes and then somehow fell asleep. It was God's mercy.

Tanner woke us up in the dark. He was like a rooster in the morning—woke up like clockwork.

I could have slept longer, but today I had no desire to. I came up out of my blanket, thrusting my gun into the holster and my hat on my head. I took a corner of the red scarf at my neck and scrubbed the sleep and dried tears out of my eye corners.

Loading gates were clicking. A cylinder spun here and there. One rifle lever jacked, and I looked over to see Slug Holch staring down grimly at his carbine. The bruises were leaving his face now. Tye's, too. I wondered if either of them even thought about their fight anymore. Even the night of the fight their only real enemy had been Jason Shilo. Now he was the only one they seemed to think of. Somewhere there might still have been a posse, in spite of the damage we'd done them. But they didn't seem important.

When we collected our horses from the livery, Chadwick and his boys were nowhere to be seen. I'd been so groggy the night before I couldn't remember what had been said in parting. Didn't know if they even meant to keep on looking for Shilo. But I wouldn't wait for them. Our best guess was that Shilo had headed north, and that's the way we rode.

We traveled in the dark for a ways, rode having no idea if we were on the right trail. As for me, something kept telling me I felt Shilo's presence. But it could have been nerves. He could have been headed south, defying the odds. Could have been headed west, too, over the Bighorns. He could have been taking a road east, or northeast, or making his own road, for that matter. We rode blind, and that was a fact. But what else could we do?

I put a mask over my face as I traveled. I looked around calmly, hoping the others wouldn't know how scared I was. I wasn't scared for me, no. I knew all too well I deserved to die for all I'd done to others. I was scared for JoAnna. I just couldn't help thinking we were her only hope. She knew what Shilo did to those Injun women, and I figured he'd use her while it suited him, and then he'd kill her. I didn't trust him any farther than I could throw an elephant against the wind.

I'd long since given up on any notion that JoAnna might have been in on the killings of those Injun women with Shilo. She might have lied to me about some things, but I couldn't have been *that* bad a judge of character. JoAnna was a misled woman, but she was no killer.

The Tongue River was marked by a thick, wandering line of cottonwood and willow trees. We saw the trees first, standing stark against the remains of drab yellow grass and the sagebrush which overgrazing had caused to thrive. We were riding the main road north as casual as you please, for as far as anyone around here could know we were just wandering cowboys. Other than Bennett's posse, and we figured them to be in pretty bad shape, we hoped no one else yet knew of our escapades. But I guess my gray horse was the red flag. We'd run the line of telegraph wires a lot faster than we'd run the road, and word about Sheriff was out.

We were crossing the bridge over Tongue River, a measly forty-foot width of water, when they hit us.

Key Bachelor had somehow wound up in the lead. Tye rode beside him, both of them carelessly staring ahead. No one saw the treachery hidden in the trees.

The first volley swept Tye and Bachelor from their saddles as if by giant hands. Spurts of smoke erupted from the trees. Five, maybe six or more rifles spoke rapidly, racketing over the water. Horses screamed, and I saw Tye's slip on the bridge and go down. I glimpsed Tye as he rolled over the side of the bridge into the water. But Bachelor lay on the bridge with blood all around. He didn't move.

Shots tore past us like a swarm of bees. The firing seemed less precise now, panicked men throwing lead before their targets could disappear. I whirled Sheriff and lay low in the saddle, spurring him off the bridge and heading for the cover of the trees. I heard a horse scream, and someone yelled. I heard Tovías Ruiz from the riverbank growth, cursing in Spanish.

Far as I could tell, none of us had returned any fire. I had got Sheriff behind the trees, and I heard a couple others thrashing through the thick cover around me. As I looked out at the bridge, I saw in shock that Slug was still there. Even as I watched, he turned his horse. He was looking out in the river, not at the far bank, and not at us. Then, with a swiftness I almost didn't follow, he jammed his spurs into his horse's ribs. The horse's nose was aimed square at the log side of that bridge. When the spurs dug in, he leaped up and forward. I don't know if he did it out of terror and surprise or if he'd been trained to it. But they sailed over the side of the bridge, disappearing momentarily in a spray of water.

Slug and his horse appeared again. He'd kept his seat and drawn his pistol. He fired blindly toward the far bank as he leaped his horse forward through chest-deep water. Covering him, we set up a harrowing fire against the far bank. Soon, it seemed it was only us firing. I could hear nothing from the far side. Of course my ears were numbed, but I saw no puffs of smoke from there, either.

I chanced a glance toward Slug and saw him lean down over the side of his saddle to grab at something. My curiosity fairly clawed at me, but I continued my hail of lead toward our attackers. The lever of the new Marlin clacked crisply with each ejected and reloaded shell. It struck against my shoulder time and again, mushrooming smoke into the still morning air. It was every bit the rifle the hardware clerk had told me it was, and I was glad for the meat on my shoulder. I looked at Slug again, and he was making his way toward the bank. Only now he was dragging a load.

It was Tyrone Sandoe.

I stopped to claw a handful of .45-70 shells from my vest pocket and jam them through the rifle's loading gate. Then I was firing again, not at figures or at puffs of smoke, only at memories of where they'd been. The other side seemed to have lost interest.

I saw a man move in the far brush. Before I could raise my rifle, one of the others fired, and the man went down hard. Even across the river I heard him groan. I looked through the trees to see Duke Rainey where smoke was drifting away. His eyes were wide, the whites showing like saucers against his inky skin.

"Hold 'em down!" I yelled as Slug's horse struggled up the muddy bank, Slug dragging his bloody burden. Dropping my rifle so I could free my hands, I sprinted through the undergrowth, jumping fallen limbs. I slipped on a mossy log and almost fell, then caught my balance and came out onto the muddy ground as Slug piled from his horse with his rifle in hand.

"Give me your rifle!" I yelled. "I'll get the horse!" Without time for any argument, the big man turned and complied. I took his rifle and flung a shot toward the far bank before wheeling and scrambling into the trees with the frightened horse.

Tying the horse's reins around a limb, I turned with Slug's rifle ready. Slug was coming up the bank at a lurching run, Tye dangling over one broad shoulder and flopping loosely. They made shelter with no more shots from the other side, and I wondered if our attackers had gone.

"Who's over there?" I yelled.

A harsh voice replied. "The boys of the EK. And you? You who you s'posed to be?"

Irritated at the stupid question, I glanced over at Slug, calling back, "We're punchers headed for Montana—ridin' peaceable, till now. You boys out to die this mornin'? Diet o' lead ain't healthy."

"Answer me. You who you s'posed to be?"

"What the hell does that mean?" I yelled over. "We're black-balled cowboys, headed to friendlier country. And none too soon, I guess; they say Montana ain't the same hellhole as here. Why? Who're we s'posed to be?"

There was a long pause. Then, without warning, a shot rang out. A searing pain in my left side dropped me to one knee, and I clutched at the wound. Within seconds, blood ran down my fingers. Letting go of my side, I fired several times at the place where the voice had come from.

The same voice sailed back. "You're cow thieves! We know that much. The name Jason Shilo mean anything to you?"

"Yeah, he's a murderer," Holch yelled back.

After a long pause, the voice replied, "Well, he's a trusted name in the Association. He set us onto you."

Chapter Nineteen
What Makes a Man an Outlaw

The Posse: Anthony Ribervo

We made our way down out of the Bighorns, nursing more wounds than I cared to think about. We'd been following that cursed bank robber and his partner for three days, maybe four. Was it five? Hell, I couldn't even remember how long. But I'd had a feeling all that morning we were getting close. Van had been riding in front, and the rest of us were just trying to keep up. Most of us weren't really horsemen, not when it came to sitting a saddle all day. With the exception of Poco Vidales, Cale Storrie and a couple of the others I didn't know very well, we were town dwellers. Being Van's deputy, I rode a little more than some, but I was no cavalryman. My rump was raw. I knew Van's had to be, too, but still he kept on.

Then out of the blue there was that crazy killer, riding the long-legged gray we'd heard tell so much about. He ran right over Van and his horse, trampled them both into the mud of the trail. The only one that hadn't chuckled about that at least a little, later on, was Van himself. All potential deadliness aside, it had been a comical sight.

Then the outlaw shot my horse, and we both went down. Firing started up all around, and with my horse on my leg I never got off a shot. I'm embarrassed to admit it, but I don't think we hit anyone. They did us, though.

It was mostly the horses that paid. My horse still carried a hunk of lead in his right shoulder. One had a slug in the neck, and one high in the rump. Cory McCabe's sorrel was dead. Then, after all that humiliation, when they were trying to get McCabe's horse up off him, some colored fellow rode back out of the trees and opened up on us with a rifle. It was obvious he was shooting to kill. But again we weren't the targets. Our horses were.

That fellow killed four of the animals before we even knew what was happening. I wished he was fighting on our side. When he rode away, Dunaven's, Spencer's, Chantry's and Cedroe's horses were all dead or dying. That boy accomplished just what he'd intended. And other than a few bruises and scrapes when they went down, he hadn't hurt a man in doing it. Needless to say, we didn't like to talk much about it. It was shameful. But a few of them had sworn a special oath of vengeance against that colored man.

When I said the colored man hadn't hurt anybody, I didn't mean to say nobody'd been hurt. Cory McCabe had broken his wrist in the fall—his right wrist. Luckily for him he was left- handed. Anderson had a bullet in his thigh from the man on the gray, and it had swelled up like a wet rawhide bag. Abe Cedroe, the poor old fellow, had a crease across his ribs that wouldn't quit bleeding, and by the look on his face it must have hurt him terribly. But the old man never complained. That wound was the bank robber's doing, too.

Anyway, we rode out of the mountains with six of us riding double. I had my horse but didn't dare ride him with that bullet in his shoulder. It looked like there'd been horses there at Boyington's place, but the outlaws had run them all off when they went by. We limped down into Big Horn City, where we were able to pick up a new crop of horses. Van just commandeered them and told the owner of the livery stable the county would send them a check if we didn't bring back the animals. I don't know if a normal sheriff did things like that, but Van always did pretty much as he pleased, and no one ever told him no. We always joked that you'd better know how to handle a hefty rock and sling if you intended to take Van Bennett on.

We stayed in Big Horn City that night for a much needed rest. We'd been a long time limping down out of the mountains, so it was well after dark anyway.

The next day in Sheridan, we had a falling-out.

We walked into the Palace of Mud Saloon, chuckling at the owner's sense of humor. Van just wanted some information, but several others, mostly Ted Burlen's bunch, had been talking about whisky for several miles. They'd also been talking about going home, although I don't know if Van had heard that talk.

All of a sudden, Cale Storrie walked away from Burlen and Cory McCabe and right up to Van. It was like some teenage kid talking to his father, their size was so opposite. Van probably stood six-foot-six, and Storrie couldn't have been over five and a half feet. But he had gumption.

"Sheriff, me and some of the boys've decided to go back to Buffalo. This is a wild goose chase."

Van's eyes got big, and he turned from the bartender to look down at the little man. He didn't speak for several seconds, and it seemed like the room was holding its breath. I know I was. The worst insult Van could have given was the one he did. He just sort of waved a hand like he was dismissing some annoying kid. As he turned his attention back to the bartender, he growled, "Then scat."

A second later, he turned back to Storrie. "And any of you who're ridin' horses the county paid for, you can leave them here at the stable and tell them to send them back to Big Horn. You can walk back to Buffalo—or ride the stage."

There wasn't any argument. When we left Sheridan, heading north, we were less six men. It was Storrie, Burlen, McCabe, Auburn, Anderson and Cedroe. I couldn't blame any of them, especially those who'd been hurt. Van wasn't mad at Anderson and Cedroe. They'd been wounded pretty badly. In fact, he even paid their doctor bills with county funds and arranged for a wagon to take them back home. McCabe had the broken wrist, but I could tell Van felt no sympathy for him. We'd found Swiss Boyington dead in his cabin, and Van still hadn't gotten to the bottom of that story. He didn't think McCabe and the other three he sent back to look for cattle were completely guiltless, but it didn't seem there was much he could prove. I had a feeling he didn't care, either.

So off we went up the road, getting closer to Montana all the while. I, for one, was starting to wonder if we'd ever see the outlaws again.

The Outlaws: Tom McLean

I cursed. Sitting here in this Mexican standoff on the Tongue, wondering if we'd ever get out of here alive, now I had another reason to make sure we did. What had the feller across the river said? *Jason Shilo, a trusted name in the Association? He'd set them onto us?* That man didn't know a thing about the First National Bank! He wasn't after us because me and Tye were bank robbers. *Mister* Shilo had been our downfall. If not for him, we'd still have been riding.

I hunkered down behind a sheltering deadfall and exchanged deadly glances with Slug Holch before sending back my reply. "Now for the truth. Jason Shilo's the cow thief. And that girl he had with him? He kidnapped her. Plans to kill her."

There was silence. Silence long enough the birds began to take their chances on talking in the trees again, and soon a fish jumped, its silver sides sparkling as it broke the mirror surface and cleared the water, sloshing back.

With a rifle in each hand, I crawled over to Slug's hiding spot. It was a move I should've made minutes earlier. Slug could've used his rifle. But I was afraid of what I'd discover there.

Down in the damp grass, Tye was propped up on roots pillowed with moist green moss. I crawled to him, reaching out to the side to hand Slug his rifle without looking at him. Tye smiled up at me. "Got my first battle scars," he said in a weak voice, his eyes flickering downward.

I followed his glance. The front of his shirt, just beneath his left breast, was soaked with a patch of dark blood that grew even as I looked. Another small hole beneath his collarbone bubbled with each breath. His left shoulder and upper arm were both mutilated by bullets and shattered bone. After that, the clean, trickling hole in his thigh looked pretty minor. So did my side wound.

I returned Tye's smile, which was the last thing I felt like doing. "You got a couple scars in the makin', all right. Too bad you can't get your lazy carcass off the ground and help us fight."

Tye started to laugh but cringed and drew up, putting his hand to the wound beneath his breast. "Just get my rifle," he said. "I'll show you lazy." He sucked for air after he spoke.

I chuckled. "I already see lazy. Now I need to see a miracle."

A voice rose across the river. "Hey, you thieves. What else you know about that girl?"

"Name's JoAnna," I said quickly. "We were up in the mountains with Shilo when we ran into a village of Crow Injuns. Shilo got in a mix-up and killed two of their women, then he took JoAnna as a hostage." It was still possible I was making that last part up, but it sounded good. "You don't believe me about the stealin', Shilo's got saddlebags carryin' a bundle of money. You get a chance to see 'im before we do, ask 'im to show you."

"Yeah, well…whatever." The voice was quieter. If the river hadn't been so narrow I wouldn't have heard. "We know you're the thieves Shilo said. He may rightly have been with you, which made him know all he did. Still, you wouldn't know what you do without you were in on it. But you killed the boss, mister. So we're pullin' out. Had enough. But you take any shots at us while we're leavin', we'd just as well stay and trade lead all day."

I looked at Slug, then scanned the undergrowth for Barlow Tanner, failing to find him. "Speakin' for me, there won't be any shootin'. Go your way. Best be lookin' out for Shilo when you see 'im again. He'll kill that girl 'fore it's over."

We watched them go, five of them, picking up horses that were concealed far back in the trees and riding straight away from us. We could see them clearly when they left the cover of the trees and climbed a bare bluff that flanked the river. They kept turning to look back, like they thought we'd start shooting. I guess none of us were in the mood to kill. We all just watched.

"If they were tellin' the truth about their boss they didn't stop to fetch 'im along," Slug said.

I just shrugged, looking down at Tye. "Your hoss is dead, Tye. Guess you'll have to ride with me. We gotta hightail it."

"What about JoAnna?" A scared look came into his eyes, pushing away the pain.

I looked away, squinting up the river. I rubbed at my six days' growth of beard. "Don't know where they are now, Tye. But we gotta make tracks, or they're gonna kill us. We'll be easy to follow now." It sickened me to realize it, but there was nothing we could do about JoAnna. We were hunted ourselves.

"Set tight, boy," I said. "I'm gonna walk around and check out the damages. Slug, why don't you keep an eye out over there? They mighta left somebody behind to pick us off when we step out of cover."

Slug just nodded, hunkering down again with his rifle. With my own suggestion in mind, I picked up my Marlin, and as I passed Duke Rainey I mentioned the same idea to him. "Sho' thing, Thomas." His black eyes scanned the far trees, and he hefted his rifle in one hand.

"Where are you, boys?" I called out. "Tanner. Ruiz. Fightin's done. You can show your yella hides."

I heard crunching in the underbrush and made out the form of Tanner coming toward me. "Stop yer yammerin', boy," he said. "I did just as much shootin' as you."

"Guilty conscience?" I asked dryly. "Don't get so riled. Where's the Mex, anyway?"

"Down a ways. Nursin' a wound in his leg." He paused and looked toward the body on the bridge. "That Bachelor?"

I nodded, not looking over there. "He ain't moved."

"Figgered. He took the brunt of it. Didn't he?"

"Him and Tye."

Tanner winced, glancing toward Slug and Duke. "Is he...?"

"No. But he will be."

We walked together past Duke, to where Slug crouched over my partner. Slug looked up and inclined his chin toward the far bank. "All quiet. I think the lot of 'em lit a shuck."

I nodded, my mind elsewhere. I looked down at Tye, whose eyes were shut. My first thought, the obvious one, vanished when I saw his chest rise with a breath, frothing his lung wound.

Me, Slug and Tanner walked out on the bridge to where Key Bachelor lay. The self-proclaimed gunman had three bullets in his torso, two in his thigh and one in his neck. He'd shed his lifeblood all around him.

I looked at Tanner. With a grimace set into his leathery face, he withdrew the makings and offered them to me. Without any real interest, I took the paper and wetted it, sprinkled it with Bull Durham and handed it all back. I finished rolling the smoke and brought it to my lips. Then, after waiting for Tanner and Slug to roll their own, I took a match from my shirt pocket and lit each of them. We smoked for several moments, Slug leaning on his rifle barrel.

"Interested in seein' who we kilt?" Tanner asked.

"Not really."

"I am. I know a lot o' these folks." With that, he continued across the bridge, weaving in through the trees where we'd seen the man drop. I followed along out of plain curiosity.

We waded into the bushes, and after walking around a while discovered the body, lying on its back. Tanner looked at it a while, then finally shook his head. He grunted, then began to speak. "Perty ironic. He's one o' the big managers. Works fer Roche and Horace Plunkett's bunch on the EK spread. You know who it is? John Chadwick. Utah Chadwick's his son."

I stared at Tanner, sucking deep on the cigarette. "Thought Utah was *fightin'* the big interests."

Tanner chuckled dryly, his expression unchanged. "He is. Fightin' his daddy, too, I reckon. But not anymore."

"No, not anymore," I agreed.

I figured we'd hit more than one man, but we didn't find anyone else. No blood, either. So we went back and gathered our horses, while I tried to figure out what to do with my partner. I'd not wanted to think about it, but now it came down to that. With my heart slamming around high in my chest so I could hardly breathe, I looked around at the others. All of them, even Tovías Ruiz, with his patched leg, gathered around my pal.

"Me and the boy came into this bunch together," I said. "It's only right we should go out that way. I can't go without 'im, but we'd only slow you up. Go ahead. I'll try to follow."

Tanner swung his eyes around the circle of faces. Slug and Duke just looked at him with noncommittal glances. Ruiz was digging in the damp soil with his boot heel, sucking his whiskered cheeks in. Tanner looked back at me. "We already done split up once, back in the mountains, an' nobody liked it. No sense doin' it ag'in. We'll stick t'gether."

"Suit yourself," I said. "Hope you don't end up regrettin' it."

After taking the time to bandage up my side, we gathered our horses, and I climbed on. With the help of Tanner, Duke and Slug, I managed to get Tye up on the gray before me, so I could hold onto him. He was bleeding all over my clothes, but I didn't care. He was my friend. And for now he was a warm body. But he wouldn't be for long. Anyone could see that.

Nearest doctor would be Sheridan, best we could figure. Didn't even know if they had one, but it was a cinch there'd be none farther north. My side throbbed, but I couldn't feel it much, because my mind was on Tye's hurting. Maybe he was numb, but fact is he never said a word of complaint. Damned if I would either.

We stayed off the road on the way to Sheridan. Chances were there'd be word out about us now, if our attackers on the Tongue had got to a telegraph. It was bad riding, for Tye, but we didn't have much choice.

Tye was turning mighty pale now, for loss of blood. He gritted his teeth and rode, saying nothing. Made me want to cry, to tell the truth, seeing him that way and nothing I could do. I wondered how I'd ever figure out any way to find his family and tell them. Maybe he didn't have a family. He'd never talked about them. Never talked much about himself at all, now that I thought on it. All he ever did was ask about other people.

We rode into Sheridan two hours later, coming up out of the draw we'd been riding in for concealment. The place was quiet. Quiet enough we could hear a dog bark on the other side of town and the steady clanging of a blacksmith's hammer. Somewhere a late rooster crowed, and the ever-present challenger cried back.

Pulling in at Winebrenner's Saloon and Eatery, we walked to the side of the building to tie our horses. Not like we wouldn't be conspicuous anyway, but with Tye half-dead on my horse I didn't want to be left sitting in the middle of the main thoroughfare.

Slug and Tanner went into Winebrenner's, and when they came out they had directions to the residence of the only doctor thereabouts. He was both a dentist and a medical doctor, or at least that's what he told folks. Seemed the bartender in Winebrenner's didn't have a great deal of confidence in him.

We rode to the doctor's house on the edge of town. He had a shingle hanging proudly from his awning. It read, B.R. KAZINSKI, M.D., DENTIST. At the back of the house, the others climbed down while I remained mounted. They tugged Tye off me, leaving me a bloody mess where he'd soaked through his blankets.

Myself, I didn't see the point of a doctor for Tye. Any fool would see he couldn't be saved. Even the doctors of Boston or Europe couldn't have worked that miracle. But I needed patching, and so did the calf of Tovías Ruiz's leg. That was reason enough. Besides, I figured we could leave Tye here with some money, and Doctor Kazinski could see to the burying.

Tanner and Slug went off to buy a drink—to Winebrenner's, they said. I was able to talk Duke into going to the dry goods store to buy me a new outfit of clothes. Even if I washed the bloody rags on me, they'd still be stained with Tye's blood, and I couldn't stand to wear them again and be reminded of this day.

It didn't take the doctor long to patch me up. Turned out he'd been a surgeon during the War Between the States, and though he tipped the bottle a little, he was proficient enough with what he had to do. Ruiz didn't want any part of the doctor at first. He stood aside while Kazinski went to Tye. The doc had figured the same as we did about Tye, which is why he looked after me first. But now his job was to make the dying as comfortable as he could.

We set Tye up in grand style on a bed with fluffy pillows. But having his neck folded up like that didn't seem to agree with him, so we lowered him a little.

"You seem a sage enough man," Doctor Kazinski said to me. "You have already figured out the same as I have." He put a hand on my arm, and I let him. I needed the touch of someone who cared. "Those bullets don't need taking out. It isn't worth the pain it would cause."

I nodded wordlessly. The lump in my throat wouldn't let me talk.

"How about some coffee, young fellow?" the doc asked Tye. "Or maybe a bowl of soup. Good Heavens, for that matter, maybe a stiff shot of bourbon. Best in the house," he said with a beaming smile. His gray eyebrows turned upward at the outer edges, pointing toward a shock of prickly hair. The old man reminded me of somebody's gran'pa.

Tye smiled weakly. His hair looked starkly black against his pallid skin, and his mustache stood out like a stick of charcoal. "Long as you're offerin', Doc, I'll take the bourbon."

The doctor went away and came back, pouring Tye a glass full. "You two talk quietly, why don't you?" he said, popping the cork back into the bottle mouth. "There's a woman just delivered her baby in the next room. I'm starting to have a regular hospital here, it would seem." Without appearing to think about it, he withdrew the cork again and raised the bourbon bottle to his own lips, taking a long swallow.

Duke came in with a new set of clothes. Didn't fit perfectly, but it didn't matter. At least the blood was gone. I sponged down and put them on, throwing the others in a heap in the corner of the room.

"I'd 'bout have t'admit I chose the wrong line o' work," Tye said after Duke had gone.

"Heck, you c'n get hurt doin' anything, pard. Takes a man to act like you have about it. Before you know it you'll be braggin' to all them women 'bout these scars."

Tye lifted one side of his mouth in a wry smile. "What makes a man an outlaw?" he asked after a pause.

I looked away, squinting against something in my eyes. Finally, I placed a hand on his wrist. "The wrong friends."

He frowned. "I got the right friends. There's somethin' else."

"I guess we're born rebels. Can't survive tryin' to live like normal folks. We got a wild bone in our bodies that makes us want to be free. This is how we do it."

What a line of bull! Truth was, outlaws were too lazy to make their own living. They were out like a bunch of vultures, living on the blood and sweat of others. Made a man sick when he really thought about it. Especially an outlaw man.

"It's pretty good to be free...ain't it, Tom?"

I grunted. "It's the only way to be."

He closed his eyes, still holding that glass of bourbon he hadn't touched. I reached down and lifted his blanket, seeing that the wound was still bleeding. He looked down, trying to see what I saw.

"You been shot worse than this, haven't you?"

"Sure! But I didn't take it as good as you. I was always after the nurses. Or beatin' the hell outta the doctor for not gettin' me on my feet any quicker. Dang sawbones should get a real job if they can't have you walkin' in under an hour."

Tye started laughing, then grimaced. "Don't make me laugh. Might spill my drink."

"Sorry, kid. Know what? Soon as you're up and about we need

to ride down Arizona way. I hear it's so hot down there it'll fry your wounds right shut. Heal you in no time."

Tye smiled and started to raise his glass, but he didn't have the strength. I leaned over and lifted his head with one hand, his drink with the other. He took an unmanly little sip. "That's all," he said, and I laid him back down. "I hurt, Tom. Somethin's diggin' in my backbone."

"Maybe a bed spring," I suggested.

"Nah—" He stopped and squirmed uncomfortably. "It's…it's on the inside. Tom?" His eyes got wide with pain, and he squeezed them shut till it went away. Finally, he opened them gingerly and looked up at me, forcing himself to smile. "You ever wonder what it would be like to kiss a girl perty as JoAnna Walker? She's a beauty."

"She sure is, Tye." I ignored his question and squeezed his arm. "I think she likes you."

He smiled knowingly. "I ain't the man you are, Tom. It's you she likes. Anybody c'n see that. Too bad…too bad—about Shilo."

My chest went momentarily cold at the sound of that name. "Yeah, it's too bad. Too bad somebody don't kill 'im."

"You think she'd hold my hand?" Tye asked suddenly.

I was momentarily taken by surprise, and I just stared at him. Then I chuckled. "Why, sure she would, kid, if she was here."

His brow knitted, and then his eyes widened, and he tried without success to sit up. He looked wild-eyed about the room, then back at me. "Shilo's got her, don't he? You need to go get her! She wouldn't leave you like that."

I frowned, leaning over to push him gently back down on the pillow. I didn't speak for several moments. Tye was starting to go out of his head. But he was right. Tye had slowed us up some, and I'd felt the least I could do was get him to a clean place to die. But now he was here. Now I could make a decision to head out for Montana as I'd planned…or find JoAnna.

My eyes met Tye's. "You're right, Tye. She wouldn't leave me. Don't you worry. I'll get her back. I'm gonna go get Duke and the others. You be all right till I get back?"

"Sure." He nodded, closing his eyes, trying to open them again and failing. "I'm always all r— always…all right…"

When I left the house, his heart still beat weakly, and he slept. I hurried down to Winebrenner's, where they told me my partners had all decided to try out the Palace of Mud Saloon. I switched locations, too, and had just stepped onto the dirty porch of the Palace of Mud when I heard the menacing voice from just inside the doors.

"There's only one way you'll walk out of here on your own. And that's immediately."

I wouldn't have gone in, except I'd heard that voice before, and I knew what it meant. It was Slug Holch. And someone was about to be hurt.

Chapter Twenty
The World Turned Over

I took a deep breath and shucked my Remington. For a moment more I stood there, and no one spoke another word. But I could almost hear the tension in that room. They were in the old sizing-up mode. Whoever it was, their silence was not out of deference to Slug. They'd have spoken by then if the feeling ran that way. No, they were deciding whether or not to take him on. Maybe I'd tip the scales just enough.

I stepped to the swinging doors with my gun in hand. Several pairs of eyes, none of them friendly, swung to me from along the bar. But until I pushed open one of the slatted doors and they could see my gunhand they had no idea I'd chose to be involved.

The long barroom was shadowed and quiet, smelling of stale smoke and sweat. Sawdust littered but didn't carpet a puncheon floor. A little Franklin stove stood in the center of the room, its pipe running toward the ceiling, then along its length. These things and the plank bar and lunch counter were standards in a frontier saloon. And so, maybe, were the four men spread out along the bar.

The bartender had edged far down the bar, almost out of my vision while I looked at those who faced me. As for the four, my attention had settled not on the chill blue eyes of the man I figured was the killer here, nor the almost black eyes of the brawny looking one I figured *thought* he was the leader. Instead, I looked at a little man with sandy blond hair and an amused smirk on his face. This was the real leader of these men, I guessed. At least the only one a man could reason with.

The fourth one was so stupid-looking as to appear ridiculous. Dull brown hair curled from beneath a hat that had been batted about his ears far too many years. He stared with his mouth hung open like a snot-nose brat. His dirty brown gopher teeth pushed out at his lip, hanging over the lower set by a noticeable bit, and his over-large eyes jumped like grasshoppers along the line of those who faced him—four of us: Tanner, Duke, Slug—and now me.

The big one settled his black eyes on me, resting them on my gun, then at last on my face. "I seen you in Buffalo. You're him—the bank robber. You're the man rides the gray horse."

"I ride a gray horse," I agreed.

"I seen you," he said again. "You kilt that stingy old banker and Lucius Bird."

That was the first time I knew for sure I'd killed Bird, and I tried to hide my disappointment at learning he was dead. I shrugged, glancing over at my partners before bringing my eyes back to the big man. He was every bit as big as Slug Holch, probably even outweighed him by ten or twenty pounds. But his bulk wasn't as hard as Slug's, and the extra weight pushed against the buttons above his waistline. He'd spent too much time lazing around in some saloon while Slug was out pounding leather—and heads, on occasion. His hair was long for the time, long and heavily curled, snaking along his ears and shirt collar like licorice whips. But it was his neck that impressed me, with its bullish broadness, and his powerful shoulders and thickly knuckled hands. He wore a gun on his hip, but I didn't notice it like I did the killing power of his body. And by the slight bend to his knees and the cock to his elbows, I could see he itched for a fight.

"Guess we stopped at the right place," he said. "The sheriff'll be along soon, but right now it's just us. Mebbe you oughtta turn your guns over so it'll go easy on you." His eyes were wide on me and kept dropping to the gun I had leveled between him and the one with the cold blue eyes and a sling holding up his right arm.

"You can't be as stupid as you sound. Nobody could," I said. "Except maybe him." I motioned with my gun barrel toward the buck-toothed one.

The big man laughed. "Buck? He might be stupid, but he's loyal as a pup." Buck grunted, turning his head to look at the big one with a grin spread across his face.

"Well, I got an idea better than yours," I told them. "You all drop *your* guns, and we'll take 'em and keep 'em safe for you. You're itchin' for a fight, and I'm not in the mood. You got us mixed up with somebody else anyway. We never been to Buffalo."

The big man forced a smile, and his eyes flickered to my gun. "Well, I say you have. And if you didn't have that gun out, I'd help you remember."

"You couldn't help a old lady acrost the street," Slug growled. "Not by the looks o' you."

The big man reddened, and the little man I'd pegged their leader laughed quietly. "You ain't gonna let 'im talk that way to you, are you, Burlen? He looks like a kid, for the kind you been used to fightin'."

The big man called Burlen looked over at the little one. Anger flashed across his eyes, but when he looked back at Slug it was cleverly hidden. "I guess we'll never know, not with your friend holdin' that gun."

"Put it up," Slug told me.

"No. You wanna fight, go ahead. But the gun stays. And all theirs go."

Slug looked over at me, eyes narrowing. "You...All right." He turned back to Burlen. "I know the man well," he said. "He won't use the gun, or I'll kill 'im for it. Mine's goin' down, if that's your game. Unless you wanna march outta here gunless, come acrost here and pit your fists. You don't look any tougher than my mother, and she's got no arms."

Burlen set his gunbelt carefully on the bar, and I turned my barrel on the cold-eyed killer, motioning for him to do the same. "Plant it or use it, blondy. You others, too."

The killer had been quiet till then. But I guess he must've been teased before over his white-blond hair; his eyes turned almost glowing with hatred when I called him "blondy." He looked at my gun again, gauging his chances to draw. I saw it in the flicker of his eyes. "I could beat you three ways from Sunday, old man. Why don't you holster that and give me a chance?"

I chuckled. "Now, do I look like a fool? You just *might* beat me, if I was stupid. As it is, I can put two holes in your fence-rail chest before you bring that halfway up. Now shuck it, put it on the bar and get away. And quit lookin' at me with those big blue eyes. You fancy men or somethin'?"

The killer bared his teeth and tilted forward, his hand going instinctively for his gun. I cocked mine and pointed it at his chest, just laughing. Laughing to make him furious—which I did. But he wasn't furious enough to draw. Slowly, he unbuckled the belt and laid it on the bar.

By then, Buck and the little man had already got shut of their guns and stood at the other end of the bar until I motioned them to go down with the killer. When Burlen looked at me questioningly and brought a thumb up to his chest, I shook my head. "Nah. You wanted to prove your manhood. Why don't you show us how you're gonna clean my friend's clock?"

He turned full attention to Slug. "By the bruises all over your face, I'd say you're about tuckered out, old timer. But you ain't seen a beatin' like the one you'll get now. I was raised fightin' wild hogs, and they're a lot harder than you."

Slug's mustache twitched in a smile. The old glint came into his eyes that told me his fists were about to turn to sledge hammers, and Burlen would soon go down.

"Sonny, I used to pick my teeth with chubby boys like you."

"I'll bet you did—back when I was a boy. What, twenty years ago? You obviously changed since then."

Slug's jaw muscles bunched as he slipped the gunbelt from around his hips and laid it on a convenient table. He tried to smile but grimaced instead. "Boy, you got a butt that looks like a face and a face that looks like a butt. Let's put 'em back in their rightful spots."

With an oath, Burlen charged, head low and eyes wild. Before he could reach Slug, my friend bent low, and he came up hard into Burlen's chest with his shoulder. Burlen staggered back, but not out of range of the right cross that slammed his cheek. Staggering, Burlen threw an instinctive roundhouse left that clipped the air a foot from Slug's head. He spun half-around in his fury, then stumbled back toward Slug, trying to recover his balance. Slug took two quick steps back, then settled himself and shook Burlen with left and right jabs as Burlen closed.

This time the blows seemed not to affect Burlen. He shook them off and threw one of his own, a blow which sank like bricks against Slug's ribs. But he wasn't fast enough to throw another before Slug stepped back and hit him—no, *slapped* him—across the left side of his face. And even the slap was enough to wrench Burlen's head sideways. But more than anything it made him mad.

Burlen came in with two impressive roundhouse blows, one of which dug into Slug's neck and made his knees crumple. But Slug didn't go down, just dodged out of the way to give himself time to recover. For a moment, he wasn't so sure on his feet, nor so ready to jump forward. It was obvious Burlen had power behind his blows when he could make them land. He just wasn't fast enough to land many.

Slug let Burlen draw near. When Burlen slung another round-house for the cheek, and it was plain he was confident of its effect, Slug threw his torso backward, tucking his chin. Then he recovered and stepped back in. He slammed a left jab, then another, into Burlen's twisted mouth. Both times, Burlen's head snapped back, but with that bull neck of his it did little but bloody him.

Blood smeared Burlen's open, cursing mouth. He just shook his shaggy head, flinging crimson across the sawdust, and came in for more. Burlen had lost his hat, and hair hung in sweaty clumps on his forehead. Slug, on the other hand, still had his hat. He appeared to be toying with the slower man.

Burlen made a rush, and Slug lunged back, but not fast enough. Burlen managed to get hold of his shirtfront, and his momentum carried them both into a table. The table tipped and fell to the floor under their weight, and both went with it. Burlen rolled and came up first, which surprised me. As Slug came up, Burlen threw a hurried kick, and his boot toe caught Slug in the breast bone, knocking him backward. He landed and rolled, and like the barroom brawler of old he started up with his eyes seeking out his opponent's next move.

The fight had degenerated. Even as Slug looked, the foot was coming again, and he dropped and twisted, the foot missing him. He threw himself and hit the planted leg. Then he grabbed it, and with all his strength heaved upward and sent Burlen crashing to his face in the sawdust.

Burlen stumbled up, shaking his head and pawing at the bloody sawdust, smearing it away from his eyes and mouth. "Come on!" He roared a curse at Slug and let out an animal-like growl, grabbing for the nearest table. Even as he started to raise it, Slug came across it to give him a thundering blow that came from above to strike him on the chin, slamming his head down into his neck. Slug rolled the rest of the way over the table, landing against Burlen.

The black-haired one saw his chance. He threw his powerful arms around Slug and squeezed mightily. With a roar, he raised him clear of the floor. Then, throwing himself forward on top of his opponent, he drove him onto the table top. It was too much for that shabby piece of furniture, and it collapsed beneath them.

They went down hard, landing on the table top, nearly flat on the floor. Being beneath the bigger man, Slug took the brunt of the punishment. He gasped for his air, unsuccessful in regaining it for several seconds as he struggled to rise and get away. Even with his breath gone, he drove a flat-knuckled fist three times into Burlen's left cheekbone until the bigger man snarled in pain and pushed back to his hands and knees, getting away from Slug.

They staggered up together, and Burlen's hand came up holding a table leg. Before he could straighten out of his crouch and use it, Slug's flat boot toe caught him in the mouth. Even I cringed that time. I'd heard teeth break free.

Burlen screamed out in pain, revealing the missing four front teeth of his upper jaw. He spit them violently toward the floor, swearing and sounding like a fool when his tongue found no teeth to push against. That seemed to madden him more than anything. With the table leg still in hand, he drove at Slug. His mouth open in a roar, his face smeared with blood and teeth gone, he looked like a madman. And no doubt he *was* a mad man.

Slug tried to dodge away, but he stumbled like he'd been tripped. They'd moved too near Burlen's friends, and I saw the man called Buck jerk his foot back as Slug started to go down. In anger, I pivoted at the waist as Slug and Burlen cleared my view, and I shot Buck through the knee cap. He went down screaming. "When this is over maybe you can give your teeth to your pard," I growled over the noise of the struggle. "Hell knows you got enough of 'em."

When I looked back, I guessed Burlen had clobbered Slug with that table leg. He had a bloody gash down the right side of his head. They rolled on the floor, punching and kicking each other, inflicting any damage they could while both of them hung onto that table leg. They drove knees against groins, boots against shins, fists against bellies and chins and noses, until I thought both would throw up from the pain.

When Burlen sank what teeth he had left into Slug's shoulder, Slug growled and slammed the top of his head against the bigger man's cheekbone. That made him let go, and he rolled away onto his back, shaking his head groggily.

Slug struggled away and came to his feet, gasping for air. His shoulder had a wicked gash where Burlen had bit him, and blood already streamed down through his shirt sleeve. The missing front teeth hadn't kept Burlen's dog teeth from being terrible weapons. But now *Slug* held the table leg. Dumping his advantage, he threw it out under the batwing doors and stepped up to meet Burlen as he lumbered erect.

Slug broke the man's jaw with the next blow. While Burlen stood there in shock, gasping, Slug sank two blows deep into the fat of his belly that slung him over double. Then, as a final *coup de grace*, Slug stepped back and gave the bigger man a solid blow to the forehead with the bottom of his boot, straight out like the kick of a mule. Burlen stumbled backward before falling and crashing headlong into the bottom of the bar. An unconscious sigh escaped his mouth.

Suddenly, boot steps pounded across the porch. Before I could even think of turning, I saw the alarm in Duke Rainey's eyes. Duke had already drawn his gun, and as he raised it I started to whirl. I heard two shots as one, Duke's and one from the man in the doorway. The other man, a large, bloody bandage already around his thigh, pitched backward and landed on the porch. His gun struck the porch and skidded away to fall off into the dust of the street. His bullet had struck the bar.

Over Buck's moaning, I heard a scrape behind me. I whirled to see the blond killer snaking his pistol from its holster on the bar. Without me even knowing my gun was up, I heard it bark and saw it smoke. The would-be killer's gun spoke, too, but he was weakened by my shot, and his bullet burned into the broken table top. I shot him again, again, again, aiming for that narrow chest behind his sling. Each shot rocked him, but he didn't want to go down. He'd set himself to kill someone.

I shot again, this time low enough in the stomach it doubled him over, and he fell on his face and lay moaning. Buck was seated in the sawdust now, his wounded knee drawn up to his chest, where he had it cradled in both hands. The third man, the little one, stood stock-still, leaned back against the bar. He tried to look nonchalant, but his face was white, and his eyes flickered uncomfortably back and forth between Duke, Tanner and me.

The would-be killer had stopped moaning. I figured him for dead. As for Slug, he leaned on the bar, still struggling to regain his wind. His face was covered with blood, and he'd torn away his ruined shirt. His muscular back and chest heaved in and out with breath as he stared at the room through the slits of his eyes. He swiped at the blood on his face, smearing it onto a pant leg.

I looked again at the little man as I stepped to the bar and slid his pistol out of its holster, sticking my empty one behind my belt. "Everybody else wants to kill us. How 'bout you?"

"Mister, my gun's a long ways away. Besides, I enjoyed the show. You boys earned your way outta here."

I nodded, still not trusting him, and walked over to Slug. Holding my pistol in one hand, I tried to help him stand away from the bar, but he stubbornly flung my hand away. "Just get my gun," he said.

I walked over and picked his belted gun up off the floor. Blowing the sawdust off it, I handed it to him as he managed to walk to me. Every step was a struggle, but he tried to look unhurt. Sort of like a skeleton trying to look undead.

Last of everyone, I looked at Barlow Tanner. He held his pistol in his hand, but his face was unreasonably pale under his scruff of beard. I was fairly certain he hadn't managed to get off a shot in the fracas. I wondered if he'd ever be good to any of us in a scrape, or if he was just there as a decoration. And not even too ornamental at that.

Not in any mood to be led, even if Tanner still felt man enough to give orders, I looked at his palmed gun. "Why don't you make yourself useful and pick up the rest of those so Shorty, there, won't get any notions?" Flashing me a hurt look, Tanner started slowly over.

The little man at the bar laughed. "You want the one in my belt, too?"

I motioned Tanner over to check it out with an insistent whip of my chin. Sure enough, he pulled a little silver derringer from the man's waistband. After looking at me uncertainly, Tanner stuffed it into his pocket.

"You coulda used that," I said to the little man. "Why didn't you?"

He laughed again, this time with a kind of dismayed look on his face as his eyes flicked about the bloodied room. "Why? And give yuh reason to kill me too? Besides, like I said—you earned your way out. This is none of my grief."

"Did you know the man on the porch?" I asked, slipping the spent shells out of my gun and new ones in.

"Uh-huh. He was in the posse, too. Name's Anderson. And there's another one about. Old man named Abe Cedroe. I hope you won't hurt that old gent. Used to give credit to my ma down at his store, when times was hard."

"I hope not to hurt him, too," I said. "I never wanted to hurt nobody."

With one last look at the shattered, unconscious Burlen, I stepped away, following Tanner and Slug onto the porch. Duke was crouched there, scanning the street warily, a gun in each hand. I was surprised to see Tovías Ruiz nowhere in sight, but soon he came from the direction of the doctor's house, hobbling on a crutch. His eyes were worried.

When he got close, he gaped at Slug, then swung his eyes to Tanner. "What in the hell happened? Ay, *Diantre!* Slug is a mess." His eyes flickered to the dead man on the porch and to Duke's two guns, then back to Tanner.

"Might have to shoot our way outta town, Tovy," said Tanner. "Just kilt two deppities."

Still angered by Tanner's inactivity in the saloon, I turned to Duke. "You and Ruiz take Slug down to the doc's. He can't go with us like this. Maybe get 'im a new shirt, too. And keep your guns out. This village is likely to explode here in a bit."

Duke looked at me uncertainly, then swung his eyes to Tanner. The older man looked away. "Go, Duke," I said louder.

Without another look at Tanner, the Negro started away, walking slow so Slug could keep up. The Mexican had drawn his pistols and walked a couple steps behind them, watching the establishment doors and windows nervously. He branched off at the mercantile, and Slug and Duke went on alone.

"Come on, Barlow," I said, turning. "Let's go get some fresh horses."

"With what?"

I thought of the gold nuggets obtained from Toy. "I got a little saved. Let's go."

We started down the street, walking fast. People were daring to come to their doors now, and when I looked back I saw a couple of them venture over to the Palace of Mud. By the time we reached the local livery stable, the porch of the saloon was crowded with onlookers, and all of them staring our way.

"You wait out here and watch them people," I told Tanner. "I'll go buy the horses. Keep your eyes peeled."

I hadn't even made it halfway down the stable aisle when I heard a familiar voice outside. "Well, hello, Barlow. It's good to see you."

My chest felt clutched by eagle talons. I whirled, unbelieving, and heard the voice again before any reply by Tanner.

"McLean is in there, isn't he? I suppose we all need to have a talk."

It was Jason Shilo.

Chapter Twenty-One
Luck of the Draw

"Howdy do, Mr. Shilo," I heard Tanner say.

I came to the doorway holding the Remington in my hand, but it was down along my leg. Shilo faced Tanner, that calm look on his face. No sign of guilt or fear, no hint that he done anything wrong. I kept my eyes on Shilo, somewhere between his face and his hands. I couldn't see what Tanner was doing. I just hoped he'd get out of the way.

It suddenly struck me that he could just as easily join forces with Shilo.

A smart man would have killed Shilo then, but I'd never shot a man that way. And I couldn't now. Not even Jason Shilo.

Shilo turned when he saw me in the corner of his eye. The day was warm, and he'd left his coat somewhere. That was probably *part* of his reason, anyway. But surely he'd thought of the fact that his gun butts would also come easy to his hand.

Somehow, when the rest of us were dusty, shabby, spent, the hard ride hadn't seemed to affect Shilo. His hat had been brushed, as well as his black pants and dark gray vest. His string tie lay just right, like a painted line against the striped white of his shirt. His boots and gun leather shone as always, and those ominous ivory butts of his Colts tilted at just the right spot against his forearms.

Shilo reached up and tipped back his gray hat with a forefinger. If there was any expression in his blue eyes it was friendliness, much as I tried to look for something else.

"Hello, McLean."

I nodded, letting my glance leave his face only enough to dart about the vicinity. "Where's JoAnna? Still with you?"

"Still with me? Well…of course." He looked almost confused, like he was surprised that any other thought could even have entered my mind. "We've been together for a long time. She couldn't leave me." His eyes dropped to my right hand, and smooth as gunmetal his hand came up to rest casually on the butt of one Colt. I still don't know why

I let him do that. I knew we both couldn't walk away. Thinking back, when I let him touch that gun butt, I was good as dead. I'd bring my gun up, and I'd shoot him, and he'd die. But so would I. He was too fast, and I gave him the edge to make sure if he died we both did.

"I had a set-to with some Arapahos one time," Shilo said of a sudden. The comment puzzled me. "We were pushing a herd—our first herd of Durhams, in fact. They came upon us on the prairie. There wasn't even so much as a clump of sagebrush to hide behind. There were five or six bucks, and five of us. And I recognized one of those bucks. His name was Tall-Feather. He had killed a white woman outside of Denver one year and escaped. I wanted to kill Tall-Feather. He deserved to die. But I had killed Arapahos before, too. Some he knew. And he wanted me dead just as much."

A long pause forced me to speak. "What happened?"

A corner of his mouth pushed up under his mustache, and his eyes crinkled. "Well, as you might expect, he turned his bucks and rode away, and we pushed our cattle on to the ranch. If we had fought, we would probably both have been killed. And that wouldn't have done either of us any good. We both wanted to live—we both had a lot to live *for*. And speaking for me, I still do."

My heart was doing cartwheels in my chest. Without saying it direct, Shilo given us both a way out. And maybe there'd be another day. Maybe I'd see Shilo again when the odds were with me. Right now, it was a Mexican standoff, which had been Shilo's whole point. Sure, Tanner was there. But who knew whose side he'd fight on? That's if he fought at all. He'd proved himself about worthless up till then. So I felt pretty much alone—and the closest I'd ever felt to dead.

"Where's JoAnna?" I asked again. "I don't see her."

Shilo sighed. "I don't think she wants you to. She's not worth it anyway, McLean. You remember all I told you. JoAnna's a nice girl, but she's really no more than a tramp."

"Where is she?" I asked, the anger rising in my voice.

"She's safe."

"Where?"

"Actually, she's over at the Bridger Hotel freshening up."

For a long time, our eyes held and no one spoke. Finally, I couldn't hold myself back. "You're damn calm, knowin' what you did back at that Injun camp."

"What'd I do, McLean?" he responded instantly. "That girl was nice, and she was sweet on me. I lay with her, and there wouldn't have been anymore to it. Not until her mother came in to interfere.

She tried to kill me, McLean. She came at me with a butcher knife, and I struck her with my revolver. What would you have done?"

I stared at him and tried to come up with an answer for that. I couldn't. Damn Shilo was always able to talk his way out of anything. "What about the girl?"

He scoffed. "Come on, McLean! What do you think? The second I killed her mother she turned into an animal. She came after me and tried to get my gun. I didn't mean to kill her."

"Didn't mean to kill her! You cut her throat!"

For the first time Shilo's eyes flickered away, the only sign I'd yet seen that I might have believed was guilt. "She was trying to scream," he said. "What would you have done? Let her bring the whole bunch of them down on you?"

"Damn you!" I said angrily. "You ever get tired of puttin' your mistakes on other people? It *wasn't* me! It was you. You murdered two women!"

"It wasn't as bad as you act," Shilo said calmly. "They were just Indians. It sure didn't keep JoAnna from coming with me when I left."

"You mean you gave her a choice?"

His eyes flickered again. I knew whatever he was going to say would be a lie. But he worded it in such a way that I couldn't call it that. "What do *you* think?" he asked.

My heart thudded wildly in my chest. My glance flickered down at Shilo's hand. He had managed to close it over his gun butt. He was too fast for me. Sure, I had my gun out of the holster. But that wasn't going to make a damn bit of difference. I given him an edge, and he was going to kill me. But I couldn't let Jason Shilo walk away. I couldn't let him go back to JoAnna, wherever she was. This was my chance. My chance to do something good with my life. To redeem myself. I was going to die to save JoAnna from a miserable existence with Jason Shilo. I was going to die, but so was Jason Shilo.

I heard myself speaking as if from a distance, not even knowing I was forming the words until they were out of my mouth. "You're the smoothest man I ever met. But you're just a cattle thief. Just like all the rest of us."

"No," he replied. "Not like all the rest—"

"Hey! You cowboys throw down your guns!" The call from down the street cut Shilo off.

Instinctively, I whirled toward the Palace of Mud. Seven to ten men armed with rifles and shotguns had just stepped off the porch and were coming toward us.

A gun makes a peculiar kind of hard sucking sound as it leaves a good-fitting holster. Man like me knows that sound, has heard it countless times when he's made it himself, and plenty of times around others who use guns. I heard the sound now and realized my fatal mistake. The sound, of course, came from Jason Shilo's holster.

But I didn't have the time to react like a man who'd gave it any thought. Shilo had me off-guard. I whirled, but I stayed glued to my tracks when I should have fallen one way or the other. I was trying to bring my gun up as I came around. I heard the shot, like a dull thud, deep inside my brain. But I felt no pain. In the confusion I saw the billow of smoke, and it came from Barlow Tanner's gun!

I was facing Shilo now, my gun up. A grimace twisted his handsome face. He fired, but it wasn't at me. Even as I saw Tanner double over from the corner of my eye, I snapped a shot at Shilo's broad chest. At ten feet my shot was deadly. Tanner raised his gun and fired again, matching my second shot. One of our bullets twisted Shilo to the left, and his arm flopped grotesquely around, shattered at the shoulder.

Shilo gave out a cry of anger and pain. He could have shot at me, but his eyes darted between me and Tanner, and in that moment of decision he shot Tanner again. Even as I returned the shot, Tanner fell to his knees.

Shilo twisted off balance just enough to drop to his left knee as he fired at me, and his bullet threw up dirt at my feet. Besides his shoulder, his midriff and chest were covered in blood now. He canted over and fell on the left side of his face, crushing the ruined shoulder beneath him.

Without looking at Tanner, I jumped to Shilo and stepped down on his right hand, which still clutched the Colt. I looked at him in time to see his eye raise to me, and a stream of blood trickled out the corner of his mouth and pooled dark in the white clay dust. I bent to pry the gun from his hand, but there was no prying involved.

Jason Shilo was already dead.

"Give up your guns!" I heard the voice from the crowd behind me say. I whirled and dropped into a crouch.

Chapter Twenty-Two
Kiss an Outlaw Like Me

As I dropped into the crouch, I felt a sharp pain in my side. For a moment, I thought I'd been hit. But it was only my wound from the river fight.

I still had my gun palmed, and those riflemen came to an abrupt halt. They stared at me in confusion. I was only one man with a half-empty six-gun against a bunch of them with rifles and shotguns. There was no contest here, but none of them wanted to be among the one or two men they figured I could kill.

A sudden flurry of hooves rolled in from my left, a bunch of horses crossing between me and the crowd of angry citizens. I looked to see Utah Chadwick and his bunch of Anti-Association boys drawing guns and reining up in a swirl of dust to face the mob.

"Hold up there, gents!" Chadwick barked, leveling a Smith and Wesson Russian on the crowd. "These are friends."

He spun his big, mottled buckskin horse around and met my eyes. "That Shilo?"

I nodded, wondering if he knew about his father yet. But I wouldn't be the one to tell.

"How's your friend?" Utah asked.

I looked down at Barlow Tanner, whose pain-filled eyes flickered up to meet mine. He was sitting back on his legs, his shoulders slouched. Blood soaked the front of his shirt and pants. A faint sour smell tinged the air.

"He's dying," I said as I turned back to Chadwick. "Gut-shot."

Chadwick grimaced. "Well, we have to get. You do what you want with him, but if you want our help it'll have to be now."

"Why help us?"

"You killed Shilo," he replied. "That's reason enough."

Duke had reached us now and was staring down at Tanner with a sick look on his face. Ruiz and Slug came limping up, gazing about warily to take stock of the situation. And behind them stood JoAnna Walker. Relief washed through me as I saw her, but we had no time to talk.

"You're dyin', Tanner," I said. "What'll it be?"

A bubble had formed at the corner of his mouth. He lowered his head to force a breath in, then looked back up at us. Weakly, he jerked a thumb toward the wall of the stable. "Hell, jus' leave me m' gun, McLean, 'n' set me up agin' the wall, so's I c'n see who-all's a-comin' at me."

Between me and Duke we dragged him to the livery wall, setting him up there like he asked. Tovías Ruiz had carried his gun over, and he handed it to me. I took it and crouched down, slipping two cartridges out of Tanner's belt to reload the two he'd spent. Then I took Tanner's hand and placed the gun gently in it, closing his fingers over it.

"What else can we do?"

He tried to smile, and tears welled up in his eyes. His gaze swung all around, and when he spotted JoAnna, the failed smile finally broke across his face. "There's m' gal," he said in his hoarse drawl. He held his hand out to her, and she hurried to his side. I couldn't help but notice a huge, dark bruise across her left cheek.

JoAnna took his hand and tried to smile. "Roll me up a smoke, Jo. Like yuh used t' do."

Her hands trembling, JoAnna fumbled the ever-present sack of Bull Durham out of Tanner's vest pocket. Slipping the pack of gummed papers from its sleeve, she pulled one loose and sprinkled the dark grains onto it, licking it and running two fingers along it to seal it. With one hand gently at the nape of Tanner's neck, she brought the quirly to his lips and inserted it. Then she took a match from the same pocket and struck it against the wall. The end of the cigarette glowed at his breath, and she threw the burning match into the dust. The tiny flame held there stubbornly, then suddenly burned out, and a little tuft of smoke lifted away.

Tanner sucked deep on the cigarette—way too deep, I thought. He coughed a little, and the smoke sputtered out of his nostrils and mouth at once.

Tanner reached up and put a rough hand alongside JoAnna's cheek. "That jasper's gone now, honey. Yer free. Now git. No more outlaw stuff."

She nodded. I could see she couldn't speak.

Tanner tried to smile, and he shook hands all around, nodding at each of us and saying "Ay-dios."

When we stood away from him, he took another puff on his quirly. "So long, boys. Hope t' see yuh t'other side."

The others started to back away, all except JoAnna, who still held onto his hand. She leaned over and kissed his forehead while tears rolled down her cheeks and spoiled her tough girl mask. I crouched down in front of him and held out my hand again. I just couldn't let go yet.

"You saved my life, Tanner. *Mister* Tanner."

He gave up a lopsided grin and squeezed my hand. The strength was still in his Missouri grip. "I'd do it again—*Mister* McLean. Now you take care o' m' gal."

We couldn't leave without JoAnna seeing Tye. Utah Chadwick and his bunch were in a stand-off on the street, and they grew restless and angry. But there was nothing for it. The woman insisted, threatening to stay there by herself if she had to. Chadwick and his men followed us down to the doctor's house, then stood watch on the street while me and the woman went inside. The citizens with the civic minds had backed off now and milled around the Palace of Mud, talking and looking toward us. They weren't going to buck Utah Chadwick.

Tye was still alive. I was surprised. He opened his eyes when I said his name. It had been days since I'd seen such a look of gladness in them as there was when he saw the woman.

"Jo— Anna," he murmured.

Still full of tears for Tanner, JoAnna fought to give the boy a smile. "Hello, Tyrone. Ready to come with us?" She tried to sound confident, but her eyes told the truth.

A weak smile spread Tye's downy mustache. His teeth weren't much whiter than his skin now. His eyes flickered to me uncertainly, and I guessed what he was thinking. By some unknown act of God, JoAnna must have too, because she reached down and sandwiched his hand between both of hers.

Tye closed his eyes with a soft sigh. He looked up again. "Could you— Could you ever kiss a— a outlaw...like me?"

JoAnna's face reddened a little, and the tears filled her eyes again. She nodded in reply, blinking the tears back. Leaning, she bent and pressed her lips to his for a long, tender moment. When she straightened up, he was smiling.

I started to turn away, then heard his alarmed voice. "Tom? Where's Tom?"

I turned back to him and took his other hand. "I'm right here, Tye. All right now."

"You two...you...should get married." His eyes flickered between us.

I just smiled. That was one I couldn't reply to.

"Don't be...a outlaw...no more," he said.

I just shook my head, struggling at the rock in my throat. Tye gave a tiny nod and smiled. He was still smiling when the spirit went out of his eyes.

There wasn't any time to trade horses. Things were too restless out on that street. I couldn't impose any more on Chadwick's bunch than we already had. We took Shilo's horse with us as an extra, along with all his gear and his horse hide coat. We also took three more horses out of the stable. I left a handful of gold bits as payment—I don't think Chadwick would have let us take them if he hadn't seen that.

We rode toward Montana without any of us discussing the route. Chadwick must've remembered us telling him that's where we were bound. I still wanted it, but now I was leery. I didn't know for certain where Bennett and his posse had gone when they split off from Burlen and the others in Sheridan. They could easily have been north of us. If they were, we were bound to run right into them on their way back from the border. And Bennett would be madder than a kicked bear after the whooping we gave him.

I wanted shut of Chadwick's bunch. They'd helped us in a bad spot, but they didn't know yet we'd killed Chadwick's old man. And when they did, it was obvious they could stomp us clear to hell, or help Bennett do it, if they chose to. It was our shot-up and beat-up bunch and one woman against their seven rested, gun-ready hands. There was no hope for us if word reached them about the Tongue River fight. And we were headed right for the bloody scene of it.

Utah Chadwick was riding in the lead, and I touched spurs to Sheriff to ride up beside him. He was rolling a quirly with both hands while his reins lay slack across the saddle horn. Chadwick wasn't a tall man, no more so than me, and I stood a hair's width below average. But setting that saddle he looked seven feet tall. In his confidence and self-composure, he seemed another Shilo, and I hoped the likeness ended there.

From head to toe, Chadwick looked the part of a cowboy. He sat like one, wore a plainsman hat with a slight down-sloped crease to the front of its crown. He kept that Russian .44 high on his hip, too, like a cowboy, and had the battered shotgun chaps and custom-made boots that hid the small feet a cowboy set so much pride in. A colorfully printed red bandana slung to the middle of his belly.

It half-covered a buckskin pullover shirt he'd traded for the red one we'd last seen on him. The tag of a sack of Bull Durham hung from its one pocket. He rode like a cowboy, dressed like a cowboy. But still he didn't seem like he should be a cowboy.

It was something about his eyes, I reckon. They were set far back behind his heavy cheeks, set so you couldn't hardly tell they were blue. But you could see them roaming, always, and not simply for a joy of seeing the landscape. Utah Chadwick was a hard man in a hard land, and fixing to be at the head of whatever trouble fell upon his bunch when the Wyoming Stock Growers Association descended on this upstart country.

With his huge mustache hanging down to surround his chin, you couldn't see much of Chadwick's mouth. But the mustache moved when he started to talk. He looked over at me through a puff of smoke, and a slight glimmer of humor showed between his slanted eyelids.

"You boys were headed for Montana, last I heard."

"Yeah, Mr. Chadwick. We were."

"No 'misters' here. It's Utah or Ute—or Chadwick, if you prefer keeping your distance. My experience, people that carry titles are all blowhards."

I had to agree there. "Then you call me Tom."

He just nodded, occupied with sucking cigarette smoke down into his toes and trying not to cough.

"Listen, Utah. I 'preciate you boys helpin' us out of a tight spot back there. But we c'n handle ourselves from here on. You best go back and keep a eye on that war they say's brewin'."

Chadwick chuckled. "That war's gonna be all over this north country. Everywhere the deer and antelope play."

"Where the buffalo used to roam," I added with a dry chuckle. "So why're you involved?" I asked.

"I'm blackballed. They passed that damn Maverick law back in '84, and it's ruined many a good man. I ran cows under my pap, while I was workin' for the EK outfit. They told me I couldn't do it anymore, and they were takin' my cows right out from under me. When I fought back I ended up blackballed. Couldn't go to the roundups. Couldn't hire on anywhere. Not even with my pap the manager of one of the biggest spreads in this god-forsaken territory. But I'm not leavin'."

"Liable to get killed," I mused.

"Maybe. You think your boy could use a rest?"

I turned and looked at Slug. His face was a big, ripe squash. He swayed in the saddle, half asleep. But I'd seen Slug survive worse fights and ride away. Fact is, the gentle pace we were keeping gave him more rest than I'd figured he'd get.

"He'll last," I said.

"We'll stop for a while at the river anyway," Chadwick decided.

I just nodded. The one that concerned me was JoAnna. She rode with her eyes on the back of her horse's head, staring, almost never blinking. That big bruise on her cheek looked even bigger in the shade of her hat. She had both hands locked on the saddle horn. And like I said before she was too good a rider to be shaking hands with grandma that way.

I left Chadwick and dropped back beside the girl. I kept my nose pointed north, but I tried to watch her out of the corner of my eye. I kept hoping she'd look my way, but she didn't. I guess she knew I was watching her. I had to admit, I was almighty curious to know what she'd seen back in the mountains. Had she witnessed the killings of the two Injun women?

Finally, JoAnna let her horse slow up from the rest of them. It slowed until she rode at the back of the crowd, and I stayed beside her. The next time I looked over, her mouth was twisted up while she fought against sobbing out loud. Her face shone with tears.

There was no comforting the woman. Especially not for a man with a mouth full of mud like me. I just rode quiet beside her, letting her know someone was there—for all the good it did. I didn't know if she was crying over Tanner, or Tye, or whatever had happened to her since Shilo dragged her out of our lives. Maybe a little of all three.

We stopped at the Tongue River, like Chadwick had promised. I was praying the ranch hands had already come and carried away their boss, John Chadwick. But then there was also the matter of Tye's horse and Bachelor's body on the bridge. What would Chadwick make of that?

By some miracle, just before we reached the river, Chadwick veered away and led us back to a shady place under the cottonwoods, completely out of sight of the bridge. He didn't explain it. I guessed he was making sure no one came upon us to upset our rest.

Slug slipped out of the saddle before anyone could offer help, almost falling when his feet touched the ground. But after standing a couple minutes with his hands on the saddle, he limped away and knelt at the river bank to dangle his scarf in and drip water over his face and head.

JoAnna walked away by herself and sat against a tree. She never looked toward anyone else. I figured she wanted to be alone, so I left her that way.

Chadwick's boys all lazed about in a broad, loose circle. I sat with them. That's where I found the best shade tree. I nestled back in the crotch of two huge cottonwood roots, rolling a smoke like everyone else. All except the big buckskin clad man, Dale Hepner. He pulled out a pipe and started tamping it full.

I had occasion to look over and meet the eyes of Flint Drury, as he touched a match to his smoke. It took its glow, and he shook out the match and held onto it so it could cool. He was watching me, not in any challenging way, but curious. Again, his eyes were smiling.

I couldn't remember where I'd seen Flint Drury, but I knew Drury wasn't his name. And Flint? Was anyone really named that? Maybe, but I didn't believe he was. I cursed my memory.

It was while I studied him, and he studied me, that I came to the sudden realization that, although I didn't recall him yet, he certainly did me. His eyes were smiling again, and I was haunted by one fact. Drury hadn't known me in my law-abiding years. This man now called Flint Drury knew me as a cattle rustler.

And I was one match too near a fuse.

Chapter Twenty-Three
Surprise Encounter

As I was racking my brain, trying to recall anything about Flint Drury, Utah Chadwick looked over at me and blew smoke away from his lips. "Tom, I was thinkin'. Telegraph reaches a ways. They might have that road north blocked by now. The army and the big ranchers around here don't look at me in a kind light already, and they sure won't your bunch either. I say we move down along the river a little farther and make a camp for the night. Try to let the storm blow over. And that one, too."

He pointed toward the western sky, and I followed his gesture. Black clouds were forming along the horizon, and just as I looked a faint stem of lightning arced across their bellies. I didn't want to wait in Wyoming any longer than I had to. But I knew for a fact there was a posse looking for me—north of there, I figured. Chadwick's instincts, at least on that count, were good.

As Chadwick suggested, we rode west a ways, toward the hulking shoulders of the Bighorns. Then we rolled out our blankets in the trees along the river bank. The trees were thick enough here for us to plan for a fire after dark.

The storm came before the sun went. It rolled in over us and left us in a weird half-light, everything gray and lonely. The river bubbled by, and the grass and tree branches tossed back and forth, some little branches cracking loose and skittering down around us.

The range needed rain, but this time it didn't get it. The lightning poked in long, jointed trails down the clouds, making thunder rumble and burst in our ears. The wind battered and slashed at us. But the rain held back.

JoAnna sat against a tree with a blanket wrapped around her. She just stared, like a woman I'd seen one time in Portland who had gone daft and didn't know anything that went on around her. Me, I didn't know what to say to her. About all I could do was sit and worry and hope she worked through it.

It was funny how in broad daylight I couldn't place Flint Drury's face, and then in the dark it sort of came to me like a revelation. When it got dark enough that we couldn't see much, Drury started up a fire with some leaves and grass and little sticks we'd piled together earlier. He added bigger branches, and the flames leaped up, swatted around by the wind. When Drury looked up, it was straight at me, and there was a strange orange light glowing on his cheeks.

I remembered him then. I remembered him as the Oregon badman, John House.

The Posse: Augustin Flagg

We reached the border of the Montana Territory. Not once had we seen any indication of our being on the trail of the bank robbers and their fiendish cohorts. I had to admit, the trail had grown old, even for me. I was weary, and all enthusiasm for my newspaper article that would shake the world was gone.

I think Sheriff Bennett knew all along that when we reached the border most of us had intentions of turning back. I wanted to ride back to Buffalo, even as a dismal failure, and share what story I had with my friend, T.V. McCandish. I wanted to sit and nurse my sorrows down at Kennedy's with a glass of buttered rum or fine Scotch whisky—or the claret of which Mr. McCandish thought so highly.

In most respects, my venture had gone well, all things considered. It might have been a touch more memorable had I been able to write of a horrible wound I had received, or of someone who had been killed. But then, I didn't really wish to have to write about either. I would just center my story around the huge, red-headed lawman, Sheriff Van Bennett, and his swarthy, loyal companion, Poco Vidales.

To the surprise of no one, Sheriff Bennett told us he would cross the border. He didn't intend to let any imaginary line keep him from bringing justice to the men who violated his town. And of course that was good for me. It would make a perfect end to my story. And who could tell? He might even yet chance onto the outlaws, and that would make a wonderful addition to my first article, no matter which way the tide might run in the battle that was sure to follow.

Again to no one's surprise, Poco Vidales stayed beside his friend. He was just like a loyal dog. I don't intend any insult against his race by saying that; it is only a figure of speech. If only every man had such a friend as Poco Vidales!

It was mid-morning when we rode back toward Buffalo. The air smelled fresh, because there was no wind. Sometimes when the wind picked up one could smell the stench of the rotted carcasses of cattle that had died the winter before. I hadn't been in Wyoming then, but I had seen the devastation. There were dead cattle everywhere, most of them rotting bones and shards of black flesh. The skins had all been removed by bands of skinners who roamed the country, trying to salvage something from the herds.

I couldn't speak for the others, but as for myself I was in a relaxed mood. I was satisfied with the knowledge that our long and fruitless chase had at last come to an end. I was sorry for the old man and Lucius Bird, who had died, and for the bank that had been robbed. But a man could only be called upon to do so much. I felt our posse had gone far beyond the call of duty.

I was riding in the lead with Anthony Ribervo as we crested a little rise in the road. We stopped at the sight of a band of horsemen. I must admit I am not as quick in discerning individual horses as many in the West. To me, this was just another bunch of cowboys, out on a jolly ride, or perhaps looking for stray cattle. But beside me Deputy Ribervo swore as he reached for and removed his rifle from its leather scabbard.

"There's the gray!" he said in an emphatic tone.

For a moment, I was disconcerted to the point of being useless. But then I heard the others dropping from their horses behind me. Swearing filled the air, and confusion abounded. All around was the sound of the grunting and whinnying horses. I looked at Deputy Ribervo, who stood hesitantly gazing out at the horsemen, holding his rifle. Before I knew what was happening, the deputy knelt and raised the barrel of his rifle to point at them.

The bellow of his rifle stunned me. But I was even more stunned when I saw the horse next to the gray, a buckskin, go down with its rider. Shooting arose all around me as I nearly fell from my saddle.

The Outlaws: Tom McLean

I rode without any thought of the posse and Van Bennett. My thoughts were on John House, the outlaw—now known as Flint Drury. I rode beside him, and our eyes met now and then. I saw only that smiling look in his glance. I wanted to talk to him, to pick his brain. Did he intend to tell Chadwick about me? I was sure he knew who I was. That explained the mysterious humor in his eyes. But so far he didn't seem interested in telling anyone. Maybe he just wanted to see me wiggle for a while.

But almost more than worry, I felt curiosity. I wanted to talk to the man in earnest. I wanted to see if maybe he had the secret I'd been searching for so hard: how to leave the outlaw life behind. He seemed to have accomplished it. I'd always said it wasn't possible, but maybe he could prove me wrong. Then again, with him going up against the Association now, his free-living days might be numbered. Chances were, he'd put himself in the middle of a boiling pot worse than any band of cattlemen who'd ever tracked a lone cattle thief across Oregon.

I had to laugh at myself for my foolish dreams. A man let his mind wander sometimes. But I kept having to remind myself—it was too late to go back. You *couldn't* go back. I was near forty. My birthday was in...hell, in two days. Man that old couldn't start over, go from a outlaw to a lawful citizen. It was plain foolishness! Flint Drury was young enough he still had a chance to build something, if he tried. But not me. Not at forty. I knew cattle, sure. But I didn't have much to show for my years of stealing, and a man couldn't start with nothing. I had a little gold. And the bank money, and the money we'd got from Shilo. (And our shares in that had taken a considerable jump since Tye, Shilo and Tanner were gone.) But was it enough? No. Not for what I wanted. I was too old to work a farm or a ranch. I'd have to hire men, and I couldn't afford it. If I left the outlaw life...well, I could just see myself winding up some toothless old geezer serving beans to a bunch of young punk cowboys who didn't know the meaning of "frontier." I'd sit around the bunkhouse when I wasn't cooking, sucking on a molasses-soaked rag and dreaming of the old days, taking out a set of false teeth and picking at them idly with a jackknife.

Besides, who was to say I'd even get out of the mess I was in now? If Chadwick didn't find out about me and kill me, what about Bennett? He seemed like a stubborn critter, not one to give up. My chances looked mighty slim.

I was still chewing those thoughts over in my head when me and Chadwick topped out of the sagebrush to see a bunch of riders up ahead, two hundred and fifty yards or so away. I saw the glint of metal off one man's blue shirt, and my heart jumped.

I whipped my eyes to Chadwick. He was just looking, sitting that buckskin. I returned my eyes to the riders. The man in the blue shirt had pulled a rifle and jumped out of the saddle. I sat my horse a moment longer, watching that man hesitate. Then he dropped to one knee and pulled up the rifle.

Chadwick swore and started to rein his horse around. Suddenly, the buckskin grunted and hunched up under him. The long crack of a rifle shot followed, and glancing toward the riders I saw smoke drifting away. All of them had come out of their saddles now and drawn rifles, all except one man, who finally seemed to come to his senses. He bailed off, nearly falling.

Several shots followed, the bullets whining around us. Horses jumped, clearing a path for Chadwick's buckskin as it started to fall. The cowboy kicked his feet free and rolled over the side of the horse as it went down. He grabbed out his Winchester, staying clear of the horse's kicking feet.

So as not to put myself without a mount, I turned and spurred back into the sage. Several of the others had climbed down and were firing at the riders, which I figured was Bennett's posse, though I hadn't seen the sheriff. While we were still trying to figure what to do with our horses, Bert Vernon started running around, collecting reins, and I jumped off and gave him mine. Then he led the horses at a run down into a little swale. That took them out of sight of the posse.

Shots whipped back and forth, five or six of them. All of us, both sides, had been too busy trying to keep our horses under control to do much shooting. But Chadwick hadn't. Seeing the hole in his buckskin's ribs, he'd drawn his pistol and smashed the animal's skull with a bullet, stilling its kicking legs. He laid across the dead body with his rifle. The Winchester boomed and kicked back against his shoulder, billowing smoke.

I just happened to look the right way. I saw the man with the blue shirt pitch sideways into the sage. I fired my rifle, not seeing if I did any damage. But the posse was scattering in all directions now, and soon there wasn't much left to shoot at.

Skinny Rail Dobray crouched beside Chadwick. "Did you see the badge? That's the law up there! The man you shot had a badge!"

"Well, he shot first," Chadwick growled. "A man can defend himself." He rolled to the side and looked around the group. They were crouched down in the sage, all except Bert Vernon, who still held the horses. "Give me your glasses," Chadwick ordered Elias Dunn.

The young puncher crawled over and held a pair of field glasses out. Chadwick took them and scanned the road and the sage before us. There was no one in sight close enough to shoot at. "What do we do now?" asked Dunn in a whisper.

"They can't hear you, Coyote," Chadwick pointed out. I guessed they called him that after the coyote dun. "I reckon we run now. I got my doubts they're in the mood to talk."

I spit in the dust. "We can't go back to Sheridan. Prob'ly a posse comin' from there, too."

"Wouldn't think of it," Chadwick said, turning his eyes to me. "What I'm thinkin', they don't know for sure who all of us are. What we do is head over the Bighorns, before they can identify anybody. I have no doubt we can lose them in the mountains. Then we head north on the other side of the range. I have friends up in Montana who'll hide us till this blows over."

He rolled the rest of the way onto his back, leaning against his saddle. He looked around at his followers and at my bunch. Vernon sat his horse and still held the others.

"You anxious to leave, Bert?" he called over.

Vernon shrugged nervously. "Since you mention it…I didn't figure to be an outlaw, Ute."

Chadwick looked away, his face turning sour as he spit tobacco juice into the yellow grass. "Nor did I. The Anti-Association League wasn't made up to be killers. And any of you boys who feel like Bert, you oughtta make it known and not go with us. You feel like you can risk stayin' around this part of the country and not end up draggin' rope down a cottonwood limb, go now. You have my blessings."

Rail Dobray and Elias Dunn looked at each other. Dobray nodded and spoke. "I figger like Bert, Utah. If we start runnin' now, who knows where we'll end up? Like you say, they don't know for sure who we are…you know? I…"

Chadwick held up a hand. "Don't need to explain it, Rail. I gave you my leave."

Red-faced, Dobray turned to look over at Vernon, who still held the horses. "Bert, if yer of a mind to go, me and Coyote will ride along."

Chadwick sat up, cradling his rifle in his lap. He slapped Dunn and Dobray on the shoulders, looking at Vernon. "It was good havin' you boys along for the ride. But you'd best go now, before the shootin' starts up again. Best of luck to you."

Chadwick shook hands with the two young men. He saluted Vernon with a smile. Then he looked in turn at Dale Hepner, Flint Drury, and Frank Colt. "How about it, boys? You stickin', or you want my leave, too? You have it, you know."

Hepner shook his head and narrowed his eyes against the dust in the air. Flint Drury smiled. His eyes swept casually along the group until they rested on JoAnna, where she lay on her belly in the sage. "I'm with you for keeps."

"Me, too," said Colt. "Fact is, I'm a little sick of Wyoming. There's nothin' holdin' me here."

Chadwick nodded with a grateful glint in his eyes. He looked at Dobray and Dunn, and at his nod they rose to a crouch and walked off to the horses. Frank Colt went with them and took the reins of the other horses from Bert Vernon. In a moment, Elias Dunn walked to us, leading his sorrel.

"You keep my horse, Utah," the young man said. His glance fluttered downward, knowing all eyes were on him. "I'll ride with Rail. Just bring the saddle back with you."

Utah Chadwick smiled, and a gold tooth winked back in his upper jaw. "Thoughtful of you, Coyote. *Vaya con Dios*, pard." He raised a hand in farewell. "Go with God, all of you."

When Vernon, Dobray and Dunn were tiny specks in the distance, Chadwick stood up and surveyed the plain. Five of the posse members had gathered together and were standing holding their horses. They were well out of rifle range, but the man in the blue shirt wasn't with them.

Chadwick turned and looked over his new horse, adjusting its stirrups to his shorter legs. All of us climbed aboard together—nine of us now. With one last look toward the posse, we cantered off toward the south, turning west only after we were out of their sight.

We cut straight across country for a peak Chadwick called Black Mountain. It was toward evening when we started into the foothills, if you could call them that. The land just seemed to suddenly rear up before us, taking us out of the dry grass and sagebrush land toward the tree-covered mountains. There was a trail there, and we took it up the steep slope. All around us, bushes grew thick and tangled. I was glad we had the trail.

I had tried to stay near JoAnna, much as I could. I figured she'd feel better with a friend beside her. Rainey, he was busy riding with Holch, making sure he was all right. And Tovías Ruiz rode alone. He hadn't said much since they killed Key Bachelor.

I guess I must have rode up to talk to Chadwick or something, and when I went to drop back beside JoAnna again, I noticed she already had company. John Hou— I mean *Flint Drury* was riding beside her. I watched for a time, and Drury made a comment here and there. He didn't get much response out of her. But finally she gave a laugh, and after that her face seemed a little brighter. I didn't know whether to be jealous or grateful.

We made camp the first flat place we found, which unfortunately was right off the road. But up here, and coming onto night, we figured we were safe for now, long as we weren't still here much after sunup.

We were out of sight from the valley below, so Flint Drury started us a fire. He seemed to be in the habit of that, and nobody argued for the privilege. Up till now it had been JoAnna's job.

Each man cared for his own horse, except for Drury. Chadwick tended to his and Drury's mounts while Drury tried to rustle up something to eat. I was the last man to go to camp, worrying at a clump of pine pitch in Sheriff's mane. The others might have figured I was too fussy. Maybe I was. But I wouldn't have wanted that clump in my hair, and Sheriff and me thought the same. I realized as I worked on the big, sweaty animal, that he was my best friend. Perhaps my only *real* friend. There was Slug, and there was Duke. But human friends changed too easy. Horses didn't.

Yet there had been one friend who had never changed. That was Tye Sandoe.

My mind drifted back to my partner, and a lump rose in my throat. Tye had died too young. Died when a man should be out discovering the world through eyes of innocence—dancing, singing, courting pretty girls. Tye could have done most anything he chose. He was handsome, he was smart, and he could charm the teeth out of a wolf's mouth. He'd charmed everyone but Slug Holch and the jaws of death.

It was me that should've died back there in Sheridan. I wouldn't have been missed much. Maybe not even by Tye, as long as JoAnna was around. I wondered if Tye was at peace, with no more worries. I couldn't tell anymore if there was a God. If there was he sure catered to the rich, not to dirt like me. And not to a near-perfect boy like Sandoe. I've said it before. A man don't cry. But I wished I could cry over Sandoe. It might have washed the ache out of my chest.

I had worked all the pitch out of Sheriff's hair when I looked over at JoAnna's horse, standing at the edge of the group with its head down. I didn't remember her working on him tonight. It didn't surprise me. Her mind was far away. I'd done it for her last night, too.

Patting Sheriff on the rump, I walked to JoAnna's horse and touched its side. The hair there was rough and matted, clumped up with sweat. I shook my head, sorry JoAnna couldn't seem to get herself together. I scratched up a handful of pine needles and started to rough them through the sweaty hair.

The wind had come up, blowing through the ponderosas so they cracked and popped, squeaking together high over our heads. Far out over the plain, I could see the other side of the night, where a rambling ridge met the star-filled sky. I watched it while I worked.

"You don't have to do that."

The sudden voice from behind made my hand drop instinctively for my gun, and my heart jumped to match. Then I realized it was JoAnna, but that didn't lessen the rate of my heart.

"I'll take care of my own horse," the woman said. It was light enough I could see her eyes, but they avoided mine. When she finally did look at me, her glance instantly fell away, and she blew derisively out her nostrils and stomped off into the dark.

That was about all I could take. I hadn't done anything to that woman, and I didn't like being spoken to as if I had. I knew she was hurt, but I didn't know what she figured I'd had to do with it. I meant to find out.

I followed her into the trees along a dim little game trail. It was darker back under the ponderosas, but the path showed pale in the moonlight. Soon, I could hear the trickling of a tiny stream over rocks. I stopped and scanned the trees. The flicker of a match, then the glow of a cigarette tip told me where JoAnna was.

I walked toward her, where she had sat down on a big boulder. As I came up she pulled the cigarette out of her lips and blew smoke. The cigarette stayed at her side for a while, and just when I thought she'd draw on it again, she flung it into the water. After my seemingly long-ago comment to her about smoking cigarettes not suiting her, she didn't like me to see her smoke.

I stopped three feet away, faltering in my resolve to get things straightened out. I didn't know how to begin. JoAnna turned and flashed me a look. I thought she was going to speak, but she turned her eyes back to the stream. Then she turned them completely away, the back of her head to me.

A stiff wind came up and hustled down inside the neck of my shirt and down my back, sending a shiver along my spine. I wondered if the wind was calling up another cloud bank, and if this time it would let down some of its rain.

JoAnna still faced the other way, and I stood there feeling like a fool. What could a man like me say to a woman like her? I didn't know what she was thinking, and she wasn't about to tell me.

Over the moaning of the wind and the rustle of the water, I heard her draw a sudden, sobbing breath. My heart seized up inside me.

Chapter Twenty-Four
I'd Marry You

I stood there for what seemed forever. I knew JoAnna was crying. I'd heard her sob again, though she tried her best to hide it and wouldn't look at me. I wished I hadn't followed her. I should have stayed in camp with the men. I knew how to handle them. But not her. Men weren't ever meant to figure out a woman, just to be baffled by them till they went daft.

Something drew me to JoAnna against my will. Even as I tried to hold them back, my feet carried me forward. I stopped behind her, and my trembling arms went around in front of her and closed, my fingers clasping together. Her reaction was instant. Tearing my arms away from her, she almost fell away from the boulder in standing up. She whirled on me with such suddenness I thought she was going to curse me. Or attack me. I couldn't see her face well enough to know what to expect.

When she came at me, I flinched. But I held my ground. In the next moment, her arms were around me, and she squeezed so hard it put me short of breath. I encircled her with my arms, and the tears came from her like the stream at her back. She cried, not softly, not a hidden sound, but in loud, wrenching sobs. In a moment I felt her tears soak through my shirt. I patted her back and held her, listening to her moans fill the dark woods.

She stopped crying once. In fact, she stopped three or four times. But each time it started up again, just as mournful as before. I didn't let her go. I couldn't. She held on too tight, her palms flat and warm against my back. I had felt the heat of her body against mine increase as she cried. She grew warmer and warmer. Even while the shoulder of my shirt got wetter, the cold of the mountains seemed far away.

The crying didn't stop suddenly. It went away slow, with great, heaving sobs that shook both of us. She kept her hands at my back, her head nestled into the side of my neck. She held me like she'd never let go.

I'd never had to comfort someone that completely, not even JoAnna herself back that night at the Flying B. But even while I realized her pain, I felt the warmest feeling I'd ever had creep up in my chest and nest there. For the first time since the last of my family died, I meant something to someone—really meant something. At least I felt that way right then. Maybe I was just a convenience, but I didn't think of that till later. Right then I felt like a god.

Finally, I dropped one hand and tugged a handkerchief out of my vest. "Here, JoAnna. Use this."

She pulled herself away long enough to blow her nose. Then she leaned into me again, and a long, shaking sigh escaped her, warm on my shoulder. I still had no words to say, so I just waited, my chest tight with feelings.

"I heard that Indian girl scream," JoAnna said quietly. I almost didn't hear her. But suddenly the story gushed forth from her, spoken half into my shirt as she held onto me. I guessed she didn't want me to look at her while she rid herself of what I could only figure was guilt.

She had gone to sleep in Shilo's tent, because she could hear him with Yellow Grass inside our tent. She had felt sick listening to them. She had felt dirty. But she had nowhere else to go. Then, sometime after she went to sleep, she heard angry voices, one of them snarling like an animal. She rolled out of her bedding and left the tent only moments before she heard the scream.

When she reached the tent, Shilo was stumbling out of it, his movements ungainly from drinking. He tried to keep her out of the tent. She ducked around him and opened the flaps to see in the light of the single, dim lantern, the two dead bodies. JoAnna had never seen anyone murdered that way before. The shock of it had made her speechless only for a moment, and when she started to cry out Jason Shilo struck her in the face with his fist. She woke up on the back of Tye's horse, moving down the mountains in the dark.

JoAnna had lied to me before. I couldn't forget that. Yet the emotion she showed as she told me that story let me know it was the truth. She wasn't that good of an actress. I ached for JoAnna, for what she had seen.

"Why didn't you come to me?" she asked. Her voice was quiet, almost a whisper, matching the rustle of water. When I didn't answer, she looked up at me. Thanks to the same stars and the moon slab that made bear-tooth silhouettes of the trees, we could dimly see each other's eyes. I didn't know for sure if that was good.

"Last night. Or in Sheridan. Why? Why didn't you come to me?

I needed you."

My throat was stiff with sudden pain. "I didn't know. I didn't know what to say."

She lowered her head into me again. "You didn't have to say anything. I needed you. I needed you to hold me."

I couldn't tell her why I really hadn't come to her. I couldn't tell her she scared me. I was an old man. She was just a kid. She stirred me, and it scared me to death.

"We better go back," I said suddenly. "They'll wonder where we went."

Nodding wordlessly, JoAnna stepped away. She started to turn, but then she stopped, still facing me. Hesitantly, watching my eyes for a reaction, she reached out and took my hand. My fingers closed over hers, and I smiled.

We walked back along the creek, silent because our sounds were hidden by the chattering wind. My heart pounded at me, telling me to take JoAnna right here. I knew she'd let me. I knew she'd never resist. But I couldn't. All she'd ever been to men was something to use. I couldn't add my name to the list.

When we got to the point where the stream veered away from the game trail, JoAnna stopped me. I'd felt her hand grow moist as we walked. Moist and even warmer than before. I turned to her, and she took my other hand, holding both of them between us. She tried to meet my eyes, and at last took a deep breath and forced her gaze to mine.

"I can't go back there without saying something. I...I..." She looked suddenly down, and I heard her swallow. "Your friendship means a lot to me." She forced the words out quickly, her eyes flickering up to mine, then away.

"I feel the same, girl. But...is that what you wanted to say?"

She hesitated. "Tom..." My name was a whisper, and it seemed to hang in the air for a long time between us. "Tom, I...I'll never lie to you again."

Her eyes held mine now, and hers, soft with tears, pleaded with me to believe her. I guessed Shilo had told her about my talk with him, and how I'd found out the truth about her father. My feelings about that worried her.

"Don't fret about it. It's okay."

"No! No, it's not okay. Will you ever trust me again? After what I told you about my father?"

"I understand."

"Then please believe me. *Please.* Tom...I...Damnit, that's not what I wanted to say. I love you! I want to stay with you." She blurted the last sentence out, as if it would cover her other words—maybe draw my attention away from them.

I just stood in silence, feeling foolish. I couldn't remember that I'd ever uttered those three words together, and if anyone had ever said them to me it had been years ago. Did people really say that out loud, anyway? Not me. Not me. But…I *did*. I did love her. Of course she'd feel it. I didn't have to say it out loud.

"Let's go away," she said suddenly. She'd waited long enough to know I wasn't going to say those words back to her. "You can have me tonight, Tom. Please."

A waft of bacon smoke reached us on the wind, adding to the flutter in my stomach—two kinds of hunger running into each other.

Before I knew what I was doing, I pulled JoAnna's body tight against mine. Our lips met, and hers were as hot as her hands. She reached up behind me and put a hand to the back of my head, crushing my lips against hers. I didn't fight her, either. I'd never kissed a girl I thought I might…have feelings for. Not until now. It had always been a game, a release. Nothing more. Kissing a girl I…a girl I *loved* was a far different thing. It wrenched my heart and turned it upside down.

When I pulled away from her, it took all the strength I had. "We better think about this," I said. It was hard to speak past my breathing. "We better think, JoAnna."

The crackle of flame on pine knots greeted us as we neared the camp. Feeling sheepish, I walked in next to JoAnna. Duke and Slug were already rolled in their bedding, as well as Dale Hepner. Utah Chadwick was out of sight, and Frank Colt was cleaning his rifle, staring blankly into the dark. Flint Drury was bent over a frying pan, and his eyes flickered up at us. A broad smile matched the look in his eyes.

"Howdy do, folks? You didn't come when I called, but we saved you some bacon and beans. There ain't much, but it's fare, anyway. Eat it slow. That's the trick to makin' your belly think it's a fiesta."

He looked back and forth between JoAnna and me. The smile sort of faded when he looked at her eyes, and I wondered if he could see she'd been crying. I hoped so. I didn't want him already sure he knew what we were up to. I didn't want anybody thinking I'd use that girl.

After we ate our meager supper, me and JoAnna sat down Injun-style by the fire. She wouldn't meet my eyes, and I didn't dare look at her. I could still feel my heart battering me. I didn't want her to see my feelings in my eyes.

"McLe— " My eyes jumped up at the sound of Drury's voice. He didn't finish my name. Our eyes held for a long moment, both of us wondering what difference his knowing my real name would make. Then he said, "I'd like to talk to you a minute."

I looked at him, knowing without a doubt now that he knew who I was. I stood up, leaving JoAnna by the fire, and walked out of camp with him.

Out in the darkness, he looked about for a minute—searching for Chadwick, I assumed, since he wasn't in camp. Then he met my gaze. "I take it there's an understanding between you and the woman."

I chuckled. "We understand each other some," I replied. "But I don't think that's why you called me out here. Is it?"

"No. I just want to know your intentions. I remember you, McLean. From Oregon."

"So where does it get us?" I asked. "Should I call you John—House?"

"You could, but John House was a made-up name. Flint Drury was the one I got from my folks. James Flint Drury."

I was surprised to learn that. Flint just hadn't struck me as a name someone would plant on a little baby.

"Whatever yer name was, you used to be a outlaw, too."

"It's far behind me, McLean. I hope the life's behind you, too. Chadwick would be sad to know he'd helped out an outlaw."

The Posse: Poco Vidales

I stayed with the sheriff because he needed me. And when I and my family needed him, always he was there. Giving us food, shelter if we needed it. He was a good man. So even though the others, they left him, I stayed. The sheriff, he needed me.

When we come back from Montana, because we had not seen the bandits, we found the others waiting for a wagon from a ranch that was near. They had fought the bandits, and Antonio, he was shot. When the wagon arrived, we said adios to the others, and they took the Deputy Ribervo back to Sheridan. The deputy, he was hurt, but they thought he could be made better. So they went. And me and the sheriff, we went too—to the Bighorn Mountains.

We did not take the road. The men who had shoot the deputy, they had gone away from the road, too, gone toward Black Mountain. I followed them, for the feet of nine horses, they are easy to see in the dry dust. Before we arrived at the low hills, a cloud of heavy dust appeared to the north. This dust, it was made by many caballos, or by cattle, maybe. Hopefully not *rustlers* and cattle. I hoped not to have to shoot again against someone. The shooting, it was getting too old.

The sheriff, he decided to wait. We watched until we could see many riders in dark coats. The dust flew away from them, because the wind, it blew hard. Four men left the others and rode to us. The dust from their caballos' hoofs blew sideways.

One man with mean-looking eyes and the nose of an eagle held up his gloved right hand and made the others to stop. He had bushy eyebrows and eyes the color of a lake of water in the early morning. I could see he was the leader.

"Good afternoon, gentlemen." The leader made a lazy salute with his glove. "I'm Captain Thomas Gregory, out of Fort Custer. This is Sergeant Cornir." He did not tell us who the other two were.

"Sheriff Bennett, out of Buffalo." My big friend leaned forward and rested his hands on his saddle horn. "You boys're a long ways from home. Lost?"

The captain, he waved like he was swatting at a fly. He frowned with his lips and cleared his throat with a loud sound, then spit into the dirt by my caballo. "Have you chanced to run across any Indians in your travels, Sheriff? This would be a traveling family group. Dogs, tepees—the whole works. Crows."

"Haven't seen any," the sheriff said.

The captain rubbed at his eyes. "Well, Sheriff, I feel certain they've gone into the Bighorns. It's not the first time. Is that where you're headed? It appears so."

"It is," the sheriff said. "We're on the trail of some killers ourselves."

"Then if it's not too much inconvenience," the Captain Gregory said, "we'll just accompany you into the mountains. I'm not very familiar with this country, and I have no patience for riding all the way to Fort McKinney to solicit aid."

"It's a free country," the sheriff said. "But I doubt your redskins are with the ones I'm searchin' for."

After the sheriff said it would be okay for the soldiers to ride with us, the captain, he went back and divided them up in four bunches. Each bunch, it had only seven or eight men in it—eight in the bunch of the captain. The group of the captain, they stayed with the sheriff and me. The other groups, they separated and went toward different places in the mountains. I knew how the Indians on the reservations lived. I am Mexican, and my people and the Indians have always fought, but I felt a pity for them. I hoped they would get the meat they must be hunting for. I hoped for them to find it before these soldiers found them.

The Outlaws: Tom McLean

We rode out before dawn, our coats drawn about us against the cold wind that kicked up the mountain ridges. We stopped frequently, having to rest the horses because of the steep incline. Up and up we went, riding into the heart of the mountains. Scattered around were outcroppings of deep red stone, pushing right out of the yellow grassland. I imagined it would be a beautiful sight in days when the grass was green, the way it should be in early summer.

Yucca in full white bloom surrounded us, along with the other flowers JoAnna had made me grow so fond of—the blue lupine; white yarrow; red Indian paintbrush; yellow sunflowers; blue penstemon; lavender harebells. It was a beautiful country. I hoped it would have rain soon. It'd be nice to come back and see it in more peaceful times.

Dark green shocks of ponderosa dotted the foothills. The mountains were a gray wall on the other side of them, rising up out of the shadows of canyons. To our left, the Tongue ran in its course, a canyon that swiftly deepened as we climbed until it must have been two thousand feet below us, smothered by green, fir-spired slopes.

Chadwick made us take a rest after the horses had started to lather, and he led us to the edge of the canyon. He pointed out across it at a huge slab of rock that dropped long and steep down the head of the canyon. The rest of the canyon was covered completely in heavy timber. Only here the trees couldn't grow. "That's the Buffalo Tongue. The Crows call it *La-zee-ka,*" Chadwick offered. "The Tongue River comes out below it."

"That's a bunch of rock," I put in.

Chadwick nodded. "Must be more than fifteen hundred feet of solid limestone. I figure there's black bear down there ain't ever seen a man."

We rode on up the mountainside, our horses breathing heavily. The beauty of the place was overwhelming, taking my mind away for a moment from the fact that we were hunted men. We climbed and stared, unable to believe the beauty of the world up here. And as we climbed, the grass greened up, and there was more of it. It was like we'd come into a sort of paradise.

After noon we passed a place of jumbled, column-shaped rocks called the Fallen City. Broken canyons lay in every direction, along with the wildflowers that at times were so thick they seemed the only growing thing. Even JoAnna, with her knowledge gained from Shilo, was surprised by the variety of it all. Some meadows were so thick with lupine they appeared to be small lakes, or pieces of sky fallen down to land on earth.

We made early camp that evening. The beauty of the country had worn us all out, I think. Of course, the five thousand foot climb probably had a little to do with it.

We camped beside a little lake deep in the timber. We set our horses out to graze on the first grass we'd seen in days that looked like June grass. Slug Holch was healing up from his wounds enough to want to be sociable. Me and Duke set up fishing poles, so's the three of us could fish along the shore. JoAnna sat on a rock, watching us, laughing like a little girl when Duke slipped and fell in up to his waist.

Finally, Duke and Slug returned to camp. Me and JoAnna had the lake to ourselves, and all we could do was stare at it. Little clouds floated in it, yellow and pink and orange as the light went down. The sunlight had long since gone away from us, but across the lake the trees glowed golden green in the light that still crowned them. I reveled in the cool scent of the fir, the water and grass, the feeling of being alone again with JoAnna.

We were sitting there like that, all quiet, when JoAnna touched my arm. I looked at her, and she held out a handful of flowers. They were all the same, tiny blue and white, delicate looking things. I was surprised she'd picked only these out of all the rest.

"Forget-me-nots," she volunteered.

Before I could reply, I spotted movement in the trees. Shushing the woman, I looked that way. Soon, we saw a doe mule deer and two spotted fawns come down to the water's edge for a drink. After they'd gone, JoAnna turned and smiled at me.

"They're beautiful, aren't they?"

"Everything here is," I said, holding up the forget-me-nots. "Especially you." Even as I said it, I felt like a fool kid in school. But it was one of those things that just slips out with no control. By the look in JoAnna's eyes, I guess she didn't think it was so silly. She blushed and looked away.

After a minute, she stood up and held her hand down to me. I used her help to stand, then fell in step beside her as she walked along the lake shore. The sunlight didn't paint the tops of the trees anymore, and it was growing cold down here by the water. JoAnna hugged her arms tight to her body and shivered. The strange thought struck me that Tye would have put an arm around her, if he'd been here in my place.

I got kind of sad, thinking of Tyrone Sandoe. JoAnna seemed to sense the change in me. She unfolded her arms and slipped a hand into the crook of my elbow. She pulled herself close, placing the other hand over the first.

I faltered in my step. I started to look at her but looked away. She only drew herself closer. My heart was hammering against my chest, and I think it had found a weak spot. It seemed awful close to the surface.

After a hundred yards or so, JoAnna just stopped, and I stopped with her. We stared out over the lake, letting the twilight fold quietly over us. A fish surfaced, making a rippling splash that seemed much louder than natural in the gathering darkness.

JoAnna reached down and took my hand. Instinctively, I started to pull away, but I stopped. "Do you mind when I touch you?" she asked.

"Of course not." I didn't dare tell her just how much I *didn't* mind. How peaceful and safe I felt being touched by a woman like her—even though she was an outlaw. The only women I'd touched or had touch me had been soiled doves, women of the night, dance hall girls. Women with false, iron hearts, carved smiles and deep, yawning purses.

"I asked because you seem afraid when I do it," JoAnna said. "Like you think I'll hurt you." I chuckled, having no reply. "Are you?" she said. "Are you afraid? Do I scare you?"

I started to say no, but I couldn't lie to her now. "In a way, you do."

"Why?"

I chuckled again, hoping it would set me at ease. It failed miserably. "Because...I can't have you."

JoAnna laughed uncomfortably, her eyes flickering away. "What are you talkin' about?"

"I'm not free. I got prison walls around me. Besides, I could be your daddy."

"My daddy!" she said with another laugh. "Just how old are you?"

"Turnin' forty."

JoAnna studied my face for several moments, as if to judge whether I was lying. She finally asked, "And what would you do if you were younger?"

"I'd marry you."

Chapter Twenty-Five
Brought Down

JoAnna just stared at me. I felt my face reddening, and the heat built up inside my shirt. I had never spoken of marriage to anyone before, at least not in a sober state of mind. And certainly never meaning it.

I hadn't intended to say the words at all. I wanted to hide my true feelings. The truth could only hurt us, before everything was done. Tears came into JoAnna's eyes, and she walked off alone, several yards from the lake. I hesitated, then followed, unsure what to do.

The forest had grown black. The tops of spired firs knifed into the star glow of the sky. JoAnna's long dark hair fell down over her shoulders to meld with the cloth of her shirt. I stopped a ways behind her, waiting. She was staring away from me, and when her shoulders shook, I knew she was crying again.

Calling up my courage, I went to her and touched her shoulder. She turned, and I drew her into me, holding her against my chest. Her cries were soft, not sobbing like the night before. The only way I knew she was crying was because of the little shudders that went through her body, and the tears that touched my neck.

Finally, she raised her face to me, and I let her take a half-step back, still in my arms. "Why did you do this to me?"

"Do what?"

She gave a sad shake of her head, wiping her eyes one at a time with her finger. She dabbed unlady-like at her nose with her shirt sleeve.

When I saw she couldn't answer me, or wasn't going to, I cleared my throat. I had to call a stop to whatever was developing between the girl and me. It couldn't go on. It would lead nowhere good. "JoAnna, I'm not sure what you're thinkin', but…you don't want me. You need someone like Flint Drury, a younger man—a law-abiding sort. You need a decent life. And it's too late for me to turn back. "

"You know that's a lie!" Her tone was near anger. "If you don't turn back it's because you don't want to."

"Listen to me," I said. "You want a father, or a husband?"

"I'm twenty-four years old," she replied. "And I don't care how old you are. I've been around long enough to seem a lot older than my age."

"Yeah, so have I. Seems like I'm sixty. And you *should* care about my age. JoAnna...I don't wanna hurt you. But I have a bad feeling. I feel like I'm gonna die out here." I hadn't voiced that thought to anyone, but it had been strong in my mind for days. With so much death around me, it was hard not to expect mine to be next.

"You don't have to die! Not out here. Not now!" She pulled away from me angrily, throwing my arms to the sides to be free of their restraint.

I looked away, letting my frustration run its course. Then I looked back and tried to take her hand, but she jerked away. "What would I be if I wasn't a outlaw, girl? Swamper in some saloon? Come on! I'm too old to work that way."

"You have money," she said. "If you wanted, you could start up some business. Tyrone told me about your money. About what the two of you did in Buffalo. And as far as I care, you can go back and give the money up. It doesn't matter. Don't you see? We...we could go somewhere together. You could..." She paused and stared up at me. "Don't you want to be with me?" she asked. Her voice had become sort of distant. She sounded of a sudden like a lonely little girl.

I guess what shook me most was her suggesting I give back the money. I thought nothing of the fact Tye had broken our trust and told her about it. That didn't matter anymore. But a woman was telling me to give back all that money, and she'd still stay with me? I wanted to believe her, but women—*people*—just didn't think that way. Did they?

"JoAnna..." The words I wanted to say, about how I wanted to believe her, and how I—how I loved her, died there in the dark. I was left feeling empty and very alone. "Let's go back to camp. I don't want 'em to think—" I stopped, not needing or wanting to go on.

We turned and walked, stepping careful in the grass and broken branches along the shore. We didn't touch. We only walked in step. My chest was full of pain. I wanted to talk more, I wanted to tell her how I felt. I wanted to tell her about the men I'd killed, and how I'd somehow have to pay to ever have peace. But what way was there to pay? What way but to die? That was the only peace I could expect.

In camp, Flint Drury was the only man up. He didn't seem to ever sleep. He sat by the fire, stirring it slowly. He looked up as we came in, and his glance went straight to JoAnna. His eyes almost always smiled, but now a smile turned up the corners of his mouth, too.

I counted the bedrolls, finding Drury's empty, and another one still rolled up. "Who's missin'?" I asked.

"Holch."

I was surprised Slug was moving around so much after such a long day, and even more so when Drury told me my friend had gone out to stand watch. When JoAnna walked off to see to her horse, I took my rifle and went to find Slug. I found him leaning against a big fir tree, his rump nested down in heavy duff.

"Mind if I sit with you?"

Slug shrugged. "It's a free forest." There was humor in his tone.

There was no tree nearby, so I just sat down Injun style. Slug spit to the side, and even in the shadows I could see him looking at me. "You sound tired."

"I ain't slept much."

He chuckled, wiping at his mouth with the back of his hand. "What's the matter? Girl got under your skin?"

I peered at him closer, wishing I could see his expression. But I could tell by his voice it was a friendly one. "She's a nice girl, Slug. And perty, to boot."

"Pertiest one I ever had. No arguin' that," he replied. "Makes you feel young again, don't she?"

"No. She makes me feel like Methuselah."

"Then you oughtta relax. She's a lotta woman, you let her be."

"Slug…what's the deal with you and her?" I asked suddenly. "Did I step on your toes? I didn't mean to."

He swore good-naturedly and spit again. "We were—*partners,* for a while." I caught a tone of wistfulness in his voice. "That's all. She's too young for me. And she wanted somethin' permanent, which I didn't. Tom, I'm near thirty-six years old! What would I do with a filly like that?"

I nodded thoughtfully. He wasn't telling me everything. Maybe he wasn't telling me *any*thing. But what he was saying seemed to make him feel better. At least it came across that way. And he was a lucky man to get shut of her. That much I knew.

What hurt most was his comment about age. Here he was saying thirty-six was too old for the woman, and I was near forty.

"Tom, you're perty quiet."

"Uh-huh. Not much to say."

"You're took with that woman," he said. "More than I was, even. And it's plain she's took with you. A man with one false eye and a patch over the other could see it."

I chuckled. "So what about you?"

"I never had plans for her," he said brusquely, looking away to spit. "Shilo had her tied up too tight."

"Shilo's gone."

"Yeah. And so's anything we had before. It's you she wants, Tom. If you're man enough. She's been through some rough times with Shilo and her pa. I know I'm not man enough to handle it. She's all yours, if that's what you're fishin' for."

We rode easy the next day. I'd only slept a couple hours or so, and I didn't have any urge to move fast. Besides, Slug was still a little under the weather. He tried to act tough, but the fight with Burlen had took its toll, and he'd never took time to get over it.

I didn't worry much about a posse. We were in the high country. There were lots of directions we could have traveled. I just didn't believe they had a tracker that could trail us everywhere we'd been. Anyway, they wouldn't be moving much faster than we were. I hoped.

We rode in high, grassy meadows full of wildflowers all day. Me and JoAnna didn't talk much. We didn't even look at each other much. But every time I looked down and happened to see a sprinkling of forget-me-nots, her face came rushing back to my mind—as if it wasn't already there.

We were climbing, climbing endlessly. Toward the rugged, snow-frosted ramparts of the Bighorns. Chadwick told us we'd cross over Granite Pass before long—more than eight thousand feet above sea level. No wonder we were sucking breath like we were, as were our horses beneath us. Sheriff was about done in. I was riding Jason Shilo's chestnut horse, giving Sheriff a much-needed rest. The chestnut wouldn't have the speed Sheriff had, I knew. But he had it where it counted when it came to climbing hills.

Mountain ridges buried in snow flanked us on either side when at last we rode through Granite Pass. It was a beautiful country, but we hardly saw it. I couldn't imagine appreciating beauty, not at least until we made Montana. I was tired of the running, tired of wondering if someone would catch up.

We made an early camp. There wasn't one of us who didn't feel beat by the climb. We rode off the main trail, back far in the timber, out of sight of anyone who might happen by. We were unloading our gear, scattering it around a central spot in the trees, the way we always did. I must have been more tired than I thought. My mind must have been weak. I took Shilo's saddlebags and was carrying them to my bedding. I stumbled on a pile of stones. I dropped the saddlebags, and one flopped open. A handful of greenbacks slipped out and landed in the stunted grass.

Quickly, I looked up, right into the eyes of Utah Chadwick. It was obvious he'd seen the money too. "What's that?" he asked.

"Uh, Shilo's travelin' money, I guess." I had a time meeting Chadwick's gaze. "Looks like he traveled well." I glanced around at the others, and every set of eyes was on me.

As casual as I could, I stooped down and stuffed the bills back into the saddlebag, trying to keep what was inside from showing. There was a lot more where that had come from. As I was straightening back up, I saw a glistening bit of gold where the cash had been. Nonchalantly, I picked that up, too. It was an earring, a crude-made one. It was gold, with some kind of bluish-gray, see-through rock mounted in its center. I tucked it into my vest pocket.

I looked up and caught Chadwick and his cronies exchanging glances. No one spoke for several minutes. We all just kind of went back to unloading our gear, trying to act like nothing had happened.

I'd already loosened the chestnut's saddle. But when I returned to him to pull it off, Chadwick stepped up behind me and spoke. "Hey, Tom. What say you and me take a ride ahead for a few miles? Scout things out?"

I was dead tired, ready to drop where I stood. But something in Chadwick's eyes wouldn't let me. It seemed like I was back with Shilo again. "All right," I replied. "A few miles. Then I'll be ready to sleep for ten hours."

We rode side by side. The country was more than open enough for it. And that was good. There was something about the way Utah Chadwick was acting that warned me against letting him ride behind me. And I guess he felt the same.

We'd rode a mile or more when I sensed the drover watching me. I turned and caught his stare. His eyes fluttered, but he didn't look away. "You weren't surprised by that money, Tom. You were surprised it rolled out, but you knew it was there."

"What're you tryin' to say?"

"I want to know what you have to say, that's what. You're name isn't Tom, is it? And you're no cowboy. What about the money? Where'd it come from?"

"Full of questions all of a sudden," I said uneasily. "I can't answer 'em all. It was Shilo's money."

That was all I had time to say. Before either of us could make another sound, or make any kind of move, I heard the rushing of feet around us. And then hands were wrenching me from my horse.

The Posse: Van Bennett

One of Colonel Gregory's soldiers fell and broke a leg. That bunch couldn't ride the way soldiers were supposed to. Held us up, even in their best of shape. But me and Poco weren't waiting. I'd had enough of the constant jabbering of those soldiers, most of them no more than kids. Drove a man half insane listening to them.

Me and Poco set off alone. As for myself, I'd have turned around by then, if not for him. That bunch of grass and rock and pine needles underfoot meant nothing to me. But Poco saw little signs in it. They kept him riding on.

I had nothing in my head but seeing that outlaw dead—that outlaw, McLean, I seemed to remember him calling himself back in Buffalo. I wanted McLean dead. Dead and rotting like he'd left plenty others. Didn't deserve a chance at jail, even. I didn't intend to give him one.

We were riding easy. I didn't think Poco was paying much attention to the trail anymore. There was only one way it could go. We were riding through Granite Pass. It wasn't like a man could turn off. And we weren't looking to run onto the outlaws just yet. It was still full sunlight; they wouldn't stop for camp till dark.

I didn't know where they came from. Don't figure Poco did, either. Just all of a sudden I was riding and then I wasn't. I was on the ground, and hands were holding me down, yelling. I didn't understand the words. I didn't care. I only cared about Poco Vidales, my little amigo.

Chapter Twenty-Six
Chadwick Learns the Truth

The Outlaws: Tom McLean

Snarling like a madman, I struggled against the hands that pinioned me. But it took only seconds to see I had no chance of escape. Crouched all around me were Injuns—Crows, I assumed. They dressed the same, kept the same hair style as the ones of Toy's village.

Grunting, three of them heaved me to my feet, and one struck me hard across the cheek with a short, heavy stick. The pain was so bad I cringed and slammed my eyes shut. But the pain didn't go just yet. Instead, it was replaced when one of them kicked me in the stomach.

I heard the almost inaudible growl of pain as Chadwick got some of the same treatment. Shaking my head, I glanced over at him. With his hat gone, thinning yellow hair spilled down over a forehead about as white as Noah's beard. A thin trickle of blood trailed down from one corner of his mouth. Even as I looked, he took another kick to the stomach. Then one of the Crows spoke, and the beating ceased abruptly.

Looking at the speaker, I saw a man of medium height and build, about Chadwick's size. His chest was broad and flat and his legs were badly bowed from years on horseback. His hair swept back in a towering pompadour decorated with two feathers, and black eyes glittered as they clicked back and forth between me and Chadwick.

That one was obviously their leader. He spoke in the Crow tongue and motioned the others into action. Before I knew it, me and Chadwick were loaded back on our horses. The Injuns had our pistols in their belts, and one of them was packing my Marlin.

After we'd ridden for what seemed four or five miles, deep into timber, I saw a movement far ahead. The Crows saw it, too, and after a quick exchange one of them took off at a lope in that direction. This one had no saddle, yet his horsemanship was incredible.

He rode with the supreme confidence of one who had grown up on a horse, dodging wildly through the trees yet staying on.

After ten minutes, the brave who had gone returned with another one at his side. The newcomer looked us over and spit at my horse's feet. We had all stopped, and he halted his pinto in front of the man I had assumed was their leader. They exchanged words briefly, and I saw a look of satisfaction, then hatred, cross the leader's face. He looked in the direction the newcomer had ridden from, then looked at me and Chadwick. With a nod at the newcomer, who turned his pinto, we continued on.

In less than a mile, I smelled the powerful scent of woodsmoke. Soon, the trees began to thin, and we came out into a small green clearing scattered with tepees. A stream ran down the clearing's middle, rattling over stones. Glancing about, I instantly recognized one of the horses from Toy's camp, and my heart took a little hope. Was Toy here? There were fresh elk hides staked around to be worked, but at the moment everyone in camp was gathered around a small band of horses. By their hackamores and a saddle or two, I assumed another bunch of warriors had ridden in just before us.

Me and Chadwick were led to the other horses, and when the village discovered us sitting there a chatter arose. Many of them started pointing at me, talking all excited. I kept looking for Toy, hoping he might come to our rescue. He was nowhere to be seen. After some of the villagers had talked to the leader for a time, he rode his horse over in front of us.

For a long moment, the Injun only stared, calculating. Finally, he stepped off his horse and motioned for us to climb down, too. We had never been tied, so we complied with ease. He ordered our horses led away, and now he stood before us, surrounded by a group of warriors and some villagers I recognized..

"Me Moon-Wolf. You name Tom?"

"Yes, my name is Tom," I replied slowly, so he'd be sure to understand. "I am a friend."

Moon-Wolf gave a growl of derision. "You, friend? You come, kill my woman. You kill my—my *daugh*-ter. You also die."

I shook my head nervously, glancing around for Toy. Suddenly, he appeared from the crowd, stepping forward. His eyes were wide as he glanced from me to Moon-Wolf. It took only a moment for him to grasp the situation, and he spoke quickly to Moon-Wolf, then turned his eyes on me. After several seconds studying the boy's words, Moon-Wolf looked again at me.

"This name Toy. You know. Him son. Him say you help our People.

You hunt, kill elk."

"Yes," I readily agreed. His English, though broken, was easy to understand. "I helped your people kill elk to eat. I told you. I am a friend."

Moon-Wolf turned again to say something to the boy. Speaking English made him seem somehow slow-witted. In his own tongue his words came straight and clear.

Toy looked at me and Chadwick. "My father says he wants..." He paused, unable to think of a word. "You must show him where is the man who killed my mother and my sister."

My glance flickered to Moon-Wolf. "His name was Shilo. He is dead. I took his life."

Moon-Wolf gave a growl, waving his hand with the same gesture you would use to tell someone to leave. "You show me. Show me man dead."

I looked beseechingly at Toy, then back at his father. "I can't show you. The man is in the village called Sheridan. Far away."

"Sher-i-dan?" he repeated slowly. "Sher-i-dan. Maybe you lie."

"I'm not lyin'," I said. I looked at Toy again. "Help us. You know I went after Shilo."

I could see the boy wanted to help, but there was nothing he could say. Suddenly, Moon-Wolf barked orders and motioned to some of his braves. Me and Chadwick were quickly led away toward some trees at the edge of camp. I could hear a large group following behind us.

There was also a bunch of people before us, and as they parted my eyes fell on a sight I never thought to see again. Tied with his back to a tree, his hair disheveled and his face resigned, was Sheriff Van Bennett. Backed up to the same tree, almost seeming of no consequence next to his partner, was the little Mexican from the saloon fight. Poco, I remembered him called.

I could never forget that look of hatred I saw in Bennett's eyes. Not if I lived past the day, which I didn't figure I would. The giant of a lawman stared at me from under those shaggy brows, and his beard seemed to twitch, to twitch with the words of hatred his lips must be forming for me. His beard hadn't been combed recent, and had grew down so's a man couldn't even see his mouth. I didn't think Bennett would have minded dying that day, not if they allowed him to see me dead first.

Without any undue ceremony, Moon-Wolf had his warriors tie me and Chadwick next to the others, backed up to a tree of our own. It was my bad fortune to be left facing Bennett. I couldn't meet his eyes for more than spurts. His fury was too intense. He stared at me, and I was sure he could break his ropes any moment he chose and come to choke me to death or tear my chest open with his bare hands. Yet he didn't move. His towering bulk remained perfectly still, unmoving. Perhaps that was the worst threat of all.

I didn't have long to be stared at by the big lawman. As soon as the warriors walked off, the village children took to pelting us with stones and branches and pine cones. We bowed our heads and tried to dodge the worst of it. After our faces were scuffed up, and Bennett's was bleeding, the children finally grew bored of their game and drifted away.

Utah Chadwick hadn't spoken in all this time, and suddenly I heard his voice from behind me. "What are you doing up here, Sheriff?"

Bennett had returned his glaring eyes to rest on me. He looked even more terrible now, with the ooze of dark red down one cheek where a rock had cut him. It almost seemed he wouldn't be able to speak, he was so furious, but slowly he loosed his tongue. He eyed me the whole time.

"What am *I* doin' here? I'm after the men that robbed First National Bank. You're ridin' with 'em. I thought you knew better, Utah. You finally crossed the line."

Hearing those words leave the big man's mouth made me almost sick in the pit of my stomach. They clinched one thing: I was friendless here now. If Chadwick had thought himself an ally, he no longer would. A lot of that money belonged to the small ranchers he'd sworn to protect. And that wasn't the worst of it. That was still to come.

"There's another thing, Utah. I don't think you could have heard. I hate you to hear it this way, but your father got killed."

"What?" It was the most emotion I'd yet heard in Chadwick's voice. "My father got killed? What are you talkin' about?" I felt him struggle against the rope, a useless attempt to free himself. But although it was useless, it was effective at feeling like it tore the skin right off my ribs.

"Your daddy's dead," Bennett said flatly. "He got shot on the Tongue River crossing by a bunch of rustlers." His deadly gaze was on me while he spoke.

The entire scene seemed to go quiet. All I could feel or hear or smell was the rage on the other side of that tree. I felt like part of a sandwich, a piece of meat trapped between two slices of putrid dark rye bread (which all dark rye bread is) whose only desire was to smother out my life. Now I'd just as well die at the hands of the Crows. Might be less painful.

There was a commotion in camp, and after a time a group of warriors came toward the trees where we were tied. They stopped before us, and I saw Toy in their midst. Moon-Wolf stood beside him.

"These men, they not with you?" Moon-Wolf asked, flicking his fingers back and forth between Bennett and Poco.

I paused for only a second, then shook my head. Moon-Wolf nodded and motioned one of his warriors forward, giving him an order in Crow. The warrior immediately responded by stepping to the tree where the lawman and Mexican were tied and then shucking his knife. The fleeting thought crossed my mind that they were going to kill Bennett and Poco quick. They didn't need to suffer since they weren't there when Shilo killed the Crow women. But Moon-Wolf was more merciful than that. Instead of cutting the men, the warrior cut the binding ropes, and suddenly, like a grizzly bear at a gypsy sideshow, Bennett was loose.

The big man didn't say anything. He didn't even look at the Crows. His only look was for me, the same burning look that had been in his eyes since our arrival. When he finally did look at Moon-Wolf, the Injun waved him over to the horse herd. "Crow always friend white man. No hurt our People, you. Me not kill. You two, go free. You horse there."

He turned to a couple of his warriors and nodded. The pair stepped forward and handed Bennett and Poco their weapons. Bennett's only answer was another nod. He shoved the pistol into its holster and balanced the rifle on his fingers, and him and his little brown shadow trooped off to the horses.

Without another word, just one long, searching glance at me, Moon-Wolf turned and strode away, followed by his warriors. Toy lingered for a moment, and sympathy glowed in his eyes. But at last he, too, returned to his fire.

At the far side of camp, I watched Van Bennett and his friend, Poco, tighten their cinches and slide the rifles into their scabbards. They climbed aboard, and as they turned their horses, Bennett jerked his mount in and stared my way. It was a long, hating gaze he fetched me, a look full of intent to kill. Then, with the Crows watching curiously, he and Poco rode away.

Then there was silence. Silence not from the Crow camp, where life went on as normal. Only silence from me and Chadwick, who no longer had anything to say. I had my thoughts to think, my fears to entertain. He had his suspicions to harbor, his plans to form.

I didn't know what the cowboy was thinking. But I knew several things, and they added up to trouble. He knew I'd lied about why the law was after us, because he knew now that I was a robber. He knew his father had been killed, supposedly in a fight with rustlers. And he knew my bunch had been involved in a battle that must have been the same morning. What did it add up to? To a man of Utah Chadwick's intelligence, and even a duller man, it added up to one thing. I was a liar, a thief, an outlaw.

And my bunch had killed his father.

We stood there until dark, until Van Bennett and Poco would be only lurking shadows, gone away somewhere to wait. Then, after dark, I saw a shape come walking toward us, bouncing in and out of the firelight. As it drew nearer, I recognized Toy. He carried a bundle of sticks and grass in one hand, a glowing fire brand in the other. He stopped in front of us and looked at me with an apologetic gaze.

"I am sorry. You helped us. You are my friend. My father, he says you must stand here all night—sleep here. But he allows me to make a fire for you—so you can stay warm. That is all I can do."

"Thanks, friend. That's somethin'."

He knelt and built our fire, and after that he returned every half hour or so to add wood to it. I shivered in the dark and tried to imagine Chadwick's thoughts.

Long before the sun came up in the morning, the fire had burned to a pile of loose gray ash. I shook my head and looked toward the east. The light was strong there, but those high, snow-pocketed mountains were going to hide the sun for an hour or so yet to come. I was frozen stiff, and numb from standing the night through. But still I was half asleep. My body didn't care about the cold anymore.

Yet I couldn't help thinking about JoAnna and Duke and Slug, as I had plenty of times through the long night. What were they doing? Did they figure me for dead? Had they moved on? Were they waiting? Were they searching for us?

I heard someone coming and looked over to see Toy approaching with a pot. He had a red and black plaid Scotch blanket wrapped tightly about his shoulders. He stopped in front of me. "I am bringing you water. Are you thirsty?"

My voice seemed unnatural loud in the still woods. "I am, Toy, but I could use a smoke even more. I'm 'bout froze stiff. Do you know how to make white man's smoke?"

"Of course," he replied. "I have done it many times."

"The makin's are in my vest," I said, glancing down.

Setting down his pot of water, Toy stepped forward and reached into my vest pocket. As he pulled the sack of Bull Durham out, something shiny came with it and tumbled onto the ground. I looked down at it and just stared for a while, not recognizing it. Then I remembered picking it up off the ground after spilling Shilo's saddlebags—the strange earring.

Toy stared at the object, too. At the same time I recognized it, he dropped into a crouch, springing back up with it in his open palm. "Where you find this? Where?"

"Shilo's saddlebags," I replied.

"Tom! Tom! This was for the ear of my sister. My father made it."

I stared at him, not grasping why he was so excited about it. Without any explanation, he turned and ran toward his father's tepee.

Shortly, Moon-Wolf returned with his son. He held the earring now, and he rolled it over and over in his hand while he studied my face. "You no show this me. Why you no show?"

"I didn't know what it was," I admitted. "Sorry. I didn't know it meant anything to you."

"Me think you...you..." Struggling with his words, the warrior turned and spoke quickly to his son, motioning for him to translate.

"Because you have this, my father says you must speak the truth. Shilo took the things that belonged to my sister. The only way for you to have it is if you killed him."

I looked on, my eyes flickering between them. I didn't know how to respond.

"How kill this man?" Moon-Wolf asked. "How you kill?"

I explained as brief as I could what happened in Sheridan. Moon-Wolf listened, then stepped back with a sigh. He said something to Toy, and Toy nodded with a look of relief and drew his knife. Stepping to me, he sliced through the knots that held me and Chadwick.

"White man, go now, you," Moon-Wolf said. "Injuns go, too. Red beard man, him tell—soldier come. Soldier come take People reservation, home. Soldier come, not happy."

My heart jumped when I realized what he meant. "The soldiers are comin'? Here?"

Moon-Wolf nodded. "Red beard say. Now you come my tepee."

Hesitantly, I followed him. I could hear Chadwick on my tail, and the only reason I allowed it was because I sort of felt like I was among friendly acquaintances now. At his tepee, Moon-Wolf stooped and went inside. When he returned, he held our two rifles under his arm, my Remington pistol in his belt, and Chadwick's in one hand. He handed them over, and I nodded to him, glancing nervously to the side as Chadwick slipped his Smith and Wesson into its holster.

Toy had gathered our horses, and we saddled them in silence as him and his father watched. We climbed on, and with a last nod and thank you, we turned back toward our camp.

Me and Chadwick didn't talk. I don't know why. I don't know why we didn't discuss our situation, or shoot it out, or something. He had to have figured out that my bunch had been responsible for his father's death, whether or not I had actually pulled the trigger. And he wasn't afraid of me. I was sure of that. So why didn't he make a move? Why did he let the mental torture go on?

We rode side by side—careful to *stay* side by side—and tried to keep an eye not only on each other, but on the surrounding terrain. The valley was narrow and boxed in by timbered slopes broken by granite outcrops on either side. Where we rode it was rutted and grassy. Looked like cows had been in here knocking things down. Sure made it easier to ride.

"Utah," I said suddenly, "we ain't talkin', but I have a suggestion to make. Didn't want you to think I was tryin' anything. But we oughtta shuck our guns and make sure they're still loaded. Them Injuns might've decided they could use some spare ammo."

He glanced over at me, then quickly away. Squinting toward the sunlight on the far, scattered trees, he nodded grudgingly. As one, we started to draw them out.

The boom of a large caliber rifle nearly made me drop my gun. My heart dove into my throat. Instinctively, my horse had started to run, and I skinned my spurs across his ribs. With little effort, the big-muscled thighs of the chestnut threw him into a gallop. But Chadwick didn't gallop beside me!

I was nearing the top of a slope I figured would take me out of sight of the attacker. Another eighty yards—less. I'd be free. But Chadwick wasn't with me. Chadwick, who'd saved my skin.

With a falling heart, I whirled my horse just long enough to look down the slope. My quick glance showed Chadwick's sorrel down, with the man trapped beneath its weight. The horse was struggling to rise, but the big rifle must have broke its back. It wasn't going anywhere, and Chadwick was firmly caught beneath.

A movement in the corner of my eye showed a horse streaming down the precarious embankment that dropped out of the timber beside Chadwick. It was a big bay horse, its hooves scattering debris each time its front feet slammed into the bank to catch its weight. Huge Van Bennett was the rider, leaned back, almost parallel with the saddle seat, fighting not to fall. I guess the momentum alone kept him there.

I was two hundred yards away now, and I thought sure Bennett would fire on me. But maybe he counted on the Mexican to do it.

Where was *he?* Bennett reached the bottom of the dirt bank and jerked the horse to a stop. Then, instead of turning to shoot my way or chase me, he pivoted his rifle on Utah Chadwick. And there was nowhere the cowboy could go.

Chapter Twenty-Seven
If He Wants My Life

Just for a moment, I stared. What was happening had no time to dig into my scattered thoughts. Here I was, two hundred yards away from Van Bennett, and he made no attempt to shoot me. Instead, he steadied his sights on Utah Chadwick. If I'd had time to think, I'd have been sure the Mexican was nearby, leveling his own rifle at me. But I didn't have time. I only had time to act.

Whisking my rifle out of the boot, I raised it and fired at my biggest target, the horse. I saw Bennett's rifle erupt with smoke a breath later. Even as it did, the legs of the lawman's horse buckled, and it went to its knees. The lawman sailed over its head, losing his rifle. He recovered quick, rolling away from the struggling animal. My first thought was to ride him down, but I couldn't let my horse end up like the other two.

With an oath, I bailed out of the saddle. I landed on a loose stone, twisting my ankle and spilling to my side. As I rolled over a shoulder and came up, Bennett's rifle spit smoke again. I snapped a shot back at him at the same instant I heard the report of his rifle. Then I was running for cover of the trees.

The steep dirt bank was a challenge. Holding the rifle in one hand, I clawed my way up, and for each lunge I made I slipped a foot back down. A bullet whined off rocks near my feet. A second later the report rolled past me. I fell forward, catching a dangling tree root with one hand. Feverishly, I struggled for footholds, and as dirt exploded near me again I turned and took a more carefully aimed shot at Bennett. He whirled and dropped to his knees.

With the split second I'd gained, I continued my scramble up the broken bank. There was a dead tree at the very lip of it, the one with the roots protruding. I grabbed at it as I reached the top. With the urgency of a man under threat of death, I jerked myself up and over, falling into dead grass and pine needles.

No time to rest. A glance to the side showed me Bennett on his knees, steadying for another shot. His horse had reached its feet and run down the valley, stopping four hundred yards away and looking around like it hadn't even been hurt. I scrambled up the hill, hearing a bullet whack into the tree where I'd just been.

Now I had the advantage. I was in the trees, partially concealed, and uphill from Bennett. He was in the open. I fell to a sitting position at the next tree I reached and turned to lean my rifle barrel against it as a rest. But Bennett had already disappeared. Surprisingly quick, he had made it to one of the granite outcrops that poked out of the bank into the valley. The only way I could get a shot would be to circle around him.

Without hesitation, still thinking of Utah Chadwick, I started through the trees. I had Poco in my mind, but I couldn't dwell on the possibility of him being up here. I had to reach Bennett before he had time to formulate any plans.

After several minutes of sneaking, I paused behind a furrowed tree. All was still. A raven made his deep, rattling cry, but it was far back in the trees. A fly buzzed near me. And then a woodpecker began to rattle his beak against a tree trunk somewhere in the deep forest. The sun beat down warm through the trees, singeing the fallen needles, softening pitch on the trees. The musty odor of the first and the sweetly resinous scent of the second made me ache with longing. It was a day made for peace. But there was none of that for me. The smell that over-powered it all was of the burned black powder in my rifle.

I could see Chadwick lying under his horse. The horse no longer struggled, and neither did Chadwick. Shifting my weight to ease a cramp in my leg, I looked toward the rocks where Bennett had hid. No movement. But there wouldn't be. My instincts told me he wasn't there, but up in the forest with me. Behind the rocks, he'd have a clear path up into the trees.

I moved on, trying to breathe quietly. But it was pointless, for the needles and cones crackled beneath my feet at every step. Once, I thought I heard a whisper of cloth rubbing on something, and I paused in mid-stride. I put a hand out to steady myself against a mossy trunk. The sun filtered through to me, but around me most of the woods were in shadow. A breath of wind oozed among the trees, fluttering the hair at my temples, cooling my sweat.

Like thunder, the big rifle shook the silent woods, slapping its blow against the far slope and rocking back to me. Bark spit at me, stinging my face. Startled, but too shocked to think, I slipped in the duff and fell sideways. My head slammed against the tree, my hat rolling away.

Fighting against sawdust in my eyes, I scrambled for cover. I was desperate beyond thinking. I crashed into another tree and fell into a crouch behind it, raking at my eyes.

Suddenly, I realized my rifle lay at the base of the other tree. As the tears washed my eyes clear, I looked that way, cursing under my breath. The rifle glinted as if taunting me. Drawing my Remington, I peeked gingerly around the tree. I saw the big lawman creeping toward me, unbelievably silent in his movements. He saw me at the same time, and I snapped a shot at him as he dove for a nearby trunk.

Again the forest was still, this time completely. The birds, wherever they were, waited silently wondering what had disrupted their world. Looking toward Bennett, I saw he'd disappeared about forty yards from me, with three or four big-trunked trees between us. If I could get to my rifle, we'd once again be equally armed. With him hidden, I had to try it.

Blinking against my stinging eyes, I stood up. I put my hand up against the tree, ready to bolt toward my rifle or pull myself back to safety. I took a deep breath.

Then Bennett leaned away from his tree. I jerked, involuntarily whipping back my hand as his shot crashed, but not before it dug into the tree trunk, too close to my fingers. I sat down hard on the exposed roots of the tree. Again, bits of bark had peppered my face, and I raised my left hand to wipe them away. I was glad my instincts had made me close my eyes that time.

As I wiped at my face, I was surprised at the warm wetness. Was it only sweat? I opened my eyes to look down at my hand.

A shock ran through me. I hadn't felt any pain. I'd had no idea. Bennett's shot hadn't just been *close* to my fingers. It had taken the third one completely off at the hand! I swore violently, looking toward Bennett, then back at my hand. Finally, I let my head fall back, thumping against the tree. Well, there was nothing for the finger now. Only a minor appendage anyway. I'd seen men take worse and go on about their lives. At least it wasn't a trigger finger.

A spiteful shot slammed into the other side of my tree, and the echo was frightening in its closeness. "Next one cuts your head in half!" Bennett taunted in a growling voice. "Ever see what a fifty caliber bullet will do to a man's head?"

There was no call to answer him. I held my place and waited.

The silence ran on, as if peace had returned. Black wood ants trekked across my pants and vest, pausing in each wrinkle like some treasure waited there. Little black flies and deer flies darted in at me, licking my skin or taking my blood—whatever they'd come for. I swatted at them for a while until I didn't care anymore. Then I just sat in listening silence, holding my scarf to my stump of finger. Finally, I tied the scarf in place. I settled into the tree, hugging my Remington to my belly.

It started to seem like I was alone. Only me, the trees, ants, and flies. A single cloud rode lazily in front of the sun. I watched until it disappeared behind the top of the tree, and the sunshine poured down again.

I started to doze. I shook myself out of daydreaming. There was a man nearby who wanted to kill me!

Just when I'd started thinking of going on the offensive, I heard needles crunch down the slope. I turned my head slowly, keeping behind the trunk this time. I keened my ears and waited for the lawman to come on.

The sudden crackle of needles *up* the slope snapped my attention that way. I imagined Poco sneaking up on that side. A fist-size rock rolled into sight—Bennett's distraction, planned for me to fire at it.

I heard clothing stir against a tree trunk, back down the slope. It was close—very close. I eased back the hammer of the Remington, cursing each click as it engaged the sear. After so many minutes of quiet, the rifle barked again, tearing up duff near my boot.

I shoved away from the tree and plunged toward my rifle. As I rolled over a shoulder and slammed into a tree trunk, I heard the rifle speak and felt the bullet wing past. Dazed, I careened to the right, stumbling and falling into a hole full of musty needles and dirt clods. My back was against the spider-leg under-roots of the tree that had toppled to make the hole.

With a sick fear, I realized I'd not only missed my rifle, I'd put myself in a position where Bennett could fire down on me. I looked toward the rifle, but my view of it was obscured by the mound of dirt around the hole. I couldn't have reached it anyway. It wasn't worth the chance.

I heard a dull metallic click. It didn't sound like a hammer cocking. It was more like a cartridge sliding home. Reloading! Without thinking, I bailed out of the hole and sprang to my left, seeking out Bennett among the timber. I saw the big red-bearded face poke out from behind a tree. I snapped a shot at it and ducked behind my own tree.

By Bennett's muffled cursing, I made a wild guess that I'd managed to either hit him or throw bark into his eyes like he'd done mine. And how vulnerable I'd felt came back strong to me. That's what made me move without reloading the spent cartridge.

I charged to my right, headed for a tree only five yards from Bennett. In running for it, I could have stooped and grabbed my rifle. But I was so close. The odds had evened up. To stop my momentum, I grabbed at the tree as I reached it, hugging it close to me as I jerked to a halt, facing Bennett.

He was leaned against his tree, his face stained with blood where my bullet must have creased it. He pulled his trigger the second he saw me. His rifle belched smoke and slammed back against him as his bullet burned the meat that joined my neck to my shoulder. Dropping my shoulder, I leveled the Remington waist high and fired. I fell against the tree, kneeling, and fired again.

I knew at least one bullet made it home as Bennett humped up and snarled. He raised that big rifle again and fired as I rolled around the tree, my back against it. The bullet exploded into the dirt nearby.

Bennett made that five yards in less time than I'd ever have figured. One minute he was hiding behind his tree, the next he was on top of me, ready to fire. The surprise of it made me scramble and fall backward, firing before he could. The bullet turned him to the side, and I shot again, from the ground. That one went through his ribcage, and his rifle fell and clattered against roots, going off on its own to put a harmless round in the trees.

Towering over me while I lay flat on my back, Van Bennett looked more than ever like a bear. Sounded like one, too, growling from down deep in his throat. As he drew his pistol and brought its bore toward me, I kicked upward into his groin. Then I fired my last round into his chest.

The lead must have broke his back, for he fell side-long into the duff, his hat rolling off to reveal a thin and graying hairline. Struggling to move his eyes, he looked up at me and cursed me one last, almost inaudible time. His last breath scattered dusty needles away from his mouth.

I stumbled and sat down hard, clutching the empty Remington like a last bottle of whisky. I suddenly realized I was exhausted. I fell over beside the big sheriff.

As I lay there, my thoughts went strangely to JoAnna, wishing she was there to hold me. I looked at the sightless eyes of my latest victim, and sickness filled the pit of my stomach. Some people claimed they'd killed so often they lost track of numbers. But I hadn't. I remembered them, each and every one. Of course I couldn't include the war, or any that might have fallen to all the crazy shots I'd flung.

Seven men dead behind me. Seven that I was aware of, and I was still alive. I wished I'd been the first one to die.

When I found Utah Chadwick, he had his head up, listening to my approach apprehensively. I came to stand over him, and he let his head down gently in the grass.

"He did this old horse in, Tom." For a moment, I thought he referred to his sorrel. Then I knew he was talking about himself. His left shoulder was soaked with blood.

"You won't die, Utah. Not out here."

He smiled, his gold tooth glinting. "Can you think of a better spot?"

"In a lady's arms," I said with a shrug.

He chuckled. "Sure. Find me one."

I found Bennett's big bay horse still down the valley munching grass. He had a bullet clean through the front of his left leg, but otherwise he wasn't hurt. Deciding I was lucky to find him and wouldn't see Shilo's chestnut again, I took him back to Chadwick, and we managed to pull the dead horse off him.

It didn't take much to see Chadwick's left leg was broken. But he had the gumption of a three-legged hog, and somehow we got him onto that big bay without no more than a grunt or two of pain. I shoved my Marlin into the boot, shucked his Winchester and climbed on behind him, and we headed back to where we'd made camp. I wondered if there'd be anybody there to greet us.

We hadn't gone no more than three miles when around the corner came Duke Rainey, and then I could see the rest behind him. Tovías Ruiz was leading the chestnut.

We camped far down the Bighorn Mountains that night. We chose a place of blown-down timber and young, new growth, short and thick enough to hide us. The blow-downs would camouflage us in case of any night attack by a posse, if there was anything left of the posse now.

I still wondered about that little Mexican. He'd been such a good friend to Bennett, we'd been told. I just couldn't help but think he was still somewhere around. But chances were he'd find his dead boss. Then maybe he'd realize his cause was useless, and he'd just go home. I'd defend myself if forced to, but I hated like hell to think of killing again. It seemed I'd been caught in a never-ending cycle of it.

Chadwick had had a tough time of it. We'd pried his custom boot off, because the leg had started to swell so bad we figured he'd never get it off if we waited. Far as I knew, he'd never talked to Drury and Colt and Hepner about me, but I was waiting for it. I always kept a gun somewhere near me, and I watched their group with wary eyes. Not only might they want revenge for John Chadwick's death, but they also knew I had a sight of money in my saddlebags.

I sat up in the shadows, keeping watch because, in spite of my exhaustion, I couldn't sleep. Too many ghosts haunted me.

JoAnna came to me silently and hugged me. We hadn't had a chance to greet each other proper earlier on. Or at least she hadn't seemed so inclined. I'd figured she was still mad.

Putting my arms up to return the hug made my shoulder burn like fire where Bennett's bullet had sliced along the flesh. But I wasn't about to admit the pain. I'd take JoAnna's form of pain deadener anytime.

A brilliant star dashed across the sky, cutting through a clot of duller ones. JoAnna turned to me and smiled when she saw I'd seen it too. She looked back up, and for a moment, she didn't speak. She just stared at the boundless sky, until at last another star rocketed into the treetops.

But this time when she looked away, it was down at her lap, where her hands were folded. "Tom, did you ever wanna wear a ring?"

Surprised, I just stared at her. My eyes flickered down at my missing finger as I realized suddenly why she had asked. I hadn't given a thought to ring-wearing until now. I finally looked back over at her. "If I had, Bennett changed my mind for me."

I heard her swallow, and she began twisting at her fingers, fidgeting. At last, she reached out and took my right hand, and hers was shaking. She guided my hand to her left one, to the ring finger, then ran my fingertips along it for a moment.

"On that star that fell," she said with a tight voice. "On that star I made a wish that your ring could be here tonight. I wished you would take me away."

"Never s'posed to tell a wish," I said quietly. I brought my hand up and ran the back of it gently across her wind-roughed cheek. She sighed like a little girl, and her eyes shut. Her head tilted back, and I leaned and kissed her softly, letting her lips form naturally against mine. Then I turned on my log perch and held her, and she looked down at my bandaged hand and began to weep.

In the morning, me and JoAnna lay asleep beside each other against the log. I felt a hand shaking me and started awake to see Duke Rainey looking down.

"I let yuh sleep long as I could, Thomas," he said. "But we gotta go. Tovías got suspicious and rode back on our trail. They's comin'. Not the posse—a bunch o' soldiers. They's a little Mexican ridin' in front of 'em, trackin'."

I scrambled to my feet, cursing. I ignored the dull pain in my wounded shoulder. "That'll be Poco," I said. "That damn little greaser's half hound."

We broke camp quick as we could, and before we got done things came down to a question of what to do with Utah Chadwick. His boys had set his broke leg the night before and bandaged his shattered shoulder. But that didn't make things all better. He couldn't ride fast. That was a simple conclusion. And it meant the soldiers could overtake us.

We gathered together away from the wounded man. Slug Holch spoke before anyone else could think of what to say. "We'll have to ride like the devil to lose that bunch of soldiers. It could come down to a fight."

I looked around the group, then shot a glance across the camp. "Chadwick ain't up to a hard ride."

Slug looked at me like he was angry. "You think we all oughtta die on account of him?"

"On *account* of him? Damn, Slug! He saved our bacon."

"And you saved his!" he retorted. "He wouldn't expect us all to stay and get killed for him. He knew the chance he was takin'."

I stared him down, and the others stood silent. "Go ahead and go, Slug," I said at last. "I'll ride when Utah can."

It was Flint Drury who finally broke in on us. "You boys better ride on ahead. I'll stay here with Utah."

I turned on him. "You? Why you?"

"Your friend's right. You oughtta make a run while you can."

I could feel Dale Hepner watching me, and now he spoke in his gruff voice. "Listen to Flint. We appreciate your loyalty, but Ute's our responsibility."

Drury turned his eyes on Hepner, flicked them to Frank Colt, then back to the big buckskin-clad one. "I'm talkin' about just me, Dale. One man can do what three can."

"You can drop it here," cut in Frank Colt. "I'm stayin' back, too."

I studied each of them in turn, then looked at Slug. "I'll ride with them, Slug. Go on ahead if you want. We'll meet up down the trail." That *down the trail* was just a way of talking, of course. I knew if we parted we'd never meet again.

It turned out we all went together, but Slug and Ruiz hated the idea. I don't even know why the Mexican stayed. He was pretty much the black sheep here. But stay he did.

Even Duke seemed itchy to be on the move. I couldn't blame him, not with a couple dozen troopers riding down our underwear. To men who weren't accustomed to anything more than lice—pants rats, as we called them—it could prove to be a mite uncomfortable. JoAnna, she wanted to run, too. I'd told her Chadwick knew about his father, and I could see in her eyes she didn't understand why I wanted to stay. But I'd never done anything good in my life, and sorry effort though it might have been, I guess staying back with Chadwick was an attempt at making up for it.

We'd rode ten miles or so, all of us keeping an eye on our back trail, some of us keeping a worried eye on Chadwick. But he was one tough wolf. He wore a permanent grimace, but he never made a noise.

Dale Hepner was riding beside me, his big rifle across his thigh. I cast a sidelong glance at him, then looked back at the trail. "Them soldiers'll have us 'fore it's done."

Hepner leaned and spit a stream of tobacco over his horse's neck. He turned to me with brown slime running into his beard from his lips. "You had your chance to run, boy. Shoulda listened to your pardner."

"I won't leave Utah after what he's done."

Hepner chuckled, looking at me with a fierce light in his eye. "I guess you don't know it, but the first chance Ute gets he's gonna hang your hide out to dry. He was mighty partial to his pappy." He turned his bright eyes away from me.

"He told you, huh?" I asked softly.

"We talked about it. He suspicioned you was bad before, 'cept then he didn't know about his pappy. He just knew Shilo was an outlaw and saw you wanted 'im dead awful bad." He paused to spit again. Then he turned a serious gaze on me. "If I was you, boy, I'd hightail it while I could. No matter what you face later, it's a better chance than you'll get with Utah Chadwick."

After several moments of silence, I just nodded. "Well, I owe him my life. I guess if he wants it now, it's his."

Chapter Twenty-Eight
Brother of the Tumbleweed

We rode for a day, and Chadwick never complained. We made it down along a rocky defile Hepner called Shell Creek gorge. The country was beautiful, but not meant for the meek. It was a land of gnarled trees and jagged rocks, dashed together and sliced down its middle by the roiling waters of Shell Creek. A country for strong folks.

We left the mountains as night fell, and where Shell Creek boiled down to become a gentle stream, we made our camp. Dale Hepner had left us to go back along the trail, and an hour after dark we heard the return of his horse's hooves.

When the mountain man walked into camp, his face was grim. "Them soldiers'll be on us before noon tomorrow," he reported. That was all he said, and then he sat down to eat.

After supper, we sat around the fire, and for a long time no one spoke. Finally, Slug cleared his throat and spit.

"It's time to do the smart thing, Tom. Set Chadwick up here against a rock with a blanket, some food and a canteen, and let's ride."

"You ride!" I snapped. "He'll be with me when I reach Montana."

Duke Rainey cleared his throat, looking down into his cup of coffee. "I'm with Slug, Thomas. We gotta ride. We can't win this here."

I sighed and looked at JoAnna, who hunkered beside me, facing the others. "I guess it's best, girl. Why don't you go too? I'll catch you later on." I looked over at Hepner, Drury and Colt. "Boys, I owe Utah Chadwick my life. Do what's sensible and go while you can. I'll wait here. No sense all of us takin' a risk."

Hepner inclined his head and spit into the fire, then looked up at me, his eyes glittering in the firelight. "Not on your life, boy," he growled. "You go."

"Take the advice," Flint Drury agreed. "Utah'll only kill you when he can."

JoAnna reached out and squeezed my arm. Her eyes pleaded with me, but she said nothing. Sadly, I just looked away. My eyes met Slug's, then Duke's. I couldn't believe they'd run. But I couldn't hardly blame them. Otherwise, they faced almost certain capture, or death. Ruiz, he was another story. He was his own man, and I expected as much out of him. I didn't give him another thought.

When I looked back at Duke, he said, "Thomas, why don't yuh go ask *him*?" He nodded toward where Chadwick was rolled in his bedding. "Might be he'd as soon you was gone."

So I did just that. I went to crouch beside Chadwick. He had his eyes shut, and beads of sweat stood out on his cheeks. I put a palm to his forehead, and his narrow eyes flickered open.

"The boys're talkin' about goin'. Now, while it's dark. What about you?"

He lay there watching me, his pistol snug against his breast. "You better worry about yourself. You don't owe me a thing."

"I owe you my life."

He chuckled dryly. "Well, you came back for me when Bennett had me down, so on that count we're even. Now the only thing between us is the killin' of John Chadwick."

"They ambushed us," I said lamely. I wouldn't tell him it was Duke Rainey who had pulled the trigger on his father. "Shilo set them on us. We fired back to defend ourself. Nobody could see where they was shootin'."

"You're a bunch of cow thieves! What'd you expect my father to do?"

"Just what he did," I replied after a pause. "Listen, Chadwick. I don't expect you to believe me, but I was tryin' to go straight. Things just didn't work out like I expected. But if I live I'm gonna take JoAnna and marry her and raise a family—if you'll let me."

He raised his head a little and looked past me at the girl, her face lit up by the fire. Her hair flowed out from beneath her hat, falling onto her shoulders, and she stared into the flames. Chadwick's face seemed to soften, and he looked back at me, then away into the darkness.

"She does need out of this. But you're not the one who'll do it." He looked over at Flint Drury. "Flint's the fellow she needs—an honest hand."

I gave him a grim smile. He was right, in all likelihood. But it was ironic that Chadwick chose Drury, when he'd been an outlaw too. I didn't have the heart to tell Chadwick about that. Drury hadn't done anything to me. But damn them all! I'd marry that girl, and to the devil with what anyone thought.

I started to turn back to the fire, but Chadwick stuck out his gun across my forearm to stay me. It crossed my mind he might shoot me right there. But he'd had plenty of chances and hadn't taken them.

"Let the woman go. You're too old to go straight. You missed your chance."

I returned to the fire and stood looking down at my friends. There were questions in their eyes, but I didn't feel like answering them. I thought back over the rides with Slug and Duke at my side. I thought of the lawless things we'd done, and how looking at them would always bring me guilt, if we stayed together. And my life was full enough of guilt.

"You boys better ride. Time's not standin' still."

Half an hour later we'd divvied up our loot, out in the darkness away from curious eyes.

Duke and Slug stood in front of me, while Ruiz waited by the horses, aloof. Duke looked over at Slug, and then his eyes flickered back to me. "Thomas, I— I sure wisht yuh'd go with us. You can't make it out of here. Not at Chadwick's pace. 'Sides, you know he'll kill you."

I smiled, putting a hand to my friend's shoulder. "Since that night in Baker I've been a bad man, Duke. I'm tired of it. I wanna do somethin' good for once."

"Doin' good's goin' git you kilt."

"No, it won't. Men with guilty consciences don't ever die. They only wish they would."

Duke Rainey's eyes filled suddenly with moisture, and he took my hand and held it for a long time, then hurried to his horse. Slug just stared at the ground, and at last he looked up with a grim nod and took the front of his hat brim between thumb and forefinger, giving it a quick dip that nearly hid his eyes. "You're the best of us, Tom. You're the winner." He shook my hand, then put his other hand up and squeezed my shoulder at the base of the neck. "Marry her, Tom. You're the winner."

I watched Ruiz and my two friends climb onto their horses and turn away from camp. Duke turned to watch me as they picked their way into the dark, and it wasn't long before the fading thud of their hooves was the only sound left but the creek.

When we woke up in the dawn, Dale Hepner was also gone.

We decided on coffee that day, and to hell with the cavalry. We were worn down to almost nothing, going on will alone. Thoughts of climbing back in the saddle were just too harsh.

Around the fire, me and JoAnna were crouched on one side, and Drury and Colt on the other. "Where's Hepner?" I finally asked.

Flint Drury pointed back up the mountains. "You couldn't guess? He's gone back to hold off the soldiers while the rest of us run."

Stunned, I stared at him for a moment. My glance flickered over to Frank Colt, but he just gazed into the fire. Looking back at Drury, I nodded grudgingly. "He'll die up there." I looked down at the fire. "He's quite a man. Quite a man."

And so it was that for the first time I came to believe we'd actually make it to Montana. We'd ride into that land of rolling prairies, the last stronghold of the Injuns. Land where Custer had met his end. Land where I'd lose myself and at last be free. If only Chadwick and his men would let me.

We couldn't expect Chadwick to ride anymore. He'd been through too much. So we rigged him up a travois, and on we went, at the plodding pace of an Injun village moving camp. But no longer did I look behind us for pursuit. I trusted that crusty mountain man, Dale Hepner. He wouldn't attack the cavalry head-on. He'd shoot from hiding, then run and shoot again. He'd hold them up, dog them, keep them off our trail. There was a slim chance he might even live through it himself.

We crossed the Bighorn River and at last turned north. Except for the mountains to our right, the land lay flat and lonely all around us. Cattle roamed in scattered bunches, but we saw no human. Roundup was over, and there was too much land for cowboys to scour it all every day. We plodded on, the travois trailing dust in streamers. Around us lay the bones and stench of drought-killed cattle.

I was riding beside Flint Drury when a gust of wind rolled a big tumbleweed across his path and spooked his horse. He cursed the thing, fighting to keep his horse under control.

I kind of chuckled at him, and when he looked over I just shook my head. "Sorry about that."

"Sorry? Sorry about what?"

"The tumbleweed. You got cause to curse a tumbleweed, you got cause to curse me. I always figured me and the tumbleweed were brothers."

Drury looked thoughtfully back at the rounded clump and then gave me a wry smile. "Sort of a funny thing to think. That's one weed that will always be hated by the cowman. Always rollin' around spreadin' bad seed everywhere it goes."

I nodded. "I know. I told you we were brothers."

It was late afternoon when we camped on a little rock-studded knoll in the middle of grass prairie. None of us knew this country.

It was all strange and new. We hobbled our horses, and then Flint Drury and Frank Colt decided to ride on north for a ways. We thought we had to be near the Montana line. If there was a way of knowing, they wanted to find it.

Chadwick lay chilling, so I covered him with a blanket. I watched him for a time while JoAnna dozed. I wondered what stupid loyalty had caused me to stay with this man. It was a sure thing Slug and Duke and Ruiz were safe in Montana by now. JoAnna should have been too, and so should I.

I guessed my answer wasn't only what Chadwick had tried to do for me. Even if he hadn't offered aid, I wanted to help his good life go on. He'd made one bad judgment in his life it seemed—trusting me. That was the only reason he found himself on the wrong side of the law.

Chadwick had experienced freedom like I'd never know. A cowboy's life might have had its share of worries, but until now he'd never been hunted. I'd told Tyrone Sandoe I chose this life for its freedom—a fool's excuse. There was no worse prison than being on the run. Never knowing, day to day, who your real friends were. Never knowing when someone would come to kill you. Never having the joy of marrying and raising a family, watching your children grow up to carry on your name. Worst of all was never being able to feel honest about taking the woman you loved in your arms and telling her you would protect her. A woman could only be so safe with a wanted man.

I walked to the edge of the hill, where it tipped downward to meet the prairie. I sat down on a half-buried lava rock and rolled out a blanket, then set my guns and cleaning tools on it, jacked all the shells out of the Marlin and started to break the Remington down.

I thought I was the only one awake, but grass rustled behind me. I looked up to see JoAnna stop beside me. She stood with hands on her hips, her chin up and back straight; yet her eyes were bloodshot and squinted half-shut with weariness. She gazed out over the far prairie, where the grasses rolled gently under shifting wind. The sun and wind had cracked her lips, and dried blood scabbed the worst spot. Her cheeks were deep red, and dead skin had begun to peel from her nose. She gazed with the look of a woman who perhaps right now didn't care what came tomorrow, as long as today could end.

But despite her battered appearance, JoAnna'd lost none of her beauty. She'd removed her hat, and her dark hair flooded back from her face, ruffled by the breeze. She wore the blue denim shirt and brown canvas pants, but none of her fine form was marred by the male duds. Her long, perfect neck, normally protected by a scarf, looked white and soft against her sunburned face.

I reached over and rested my hand on the back of her leg. She looked down and smiled, making her tired eyes go almost shut, and those attractive little wrinkles form at their corners. She sank down in the grass in front of my rock. Closing her eyes, she rested her head against my leg. I studied everything about her face, which I'd come to figure was nigh perfect. From the dark eyebrows that slanted low over her eyes; to her nose with its hint of a button on the tip that was so cute it even made an unromantic man like me want to kiss her there; to her firm chin and perfect neck with its one little brown mole that set just a touch to the right of her Adam's apple. I'd just about put every detail of JoAnna Walker's face in my memory, and still I didn't believe I could ever tire of watching her.

Suddenly, she pushed herself a little ways away and looked up at me. "Today's your birthday!"

I thought for a moment, then chuckled. "You actually remembered that. You're right. I'm officially a old varmint."

"Not until I say so," she said with a teasing smile.

"Yeah? Well, you're not old enough to know."

I guess I won that one, because it quieted her. Instead of talking, she maneuvered around on her knees until she could lean between mine and look up at me. I set my gun down on the blanket, and she took my hands.

"Remember the falling stars?" she asked. "And how I wished I could wear your ring?"

I smiled and nodded.

She looked down, and though I couldn't see her blush beneath her sunburn, I could see embarrassment build around her eyes. "I saw another one last night," she said. "And I made another wish." She forced herself to look up at me, and the tiredness in her eyes seemed miraculously vanished. "I wished for your birthday I could give you a gift. Me."

Her gaze flickered, and though I could see she wanted to look away she managed to keep her eyes on me. They flashed only for a moment to Chadwick, then back. "He's asleep, Tom. If you want me..."

I felt the pulse in my throat as she lifted my hands and placed them at the top button of her blue shirt. She swallowed nervously and tried to smile, glancing down at my hands, then back up at me. Her hands came to rest on my knees.

It had been so long since I'd made love to a woman—any woman, but especially one I was in love with. I didn't know that I remembered how. And worst of all my hands seemed paralyzed.

She was watching me, waiting. Too many seconds went by, and at last her eyes flickered and fell. She tried to hold her smile, but I could see the hurt seep into her eyes, and then the glistening of tears.

"What's wrong?" she asked. "Don't you— Don't you want me?"

My voice started without me planning any words. "JoAnna, we'll be free tomorrow. We'll be in Montana. I'm sure we can see it from here. Out there." I pointed north. "You know that. Don't you?"

She nodded, her eyes asking why it mattered.

"I'll take your gift then, JoAnna. We can even find a preacher. Please don't feel hurt. I— I think the world of you."

I cursed myself. I'd been so close to saying I loved her! I'd worked on that since the day she said it to me. But no matter. I'd tell her tomorrow. I'd tell her when she became my wife. Anyway, she must have known it. She must have felt it.

"Do not touch your guns, *Señores*."

The words caught me with my rifle on the ground, the action open, and the Remington with its cylinder removed. JoAnna had taken her gunbelt off before she came to me. And her presence took away any chance I had to move anyway. I couldn't risk her life.

"*Señorita*, you raise up your hands, and you, too," the voice ordered.

JoAnna looked at me as she took her hands from my knees and brought them to the sides. I did the same, wishing I could calm her fear.

"Now both of you stand and turn to me."

We stood, and I turned and stepped back so I was at JoAnna's side. I wasn't surprised to see Van Bennett's Mexican companion standing there with a shotgun trained on me.

"Howdy, Poco."

His eyes flickered surprise that I remembered his name, but he only nodded. A glance behind him showed he was alone. The vast prairie was empty, even of any strange horse.

That side-by-side shotgun the Mexican carried was more than enough to make up for his size. If I tried to buck it, they'd have to pick me up with a blotter. It was a brutal, sure-fire way to end the life of man or beast. And I'd never have thought to go against it. I'd never have challenged it...except that I knew a rope awaited me...and JoAnna was out of the line of fire...and...and I couldn't spoil her dreams while there was still a chance.

And then a soft moan broke from Utah Chadwick, and he rolled in his sleep. Poco whirled, and I dove for his shotgun.

Success was within my grasp. I wouldn't kill the Mexican, just overpower him. There would be no more killing. As I came within inches of grasping the barrels to thrust them skyward, he turned back. The gun exploded in his hands. I felt a force like the butt-end of a log striking my chest.

The buckshot load threw me backward, and I landed jarringly against my rock perch, then flopped sideways into the grass. JoAnna, screaming, dropped down beside me on her knees, pulling my head into her lap. She was saying something, but I couldn't understand her. I could taste blood in my mouth and smell the scorched odor of my smoking shirt. I couldn't feel my feet.

From the corner of my eye, I saw Chadwick, his eyes open. He pulled his pistol and rolled so its barrel pointed at the Mexican's head. I looked back at the Mexican, and he had turned to stare at Chadwick. The barrels of his shotgun had turned, too, and he still had one barrel left. They held the guns on each other, and I waited for them to fire, but neither did. I looked over at Chadwick, who was watching me now. With a grimace, he let his pistol sink to the grass.

JoAnna wept uncontrollably. I looked up at her, my eyes flickering. They sort of fogged over until her face was all I could see. And it was dim. A teardrop splattered on my cheek and another on my lips. She wiped them away almost frantically, like it was acid and would burn me. I reached up and took her hands, and the next tears that fell on my face stayed there—where I wanted them.

Starting to rock slowly back and forth, she repeated my name over and over. I could hear that clearly, but I could hear nothing else. I could feel it when she pulled her wrists away and squeezed my hands. But when she put a hand on my chest I couldn't feel that.

I smiled, my breathing coming hard. "Give me—" I couldn't form the words I wanted. Something mushed in my throat.

The Mexican appeared in my sight and crouched over me, and him and JoAnna lifted me up against the rock. JoAnna sat against it, too, one arm around me while the other hand rested along my cheek. At least I could breathe now—not good, but better than before.

"I wanna smoke," I said in a croaking voice. I was embarrassed by its weakness.

With merciful eyes, Poco dug into his vest pocket and pulled out the makings. He had placed his shotgun aside. He rolled me up that smoke and lit it, putting it between my lips. When I drew on it, I coughed. I opened my eyes to see a thin drift of smoke lifting out of the hole in my shirt. I had to smile at that. It was coming through my wound.

JoAnna had stopped her hysterical crying. Her voice was now a whisper, but still it carried my name. And she kept saying, "I love you, I love you, I love you." She never asked me not to die. Guess she didn't believe in miracles.

I looked at her eyes, and for a moment they seemed to be all there was. No blood, no killing, no wasted life. Just dark brown eyes full of tears. "Jo—" I coughed on the rest of her name. It hurt me not being able to say it. My throat had filled up. I tried it again and couldn't even say that much. I tried to draw on the quirly, and I tasted nothing. So I opened my mouth, and the smoke fell down onto my blood-soaked shirt.

I wanted to clear my throat. Wanted to spit. Didn't have the strength. Wanted to say those three words. Those three words, words JoAnna hadn't heard me say. I looked at her, begging for help. But she didn't give any. She just put her cheek against my forehead, let tears run down my face.

Breathing seemed to stop. I gasped for air—there wasn't any. I was choking. I opened my mouth to struggle for more of that precious breath of life. My eyes dimmed as I arched my back violently. I could hardly see my girl anymore.

I heard horses gallop in, then the voices of Flint Drury and Frank Colt, cursing helplessly. Poco's voice spoke too, a sad, apologetic sound. No gunshots ever came. No one died.

I was struggling on the ground, gargling. No breath… Felt hands pull on me. Crushed against JoAnna's breasts. Tears fell down on me like the scarce rains of that fatal summer. Didn't care about breath anymore. Too late. Tried to…remember her face…face the way it looked—earlier. When she…when she looked across the prairie.

Heard a distant voice. John House…Flint Drury… "You're safe now, girl," it said. Muffled like in a windstorm, but there wasn't any windstorm. "We're all safe. We crossed into Montana some time back."

No More an Outlaw: JoAnna Walker

My hopes lay shattered there. Broken among the few seedpods of flowers that had bloomed in spite of the drought. One man had loved me—at least I thought he had. One man had truly cared for me and kept me safe. Now he was gone.

Had he loved me? He never said. But I wanted to believe he tried. No one ever told me that before. I didn't know what it sounded like to hear someone say "I love you" in the same breath which spoke my name.

There was wind blowing in my hair, drying tears on my face. It was dark, and still I could hear them digging. Three men: Flint Drury. Frank Colt. And a little Mexican man they called Poco who had killed the only person I'd ever loved.

I didn't move from my spot. I still held my man. I let my fingers brush through his hair. It had to be straightened. It hadn't been washed for so long, and that hat had frozen the snarls in place.

A horse came in long after dark, while I still held onto…to Tom. A man walked into the light and stood looking down at Tom, and I watched his bearded face. It was Dale Hepner. He just stared and never said a word, and then he walked back off into the darkness.

When morning came we were still on that hill. Someone had covered me and Tom with blankets. I was still sitting up. My backside ached, but I didn't want to move. To move meant I was real. I was not a dream.

Flint Drury went away for a long time and came back with a log a little over three feet long. No one said anything. He just sat down and took out a hatchet and a jackknife. Then he started to carve.

I couldn't cry anymore. When they lifted me off the ground, I let them. Tom fell away from me, and I didn't look. I stared northward, into that lovely Montana he'd wanted to see. I could hardly stand now. I'd sat so long. Flint Drury put his arm around me and held me up, talking softly, then singing. He sang "Amazing Grace" like Father Rimes did, back home in Lawrence.

Poco and Dale and Frank put my man down in the hole they dug. A blanket was over him now, and he looked so small down there. Too small to even be my man. They covered him with dirt while Flint Drury held me. I began to cry, and I don't know where those tears came from. I thought I was dried up. Flint pulled me into him and let me cry on him. He was a kind man.

I heard the rattle of stones being piled together, but I didn't look. My man was gone. When I heard the horses being saddled, I looked. Poco quietly stepped onto his horse and glanced down at the grave. Then he looked at the others. He still didn't say anything. He just rode away.

Dale and Frank watched Flint, but they wouldn't let their eyes meet mine. They nodded and got on their horses. Then Frank looked down at Flint, and his eyes flickered to me. "We'll travel slow. It won't be hard to spot us."

I watched them ride down the hill. They led our spare horses, including one that pulled a litter. It made thin-scraped lines in the dusty grass as they went away.

I pulled away from Flint Drury and sat down by the pile of gray rocks. There was that little log poking out of the pile, and I looked at it for a long time before the tears started up in my eyes and made the words blur. There was a name on the log: TOM MCLEAN. His name, the date, and four simple words: BROTHER OF THE TUMBLEWEED.

THE END

LEGEND OF THE TUMBLEWEED

Who are you, Tumbleweed? Where are you going to?
An outlaw without a name, what are you gonna do?
You rode out of town with a posse behind—fourteen vengeful men;
If they catch you now, while you're riding away, you won't ride again.

Tumbleweed, there's a lady waiting for you;
Tumbleweed, she'll be a-weeping o'er you.

You're riding with a band of men who tell you they're your friends;
They say they will ride with you until the bitter end.
But you know better, 'cause you've been there—you've heard those
words before;
If that posse ever captures you, they'll be your friends no more.

Tumbleweed, there's a posse searching for you;
And you'll die, like your partner gone before you.

Who are you, Tumbleweed? Where are you going to?
An outlaw of growing fame—what will become of you?
Why can't you heed her words? You don't have to die;
They say that you can't go back, but you know that's a lie.

Tumbleweed, there's a lady who adores you;
Tumbleweed, she would give her own life for you.

A burning rush of red-hot lead, the blood upon your shirt;
Now just like this tumbleweed, lifeless in the dirt;
That lady loved you with all her heart, but you just couldn't see;
Now gunsmoke boils, and your blood runs cold—her love can never be.

Tumbleweed, there's a lady weeping o'er you;
Tumbleweed, now she cries her heart out for you.
Tumbleweed, Tumbleweed, Tumbleweed...

Glossary

It has come to my attention through many of my readers that a lot of the old Western terms are becoming lost to modern generations. As a Western novelist and a lover of all things Western, I hate to see that happen. So rather than pattern my dialog and narrative toward the way people talk now, thereby taking away much of its authenticity, I decided to add a glossary of many of these words to help the average reader along.

It is for this same goal of authenticity that my characters, and even my dialog, in this novel written in first person, are not what one would call politically correct. I have no desire to offend anyone of any race or religion, and I apologize in advance if some of my readers take it that way. But we all must realize that times have changed drastically in regards to the way different races are treated. People of a hundred years ago had no concept of what I know lovingly today as "political bootlicking", a.k.a. political correctness. The word "Nigger", for instance, was used freely even in big name newspapers of the day. Please take that for what it is worth and read this 1880's story through the eyes of the times.

Ándale: Spanish. Hurry.

Arbuckle's: Arbuckle's Brothers coffee, a brand so common in the West it became a generic name for coffee, just as Levi's for jeans, Winchester for rifle, Colt for pistol, Stetson for hat.

Boot: The tarp-covered area that was used to store valuables at the front or back of a stagecoach.

Buffalo: To strike a man over the head with a gun.

Caballo bayo: In Mexican-Spanish, a dun, brown or sorrel horse with dark mane and tail and a dorsal stripe.

Caballo rojo: A red horse, a bay, chestnut or sorrel.

Calico: A cowboy's term for a woman.

California plaid: a favorite style of wool pants worn by cowboys.

Camprobbers: Nickname commonly applied to the gray jay. In this particular case it was used to refer to the Clark's nutcracker, which was also referred to as a whisky jack.

Cash in one's six-shooter: To rob a bank.

Catamount: A wildcat, commonly referring to the mountain lion.

Charro: A Mexican word for cowboy.

Chili-eater: A derogatory term for a Mexican.

Clear-footed: Said of a sure-footed horse.

Coffin paint: A term for hard liquor. Not necessarily a complimentary term!

Cows: Name used by cowboys to refer to a herd of bovines, even a mixed herd.

Curly wolf: A tough guy. Somewhat of a compliment.

Fish: A slicker, so-called because the trademark on the label was a fish.

Greaser: Another derogatory name for a Mexican.

Gallowses: Suspenders, also known as galluses. Cowboys didn't like to wear them in the early days because it gave them the look of a sodbuster—a farmer.

Hijo: Spanish for son.

Hooley-ann: A rope throw for catching a horse out of a herd that is milling in the corral. Also known as Hoolihan.

Jehu: Stagecoach driver.

John Law: A common name for a lawman.

McCarty: A horsehair lead rope. A typical American slaughter of the Spanish word, mecate.

Mercado: Spanish for market.

Mes Amis: French for "my friends."

Outside man: During roundup, a man who would work with other ranches to keep track of animals from his home ranch.

Owl-hoot trail: Outlaw trail.

Prowler: A cowboy sent out, often after general roundup had ended, to hunt up cattle that might have hidden in draws and thickets and been missed.

¿Quién sabe?: Spanish for "Who knows?"

Quirly: A hand-rolled cigarette.

Ranny: A tough cowhand. Short for ranahan.

Riding among the willows: To hide. To be an outlaw.

Shad-bellied: Said of a scrawny horse.

S'il vous plaît: French for please. Literally, "if it pleases you."

Shaking hands with Grandma: Holding onto the saddle horn while riding.

Skin it: Draw one's weapon.

Slap one's tree on: Saddle a horse. The saddle was often known simply as a "tree."

Street howitzer: A shotgun.

Throw a wide loop: Said of a man who might be a little too free with his rope, drawing in a few cattle of questionable ownership.

Underbit: A type of earmark.

War bag: A bag for personal possessions. Also called a tucker bag.

Whisky jack: Nickname for the Clark's nutcracker.

Wyoming Stockman's Association: Organization based in Cheyenne. In the late 1870's through early 1900's, the bane of the small Wyoming rancher and cowboy, who were often labeled rustlers and sometimes became such because of it. The Association was made up mostly of affluent cattlemen from the East, Scotland and England.

For anyone interested in learning more obscure terms of the Old West, check out Winfred Blevins' Dictionary of the American West, Peter Watts' Dictionary of the Old West, and Ramon Adams' Western Words: A Dictionary of the American West. Also, to learn about the way people lived in the Old West, see Candy Moulton's new book, Everyday Life in the Wild West, put out by Writer's Digest Books. Without these great writers and others of their breed, much of the flavor of the West would be lost forever.

About the Author

Kirby Frank Jonas was born in 1965 in Bozeman, Montana. He lived in a place called Bear Canyon, where sagebrush gave way to spruce and fir, and the wild country was forever ingrained in him. It was there he gained his love of the Old West, listening to his daddy tell stories and sing western ballads, and watching television Westerns such as Gunsmoke, The Virginian and The Big Valley.

Jonas next lived on a remote farm in the middle of Civil War battlefield country near Broad Run, Virginia. That was followed by a move to Shelley, Idaho, where he completed all of his school years, wrote his first book (The Tumbleweed) in the sixth grade and his second (The Vigilante) as a senior in high school. He has since written five published novels and two which are forthcoming, one which was co-authored by his older brother, Jamie.

Besides writing novels, Jonas also paints wildlife and the West. He has done all of his cover art and hundreds of other pieces. He is a songwriter and guitar player and singer of old Western ballads and trail songs. Jonas enjoys the joking title given to him by his friends, "The Renaissance Cowboy."

After living in Arizona to research his first two books, and traveling through nine countries in Europe, to get his glimpse of the world, Jonas settled permanently in Pocatello, Idaho. He has made a living fighting forest fires for the Bureau of Land Management in five western states, worked for the Idaho Fish and Game Department, been a security guard and a guard for Wells Fargo in Phoenix, Arizona. He was employed as an officer for the Pocatello city police and currently works as a city firefighter. He and his wife, Debbie, have four children, Cheyenne Kaycee, Jacob Talon, Clay Logan, and Matthew Morgan.

Buy these books at your local bookstore, or use this handy coupon for ordering:

Howling Wolf Publishing,
P.O. Box 1045, Pocatello, Idaho 83204

Please send me:

❑ _____ copy/copies of: Legend of the Tumbleweed ($12.95)

❑ _____ copy/copies of: Death of an Eagle ($12.95)

❑ _____ copy/copies of: The Dansing Star ($10.95)

❑ _____ copy/copies of: Season of the Vigilante, Book II:
                                          Season's End ($9.95)

Send check or money order—no cash or C.O.D.'s please.

Idaho residents add 5% sales tax

I am enclosing $_____.

Name _____

Address _____

City, State, Zip _____
Please allow three weeks for delivery.

Author photo by Debbie Jonas. 100% beaver hat courtesy of Rocky Mountain Hat Company—"Cattle Baron Quality at Cowboy Prices!" The Morrises, John Sr. and Jr., make a terrific product. They made the hats for THE HORSE WHISPERER, as well as other movies, and all of their hats are custom made in 10 to 100% beaver. I highly recommend them! Contact them at 2742 W. Main, Bozeman, MT 59715. Phone: (406) 587-7809.